THE HOUSE THAT SAT DOWN

Omnibus Edition

Including:
'Accidental Damage'
'Restoration'
and
'Redemption'

with love
Alice May

Copyright

First Edition February 2019

Published by GW Press
www.gwpress.weebly.com

Cover design by Genevieve Alice May Tomkins
The original painting 'Guardian Angels' used in the cover design was painted by Genevieve Alice May Tomkins (née Walshaw) © January 2019.

ISBN 978-1-9160872-0-0

Welcome to the house that sat down...

I love books!

However, if you had told me a few years ago, that I would write even one book, let alone three, then I would not have believed you. Yet that is exactly what has happened.

It all began the day that my house sat down. Just to be clear, when I say that my house sat down, I mean that it started to disintegrate one day before my eyes. Within an hour and a half, more than 80% of my home was uninhabitable and the remaining 20% was looking distinctly dodgy. My husband, four children and I were effectively homeless. It was a bit of a shock to say the least! However, it was also not the end of the world, even though it felt like it was at the time.

In that moment, when I stood on my drive watching both my house and my life falling apart, I could not possibly have known that it was, in fact, the beginning of something quite incredible. It was the first step on a journey that was to ultimately take me in a direction that I could not possibly have dreamed of, proving that amazing things can come from complete disaster.

I used the subsequent events as the inspiration for my first novel 'Accidental Damage', which went on to win two *'Chill with a Book'* awards. It was so well received that there was a significant demand for a sequel, which led to me writing 'Restoration.' A year later, I realised that my story was not quite finished, so I wrote 'Redemption'. I still can't quite believe that any of this has actually happened.

Here they are, my three novels, all together as an omnibus.

My little bit of triumph over tragedy.

This is the story from 'The House That Sat Down!'

With love from Alice x

Acknowledgements

There are so many people without whom this story would not have seen the light of day and I would like to take the opportunity to thank some of them here, so please bear with me.

Therefore, I would like to thank my family, including my parents, my siblings and my parents-in-law for all their support throughout the events that inspired this story. I don't know what my husband, my children and I would have done without them.

After that I must thank my fellow author H. T. King for her excellent advice, Rose King for her encouragement and patience with primary edits, and Liz Gordon, of Brilliant Fish, for not only her invaluable editing advice but also her amazing PR skills.

In addition, I would like to thank three of my lovely neighbours; Nelly for telling me that I should write a book, and Karen and Jacqui for keeping me supplied with fresh fruit and veg while I did as I was told. I also thank my husband, my daughters, my parents and my good friend Catharine for being extremely patient in reading the very earliest drafts. All comments and feedback were very gratefully received. Thank you also to my friend and former colleague Andrew, for some excellent ecological advice dispensed over a pint or two at the local pub.

My thanks go out to our friends, colleagues and neighbours as well as the fantastic staff members at the Barbarians' schools who were all so kind and supportive throughout the time that our house really did 'sit down'. Special thanks to the Barbarians' Godfather Neal, for turning up out of the blue one day armed with a day off work, overalls, rollers, trays, paint brushes and endless energy.

The Dorset Taekwondo Association deserves a massive thank you for making the whole family so welcome at training sessions. Who knew Taekwondo would be so therapeutic? http://dtkd.co.uk/

I'd also like to thank my local Women's Institute for making me so very welcome.

I have met so many fantastic people on this 'author journey' of mine, including Gill Donnell (MBE) of the Successful Women in Business Network, and Beverley Hepting, The Message Maestro, both of whom have been a tremendous support.

Finally, of course, I thank my Beloved Husband and our Barbarians for everything. x

Contents

This is the omnibus edition of the story from the house that sat down and comprises all three novels in the trilogy.

If you think the normal school run on a Monday is entertaining, then you should try doing it from a tent in the back garden, surrounded by the jumbled-up contents of your entire home. It's vastly more diverting. Our heroine has survived the sudden collapse of her home – or has she? Certain events two and a half years ago led her to deliberately destroy an important piece of herself, hiding away all evidence that it ever existed. What happens when she decides to go looking for it? Does she really deserve to be whole again?

Let us return to the crumbling, cob cottage in the country, with our intrepid heroine and her hilarious family! They are about to start rebuilding their home and their lives. Of course, nothing is going to go smoothly for them, is it?

In this sequel to 'Accidental Damage – tales from the house that sat down', we accompany our heroine on her journey as she bravely battles to restore everything that she loves; often against the odds and with a liberal sprinkling of humour, art and home-made cookies along the way. One thing is for sure, it's going to be a bumpy ride!

BOOK ONE

ACCIDENTAL DAMAGE

Tales from the house that sat down

For my Beloved Husband and the Barbarians

Part 1

'No one saves us but ourselves.
No one can and no one may.
We ourselves must walk the path.'

Buddha

Preamble

Definition: a preliminary statement by the author to the reader

Please allow me to introduce you to our heroine.

Unfortunately, I am forced to admit that she is not at her best at the moment. An honest raconteur would tell you that, in fact, she is a complete mess.

However, that is rather the point of this tale!

There is the mother of all tempests raging outside and she is trying to pretend that she is not absolutely petrified. (Between you and me, she is not hiding it terribly well.) As a person who does not know her, you would be forgiven for thinking that she is a bit of a wimp.

You are entitled to your opinion of course, but perhaps you might consider giving her the benefit of the doubt. After all, she used to be a very different person.

There was a time when she was a strong and confident individual and found such squalls exhilarating. She remembers running along a beach in Spain one stormy night (more years ago now than she cares to recall), hand in hand with the love of her life, drenched with heavy rain, laughing as angry waves snatched at their ankles while thunder and lightning cascaded down around them shattering the darkness.

In short, she used to love storms.

Once upon a time she felt indestructible. Sadly, our heroine cannot claim to possess such an indomitable spirit anymore. That person is gone.

What on earth happened?

You might well ask!

There are countless ways that hearts can break and now, when the lightning flashes and the thunder roars, our heroine jumps in terror. She tries valiantly to pretend that she is not hiding away and whimpering quietly deep inside herself like a wounded animal. Unable to rest, she paces her home from room to room looking for somewhere safe to hide, searching desperately for something to divert her attention so that she can ignore what is happening outside.

Today, she is in luck! Something fairly momentous is about to happen to her which will distract her completely from the stupendous meteorological conditions currently stomping around outside.

She is about to revisit the past.

I will leave her to tell you all about it now.

After all, it is her story to share, not mine.

1: Compulsion

Definition: an irresistible impulse to act.

Present day....

It was late in the evening on a seriously scary, stormy night when I finally had to admit to myself that I was a wreck.

A well-known pop diva was letting rip at full volume from the radio in the corner (a vain attempt on my part to drown out the noise from outside). Yet I was still jumping with fright at each new flash of lightning and then again for the subsequent growling thunder.

As the aforementioned diva vociferously queried the whereabouts of all the more admirable gentlemen in the world, a small part of my brain was muttering, resentfully, that they were all probably comfortably ensconced in the lounge, watching the football with a tinny, like my Beloved Husband, and having a fine old time without us both.

Nevertheless, as the wind howled and the rain pulverised the ground (and the diva continued to lament at length), there I was, a fully-grown woman, cowering in the kitchen. I really couldn't pretend anymore. I knew, without a shadow of a doubt, that it was high time I sorted myself out and in order to do that I needed to find something, or, more accurately, a box of somethings.

This sudden compulsion to act was unexpectedly and entirely overwhelming. It was so all-consuming that it made the noises of the storm, and even the deafening diva, fade into insignificance.

Incapable of preventing myself, I left the kitchen at speed and dived headfirst into the dark and dangerous space that constituted the understairs cupboard, in a desperate attempt to excavate long-buried treasures. Things that had once been so important to a previous 'me', things that I had since told myself I wanted nothing more to do with. Ever!

In spite of my dogged assertion that I was done with them, these gems had somehow been spared the destructive fires of two years previously, when so much of the old 'me' was deliberately and systematically obliterated. I had stood in the darkness back then, completely devoid of all emotion, watching as so many things I had loved were engulfed in the heat and crackle of dancing flames.

Yet, secretly packaged away in the deepest darkest space I could find, these select items had been purposefully forgotten.

A line had been drawn. A door closed.

That part of my life was over.

Well, until now obviously!

The urge to be reunited with them immediately was so strong that I was heedless of the potential threat from the enormous eight-legged occupants, the presence of which usually prevented me from venturing very far into this uncharted territory.

Out came old sleeping bags, wellies of assorted sizes and a plethora of ancient coats and shoes that I vaguely recognised as having been worn at some point by one or other of the smaller humans that roam through the house from time to time in search of food and electronic entertainment.

Right at the back was the box. I dragged it out eagerly, notwithstanding the unwieldy size and sheer weight of it, and pulled it right across the hall into the little study, oblivious to the trail of abandoned detritus that I was leaving in my wake.

At last I had them.

Nothing else mattered.

Opening the box, I released my treasures, carefully extracting one thing after another. Each item unearthed generated a tingle down my spine, a spark of recognition, a brief flash of the person I used to be, as I cautiously arranged them on the desk by the window.

Time passed.

I was so utterly enthralled that I did not notice when the storm outside had blown itself out. I did not even register that the radio had been switched off. Wave after wave of memories hit me as each item was excavated, examined and set down. This was what I had been missing. How could I possibly have thought I would survive without them?

What on earth had I been thinking?

No matter! We were reunited at last.

A tentative shuffling and a quiet, yet deliberate clearing of the throat broke into my bubble of contentment. Beloved Husband was leaning against the door jam, the now silent radio in his hands. There was a deliberately neutral expression on his face as he surveyed the room. (The football must be over. The storm certainly was.)

"So," he said cautiously, "it's starting again."

A statement.

Not a question.

I looked guiltily at the mess I had generated in the hall behind him and then at the pile of things on the table beside me.

"It does rather look as though it might be," I agreed.

I couldn't deny how happy the sight of my easel, brushes, pallet knives and sponges made me. Not to mention the way the sheer range of brightly coloured paints before me lifted my spirits.

My old friends were back!

Was that a hint of fear behind the carefully non-judgemental expression on Beloved Husband's face? Quite possibly!

Thinking back, I can't really blame him. He was no doubt remembering what life was like when I painted before. Wet canvasses littering every surface in the house, my obsession with painting invading everything, the forgotten meals, the late nights and early mornings spent throwing colours at canvasses because little things like food and sleep just weren't as important as capturing a particular image in paint.

Could he be recalling the time he came home from work to find that a moment of inattention on my part had allowed our youngest offspring, dressed only in a nappy, to express his artistic side with an entire tube of Alizarin Crimson oil paint all over himself and our brand-new conservatory?

Perhaps he is remembering the moment when we stood side by side staring in paralysed horror at what we initially thought was the scene of a bloodbath (Alizarin Crimson really does resemble that most red of bodily fluids) before we realised that the semi-naked two-year-old, writhing on the floor at our feet was not suffering a terrible death, but was in fact enjoying himself immensely.

It is sad to say that the split second of intense parental relief that he was unharmed was swiftly followed by our homeowners' instinctive urge to inflict bodily harm on the little vandal. This impulse was thankfully quickly superseded, primarily by Beloved Husband's compulsion to rescue the conservatory and secondly by my guilty need to extract the miniature criminal from the scene and clean him.

I rather think Beloved Husband got the easier job because at least the conservatory didn't wriggle around and protest vociferously at the liberal application of appropriate cleaning products.

Given our youngest child's total aversion to bathtime on any given occasion, the extended period of cleaning time it took to remove all traces of crimson oil paint from every nook and cranny of his person was probably punishment enough.

For both of us!

Thank goodness the little ruffian's older sister was around to help hold him still. Wet two-year-olds are slippery little critters. Then to add insult to injury I had to clean the bathroom and myself afterwards. Fortunately, his sister was old enough to clean herself.

It was my own fault really, for taking my eyes off him. This particular child was exceptionally good at getting into mischief. Thank heaven oil paint takes such a long time to dry.

An extended telephone call to the GP followed as we tried to decide whether the offender had actually consumed any paint and might therefore require some form of medical attention. The conclusion was that, as he appeared entirely unaltered from his customary destructive self (apart from an unusual degree of cleanliness), it would be kinder to spare the casualty department. The doctor politely suggested that we keep a close eye on him at home.

Beloved Husband was remarkably restrained under the circumstances and did not point out that I should have been doing that in the first place.

That particular event rather marked an important moment in my painting career as I locked the oil paints away and invested in water colours and acrylics, which are altogether less toxic and less permanent. I painted quite contentedly with these new materials until that terrible day when I turned my back on my art completely.

Now they were back!

All of them.

Watercolours, acrylics and oils were all jostling for space on the study table.

My Beloved Husband could be forgiven for being somewhat concerned at such a development.

"I'll be careful," I said earnestly.

There was a moment of silence before he shook his head, rolled his eyes to the heavens and said with a wry smile, "Of course you will!"

He walked over and placed the radio carefully down on the windowsill, switching it back on at a more moderate volume than before. Then he turned to go, shoving the pile of discarded items back into the understairs cupboard and wedging the door closed as he went past.

Looking back at my old friends on the desk, I couldn't wait to get started. Within minutes there was a canvas clamped to the easel and my fingers itched to get hold of a paintbrush as I rummaged through tubes of colours.

It crossed my mind to wonder how on earth I had survived without doing this for so long. Painting had always been my comfort, so perhaps now, with all my materials around me, I stood a chance of working out how to feel better about myself.

With absolutely no idea what I was going to paint I simply picked up a brush, selected a pot of paint at random and set to work.

2: Barbarian

Definition: a member of a primitive or uncivilised people.

Staying with the inspired artist in the present day…

The next morning, having fallen into bed incredibly late and then risen insanely early in order to continue painting, I was contentedly immersed in shades of Sap Green. I became aware of a rhythmic crunching sound coming from behind me. Gradually surfacing from a cocoon of colour, canvas and comforting brushstrokes I turned and focused on the figure looming in the doorway. Systematically spooning milk and cereal from a bowl into his face, my older son was observing me with interest.

He is the third in the series of small people that my Beloved Husband and I had created several years previously. At 15 he is getting surprisingly tall, which might have something to do with the fact that he is *always* eating.

Sporting pyjama bottoms and nothing else, he obviously hadn't stopped to get dressed before initiating his primary raid on the cereal cupboard this morning. I resisted the urge to tell him to go and put a top on and made a mental note to turn the heating down. It's mid-January for goodness' sake! If people feel comfortable walking round in their scanties in the middle of winter, then we obviously have the thermostat set far too high.

Now, it should be remembered that this son of ours is not someone who talks very much. This is potentially related to the fact that he is always mid-way through a snack. (I would like to believe that my numerous nags concerning not talking with your mouth full were inwardly digested, but I rather think not.) It's probably got more to do with the fact that I created two rather gobby older sisters for him before I got around to the job of manufacturing boys.

Don't misunderstand me, even though he is known affectionately to the family as Quiet, he can definitely talk. He just doesn't. Not very often and, when he does, it's generally so brief you can easily miss it if you aren't concentrating, so I simply looked at him and waited patiently in case any utterances were imminently forthcoming.

He munched thoughtfully and then nodded slowly.

Then he chomped some more, while a kamikaze droplet of milk made its way down his chin and quivered momentarily before launching itself towards the floor. Yet still there was no obviously impending comment. I got bored of waiting and raised an inquisitive eye at him, effectively inviting him to either speak or naff off. Two could play at being uncommunicative.

Getting the hint, he finally swallowed and said, 'You're painting!'

Such a bright boy! It's no wonder that Beloved Husband and I are so proud of him!

Usually, when Quiet finally does express himself, I generally think it is worth listening to as so much thought goes into it. Unlike most of the population, he usually only speaks when he has something useful to say.

Still waters run deep and all that.

On this occasion, however, I realised that I might have to lower my expectations, so I nodded and turned back to my canvas.

"Good," he surprised me by continuing. I had thought I'd had my quota of words from him for the day.

"Really?" I enquired, deliberately not looking at him in case he stopped interacting altogether, "and why's that?"

This should be interesting.

Silence! I could almost hear him shrugging his shoulders – a favourite method of communication for most teenage boys.

He sighed heavily and I looked round meeting his eyes. They were sparkling with supressed humour and I could tell that he was calculating whether or not he would get away with his next statement.

I braced myself.

He tipped his head to one side and obviously decided to go for it.

"You're a lot less grumpy when you paint." He gave me a wicked grin and ambled off to find someone more entertaining to torment with his silent presence.

Cheeky beggar!

I returned to my soothing Sap Green canvas.

Grumpy? Hah! I'll show him grumpy!

Green, lovely green. Now what? Purple? Deep, dark purple! Hmmmm. Yes, purple will do nicely.

***

Sometime later, I noticed that a steaming hot cup of tea and a small plate piled high with chocolate chip cookies had magically materialised on the table to my left. Could this be a peace offering to appease the painting spirits? Probably not! It's more likely to be my daughter's attempt to remind me that I have to eat. Logic is nearly 18 and is the second oldest in our tribe. As her nickname suggests she is blessed with common sense, rationality and sound judgement. In short, she is incredibly sensible, or might she only appear so when compared to her siblings? I couldn't possibly comment.

She is also the one of all my offspring that resembles me the most in looks. Poor child! In other words, she is short and dark. I have no idea how her older sister got to be so tall or so naturally blonde, it must therefore be Beloved Husband's fault.

When faced with a situation she can't control, Logic resorts to calories. I don't mean that she eats them (although she is perfectly capable of demolishing her own body weight in chocolate if she feels like it, I've seen her). I mean that if someone has a problem she can't fix for them then her solution is to produce food. A trait she has inherited from me.

Once I realised that cute little babies turned into uncivilised little savages, I accepted that I might have bitten off more than I could chew. Beloved Husband and I had foolishly outnumbered ourselves by initially having three of the little monsters in fairly quick succession, so we set about working out how to contain the situation, swiftly establishing the fact that feeding them on a regular basis kept them relatively content and made them less likely to tear the place and each other (not to mention us) apart.

Having instigated a degree of control over the first three, Beloved Husband and I, lulled into a false sense of security, then decided a few years later to have number four. We thought that it really couldn't have been that bad.

Then, we remembered.

Four was definitely our limit. Luckily, a regular input of food tamed this last arrival as well. To a point anyway!

Thus, over the years whenever one of my small hooligans has approached me with an issue, my first act is to open the biscuit tin, place it between them and me and then stand well back.

Over the years, a degree of civilisation had been established within our little band. In fact, a peace treaty, successfully negotiated between the grown-ups and the Barbarians, was flourishing.

This agreement involves basic things such as the production of relatively adequate grades at school, not swearing in front of grandparents and the use of rudimentary table manners in exchange for an unlimited supply of food (including fruit and vegetables), donations of cash on occasion and lifts to their mates' houses when needed. After all, we do live in the middle of nowhere.

On the whole a happy medium has been achieved and the Barbarians cannot, in truth, be referred to as Barbarians any longer. But that's not going to stop me. Who said life was fair?

***

Anyway, where was I? Oh yes, I was drinking my tea in the study and chomping contentedly away on cookies. I studied the large canvas before me with a degree of bemused surprise. It was now sporting a selection of gigantic bluebells. Rather different from my old style, a bit outlandish maybe, but definitely quite relaxed and free. While I gazed at it I was surprised to experience an emotion that I struggled to identify. It was so long since I had felt anything like it, but could I possibly be relaxing just a little bit? I wasn't really sure, but thought I'd better paint a bit more and find out. Any excuse!

Now that I was starting to feel a bit better about myself, I decided that it was high time I examined the events of two and a half years ago to try and work out at exactly what point the old 'me' had become broken and why.

Concluding that I rather liked the bluebells, I leaned in to sign my name at the bottom, before reaching for a fresh blank canvas and casting my mind back.

3: Cob

Definition: an ancient construction material used for building since prehistoric times. Traditionally, English cob consists of clay-based subsoil mixed with sand, straw and water and trampled by oxen.

Two and a half years previously….

When you buy old properties, you can expect them to be a teeny bit troublesome.

Our house was no exception. Young and naïve as we might have been when we bought it, we weren't completely daft. We could see that work was required yet we could also see that the rather random conglomeration of structures that encompassed the sweet old cottage, presented us with the opportunity to build an idyllic life in the countryside for our growing band of marauding Barbarians.

There were plenty of bedrooms upstairs and a huge garden for prowling around, surrounded by fields and streams to explore. Loads of fresh air so the asthmatics would thrive, plus it was miles away from the hustle and bustle of main roads and big cities.

In effect, by living here, we could be said to be protecting both the Barbarians and society at the same time.

The house consisted of a motley selection of extensions of indeterminate age around a central cob cottage. The original structure had been present on the site for at least 350 years, but had been altered to a sufficiently unrecognisable degree that the local planners were not skipping round it trying to put it on one of their lists of historical significance.

This was a good thing as it meant that we would be able to get planning permission to make some alterations. Nevertheless, we still had National Park (NP), Area of Outstanding Natural Beauty (AONB), Site of Special Scientific Interest (SSSI) and River Corridor designations to contend with so no changes were going to be particularly straightforward. (We wouldn't want straightforward, would we? That would make life far too boring!)

Over the next ten years, we slowly spruced up bits of the cottage as our finances allowed, but the original section remained much as we had found it. Lovely thick, solid walls, warm in winter and cool in summer. There was a charmingly rickety staircase that would never pass building regulations these days and a huge open fireplace with old foot and hand holds leading up the inside of the vast chimney stack. (No, we never sent any of the Barbarians up it, even though it was very tempting to save on the chimney sweep bills!) The whole thing was topped off with a very pretty thatched roof.

We had been assured by the detailed structural survey that it was all completely sound and thus no concerns were raised. The general consensus from all consulted was that it had stood for 350 years already and it would stand for 350 more.

Therefore, you can probably understand my total incomprehension as I stood on the driveway one July day and watched as two massive, jagged cracks tore their way up the walls of my home from ground level right up to pretty thatched roof, and a section of cob started to move very slowly away from the rest of the house.

"How peculiar!" I remember thinking, as my Friendly Local Builder and his mate, who had fortuitously popped by at that exact moment to pick up some previously forgotten equipment, frantically swung into action. An amazing co-incidence it is true, but there they were, builders, just when I needed them the most. How often does that happen? Perhaps someone was smiling on me from on high that day, despite all evidence to the contrary.

Experienced in construction work as these builders were, they were able to size up what was going on in lightening quick time. Thus, while

I was staring in incomprehension, my companions were hastily trying to erect some props that they happened to have in the back of their truck, in order to prevent the wall collapsing completely.

Standing rooted to the spot, I could not believe my eyes. This couldn't possibly be happening! Yet it clearly was. That second 350 years was rather demonstrably off the cards now. In fact, the house looked as though it had got rather tired and had a little sit down. I didn't really blame it. I was feeling rather faint myself.

My mobile warbled and I answered it on automatic pilot.

"You alright?" chirped my blissfully unaware Beloved Husband.

"We have a slight problem," I croaked out.

***

Twenty minutes later, Beloved Husband and I were both standing on the drive looking at the damage to our home in total silence. Words cannot begin to describe how dumbfounded we were.

I do remember thinking irrelevantly that at least it was rather a nice day. Blue sky, sunshine, tweeting birds, you know the kind I mean. Always looking for a silver lining, that's me, or at least it was. It probably would have been worse if it had been raining, but let's face it, things were pretty bad already.

Friendly Local Builder came over to us, dusting off his hands, and said, "OK, it's stable for now, but it's going to need a bit of work." A well-meant understatement, I think. Just like when the nurse says, "You won't feel a thing."

"I take it there's no-one inside?" he continued.

Oh damn! Was there? (No, you're right I said something much worse than that but I am not admitting to it in print.)

The Barbarian Horde! Frantic mental mechanics ensued.

Phew! Panic over.

"It's OK," I stammered after a moment of carefully cataloguing the probable whereabouts of our offspring. "The kids are all at school, and the cat is asleep in the back garden."

"There's lucky then, could have been worse," he said cheerfully.

Beloved Husband and I looked at him in complete astonishment. Could there possibly be something lucky about this? Maybe he was right, after all no one was actually dead, except possibly the cottage. It all rather depended on your perspective I supposed.

"Best ring your house insurance then," he prompted helpfully.

We nodded. That did seem like the only thing to do under the circumstances.

***

A surprisingly short while later, Beloved Husband had achieved a degree of communication with the House Insurance Company.

With my hands wrapped around a warm cup of tea (we're British, what else were we going to do in a crisis?), I listened as he calmly agreed with the sweet young thing on the end of the line that it really was highly inconsiderate of us to allow the house to fall down on a Friday afternoon. However, after he had politely insisted that yes, the situation was fairly critical, and no, it really couldn't wait until Monday, arrangements were eventually made for a structural engineer to visit the property to assess the situation later that evening.

Fingers crossed there was something of the house left standing for him to assess when he got here.

There had been rather a lot of haphazard development at the property over the course of its 350-year existence. The most useful addition at this present time was a fairly large, relatively modern, single storey extension at the rear of the original two storey cob section.

This was a very useful family room designed around a kitchen with a lounge-style seating area by an open fire to one side. The room then morphed into a conservatory / dining area towards the garden. There was also a door that led to a tiny ground floor bathroom with a miniscule utility area. Fortunately, this part of the house could all safely be accessed via the conservatory doors by the back patio without risking our necks going near the worryingly, wobbly walls at the front.

As a result, we were able to corral the Barbarian Horde, on their return from various educational establishments, at the back of the house with sufficient edible supplies, a selection of electronic entertainment equipment and a stern lecture about venturing no further than the bathroom and back on pain of death. Literally!

We bravely decided to survey the damage. On reflection this was probably a rather foolish idea, but I never have claimed to be terribly intelligent.

It was a very surreal experience. The cracks had widened considerably in a very short space of time, allowing loads more daylight to penetrate the small cottage rooms than we usually got from the tiny old windows. Sadly, this additional lighting allowed us to see quite clearly the resultant substantial internal damage.

Friendly Local Builder had stuck around, not only for the entertainment value that we were offering, but also from a genuine desire to help out. He muttered something about needing some more support and disappeared back outside to his truck. He returned shortly with a couple of metal props and a stack of three yellow hard hats. Beloved Husband and I accepted the hats in wordless disbelief and rammed them on our heads obediently before turning towards the stairs.

It was at this point that we began to get an inkling of quite how big a problem we now had. The previously charming, yet slightly rickety, staircase was no longer charming and was significantly more rickety. In fact, we would be hard put to describe it as a staircase at all. It had been built into the corner of the cob cottage where the slightly smaller of the two massive cracks now ran right up the stairwell towards the roof. (Not an interior design feature I would recommend.)

As Friendly Local Builder did something useful with his props downstairs, we ventured cautiously, and no doubt imprudently, up what remained of the staircase. I challenge anyone to make sound decisions under similar circumstances.

The damage to the upstairs was comparable to that downstairs, if not significantly worse. Windows had fallen out and ceilings had fallen in. Plaster was still falling from the walls in huge chunks, leaving thick dust swirling. Early evening sunlight poured in through a significant gap between the wall and the roof at one end, highlighting a scene of utter devastation.

Bedtime was obviously going to be a bit of an issue.

4: Insurance

Definition: a written agreement by which a company provides a guarantee of compensation for loss, damage, illness, or death in exchange for payment of a premium

Staying in the past with the disintegrating house…

Having finished our rather terrifying inspection of the first floor of our cottage, we heard the crunch of tyres on the driveway. It was clearly audible through the gap in the wall and, peering out, we could see a four by four pulling up. Carefully picking our way back down what had previously been the stairs, we went to greet the new arrival.

A tall, rumpled and rather tired looking gentleman wearing an Aran jumper, corduroy trousers and walking boots, was standing on the drive, an air of complete exhaustion emanating from every pore and a black Labrador sitting obediently at his feet. It had no doubt been a long day for him, if not a long week and we were unbelievably grateful that he had added this one last site visit to his list.

He politely identified himself as the structural engineer from the house insurance company and shook hands with us before grabbing a clipboard and hard hat from his car.

He took his time examining the outside of the house, taking photos, walking up and down, inspecting the cracks closely and scribbling notes with the dog hard on his heels. Then, to my surprise, he stepped through the larger of the cracks and straight into the cottage.

Beloved Husband and I looked at each other in silence.

In a matter of hours, the cracks in the side of our house could no longer be described as 'cracks'. They were now such significantly large chasms that a grown man could walk through them.

With his dog!

In the general scheme of things, I would usually expect a visitor to ask if it is ok before bringing their dog onto (and into) my property but, having never had a house with a yawning crater in the wall before, I didn't know if the accepted etiquette was different so I decided to let it slide and simply followed them in.

Such a surreal feeling walking through the wall! What a shame we didn't find ourselves on a magical platform heading for our first term at a school for wizards when we emerged on the other side. Perhaps we should have taken more of a run-up.

Structural Engineer Man then proceeded to crawl (quite literally in the case of the stairs, the first-floor bedrooms and the loft) all over the interior of the cob section of the cottage making copious notes. He made several rather loud unfathomable comments which Friendly Local Builder appeared to comprehend. Beloved Husband and I got the impression that these remarks concerned the additional propping materials which would be necessary in order to prevent any further slippage and so we eagerly agreed when Friendly Local Builder asked if we would like him to arrange it all. Obviously pleased to have something practical to do, he beetled off to hire and install the necessary paraphernalia.

Eventually, Structural Engineer Man ground to a halt and rumbled that he now had sufficient measurements recorded to make an initial report but that he had rather a lot of questions he needed to ask us as well. In view of the instability of the property, he suggested that we retreat to a safer location at the back of the house.

"Of course, I am not really an expert in these old buildings," he said ominously. "Nevertheless, I can confirm that your cob is in serious trouble."

I could hear Beloved Husband making a concerted effort to bite his tongue and no wonder. We had spent a small fortune on house insurance over the years with a company that was supposed to specialise in old buildings and then when we actually need them, they send us someone who is 'not an expert in old buildings'!

Great! It's taken him two hours to conclude that we are in trouble. We already knew that!

I took a deep, calming breath.

"I must strongly recommend to you that no one should access this part of your home," he continued. "You really should ensure you keep your dog out of here, too."

"That's OK," I reassured him. "We don't have a dog."

He gave me a very odd look at that point and then regarded the canine between us on the floor. The Labrador was looking up at us, tongue hanging out, panting cheerfully.

"It's OK," I continued, hoping I hadn't offended him. Whether he was an old buildings expert or not, we really needed a helpful report from him. "We really don't mind that you brought your dog in with you. We do like dogs," I insisted. "We just don't own one."

He raised a quizzical eyebrow at me before looking down again and saying emphatically, "THAT is not my dog."

"Ah!"

I didn't really know what to say then and Beloved Husband was not much help either, having apparently lost the ability to speak entirely. (Between you and me, not a bad thing just at that point.)

All three of us stood and looked at the dog for a moment before we heard a sharp whistle from the road outside, and the dog shot off through the hole in the wall and disappeared.

"Shall I make us a nice cup of tea?" I suggested brightly, changing the subject.

5: Chaos

Definition: a collection of elements without organisation or connection.

Back to the future. Please note that I am not referring to the film, merely indicating that we are returning to events in the present day…

Having completed a rather hectic school run (yes, we were late as usual) the next day, followed by a hasty supermarket trip to restock the cupboards with relatively healthy provisions after a weekend of plundering by my starving teenage savages, I was energetically engaged in priming another canvas.

The breakfast show was emanating from my battered old radio. It was still sat on the windowsill where Beloved Husband had left it, and had since been joined, at some point, by the cat. Extremely elderly and looking decidedly scruffy these days (a bit like the radio), the aforementioned feline was enjoying the January sunshine whilst politely ignoring me.

Having carefully hidden my feelings about what had happened for so long, I was amazed at how quickly I was changing my mind. The more I thought about it, the more I wanted to get these damaging emotions out so that I didn't have to waste energy trying to suppress them anymore. While I didn't yet actually want to talk to anyone about it, transferring my emotions onto the canvas before me was definitely helping.

Luckily, I had found several large, abandoned, blank canvases stuffed behind the freezer in the garage. (No, I don't know how they got there.) I reasoned that as they weren't costing me anything, I would just let my rediscovered creative spirit wander across them and see what resulted.

The insistent 'bing-boing' of an unexpected Skype call interrupted some fairly intense concentration on my part.

Reluctantly I put my brush down, muted the radio and flicked the iPad open to accept the call, absentmindedly taking an enormous bite from the piece of chocolate fudge cake that had materialised on my desk next to a huge cup of tea. I wondered where on earth they had come from and concluded that it must be a Tuesday. Logic gets the day off college on a Tuesday and therefore was capable of making tea and cake appear out of the blue.

How had I not noticed that she wasn't in the car when I did the school run? Was the need to paint fogging my brain quite that much already? (Note to self: I really must try to pay more attention!)

"Hello Oldest Offspring!" I said cheerfully to the iPad screen.

No, I am not psychic! At that time, Chaos was the only person on the planet who ever Skyped me. Her nickname is appropriate for one who lives her life in fast forward. She is a wonderfully gifted individual but, believe me, you never quite know what she is going to do next.

Skyping was a technological advancement that I had studiously avoided until one of my Barbarians actually left home for university and I was forced to embrace the world of modern communication systems in order to reassure myself that she was OK.

"Hi, Mum. How are you?" she asked sunnily, and then immediately froze in an unflattering pose that meant I could see right up her nostrils. Usually the internet here is very good but occasionally there are minor blips that make Skype calls more entertaining.

Internet aside, there were a number of things that Beloved Husband and I should have considered before we naively bought a ramshackle property in such a remote area. Luxuries like mains drainage, a gas supply, reliable telephone and electricity connections, not to mention pavements, street lighting and public transport should have been given at least a passing consideration, but we were young and foolish. We're still foolish, but sadly not so young anymore.

Nevertheless, the very rare drop-out of the internet signal has had its uses in the ever-constant parental battle against the terrible teens' insistence on living their lives entirely through social media.

"Oh dear!" I have been known to cry on occasion, having accidentally (on purpose) switched the internet off. "The internet is down! What a shame! Never mind, it's dinner time, let's all come to the table. Maybe the signal will be back up by the time we've finished eating."

This approach does, however, require the co-operation of Beloved Husband, who, if not pre-warned that this is an intentional tactic, has been known to race through the kitchen flicking the appropriate switch to re-establish connection and then claiming loudly to have 'fixed it'. What follows are rapturous cries of delighted hero-worship from the Barbarian Horde. Then both he and they all immediately return to the act of frying their brains through electronic media whilst simultaneously developing deep vein thromboses.

The lovingly prepared, healthy dinner goes cold and dry on the table and Beloved Husband (eventually) wonders why I am not talking to him.

But I digress….

"I'm good," I responded when her image started to move again, indicating that we had an active connection once more. "You?"

"Yeah! Good," she said.

There followed a silence that I eventually broke. "Go on then, Chaos, what are you calling me for so early on a Tuesday morning? I know you don't have lectures until twelve so it must be important for you to be awake this early. Spill!"

"I heard on the grapevine that you are painting again."

"And?"

"Well, I was just interested…..Can I see?"

I turned the iPad around so she could see the barmy bluebells propped up in the corner.

"Wow! That's a bit different from your usual style. It's true then."

"So it would appear," I confirmed dryly. It's rather gratifying to realise that, contrary to appearance, the Barbarian Horde do actually pay attention to what's going on in this house, and also choose to communicate with each other voluntarily. That includes those who no longer live here permanently any more.

Like most mothers I could be forgiven for thinking that no one would actually notice if I were to disappear off the face of the planet, until the supply of food and clean clothes ran out, of course.

"That's good," she continued. She doesn't mean my bluebells, but I don't take it personally.

"Yeah, I know. Your brother already gave me the 'you'll be less grumpy if you're painting' line, thank you very much."

"Ha!" She let out a delighted squeal. "He never did? Is he still breathing?"

"I was remarkably restrained," I agreed, mentally congratulating myself on my older son's continued existence on the planet (for now).

"There you go then, that proves his point," she said triumphantly and paused before continuing in a more serious tone, "I always wondered why you stopped… you loved it so much. Can I ask …was it me?"

There was a pause while I looked at her blankly. 'Typical teen' one might be forgiven for thinking. Obviously, the world *does* revolve around them. However, in this case, I got the impression that there was a bit more to it than that.

"What do you mean?" I asked.

"You stopped painting nearly three years ago, around about the time that I…" she tailed off rather sheepishly.

The penny dropped, "Oh!" I said, seeing where she was going with this. "No. Don't worry it wasn't you."

"Are you sure?"

"Yes, I promise."

"Really? Because I …"

"Chaos," I broke in forcefully, "I promise you that your little flirtation with the Grim Reaper did not make me stop painting, OK? It was all that other stuff that came afterwards, and that was nothing to do with you."

"OK." She smiled. "Well I'm glad you have started again and I rather like the bluebells. They're big and a bit bonkers but they're still kinda cute. Anyway, gotta go, lectures and all that. Love ya."

With that typically casual goodbye, she was gone.

Quite clearly, now that she'd been absolved of any responsibility for the cessation of my painting career, she was not really that interested in the real reason why I had stopped.

I was though. At the time it had seemed like the only option.

Practical.

Necessary.

In fact, essential.

I am not sure I had ever really acknowledged it even to myself. It had been an immediate, unconsidered knee jerk reaction to circumstance and all stopped thereafter.

Now that I was painting again though, it seemed unbelievable that I could ever have considered stopping. I looked at my bluebells thoughtfully. They were not bonkers. Admittedly the style was far more casual than anything I had painted before, but I liked them. Nevertheless, I pondered if I would ever paint like I had before; precise, meticulous, detailed pieces of work.

Probably not was the answer. I was a completely different person now. I'd been emotionally bashed and broken, but perhaps I could now hear a little voice calling quietly from way down deep inside me, "I'm still here!"

In a small way, Chaos was correct that her little dalliance with death a few years previously had inevitably had a massive impact on us all. This was about six months before the house fell down. (Yes, I know, it probably wasn't the luckiest of years for us!) She went from being 100% healthy and never ill a day in her life, to 99.9% extremely not very well at all.

Overnight.

I won't go into details, mainly because other people's health issues are always so boring. (Anyway, she'd totally kill me and, more importantly, I might need to blackmail her with the information at some point in the future. I am not giving away that particular advantage here.) Suffice to say that she suddenly required emergency surgery. We did our bit and transported her to hospital. We've seen Casualty, we know the drill! Once there, we waited, confident that the good old NHS would roll in and save the day.

Only they nearly couldn't, as the contrary little madam developed unexpected complications.

It's a soap opera every minute in this family. A little bit of emergency surgery couldn't possibly go smoothly for us now, could it?

Beloved Husband and I were left to ferment in her allocated hospital bay on the paediatric ward. We'd seen the bed, with her in it, being wheeled off to theatre. The curtains were drawn round where the bed used to be and we sat inside the bay on orange plastic chairs (the sort that can be wiped down if you have an unfortunate accident), looking at the big empty bed-sized space and we waited.

And waited.

And waited some more.

Eventually, totally stressed (and also desperate for the loo as we hadn't dared go anywhere in case we missed someone arriving with news, so no wonder they have wipe-down chairs), we were relieved to see the Eminent Surgeon whisk through the curtains with several members of his team and start to talk to us.

I noted with concern that he was looking alarmingly pale, sweaty and exhausted before I tuned into what he was actually saying. I struggled to get my confused brain around the words he was using. There were quite a lot of references to 'unfortunate ruptures'… 'internal bleeding'… 'difficulties suturing'… 'loss of several pints' etc… before he finished with "but she's going to be OK now."

Phew! Honestly, I ask you, could he not have started the conversation with that last bit?

It all happened so fast that we didn't really realise that the whole event had been touch and go until it was all over. I probably could have gone into a flat spin about it but there wasn't really time to have a nervous breakdown just then.

There followed an extensive period of recovery, more surgical procedures and months of rehabilitation, physiotherapy etc, which meant that I was constantly driving her to follow-up appointments and therapy sessions, as well as trying to juggle the other Barbarians' schedules.

Oh! Not to forget going to work and doing my job too. There seriously was no time for anything else. Thus, from a purely practical point of view, it did essentially physically stop me painting. But it wasn't what stopped me actually wanting to paint.

The house falling down wasn't the reason either. Nothing is ever that simple and Beloved Husband would be the first to assure you that I am a very complicated individual.

The event that stopped me actually wanting to paint came later and it was that which came so close to destroying me completely.

Part 2

That which does not kill us makes us stronger.

Friedrich Nietzsche
1844-1900

6: Serenity

Definition: The state of being trouble-free, peaceful and calm.

Present day still….

Contentment comes in many forms. In my case, I had always had the ability to become so absorbed in laying down colours on canvas that the troubles of the world would simply fade away. Problems became non-existent and my spirits were lifted. Mucking about, elbow deep in paint, had always enabled me to sort things out in my head, as if by inspiring the imaginative part of my brain through painting I was able to understand other areas of my life more effectively. It gave me control and peace simultaneously, regardless of how successful (or not) I felt the final piece of work was.

Whilst contemplating Chaos' illness and recovery, and also the initial collapse of our house a few months later, I had subconsciously and systematically filled a second canvas with colour. This time when I finally surfaced from my thoughts I saw a dark series of rather demented and dishevelled-looking daisies staring back at me.

No doubt about it, psychologically-challenged flora was my new theme.

Nevertheless, I was beginning to delve tentatively deeper into the question of why I had stopped painting. I had always refused to let my mind wander into that murky territory. Perhaps I was afraid of what I would find.

Time to finish that fudge cake perhaps?!

Now where did I put it?

I had deliberately shut my painting down two and a half years ago, immediately, completely and absolutely. A realisation so terrible had dawned, one that I couldn't control or fix.

My fundamental belief that everything would be alright if you just did your best was whipped away from me like a rug being literally pulled from beneath my feet. Everything I held dear was threatened. Beloved Husband, the adored Barbarian Horde and our cosy protected home life were all in jeopardy, and I had not been able prevent it. In fact, I had potentially contributed to events, inadvertently making the consequences far, far worse.

In response, had I amputated an essential part of myself as a punishment? No one had made me do it. The decision was entirely mine, a calculatingly measured action at a time when I had so little power over anything else that was happening.

The price I had paid personally as a result of that whole event had been so very far reaching. Even now, over two years on, I was still damaged. I found it hard to trust myself to make the right decisions.

To put it bluntly, because of what had happened, I was living in fear.

Nonetheless, the world continues to turn, and we must move forward. I can't stand that ghastly American term 'closure'. This is not about 'closure' it's about survival.

Eventually we must face those things that scare us. We need to confront them head on, because only then can we stand a chance of defeating them so that they can't dominate the rest of our lives.

Setting the disconcerting daisy canvas to one side I reached for a blank one. I wondered if I was strong enough to revisit the source of my deepest pain. Perhaps, accompanied by my art to protect me, I could deal with this massive mental monster at last.

There was only one way to find out.

7: Expert

Definition: A person who has gained a high degree of skill in or knowledge of a particular specialist subject.

Returning to the somewhat wobbly cottage in the past…

While I put the kettle on, Structural Engineer Man settled himself into a chair at the kitchen table for what looked like it might be a relatively lengthy stay.

He dumped his clipboard down and suddenly took off his jumper in that rather incredible way that I have only ever seen men do. He reached behind his head to the middle of his back, grabbed a handful of material and yanked it up and over. I watched this manoeuvre with fascinated bemusement, wondering how he managed it without dislocating something essential.

It's probably the same for fellas when they see a woman remove her bra (let me finish!) *without* taking off her top first. They just can't work out how we do that, can they? We unclip, wriggle about a bit and suddenly out the bra pops from a sleeve. Not that I go around doing that in public, you understand.

His head eventually reappeared from the folds of fabric and all his floppy, blond hair stood on end with the static, forming a crackly, golden halo. I placed a large mug of caffeine and a sugar bowl on the table before him while he hurriedly tried to make his hair behave in a more acceptable and professional manner.

Meanwhile, Beloved Husband had recovered the power of speech and was making a hasty phone call.

As he had left work in a hurry earlier that day, muttering that his house might be falling down, a helpful colleague had jokingly said that he had an eight-man tent if we needed it. This phone call was to ascertain how serious Helpful Colleague actually was with regard to the lending of the tent as it was now patently obvious that we had nowhere to sleep. It was getting late and there was no sign of a Helpful House Insurance Man to whisk us off to a comfortable hotel. Wouldn't that be nice?

To be totally fair, if a Helpful House Insurance Man was to have appeared at that point, he would have had quite a job to whisk us off to a hotel without having to build one first.

It was July and the height of the summer silly season in the nearby coastal town was upon us. By that I mean that the school holidays were just beginning and every hotel, travel lodge, caravan park and bed and breakfast within a thirty-mile radius would have been booked solid months in advance. Even if a few cancellations had been available, there was just no way that a Helpful House Insurance Man would have been able to find accommodation for six of us together in one location.

Probably just as well he didn't exist. It would have been a shame to raise our hopes.

As it happens, Helpful Colleague kindly dropped round the tent. The Barbarian Horde pounced on this new form of entertainment and set about erecting it in the garden before the light faded.

While that was going on, Beloved Husband and I did our best to answer all the questions that Structural Engineer Man asked us. He carefully noted all our answers down on his clipboard and eventually took himself off, telling us that he would file his report as soon as possible and that we would shortly hear from the Insurance Company with regard to our claim.

Both statements, though no doubt well intentioned, turned out to be somewhat divorced from the truth.

When his report finally did materialise, nearly three weeks later, it blamed the wall collapse on the fact that the roof was too heavy.

I have to confess that I had real trouble believing that this was the cause of the damage. One could point out at this juncture that the roof had been in place for many, many years and logic would surely dictate that there would have been an issue with the wall long before now, if it had genuinely been too heavy.

But what do I know? I am not an old buildings expert either.

Interestingly though, the roof was actually still in place, having not moved an inch in spite of a significant part of two walls giving way. Probably not 'too heavy' then, as Genuine Old Building Expert was later to confirm in his subsequent report.

However, I am rushing ahead. We hadn't met Genuine Old Building Expert at that point, and we wouldn't for quite a while.

Unfortunately.

In the meantime, we had more delights to come from the House Insurance Team, including the arrival of Loss Adjuster Number 1.

But not for a while.

We had several days to survive first before he showed up.

Several days during which Beloved Husband and I started systematically stripping the cob section of the cottage of all the important articles we could get to. Each trip up the stairs involved keeping a careful eye on the cracks to see if they were still moving before grabbing and bolting with whatever essential items we could get our hands on.

Mattresses, bedding, clothes and school work came down in a random sequence. Chaos, at 17, was about to embark on her second A level year and Logic, at 16, was soon to start AS levels, not to mention Quiet's GCSEs, so school work definitely counted as essential. Then there were things like tooth brushes, pants and socks, sports kits, shoes, musical instruments, books and general bedroom paraphernalia; all were dragged downstairs and deposited in jumbled heaps on the covered patio at the back of the house.

Then we got to work dismantling furniture and bringing down bed frames, wardrobes, desks, anything we could get access to really, and hauling them down, a piece at a time, to dump in piles in the garage, while trying to keep all the relevant screws and bolts together in small sandwich bags taped to each item.

This furniture dismantling operation was the scariest bit so far, as it involved staying put upstairs for fairly long periods of time during which the creaking and settling of the 'possibly' (i.e. definitely) still moving house happened loudly around us.

We weren't daft … well … apart from the fact that we were repeatedly entering an unstable building that we had been specifically warned to stay out of. We could see that the cottage was not going to be habitable for quite a long period and may in fact need to come down entirely. Regardless of what the house insurance did or did not do, we had to find a way to establish a reasonably acceptable, temporary (we hoped) existence.

***

Friendly Local Builder popped back several times over the weekend, having managed to procure yet more propping equipment. He merrily installed lots more metal scaffolding poles, wooden wedges and other strengthening apparatus.

"Better safe than sorry," he said cheerfully, as we all consumed yet more tea whilst watching the walls for any sign of further movement.

Sadly, I am not joking!

When you've seen them move once you can't help but keep watching in case they do it again. It's somewhat ominously addictive.

Our poor little home looked like it had suffered a major stroke. It's formerly pretty, little, cottagey face sagged alarmingly all down one side, with an upstairs window hanging at a wonky angle and the previously central porch roof tipping over rather drunkenly. After so many years of chocolate-box beauty, she now looked sick, old and so very tired that it made my heart ache with despair.

Inevitably, our Friendly Local Builder was keen to be invited to quote for whatever work might be necessary to fix the current situation but we were at the mercy of the Insurance Company procedure before we could make any such decisions. Off the record, though, we did discuss vague potential building options and he gave us some very scary costings.

It basically boiled down to the fact that we were possibly looking at a bill of well over £200,000, if not much, much more.

Beloved Husband had to take himself off for an extended lie down.

I couldn't really blame him.

Friendly Local Builder eventually exited stage left, issuing the helpful suggestion that if we were determined to risk our necks by repeatedly entering the unstable structure, which he wouldn't advise, it would be a good idea to empty the loft while we were at it.

Righto!

Thus, I found myself up a ladder, in the dangerous bit of the house, explaining the disastrous situation to the spiders squatting in the loft when Beloved Husband eventually felt up to rejoining the party. Thankfully he then bravely took over all loft jurisdiction and spider taming duties. He's my hero! I really hate lofts.

We made a pact between us that we should only be present in the unstable section of the house one at a time. This decision was based on the general consensus that it would be preferable for the Barbarian Horde not to lose *both* parents in one fell swoop, should the house fall completely.

Admittedly not very happy logic, but we were trying to be relatively sensible. Obviously, the Barbarian Horde were banned from the wobbly bit entirely but, keen to be useful, they formed a line along which to pass items through the rest of the house and out onto the patio. The piles of stuff were getting very large and extremely random now, spilling some significant distance out onto the garden. Happily, the weather was reasonably fine, but we did try to keep the most fragile items under cover and dragged large sheets of polythene, unearthed from the garage, over all the rest in case it rained before we could sort and distribute items to as yet undisclosed and unidentified storage locations.

It is a very sobering thing to see your entire home contents laid out across your garden. It definitely made us want to reach for neat alcohol, and lots of it. However, we restricted ourselves to one small beer each that evening. We potentially had £200,000 to find now, so there would be no spare money for sufficiently strong spirits to anaesthetise us. Current supplies were going to have to be rationed carefully.

Beloved Husband and I eventually stopped sorting things and sat on a pile of boxes in the conservatory, exhausted, having ensured that all the Barbarians were as cosily wrapped up in the tent as possible. He still wasn't saying very much at all. Periodically he would mutter "£200,000" and shake his head in disbelief, rocking backwards and forwards disturbingly, but nothing else terribly coherent was forthcoming.

After a very long heavy silence, I remember saying, "if you are thinking of driving to Beachy Head and jumping off, can I come too?"

You could hear a pin drop the room was so quiet.

"Hmmmm." He said vaguely.

There was a deathly silence.

"Of course," I eventually continued thoughtfully, "that probably wouldn't be very fair to the Barbarian Horde would it?"

More pins dropped.

"Hmmmm."

"No, you're right," (me again,) "and I suppose that, house insurance claim issue aside, we can guarantee that the life insurance would *definitely* not pay out if we do jump off."

A whole tin of pins went crashing to the floor.

"Hmmmmmmmmm."

"So, probably best not eh?"

"Hmmmmmmmmmmmmmmmmmmmm."

"Yeah," I agreed, "You're right!"

8: Soon

Definition: taking place within a short period of time, promptly or speedily.

Still in the past…

The next day was a Monday. Wonderful!

If you think the normal school run on a Monday is entertaining, you should try doing it from a tent in your back garden. It is vastly more diverting.

Especially, when that tent is surrounded by the dismantled and jumbled up contents of your entire home! Added to that, we were down to one extremely small bathroom for six of us and we all had to get ready for work and school in a very short space of time.

Under normal circumstances the first hour of our weekday mornings consists of a tightly scheduled bathroom rota system, worked out carefully to enable all six of us to utilise one of two showers, get dressed, clean teeth etc. Then a short period of time follows for breakfast, the finding of lost shoes, ties, bags, homework and other miscellaneous items before we eventually tumble into the car with almost everything we need for the day; finally setting off for school and work with something resembling a packed lunch each and a vague hope of arriving in time.

Slightly more complicated from a tent in the middle of a disaster site.

Nevertheless, we managed it and I finally arrived at work only mildly more late than usual and sat with a hot cup of tea looking numbly at the pile of paperwork awaiting my attention.

"Lucky me!" I thought, and then jumped as my mobile sprang into life.

A brief conversation ensued, after which I rattled off a quick text to Beloved Husband as follows: 'Loss Adjuster on way to our house now, ETA 15 minutes, meet me if you can'. Leaving my computer on and some papers strategically placed so as to appear as if I were in the middle of something but had been called away on legitimate office business, I swiftly exited the building, hoping no one would notice I was moving in entirely the wrong direction for that time of the morning. Then I drove hell for leather for home. (Or should that now be tent? It hasn't quite got the same ring to it!)

Beloved Husband and I arrived home simultaneously and waited in suspended animation for Loss Adjuster Number 1 to turn up.

Forty minutes later, a car squealed around the corner and onto the driveway scattering pea shingle in a multitude of directions. Normally that really bugs Beloved Husband. I only ever do it as a subversive form of revenge when he's really winding me up.

The driver, a short, rotund gentleman with thinning hair worn in an ambitious comb over, opened the car door forcefully and stepped out onto one leg, leaving the other foot dangling in the foot well. He was obviously not planning to stick around very long.

After a cursory glance at the crumbly cottage walls he nodded at us in acknowledgement.

"Yes, well," he said rapidly, "all very unfortunate of course. I'll be in touch soon to let you know if you're covered."

With that, he flung his capacious backside down into the driving seat, slammed the door and reversed off the driveway at speed.

Obviously a very busy man!

Not quite what the TV ad had implied was standard behaviour for Insurance Company personnel in a crisis scenario.

Hey ho! Let's not get too hung up on semantics.

After a several moments of stunned silence I ventured to speak.

"That was...um...promising...!?!"

"Hmm!" replied Beloved Husband, nodding slowly before patting my arm gently, then heading back to his car and driving away - hopefully back to work and not towards Beachy Head. I didn't have the energy to check, so started my car engine and set off for my own office.

***

It quickly became patently obvious to me that Loss Adjuster Number 1 and I held wildly different definitions of what "I'll be in touch soon," actually meant, as the days drifted into a week.

Then longer.

In the interests of being fair, it probably is a relatively short period of time if one is living in a nice, warm, dry home rather than camping out in ruins.

Normally I would have been on the phone to him within 48 hours, and again every hour after that until I got a response, if I hadn't had Beloved Husband (in surprisingly reasonable mode) saying patiently, "Give the poor chap a chance, he probably hasn't even received Structural Engineer Man's report yet."

Now you might think that Beloved Husband is the epitome of calm, rationality, but I know better. He had stuck his head quite firmly in the sand. He was completely convinced that the House Insurance Company had no intention of helping us and he simply couldn't cope with having that fact confirmed, because then we'd have to come up with a plan of action on our own. He knew that neither of us had a clue what that plan might be.

Yes, he is occasionally a glass-half-empty kind of guy, but not always and under the circumstances, can you blame him?

I couldn't.

He is usually the person I turn to for help fixing problems when I can't work them out for myself. He has a real skill for finding solutions and often comes up with some remarkably ingenious ways to sort things out.

Only not today! This particular issue was a bit beyond us both.

Having waited impatiently for two weeks, I finally caved and rang Loss Adjuster Number 1 to find that Beloved Husband was entirely correct. How galling! The Structural Engineer's report was still unavailable. This was nearly two and a half weeks since he had crawled all over the remains of our disintegrating house. How could it possibly take that long for him to write a report?

Immediately after placing (note the impressive physical restraint) down the telephone receiver to Loss Adjuster Number 1, I called the mobile number that Structural Engineer Man had foolishly provided me with on that day, so long ago, when he had visited our property. I didn't have the time to be patient and just wait and see. That report needed writing.

He answered relatively quickly, I thought (on the twentieth ring), and snuffled down the line at me that he had been ill. I sympathised briefly, with remarkable sincerity, and mentioned that we were still in the tent that he had seen our children erecting when he visited. Including the eldest, who had only recently been discharged from hospital following her latest bout of major abdominal surgery and had fairly significant mobility problems associated with her recovery. None of which were helped by prolonged tented accommodation. (Well, he was the one who introduced health issues into the mix. I was just following his lead.)

Was that laying it on bit thick, do you think? It was all perfectly true. He was a grown-up after all and I didn't think he needed sheltering from the very real situation facing our family.

We needed him to do his job. Things were not going to move forward until he did.

As it was, events did stumble forward, or backwards in fact, it depends on how you look at it. Very shortly afterwards, I received a fleeting telephone call from Loss Adjuster Number 1.

These transitory communications appeared to be his speciality, as were momentary visits to properties for insubstantial meetings it would seem.

I was to wonder later on whether this was a deliberate tactic employed for personal safety reasons in case his clients became unreasonably enraged and attacked him. One should remember he would regularly meet with people enduring all sorts of personal crisis situations and perhaps short encounters limited the chance that he might be verbally or even physically abused whilst performing his duties.

While I definitely understood the impulse to indulge in a bit of verbal abuse, there was absolutely no chance of him being shouted at by me. In recent days, I had found that a hard, constricting lump had settled in the region of my throat and wouldn't be dislodged. Its presence was making breathing and swallowing difficult, so speaking was almost impossible.

My mobile phone rang late one afternoon, two weeks after my rather firm chat with Structural Engineer man about his missing report. It was my day off, and I was sat on the wonky floor upstairs in the master bedroom attempting to dismantle a chest of drawers so that I could fit it down the stairwell. Loss Adjuster Number 1 stayed on the line long enough to laugh jovially as he told me that we were not covered for the structural issues at our property as we didn't have accidental damage cover included in our policy. He would send me an email to confirm.

I listened to the ended call tone for a long time after he had swiftly disconnected. He had hung up so quickly in fact that I hadn't had a chance to speak at all, which was useful really as it spared me the trouble of formulating a response.

Well! What on earth was Accidental Damage?

Accidental Damage

Definition: damage to an individual's home or its contents that transpires inadvertently during the course of everyday life.

I was to learn that accidental damage is something that you opt *into* when you take out house insurance. It doesn't come as standard, and basically if you don't have this, then you are in trouble. Or at least that is what I understood from the brief call. I may be wrong.

I clearly remember talking to the bright young thing on the phone when setting up our house insurance several years earlier. The conversation was really very speedy. How many bedrooms did the property have? How old was the property, did it have a thatched roof etc....? She spoke incredibly quickly, rattling off reams of information as well as the terms and conditions, which made it all quite hard to follow. I kept on having to ask her to repeat things in an effort to understand. She complied, very patiently, but she seemed completely unable to actually slow down the verbal torrent of information or explain it any other way. In the end, she gave me a quote that sounded reasonable and I accepted it.

I certainly don't remember being given the option of having accidental damage and then (wait for it...) *deliberately and actively turning it down.*

But I must have done.

Why on earth would I do that?

I have a highly developed sense of paranoia. If it can go wrong, it definitely will. That is my life. Added to that, I cohabit with a small tribe of Barbarians. Why on earth would I not take out accidental damage insurance?

9: Courage

Definition: the capacity to do something that terrifies you, fortitude when confronting pain or grief.

Fast forward to present day, two years later…

Finally, painting away in my little study, I was beginning to realise that this particular issue with the insurance was probably the main root of my problem.

Could this really be the reason that I had not been able to forgive myself? Although innocent of the main event, in some respects I had to admit that I had been responsible for a significant element of the subsequent ramifications.

Somehow, in the course of that telephone call to set up our house insurance so many years previously, I must have got it wrong! I had made a mistake that was to affect all my precious people massively and so very detrimentally for months if not years to come, possibly permanently.

Had I genuinely reacted to subconscious guilt by damaging myself so effectively for so long? Punishing myself by intentionally cutting off a major source of comfort because I didn't think I deserved it? Perhaps all this time I was carrying on as if everything was fine, while the hidden cracks in my own personal foundations continued to throb with pain.

The cat gave a jaw-cracking yawn from the window sill, obviously finding my company immensely boring. She lazily turned her back on me while Adele's dulcet tones floated up from the radio.

I took a large swig from the cup of tea that sat steaming away unobtrusively at my elbow, next to a large chocolate crispy cake, and wondered.

***

Looking back at that awful time again, I remembered that, later that same day after Loss Adjuster Number 1's phone call, I had been forced to confirm to my Beloved Husband that we were completely on our own. That the house insurance policy, for which we had paid so much over the years, was not going to help us now that we needed it. I remember watching in desperation as the last tiny flicker of hope in his eyes flared briefly before going out.

He is the strong and silent type and didn't utter a word of recrimination. Not one to wail and moan at life's problems, he just gets on with what needs to be done. Now, regardless of his personal feelings of despair, not once did he blame me for our predicament. Yet I wondered how I was going to live with myself?

Lying wordlessly side by side with him under a pile of cold, damp duvets in the tent that night, both of us beyond completely exhausted and staring sightlessly up at the canvas roof in shock, I felt as though my heart was being crushed beneath many tonnes of concrete.

I knew that he was there next to me, sharing the heavy weight that was pressing down and I was struck by the supreme contradiction that this represented. The immense comfort of knowing that the person I loved the most was with me, that I wasn't alone in my misery, was countered by the devastating knowledge that not only was he suffering too, but that I had inadvertently added to that suffering.

Had I been given a choice I would simply have turned my face to the wall and died. Yet obviously I couldn't, and now I wonder if it is truly a sad state of affairs if your only will to live is derived purely from the existence of another? Perhaps not, for in truth my Beloved Husband is the only thing that got me through that awful night, a light in the deepest darkness.

At that moment of utter hopelessness, in a state of complete physical and mental exhaustion, there had been an almost imperceptible rustle, a minor movement as the little finger on his right hand entwined itself with the little finger on my left and held on tight.

***

Returning to the present, I shook myself away from those dark memories and looked at what I had created while my mind wandered through the past.

Ah!

All black!

Ninety by sixty centimetres of complete and utter black.

Not a nice shiny black either. I had just spent the last hour and a half covering the whole surface in several layers of deep, unrelieved, devastating, matt black.

If it reflected my thoughts accurately then perhaps it was apt. That moment in the past when I realised that our appalling situation was my fault had probably been one of the bleakest times for me, especially as I was then finally coming to understand just how momentous the resulting consequences from my mistake might be.

More of that to follow…

I wondered where I was planning to go with this painting and reached for another pot of paint before forcing my mind back to those terrible times, determined that now I had started stirring this whole thing up, I would see it through to the bitter end.

10: Silver Lining

Definition: a comforting or positive aspect of an otherwise fraught situation.

Back to the past…

We should consider that the responsibilities of adulthood can frequently make us neglect the true meaning of life as we become swept up in the pursuit of ephemeral goals, forgetting to enjoy every moment for what it is.

Taking a lesson from the supreme wisdom of Monty Python, I would suggest that we must attempt to look on the bright side of life, and it would be a major mistake to think that everything about that fateful summer was to be doom and gloom for our intrepid little band, for it most certainly wasn't.

As always, life with the Barbarians was never boring. Over the years it has been a profound privilege to bear witness to them evolving. Observing them throwing themselves into new life experiences with a joyful exuberance has been truly awe inspiring, if simultaneously exhausting and terrifying from a parental perspective.

That summer proved that our Barbarians definitely had living in the moment sussed, possessed as they are of a highly developed sense of the ridiculous leading to frequent bursts of hilarity, no matter how bleak the prospects around them.

The prolonged period of warm, dry weather provided the most

delightful of rare but perfect British Summers, which resulted in our protracted garden camping existence definitely having its more positive moments. After all, we were taking our inspiration from Enid Blyton's Famous Five and camping in the ruins of our home, much as they had camped in the ruins of a Castle in their very first adventure. An Englishman's home and all that, although there were no lashings of ginger beer, we can't stand the stuff.

As soon as the school holidays commenced officially, our Barbarians, the boys in particular, were able to indulge their wilder sides on an almost permanent basis, thoroughly enjoying being out of doors.

The fact that the PlayStation and TV required acts of extreme exertion to access almost all of the time, given the piles of boxes stacked haphazardly every which way in the house, they swiftly ceased trying and instead indulged in their own personal re-enactment of FIFA12 on the little patch of muddy ground near the stream, beneath the oak trees at the bottom of the garden.

Probably the single most enjoyable aspect of this football fest was the careful transfer of the previously mentioned mud from the ground to large areas of their own persons. What could be more fun?

Let's face it people do pay large amounts of money to be covered in mud for health benefits. Could this be a possibility for raising the missing £200,000? We certainly seemed to have an unlimited supply of mud. (Hmm! That's not a bad idea, I think I might start making a list of potential money-making schemes.)

The mud, once acquired, was then removed in a somewhat haphazard yet fairly effective manner by chasing each other through the sprinkler in the early evening before the heat of the day waned. Regrettably, the neighbours would be forgiven for thinking our mini marauders were committing multiple acts of murder given the amount of squealing that this activity generated. We are very remote here, but there are a few rural properties with the misfortune of being located just within earshot of our makeshift encampment. Nevertheless, our dear neighbours were very patient through all of the nonsense that went on that summer, as well as what was to follow.

At night though, in spite of the bright sunny days, I have to admit that I still felt the cold. Perhaps it was the contrast of the night time temperatures with the daytime warmth. However, this didn't seem to affect the Barbarians at all, no doubt helped a little by the hot water bottles I would stuff into their sleeping bags last thing at night while they snored away peacefully, just before I collapsed into my own bed.

Conceivably, it was my age that meant I felt the cold more than they did, or maybe it was the chill weight of sheer dread I was carrying around in the core of my being like a block of ice slowly freezing my heart, which made it impossible to warm up.

There is no doubt though, that for the adults, the nights passed in a blur of the following: struggling into a chilly sleeping bag and then trying to insert yourself under several layers of duvets on a slightly damp mattress in order to get to bed in the tent, then lying awake all night feeling cold and worrying, trying to remember to breathe. At three AM most nights, I would wonder if I had the energy to keep going. Was I even going to able to get up in the morning? During those long dark nights, it definitely felt like it would be a kindness if I could simply choose to never wake up again rather than face the months ahead. Sleep would eventually claim us, but it wasn't the restorative kind.

We would wake up unbelievably early from brief, unrestful slumber and for just a few seconds each morning everything would be alright. Then reality would come crashing back in as we realised that it hadn't all been just a bad dream. Our house genuinely had fallen down, and we truly were living in a tent in the back garden. This was our reality.

Beloved Husband and I would force our aching bodies and bruised spirits upright, to keep going, to survive another minute, then another hour and eventually another day. Pretending to the Barbarian Horde all along that we had slept just fine and wasn't the whole thing just an exciting adventure?!

I don't think for one minute that they believed us because, frankly, we're not very good actors and they are all pretty smart.

In an inspired move, the girls started switching the radio on almost immediately on waking each morning so that the music, the routine of regular traffic and news announcements, as well as the light-hearted banter between the co-presenters could bring a welcome distraction and a much-needed air of normality to our al fresco early starts.

Chatting away in a studio somewhere, there is no way that those two complete strangers and the production team supporting them could possibly have known what an important lifeline they were throwing to one displaced, desperate little family unit.

Nevertheless, in spite of that, trying to accomplish anything at all continued to feel like we were wading through treacle. Slow, painful and messy.

I continued making meals for all but would then just push my portion round my plate. Speaking was hard, swallowing impossible. I wasn't the only one struggling. Beloved Husband was doing the same. Without a single word of reproach sent my way.

All the time we kept reassuring the Barbarian Horde that everything would be OK. They knew we were lying and so did we, but everyone pretended for each other's sake and we just kept calm and carried on wading.

***

Eventually, one day, the nice lady who rented the field next door for her horses beckoned to me from her side of the fence.

"What a lovely idea to camp in the garden. Your kids must be having a wonderful time. Aren't you a great mum?" she said.

I think it was probably the parenting compliment that demolished any stiff-upper-lipped pretence on my part that all was hunky dory. I sighed heavily and filled her in, even though I didn't really know her from Eve and she probably wished she had never asked. I had no polite filter in place to be anything but brutally blunt.

House falling down.

Potential £200,000 bill or more.

House Insurance refusing to have anything to do with it.

Don't know what to do.

Shrug!

She was genuinely shocked and sympathetic. I didn't realise it at the time but this encounter was going to prove to be fairly pivotal for the remainder of my story, but there's more of that to come later on.

Smiling a sad goodbye, I walked away from her towards the sheds at the bottom of the garden and thought no more of it.

***

At that time, we were desperately in need of storage. Having emptied large amounts from the houses into the garden, we need to get it all sorted and stored before the spell of good weather broke. At this time, the useable parts of the house contained piles of boxes of displaced belongings with other larger items in heaps outside on the grass under tarpaulin.

Now that we knew there was definitely no help coming our way from the house insurance, we would need to find £200,000 all by ourselves. There would be no extra available to pay for additional storage. The current plan was to sort through everything including the double garage and several sheds to get rid of anything that wasn't absolutely essential so that we could free up space for the things we needed to keep.

Thus, began the first of countless trips to the tip, recycling centre and charity shops as much of the family's historic treasures were eliminated.

Looking back on it, we probably should have tried to sell some stuff online too, but we didn't have the time, the know-how or a suitably reliable internet connection to achieve this effectively. As it was, Beloved Husband sorted the tip items and I arranged the charity shop trips and recycling. Neither option was a walk in the park due to the staggering volume of stuff to be purged.

Understandably, if you take too large a donation to one charity shop the ladies in charge start to get quite twitchy, mainly because they don't usually have room for you to unload your entire house into their little stockroom cupboards.

I began to take longer and longer trips out, combing local towns and villages for charity shops that I had yet to donate to. Feeling immensely embarrassed, I would walk in quickly and leave several bags of good quality items before trying to escape as fast as possible before some sweet old lady could ask me about gift aiding. Not that I normally minded gift aiding, I just found that my voice wasn't co-operating, which made communication of any sort very difficult. I had also been warned that apparently you can only gift aid so much before the tax man starts getting stroppy and, believe me, I had enough problems on my plate without upsetting Her Majesty's Revenue & Customs.

Similarly, if you turn up at the tip too often they start getting suspicious and think you are dumping stuff from a business, or perhaps operating as a professional house clearer on the sly. (Now there's another idea for earning the extra £200,000. I am on a roll here!)

Beloved Husband finally started a bonfire at the bottom of the garden in order to burn what rubbish we could in order to save on the sheer number of tip trips. The Barbarians had leapt on the idea and thoroughly enjoyed throwing on things like old cardboard, broken chests of drawers, piles of school jotters and exercise books. (I promise that we checked they were the old ones before allowing them to do this.) Eventually they chucked in huge foil-wrapped packages of potatoes with chunks of butter inside and also cored apples stuffed with raisins and syrup, to be raked from the ashes later and consumed whilst we all sat on or around the old swings in the sunset.

Ultimately though, we exhausted the tip, fire and charity shop options and what remained were all the items we needed to keep, and therefore to store.

The sheds and the garage (Beloved Husband had collected a few sheds over the years fortunately) had all been cleared of unnecessary junk and our more essential possessions stored carefully in the space created.

This work was achieved in silence.

There was nothing to say.

It wasn't an angry, accusatory silence; it was merely an empty exhausted one as talking would require oxygen and there simply didn't seem to be enough of that. Every breath required supreme effort. We just had to keep putting one foot in front of the other in that deep, ever present treacle. This was merely the first of so many tasks that we were going to have to complete in order to move forward.

The sorting process, in its entirety, took several solid weeks of hard work, interspersed with actually going to work and trying to keep our jobs. During this time, Beloved Husband periodically disappeared into the house to rummage around inside the computer, investigating our finances and exploring options for locating £200,000.

On one such occasion, left alone in the garden, I approached my little wooden summer house (in other words, a shed with a slightly bigger window than normal) and unlocked the door. Inside was my sanctuary, my painting space crammed with all my work, stacked neatly after my latest exhibition. My favourite pieces were on the walls but a relatively large storage area would be available if I moved all the other paintings out.

For the first time in weeks I felt something other than emptiness and despair. Here was something I could do. A tiny thing in relation to the problems before us but at least this was one issue within my power at last. We needed space. I could create a bit of space. Right here, right now.

Before I could stop myself, I had started to haul canvasses roughly out on to the grass. It wasn't long before I couldn't prevent myself from throwing them onto the nearby bonfire. Huge paintings, one after the other, crashed into the flames while I stood and watched.

A strange thing happened.

Gone was the anaesthetising numbness, in which I had barely existed, and in its place was genuine sensation. Admittedly, it was unbelievably painful at first but, weirdly, it was good to feel something, anything at all. In some ways the pain helped. I deserved to suffer for my mistakes. If I had not been distracted with my paintings all the time, so obsessed with getting back to them, then perhaps I wouldn't have made that disastrous mistake when I was setting up the house insurance. If I'd paid attention to more important things then maybe we would be fully covered. Maybe everything would have been alright.

I threw another painting to join the others in the growing inferno.

At least I was feeling something legitimate at last. I was so angry with myself. It was the very first spark that would eventually become a seething anger that was to mature and develop into a raging fury, one that I could eventually turn outwards and use to get us all through this. A force to be reckoned with! When I was ready, anyone who got in my way was going to seriously regret it.

Beloved Husband came running out of the house. (Anyone except him, of course.)

"What are you doing?" he asked in astonishment. "You don't have to do that, we'll find somewhere for them."

"There is nowhere else," I replied forcefully. "I'm just being practical. They aren't likely to sell at the moment anyway. The downturn in the market has affected everyone. People just aren't buying art anymore. We don't have the luxury of space right now so let's get rid of them. It's more important that we sort our home out for our children."

"At least keep some," he insisted. "Surely there's no need to destroy them all?"

"Yes, there is" I replied and flung yet another canvas into the flames. "There's every need."

Part 3

Legend states that the phoenix must burn before it can rise from the ashes reborn.

Alice May

11: Millstone

Definition: rounded stone used for grinding, or alternatively a weighty load that crushes.

Returning to the present.......

I resurfaced in my little study and looked at the canvas before me.

"That's interesting!" I thought, looking at the dark display. Not quite so black as it had been though.

Of course, that was before I looked at my watch and realised I was late to pick up the Barbarian Horde. Oooops! Very late!

I threw a large cloth over the easel to hide the painting. I was going to need to think about this before I let anyone see it.

Hurling myself into the car I sped off to retrieve the tribe from their establishments of enlightenment and returned shortly to throw tea at them, (not literally, although sometimes it is tempting). Then I fed the dishwasher and the washing machine, before setting off yet again to post appropriate people to the various after-school activities on the schedule for that evening.

Driving along humming to the radio, I caught Quiet's eye in the rear-view mirror. He was grinning smugly to himself.

"What?" I asked.

"Told you you'd be less grumpy."

He wouldn't say that if he could see the sinister, metallic sunflowers I had just painted on that extra-black canvas. It really was quite psychotic. Perhaps I should hide it somewhere very permanent so that no one could decide I needed carting off to the funny farm for a lengthy stay of respite care. They might never let me out.

I felt absolutely and completely fine, but that didn't mean my behaviour, or my artwork, matched.

The next day though I was surprised to acknowledge that I had slept extremely well, probably for the first time in ages, and I wondered if the act of creating these rather menacing images had, in fact, allowed me to express feelings that I couldn't speak about aloud, feelings that had hung on me like a heavy millstone for a very long time.

"Who needs a psychiatrist when you've got a large canvas, a ready supply of Daler Rowney and a four-inch brush?" I thought to myself, in amusement.

Better out than in, I supposed.

Might as well see where it took me. Anything was worth a try in order to get a good night's sleep around here.

It so happened that I had two weeks of time owing from my job that needed using up. You know what employers are like, they tell you that you can take 20 days annual leave and then throw so many projects at you that actually taking the time off is extremely difficult. Then, at the end of the year, they say that as you haven't taken the time off you obviously enjoy your job so much that you didn't need it and then they take the days you haven't used away from you because it's now a new financial year (as if that matters).

Ok, I will admit there is probably some sensible business reason for not being able to carry over annual leave into the next year. It's the same where I work if you do unpaid overtime. You have to take any unpaid overtime back pretty sharpish or it gets forgotten. I was determined not to lose my time off and so had taken the next two weeks off work, even though no one else in the family was going to be around to share the time with me.

Occupational options for today included numerous housekeeping tasks, none of which I had any intention of attempting. I had decided that I was going to paint again. All day! Perhaps all this thinking back though old events was doing me some good.

As I dressed, I pulled on my favourite comfort jumper as a talisman.

It was an old one of my mother's that she'd been about to throw out two years ago but, as she knew I had always liked it, she had offered it to me first. My Ancient Parents (A.P.s for short) are not, in fact, remotely ancient, I just call them that to wind them up.

The A.P.s had been most concerned to hear of the disaster that had befallen our lovely, rustic home but, as they lived in deepest darkest Devon, some three hours away by car, they were unable to be of much practical help. Or financial help either, come to think of it, not that we expected them to bail us out anyway. Believe me we are not the sort of family that has a spare £200,000 plus lying around although, if they did, I know they would have offered it. As would Beloved Husband's parents, had they been able.

All the A.P.s could really do was to patiently listen for hours as I sobbed down the phone, and I was grateful for that.

Having suggested that I meet them halfway for lunch so that they could be reassured that I wasn't about to top myself, they fed me, dried my tears and handed me mum's old jumper, which I immediately put on. I didn't take it off for days because it smelled like my childhood home (she hasn't changed her washing powder in all this time), which is a scent I still associate with being protected and safe. It felt like a permanent parental hug and I needed all the comfort I could get.

Ultimately though, after about a week, it started to smell like mouldy old tents and even though people expect you to whiff a bit if you are camping out, I finally gave in and washed it, putting it back on immediately it was dry.

It is still my favourite item of comfort clothing today, even though it is getting extremely threadbare. As such, it seemed fitting to wear it now as I planned to return to face the demons of the past.

Speaking of demons, the Barbarians needed relocating back to school before I could have the luxury of rummaging through my memories again.

12: Fairy Godmother

Definition: a person who comes to the assistance of someone in trouble.

Back in the past…

As I understand it, Fairy Godmothers come in many different forms and have a habit of popping up when you least expect them. Cinderella didn't recognise hers when she appeared disguised as an old crone at the kitchen door before the ball and, two years ago, I certainly didn't expect mine to arrive wearing muddy Hunters and a battered Barbour jacket over a smart business suit. But there you are. Life is full of surprises!

In the interest of political correctness, I should probably refer to this welcome visitor as a Fairy Godperson, even though the spellcheck doesn't like it; if I wished to be totally fair, perhaps I should drop the 'fairy' bit too as there were no signs of wings, wand or anything else and I wouldn't want to be sued for slander.

Never mind, I am sure that you get the general idea. All I am trying to say is that a benevolent stranger turned up completely out of the blue and tried to help.

I am referring to the day after my major oil paint fuelled bonfire, when the lady who owned the horses in the field next door hailed me for a second time. I was engaged in raking over the smouldering bonfire ashes. (Do please note the continuing Cinderella analogy here. I am rather proud of it.) At the same time, I was contemplating the steely determination to take action that had been forged in my heart while I watched my artwork burn.

The only problem was that I wasn't exactly sure what action to take.

Putting the rake to one side and dusting ash off my hands, I ambled over to the fence, expecting some more sympathy but she was eminently more practical and briskly introduced me to her husband (who was wearing the aforementioned Hunters and Barbour jacket). "I hope you don't mind, but I told my husband what you said yesterday. He says he's got some information you might find useful."

I shook hands and smiled politely.

"I don't mean to intrude, but I couldn't believe what my wife told me yesterday. It's so staggeringly awful."

I nodded in agreement.

"I know there's probably nothing practical we can do to help you so I've made a few enquiries instead," he continued. "Don't worry, I kept it all anonymous. Just asked theoretical questions, you know? I don't deal with insurance myself, but I work with a lot of people who do. Did you know that you can reject the Insurance Company's decision?"

I shook my head, wondering precisely where he was going with this.

"Are you actually sure you're not covered? Have you looked at your detailed policy document? After all, they might just have made a mistake? Overlooked something? Have you read the small print?" he asked intently. I stared blankly at him, trying to keep up.

"Look, tell me if I am teaching my grandmother to suck eggs," he continued hurriedly, obviously keen not to have offended me. "You and your husband are probably dealing with all of this very competently, but it just seems unbelievable that you can simply have the door shut in your face like that. It has to be a mistake, surely?"

I didn't like to mention that my Beloved Husband was currently busy practising his excellent verbally-challenged-ostrich impressions and I wasn't sure he was competently dealing with breathing, let alone anything else.

I also resisted pointing out that I was a strong, independent woman and could solve my own problems without a man. Mainly because right then I wasn't, and I couldn't, so I didn't.

This really nice, compete stranger was genuinely trying to help and

I was very grateful indeed.

"I looked at the insurance certificate," I said, struggling to get my rusty voice to work after a period of disuse. "They're right, we haven't got accidental damage."

"But you have got basic house insurance, haven't you?" he insisted patiently. I have to admit I wasn't in great shape for processing any information at that point so he could be forgiven for thinking that I was a bit dim.

I nodded.

"OK, good, so you just haven't got accidental damage. Well what's accidental about this whole thing?" he asked. "Who decided it was an accident? And why? You didn't accidentally do something like drive into your own house, did you?"

He stopped and looked uncertainly at me for a moment.

"You didn't, did you?"

I shook my head. "Of course not," I replied. "The cob gave way, apparently it can do that, but I have no idea why."

"Well then. Accidental damage is only a small part of house insurance. You need to find out what you are covered for. Otherwise what on earth have you been paying them for? You took out a policy with them in good faith. You trusted them to sell you something that would protect your home for you and your children. You had every reason to believe that you were covered. They have a duty of care towards you that is not being met. You must go back to them. Start asking questions. Get them to listen to you. Fight back."

He was getting quite frustrated with me now and, from a logical point of view, understandably so. However, in my defence, unless you have actually been in our position, no one could possibly understand how helpless and feeble a previously active, dynamic and relatively intelligent person can become when faced with such catastrophe.

It was true though, that at that point in time Beloved Husband and I had simply accepted the primary decision as final and given up. We had absolutely no idea how to move forward. We were both in shock at losing our home, and utterly terrified about the potential consequences of this disaster to our growing family. In that paralysed state we were really not capable of making important decisions.

We both oscillated between siting in a heap and staring into space for ages (trying not to cry, in my case), sometimes rocking silently or twitching uncontrollably, while at other times we were manically working on emptying damaged rooms and storing salvageable items, all the time lying cheerfully to the Barbarians saying that everything was going to be just fine. Not that they believed us.

"But how?" I asked eventually.

"Refuse to accept their decision, write back to them saying they are wrong and must reconsider. If they still refuse to help you, then you can go to the Financial Ombudsman, but you have to go back to the Insurance Company first. They have to have turned you down a second time before the Financial Ombudsman will look at your case, but there is a real chance that the Financial Ombudsman will rule in your favour."

I didn't like to ask what the Financial Ombudsman was. I had never heard of, or needed, one until now. I made a mental note to Google it. I nodded slowly trying to think through the thick fog of tiredness that was smothering my brain.

"What have you got to lose?" he asked. "It can't get any worse, can it?"

Now there's a silly question!

Things can always get worse.

13: Guardian Angel

Definition: A person or spirit that watches over protectively.

Still in the past…

Up until then we had enjoyed clear skies and warm balmy days. Unusually for Britain, this occurred during the first few weeks of the school summer holidays and the whole country basked in sunshine as we toiled at our salvage operation.

You might be interested to know that the nights in the tent were still very cold though, in spite of the mini heatwave that was roasting the daytime hours. Or have I mentioned that already? We had managed to drag several mattresses out of the house and inserted them with considerable difficulty into the sleeping compartments of the tent, followed by a selection of sleeping bags, blankets and duvets. These, coupled with hot water bottles, full nightwear, fleeces, dressing gowns and woolly hats, made up our night time attire. I drew the line at wearing a coat to bed, although I did seriously consider it at one point.

Each evening started out sufficiently snug and then slowly deteriorated as the darkness deepened, into a series of hours during which one debated whether getting up to put on yet another layer of clothing would result in too much body heat being lost in the process or would staying still and ignoring the increasing chill be a better option? (I never did work out the answer to that one.)

This was inevitably followed by pondering whether one needed to go to the loo sufficiently badly enough to warrant the effort involved in extracting oneself from sleeping bag and tent to trot across the garden into the house, waking everyone up in the process (why are tent zips so noisy?), and once again losing all body heat into the bargain.

Added to these personal night time deliberations I also felt obliged to accompany Small, the youngest Barbarian, into the house whenever he required the bathroom, because I reasoned that, as he was only seven, it was unacceptable to let him cross the garden and enter a house with stability issues, in the dark, on his own.

What disaster might befall him on this quick journey (the loo is right by the back door after all and the tent was very close to the house) was undetermined, but, as I am sure I have mentioned previously, I am blessed with a highly developed sense of paranoia that had not been helped by recent events. Now might be the exact time that savage wolves or grizzly bears decided to announce their secretly reintroduced presence in Britain, just in time to snaffle a sleepy seven-year-old-boy-sized snack.

Of course, once all these night time issues have been endured, it should be remembered precisely how early the day starts when you are camping, especially in summer. Dawn is volubly welcomed shortly after 4am by the birds, making the nights so short that really there was no time to grumble about the lack of sleep before it was time to get up again.

As it happened, Chaos had found it impossible to negotiate the tent as a sleeping accommodation option due to her 'recently-discharged-from-hospital-following-major-surgery' condition (stitches, four hourly requirements for medication taken with food, post-operative pain, and mobility issues will do that). As a result, she stayed in the house for the nights. Those mattresses that we had been unable to stuff into the tent were piled up along the far wall in the lounge area and she had made herself a cosy nest on the top like some modern-day princess and the pea.

Inevitably my paranoia came into play here as well, as I was convinced that given Chaos' aforementioned 'recently-discharged-from-hospital-following-major-surgery' condition, she shouldn't really be in the house on her own in case she fell or suffered a relapse and required rescuing.

OK, I agree, I was definitely looking for trouble now as at 17 years old, she was perfectly capable of looking after herself, or at least ringing my mobile if she had a problem, but give me a break! These were very extenuating circumstances. After all, there was still a blooming great hole in our wall that would not stop strange people (or their dogs) from wandering in off the street without so much as a by-your-leave.

The result was that I spent most of the nights wandering from tent to house and back again checking that my chickens were all present and correct, whilst systematically putting on any number of additional layers of clothing. No wonder I was behaving strangely.

Then the weather broke and things got worse.

This was, without a doubt, the moment when my dread of storms was born.

The night following my encounter with my fairy godparent (or whatever we decided he was), the good weather announced an abrupt departure in truly spectacular fashion. In came the rain with a vengeance. As if to punish us for the unaccustomed sunshine, water fell in torrents, making trips between tent and house extremely unpleasant. Nevertheless, we persevered. What choice did we have?

Even after that first flash of lightning, followed almost immediately by a deafening crack of thunder, right overhead. There we were, frozen with shock into our sleeping bags.

The most colossal thunderstorm was upon us so quickly that there was very little time to consider where the safest place to be actually was. It was definitely not in a flimsy tent pitched underneath a large oak tree. Then again, it probably also wasn't in a crumbly, old thatched property encased in countless long metal scaffolding poles and other excellent lightening conductors either.

The next crack of thunder decided it and, once the first of us had made a break for the house, the rest of us didn't hang about. Fortunately, as the last one out, I did remember to zip up the tent behind me in a somewhat vain attempt to keep all the abandoned bedding dry. (Or do I just mean 'less wet'?)

The Princess of Chaos had descended from her mattress tower and met us at the conservatory doors with a strong torch and some thick towels.

"I wondered how long you'd last out there in this," she said, handing the towels over. "It's probably a bit dodgy to have electric stuff on in here, so I turned off all the lights, unplugged the computer and TV and found a few torches. I also think it might be a good idea to get the fire going for heat as well as light. That way we don't increase our chances of attracting a stray lightning bolt given our current circumstances. It's not like we are going to get much sleep with this going on anyway."

I'm sorry, but who kidnapped the Princess of Chaos and replaced her with Captain Sensible?

Not to be outdone, Logic started shifting the piles of boxes around. "If we shove all this out of the way we could move the sofa over and put some of Chaos' pile of mattresses down by the fire. We're going to need some rest, even if we can't sleep. It'll be nice and cosy soon, probably the warmest night we've had for a few weeks."

In the end, we decided to block up the back door by the bathroom with the boxes as there was nowhere else to put them. After all, we weren't actually using the back door just then, and if we needed to get out in a hurry the conservatory doors were so much closer.

You see we were all thinking like proper paranoids now.

It is very true though that it is an ill wind that blows no one any good. We were surprisingly comfortable, snuggled up on mattresses by the fire as the storm raged outside. It wasn't long before Small fell into a deep sleep as demonstrated by some rather remarkable snoring. As for the rest of us there was a powerful sense of security and reassurance in staying together and looking after each other. I would pinpoint that night as being one when perhaps healing began. Admittedly, the wound that had been dealt to our home and family life was hideous, but we were actually surviving spectacularly well under the circumstances.

As sleep was out of the question, given the combined impact of the storm and the seven-year-old snoring, we eventually started to chat amongst ourselves; something that there hadn't really been time for in recent weeks. The conversation inevitably turned to our situation and I made the mistake of suggesting that perhaps given the stormy weather forecast for the week ahead, we should take the A.P.s up on their offer to house the children in their spare room in Devon, at least for the rest of the summer holidays. Beloved Husband's parents had also kindly offered to help out in a similar way.

The atmosphere in the cosy room changed instantly as the three wakeful Barbarians looked at me reproachfully and a huge wave of chilly silence washed around the room.

"What?" I asked.

"You are kidding, right?" Such immediate eloquence from Quiet rather indicated his strength of feeling on the matter of an imminent departure for Devon.

Then the others waded into the fray.

"Like that's happening!" snorted the Princess of Chaos delicately.

"You're always telling us that if we stick together we can do anything," said Logic, "and now, at the first sign of trouble, you're telling us to abandon ship. I wish you'd make your mind up!"

The first sign of trouble?

Seriously?

Did she genuinely think this lightning storm was the *first* sign? I think we were well past sign number one, don't you?

"Anyway, Grandma doesn't have a PlayStation," said Quiet, as if that concluded the arguments for the defence. Wow, two statements from him in less than two minutes! He obviously had fairly intense feelings on the matter.

It was an established fact that the rest of the house could crumble to dust for all the boys would care, as long as the lounge remained intact so they could play FIFA. (Note the PlayStation was now accessible since moving all those boxes to the back door, a fact that had been carefully observed by Small before he fell asleep.)

It would appear that our mini marauders were staging a mutiny.

Unexpectedly, my Beloved Husband leapt immediately to my defence.

"Your mother is only trying to keep you safe," he said quietly. "I don't think you realise just how scared we both are that if we send you to grandparents, no matter how temporarily, we might not get you back anytime soon. We are in serious trouble here. You three are old enough to understand that surely?"

He took a long, steadying breath before trying to explain as calmly as possible.

"As your parents we have a duty to supply a safe home for you all, and we're currently failing to do that. If social services find out, they could potentially take you all away and put you in care.

The Insurance Company has refused to help us, we have barely any savings after the last lot of building work we paid for. I can't ask the mortgage company to lend us any more money on credit because when I enquired about it they said that they would want to do a drive-by to check the condition of the property before agreeing to anything. As the house is currently, very obviously, a wreck, they will then understandably refuse and might start to question the security of the existing mortgage. Maybe even call it in. So that's not an option.

We can't sell the property as it is, as we will make a massive loss because it is currently only worth a fraction of its true value in this condition. Finally, we can't go into hotels, bed and breakfasts or rented accommodation, because everywhere is booked solid till late-September.

Believe me when I say that I have looked at all of these options in detail. Unfortunately, we have no money available to pay for any of them."

We all looked at him, stunned by the sheer number of words coming out of his mouth after such a long period of silence. Obviously, a great deal more than any of us had suspected had been going on inside his head whilst he had had it figuratively buried in the sand during all those incredibly outstanding mute ostrich impressions.

He wasn't finished.

"The only reason we haven't had to send you away up until now is the fact that it is the summer holidays and camping in the garden is a perfectly acceptable thing to do as a holiday occupation. People pay a fortune for that sort of thing, especially here in the New Forest.

But come September when school starts again, then we have to have adequate accommodation for you. There's a very real possibility that we'll have to enrol you in schools near your grandparents or your aunts' and uncles' homes so that you can continue your education in a proper environment, while your mother and I fix this mess.

We can't even guarantee that you will be able to stay together, as there are so many of you. At least we have kind relatives, that we know would treat you well. They have all asked if they can help, which is very kind of them, even though they live so far away.

We also have wonderful friends locally, who I know would offer to have you, but I can't think of anyone who would have space for all of you together, let alone for months on end. Even if our friends can offer to put you up, there is the potential for our misfortune to then damage their family life, which is unthinkable. How can we ask them to do that? It wouldn't be fair to anyone.

As an extreme worst-case scenario, there is a very real danger that the State might step in, taking you away from us to put you in care. You might all be placed in different foster homes. We may never be allowed to regain custody of any of you again.

So, however you look at this situation, unless we can find a workable solution, quickly, our family unit, the six of us, will be a thing of the past.

That is what is breaking your mother's heart."

I shuffled closer to him, tucked my arm through his and rested my head on his shoulder before adding quietly, "And your father's."

Now some people might say at this point that we were overreacting. You might think that such a scenario would never be allowed to happen. To those of you who think that, I can say only this: I never for one second thought my house would fall down. From that moment onwards, I will never ever think that something terrible could not happen.

Believe me, anything is possible. Unfortunately!

There was a lengthy silence while the Barbarians digested Beloved Husband's words.

Then:

"As I said," stated the Princess of Chaos defiantly, "that's not happening! You two won't last five minutes without us to look after you. You need us. So, basically, we have less than four weeks left and we need a plan. Forget sending us away for now, and let's be practical. What are we going to do?"

"Yes, we can help," said Logic.

"Well, I am all out of ideas and totally open to suggestions, so go for it," Beloved Husband shrugged.

There was silence.

"Um," I said tentatively, wondering absently when exactly he and I had stopped being the ones in charge. "There is one thing," and leaving out all references to fairy godparents, I relayed the information I had learned the previous day.

"That sounds interesting," said the Princess of Chaos, pulling her laptop out of a bag near the sofa and booting it up. "Let's put 'Financial Ombudsman' into a search engine and see what comes up."

"And 'Accidental Damage', see what you can get on that," said Logic, before looking at me and continuing, "While she's communing with the internet, let's take a look at the small print in those house insurance documents."

Beloved Husband was way ahead of her and already digging in the filing cabinet that was wedged at an odd angle between an armchair and the piano. (I told you the crumbling part of the house had been emptied in a rush and rescued items stuffed randomly in the remaining space.) The cabinet had a couple of printers, a wilting pot plant and a sleeping cat balanced precariously on top.

The cat! Just who had been feeding the cat? I had totally forgotten about her in the last few weeks! What a dreadful owner I was. Still, she looked happy enough so someone must have remembered, unless she was catching mice of course.

"I can't believe you haven't done this already!" Logic continued exasperatedly.

She had a point.

Thus, our own personal choir of guardian angels rallied round to organise their rather shell-shocked parents into developing a plan of action.

14: Healing

Definition: the process of becoming strong or complete again.

Returning to the present ....

I sensed that the tenor of my painting was changing. Was the initial irrational, 'edge of madness' feeling to my artwork possibly disappearing? I felt the darkness was beginning to show signs of fading. One might even go so far as to suggest that, if this continued, they might soon start to look relatively sane.

I have heard it said that you have to suffer for true art. If this is what they meant by that, then I really wouldn't recommend it.

Thinking back, Beloved Husband explaining to our older children what the true cost of the loss of the house might mean, had finally dragged the shapeless, nameless monster that was haunting us both, out into the light so that we could see it clearly. This enabled us to start working together to find a way to beat it; to overcome the paralysing power that it held over us. The Barbarians' determination not to be sent away but to stay and fight for our way of life alongside us, gave us the additional strength we needed to hold on; to focus on a solution to the problem.

We were still a staggeringly long way off success, but the first tentative steps were being taken. The burden of responsibility was shared and became lighter with teamwork. Our little clan truly had its' back to the wall, but we were stronger together. Standing shoulder to shoulder against adversity, we were going to come out fighting.

Suddenly, an image that I remembered from before this whole fiasco started to dance across my mind. A concept that had been dreamed up during the long hours sat in hospital waiting rooms with Chaos. The existence of this idea was one that I had resolutely denied for nearly three years, closing my thoughts off to it each time it had tried to resurface. I used to tell myself that I didn't do art any more. Yet now, here I was surrounded by painting materials.

Looking at my watch I realised there was no time to start on anything new right then as parental duties were calling (and also my feet had gone to sleep so I thought I had better walk around to wake them up a bit before I had to drive anywhere). I contented myself with grabbing my last blank canvas and inserting it into the easel for next time. Perhaps I would try something a little different with this old idea and see where my new style would take it.

But for now, I had my Barbarian Horde's relentless food requirements to facilitate and I cheerfully set out to the supermarket with a lightness of heart that I was truly grateful for.

I should probably confess here that motherhood did not come as easily to me as I had naively expected it to. Right from the very beginning, it wasn't quite what I had imagined. The babies were amazingly wonderful, just as expected, if somewhat noisy. It was me that was the problem. I failed quite miserably to do the most fundamental things, like breast feeding. It's a lot harder than you'd think. I was forced to resort to the dreaded bottle after only five days. (No, not alcohol. Formula!)

Feeding continued to be an issue even when we progressed to solids. I spent days pureeing cooked vegetables, (yes, yes, I know about freezing it all in conveniently sized ice cube containers too – it all sounds so eminently reasonable and easy), only to have my little food critics spit it all back at me, so I made the heretical decision to resort to those handy little baby ready meals in tiny tins and jars. It must be remembered that this was way before the lovely, healthy, organic, easy open sachets you see in the stores today. So, my baby Barbarians were packed full of preservatives from a very early age. Which does explain a lot!

Understandably to some people, of course, this means that I am totally worthless as a mother and should be taken out immediately and shot. Not surprisingly, I don't subscribe to that theory. Life is hard enough so let's allow ourselves to take the little shortcuts that work for us and run with them.

Luckily, with increasing age, my Barbarians have developed fractionally more healthy food preferences and ready meals no longer feature on the menu. I spend a great deal of time generating colossal quantities of edible offerings from scratch, packed full of nutritional goodness, to put before the tribe. Gratifyingly all is generally demolished in the blink of an eye.

On a good day this is achieved with full use of table manners and 'team-clearing-up' activities afterwards. Good Parenting Points to be allocated here please!?

Regrettably, it is usually only ten to fifteen minutes before the little savages (generally the boys, but not always) start wandering round again looking for more sustenance, which could leave a lesser parent than I feeling quite despondent with the knowledge that she has, yet again, failed to fulfil her basic nutritional supply duties. I got over that particular guilt-fest a long time ago. Three meals a day is what I signed up for, after that they are on their own. Ish!

My solution has been to designate several large, low level cupboards as acceptable foraging ground. I attempt to keep them packed with accessible, mostly healthy, but not always (depends how desperate I am getting), snacks and they make a sustained attempt to empty them on a regular basis. The situation is assisted by Logic's handy obsession with baking. She has simply trained me to regularly supply basic ingredients for all main cookie / cake options in her repertoire.

Honour is satisfied all round and a degree of parent versus Barbarian balance is achieved as long as I can get to the supermarket before closing time. It's the country, for goodness sake; there are no 24-hour opening times here, of course it's difficult, but a deal is a deal. Anything worth doing is worth doing well.

Fortuitously, at this precise moment in time, the supermarkets are currently open because Mother Hubbard has more sustenance in her cupboards than I do right now, so a swift 'smash and grab' is in order at the local food emporium.

15: Treatise

Definition: a methodical discussion or argument in writing including a systematic account of facts, concepts involved and conclusions reached.

And so we return to our adventurers in the past...

It can be a bit like buses really (not round here of course because there aren't any buses, it's too remote, you see). I am talking about luck. You can have all this rotten luck going on and then all of a sudden, several fortuitous things can happen. Like the advent of my fairy godparent.

The trick is to recognise the stroke of good luck when it happens and then make full use of it.

During one of my less frequent forays into the damaged section of the house I happened to notice a man standing still at the edge of our driveway with his arms crossed over his chest, having a jolly good look at the house. (Yes! Ok, I admit I was looking through the biggest crack in the wall.) Now this wasn't that unusual. Not a lot happens in the country entertainment-wise you see and it was currently our turn to amuse everyone. Every Tom, Dick and Aunt Sally had trotted along the lane for a bit of, what my father would term, 'nosy-parkering'. No one actually meant any harm, so we generally just smiled and waved before carrying on with what we were doing.

Our lovely neighbours had all popped along at some point to sympathise and let us know that if we needed anything we had only to ask. This was extremely kind of them but, unfortunately, the solution to this particular issue wasn't quite the same as borrowing a cup of sugar or some tea bags. Not many people have a warm, dry home for six going spare. So, while it was fantastic to know that people wished to help, we were all pretty powerless in this scenario which is not a nice feeling for anyone.

We had put up numerous signs and a lot of red tape to indicate to those passing by that the site was dangerous and not actually a new amusement park. We strongly suggested that close proximity to the walls be avoided, because we were a bit concerned that we might get sued if any of our new fans got too near and were injured by falling masonry. Nanny State and all that, you can't just say that it's someone's own fault they got hurt because they went near an obviously unstable structure anymore.

Added to that, there were several incidents of people driving past and trying to look at the damage to the cottage at same time. This frequently resulted in the rubberneckers' cars landing in a rather deep ditch on the sharp bend, just along the road from the house. It turned out that the local farmer was making a tidy profit hauling these vehicles out with his tractor on a regular basis. I certainly missed a trick there, I should have sent the Barbarians along to help so they could claim a share of the profits. After all, I have £200,000 to find, remember?!

On this occasion though, things were different, as I recognised this particular nosy-parker and I wanted a word with him. How fortuitous!

Hopping through the wall (it's quite useful having a hole there when you are in a hurry, not that I am recommending that you get one of course!), I scurried over to him.

A tall, good looking, muscular man in his prime, he frowned down at me in a concerned fashion. "Should you be doing that?" he rumbled at me in a deeply reassuring, bass voice. "It looks rather dangerous!"

I looked back over my shoulder at the gap in my lopsided house and shrugged. "Probably not," I agreed, "but it saves ever such a lot of time."

After passing a few pleasantries back and forth, he finally nodded at the house and said, "Not looking too smart is it? Still, I've seen worse."

"Really?"

I was surprisingly torn by his comment. Part of me was reassured that he didn't think things were too bad. Yet, at the same time, a tiny piece of me was also mortally offended that he didn't think my tumble-down cottage was absolutely the most impressive tumbledown property he had ever seen in his life. (Please note that, once again, I was not behaving entirely rationally!)

Nevertheless, this was the opening I was waiting for.

"Did you know that the insurance assessor is saying it's all because the roof is too heavy. Can you believe that?" I asked with studied care, and stepped back slightly to observe his response with interest.

He didn't disappoint me.

I should explain for clarity at this point, that the man I was talking to, had actually been personally involved in the construction of the very roof that was being blamed by the house insurance's Structural Engineer.

Periodically, old thatched rooftops need completely replacing with new timbers and fresh thatch etc. This had last been done just as the gentleman before me was starting out as a very Junior Roofing Apprentice in the family firm. He had a very well-deserved reputation for being absolutely the best Master Roofer for miles around, and you could forgive his outrage at the mere suggestion that one of his works of art had actually damaged a property.

I must admit that he displayed a most impressive command of ancient Anglo-Saxon in response to my comment about the house insurance report. This colourful invective was not aimed at me personally, you understand, the poor chap was venting in the general direction of Structural Engineer Man, who (fortunately for both of them) was not present. This descriptive verbiage was immediately followed by a very detailed and specific description of exactly why the roof couldn't possibly have caused damage like that observed before us.

I won't mention where Master Roofer felt Structural Engineer Man should insert his report, but I think you can probably guess.

Having not really understood much of what he had just said, apart from the last bit of course, I offered him a nice cup of tea. I felt it would help with the shock of having had his work disparaged, so I tentatively took the arm of this enormously cross gentleman and steered him around to the back of the cottage where I parked him on a comfortable seat in the conservatory with a restorative brew. Then, armed with pen and paper, I asked him to repeat exactly what he had said before (not including the Anglo-Saxon bit or the other bit about where to shove…oh, you know what I mean!) so I could write it all down.

In the end, I showed him the email that I had received from Loss Adjuster Number 1 in its entirety and he was able to categorically discredit everything mentioned in it using impressively technical, roof-building jargon that I could never have made up in a million years. By the time he had finished venting his outrage, a large proportion of my letter rejecting the Insurance Company's decision had been created.

Then he said something that was to prove even more noteworthy.

I opened the biscuit tin, sending a small thankful prayer to heaven that the Barbarians had somehow left the contents unmolested, and set it on the table in front of him before picking up my pen again.

It stands to reason that, as a Master Roofer, my new best friend would also be very experienced in dealing with old buildings in general.

Now, it would seem that the previous winter had been one of the wettest on record for the country and, like many others, I had watched news reports in horror as large swathes of the next county disappeared under rising flood water. So many people were facing the loss of their homes, something I now had a little more experience of.

As it was, we had been in no danger of flooding here, but we had still endured massive amounts of rain falling under the action of extreme winds.

Master Roofer pointed out that cob cottages do not generally have foundations, and are therefore in danger of their footings being washed out should they experience significant storm conditions over a prolonged period of time. Such an event would precipitate the sudden collapse of a cob wall.

Aha. How interesting!

One word in particular, stood out.

Storm.

We might not have accidental damage cover, but we certainly had house insurance for *storm damage*. I had seen it in black and white by the light of a flickering fire at four o'clock that morning.

A slow smile spread across my face. This just might be the key to moving forward. I believed that I potentially had all the ingredients I needed to put a reasonable request to the house Insurance Company to reconsider their position on our claim.

I was ready to start fighting back now and, armed with my newly-discovered core of steel, I started to do some investigation. Countless research papers, several lengthy telephone conversations and reams of wind speed data and rainfall statistics later, it turned out that there had been more than four major (and well-documented) storm events in the area that previous winter. The last of which had occurred only six weeks prior to the cottage walls failing.

One storm had been identified by the Met Office as the most significant storm to occur in the previous 250 years. A second one had been reported as being worse than the storms of 1987. A third was termed the most noteworthy in 40 years. One local planner helpfully informed me that there were at least two other cob cottages within a five-mile radius of ours that had been significantly influenced by storm damage. Fortunately for them, neither of these two was affected to the degree of actual collapse like ours was and remedial work was underway to fix them.

It didn't take a genius to work out that the most prominent part of our cottage, the section that was most exposed to the prevailing winds and unprecedented driving rainfall, the section which had taken the brunt of all those significant storm events, was the corner section where the two main load-bearing walls had failed.

Our beautiful cottage had successfully survived over 350 years in remarkably good condition, only to be finally vanquished by successive destructive storms arriving one after the other in a single final tempestuous winter period. She had tried valiantly to hold herself together to protect the family living within her, but the burden had proved too much. Waiting until everyone was safely out, she had surrendered her heavy load and crumpled to her knees in defeat.

Several hours later, following a fair bit of time on Google, a quick call to a friend at the Environment Agency for specific local storm data to back up my arguments, a really close reread of the insurance policy document and some extremely furious typing (that keyboard will never be the same again), finally my treatise was ready, attached to an email and sent, followed by a paper copy via snail-mail.

A baby step really but, in view of how little progress we had made so far, it was a very triumphant baby step indeed.

Cue: flourishing trumpet fanfare, or maybe not!

***

No response.

Not a dicky bird!

No acknowledgement, no receipt, nothing.

After two days, I telephoned the Insurance Company only to be told that all correspondence, including incoming emails and letters, goes via a department in another county entirely to be scanned before being distributed and that this could take up to a week.

Seriously?

I do realise that the lady on the phone had no idea what our living circumstances were and was not personally responsible for our situation, but the complete lack of concern was a bit much. I was fast running out of the ability to be reasonable.

In the meantime, electrical storms were repeatedly battering the English countryside.

And us.

As I mentioned before, we were aware that electrical storms were quite risky and, in order to lessen that potential danger, we didn't use any electrical equipment while the storms were in progress.

Just as we were getting used to sleeping in a cosy, warm huddle by the fire for the fourth night in a row, an interesting new development occurred. All of a sudden there was an almighty flash of light followed by what sounded like a firework going off inside the front abandoned section of the house. The Barbarians were actually managing to sleep through this, but Beloved Husband and I were definitely not, so we decided to investigate.

During the previous four nights, the stormy weather had resulted in vast quantities of water pouring through the cavernous holes in the broken walls causing lots of water damage. You would be forgiven for wondering why on earth we had not attempted to cover them with something, but you must understand that this was a 'Catch 22' situation. If we did anything at all, then we risked the insurance telling us that we had made the situation worse by our actions and refusing to help us.

Admittedly they were already refusing to help us, but there was still a remote chance that we might be able to persuade them to reconsider. Therefore, apart from some polythene sheeting and a few sandbags to limit how far into the ground floor the incoming rainwater could flow, we had not touched the cracks at all. After all, we had been strongly advised to stay away from them by the Insurance Company's own operative.

Anyway, the situation that faced us that night was the fact that every flare of lightning generated a surge within the electrical wires in the damaged walls of the cottage, which would cause a blaze of sparks to burst out and fly right across the room. Beloved Husband and I hastened to turn the electrics to the entire cottage off at the mains. We then retreated to a safe distance to watch carefully for the rest of the night, with several fire extinguishers handy. Heaven help us if the sparks took hold in the thatch!

I believe that this was the final straw for Beloved Husband, who is usually the soul of reason, diplomacy and discretion.

Not this time; the blue touch paper had been lit and it would be prudent for all to stand well back.

He and I were both done with hopeless despair and self-recrimination.

We had also done rather a lot of polite yet patient exasperation.

In an extremely short space of time, we skipped mild irritation, hopped over progressive annoyance, fast-forwarded through extreme aggravation to arrive at complete and utter raging-inferno outrage.

Enough was enough!

Shoving the cat off the laptop, what followed (at six o'clock that morning, i.e. as soon as we were able to safely turn the power back on of course) was a terse email to the house Insurance Company, to the effect that our house was falling down! They, the Insurance Company, were refusing to acknowledge their responsibilities. Under the current circumstances there was a very great likelihood that someone might be killed, or seriously injured if the property fell any further, and in our opinion, they were absolutely and completely in breach of their duty of care to us, their customer.

We also drew their attention to the fact that the front wall of the house, which was definitely still moving, would probably sever the oil line to the boiler, which ran at its base, should it succumb to the influence of gravity entirely. This might not only generate an environmental disaster of a significant scale, it would also probably bring the mains electric power and telephone lines to the house down at the same time, with potentially unthinkable consequences. We suggested that they might like to consider communication with us with regard to these matters.

We finished our email with the promise that if we had received no response from them by noon that day we would be taking legal action and going to the press. Attached to the email was another copy of my treatise rejecting the original decision and explaining why. This was sent to every single email address we could find on the Insurance Company's various letters and documents, including those located on the company's website, from local offices to regional, all the way up the ladder to head office.

They couldn't all go somewhere else for scanning surely?

Obviously not! At precisely 9.01 that morning, the telephone rang.

16: Storm Damage

Definition: damage to a property caused by violent winds, usually in conjunction with rain, hail or snow.

Staying in the past….

Let's take the positives where we can find them.

The news was good, not brilliant, but it was still good. The door that had previously been slammed forcibly in our faces had been reopened just a teeny, tiny crack. Our caller, who identified himself as someone really incredibly important from somewhere exceedingly lofty, politely accepted that while we were in a very difficult situation, he did not necessarily agree with our opinion that Loss Adjuster Number 1 might have either made an error in judgement or could potentially have been misinformed.

Nevertheless, he did concur that perhaps the situation might require a minor review in order to satisfy both parties that no misunderstanding had occurred.

Might we be free, perchance on Friday at 10am for a meeting on site to discuss the issue?

Well, we certainly had nowhere else more pressing that we needed to be.

A swift confirmatory email followed, outlining that a Professional Gentleman, all the way from Birmingham, would be attending a meeting at our property. Loss Adjusters Numbers 1 and 2 would also be joining us. Very interesting! Amazing in fact!! How very keen they were to communicate with us all of a sudden. I felt it was a shame that we had to resort to threats to get their attention. Rather sends the wrong message, doesn't it? However, needs must.

Given the sheer number of people coming from the Insurance Company, we decided that there would be a degree of safety in numbers and invited our Friendly Local Builder and the knowledgeable Master Roofer along to ensure that any technical talk did not go completely over our heads. The last thing we needed was to be blinded with building science and lose this opportunity to be taken seriously.

The Barbarians were all keen to observe proceedings too, and were most helpful over the next few days as we attempted to generate enough space in the kitchen, lounge area and conservatory to put up the dining table and locate enough chairs for the forthcoming meeting. We worked very hard to make the useable part of the house look as clean and tidy as possible, despite the fact that it was stacked to the rafters with all our displaced worldly goods.

As the day dawned, having been persuaded by their father, as Commander-in-Chief, that they must remain silent while the meeting was in progress, the Barbarians arranged themselves in their pre-agreed battle formation.

Logic had opted to be in charge of hospitality and positioned herself on a stool in the kitchen so that she could discretely produce tea, coffee and biscuits for all present should the opportunity arise.

Due to her ongoing mobility issues, the Princess of Chaos settled herself on the sofa by the fireplace with her iPad primed, ready to look up anything technical. She was close enough to hear everything said and had an excellent view of proceedings.

The boys opted for an external surveillance operation and carefully selected two lookout positions up oak trees that provided good visibility of either the front or the back of the property. Together they formed our very own personal reconnaissance team. Quiet was armed with his iPod and Small had an ancient walkie-talkie so they could maintain communication with us should it prove necessary.

Beloved Husband and I simply walked up and down the driveway, unable to settle anywhere, we were in such a state of anxiety and anticipation. Eventually we stopped near the gate and huddled together like a couple of penguins, looking for comfort rather than warmth. Beloved Husband repeatedly removed my fingers from my mouth to stop me chomping on my nails with the stress, and I kept stuffing them right back in until he wrapped both of his arms around me and held me so tight that I couldn't move at all.

***

Loss Adjuster Number 1 was the first to arrive with another dramatic spray of pea shingle. We were gratified to notice that he removed his entire body from the car this time, including both feet, which we felt was a promising indication that he intended to stay for longer than two minutes.

Having greeted him politely, we found we had very little to say to him. It would seem he felt similarly towards us, so we waited in awkward silence until the Professional Gentleman from Birmingham arrived with another gentleman who he introduced as Loss Adjuster Number 2. Both of these new arrivals were dressed in very smart pinstripe suits and looked incredibly business-like and, well, professional. They were gentlemen who looked like they made important decisions. We rather felt that our situation warranted an important decision, so hopefully they were in the right place and would make the right decision.

They shook hands politely with us and then asked if they could inspect the property. It was made respectfully clear to us that they would come and find us when they wanted to talk to us.

We had been effectively dismissed, in a charmingly inoffensive manner (it takes quite some skill to do that), from our own driveway. We were still mildly miffed though, but dutifully complied, retreating to the conservatory to deploy our secret weapons. Our lookouts were going to come in useful!

We realised at that point that we had made a school boy error. Literally! We had put the wrong school boy in the lookout for the front of the property. Quiet was his usual uncommunicative self, in spite of the critical nature of the situation. His habit of sending single word (in some cases single letter) text messages was infuriatingly obscure. After several indecipherable messages I snatched Logic's iPod and typed 'more words needed, in English, or NO FOOD ever again!'

There was a short silence followed by:

'K'

'I MEAN IT!!!'

'OK. Cool tape measures'

'What?'

'Dad would appreciate their tape measures.'

'?????'

'They have really cool tape measures. Electric.'

'OK I GET THAT BUT FOCUS, WHAT ARE THEY MEASURING WITH THEIR REALLY COOL TAPE MEASURES?' (Yes, it was all in caps, can you tell I was cross?)

'The house,' came the reply.

'DID I MENTION THERE WOULD BE NO FOOD?' I said.

'No. I am serious. They are measuring the house, all of it. The outside, really, really thoroughly,' he said.

That was interesting. I wondered why.

'And they seem to be arguing.'

Even more interesting!

'The man that arrived first was waving his arms around a lot and then he left.'

We had no idea what to make of that, but it sounded like Loss Adjuster Number 1 was now out of the picture.

I can't pretend I was terribly sorry about that. I don't think you can really laugh at someone while you are destroying their whole world and then expect them to like you, can you? Not that I am one to hold a grudge, he was only doing his job. Maybe he hadn't intended to laugh, perhaps it was a nervous reaction, but I could have done without it.

There followed a message from Small who was engaged in surveillance of the back of the property, letting us know that the other two men were approaching the back of the house.

We braced ourselves.

***

Beloved Husband and I were gratified to note that both Friendly Local Builder and Master Roofer had pitched up for the meeting as well, in order to sit very firmly on our team at this critical event. It is at times like these that one is surprised and eternally grateful for the kindness of strangers. Both were busy men and could easily have left us to sink or swim on our own yet, with no guarantee of recompense for their time, they were here standing up for what they felt was right.

I am not totally naïve either though; one wanted to defend his workmanship, the other was quite keen on the contract for the repair but that didn't matter. Neither of them was being deceitful in any way. The fact remained that they were here supporting us and our family. When you are the underdog, you take any help you are offered and you are very, very grateful.

After a certain amount of shuffling and shifting of chairs, eventually all those present were established in a suitable seat around the table in the conservatory, with the hot drink of their choice. Believe me it was important that everyone was comfortable because this was going to be a very long meeting. The boys had extracted themselves from their eyries and followed the two men in; and, after quietly ransacking the biscuit tins, they settled themselves in the lounge area with their sister, well within ear and eye shot to watch as events unfolded.

There was a moment of tense silence as we all regarded each other.

The Professional Gentleman took a thoughtful sip of tea before opening proceedings. He leaned forward, looked at both Beloved Husband and I in turn and then said most earnestly "May I say, personally, how sorry I am at what has happened to your lovely home. It must be very difficult for you under the present circumstances."

Well! You could have knocked me down with a feather! There must have been a mistake. Surely, they wouldn't have sent us a real-life-human-being?

What a sad state of events it was that I had honestly not been expecting genuine compassion! As a family we were braced for sweeping denials of liability, mountains of legalese, and ultimately an outright dismissal of our claim. This kind man could not have made a more effective opening statement. Immediately any defensive feelings of outrage, resentment and hostility that we held towards the unfeeling, faceless company were totally demolished.

Empathy aside though, let's not forget that he was here to do a job and we were still in trouble. As the meeting progressed, it became evident that we were dealing with a number of rather tenuous and undefined elements. I must ask you to bear with me at this point as I try and explain. Please remember that the following paragraphs are a note of how I understood the discussions that took place during that meeting. I may not have been entirely correct in my comprehension as it was a very complicated situation.

Primarily the Insurance Company had yet to determine whether our assessment of storm damage was accurate. It was suggested vaguely that this would require a number of independent assessments to be carried out by specialists. Whilst they stood by Structural Engineer Man's original report, they did agree that, under the circumstances, an assessment by an independent structural engineer, this time one who was definitely an old buildings expert, was required.

This would need to be followed by an assessment to determine whether any of the recent works carried out on the cottage could have been responsible for the collapse (i.e. had any of the work we had had done over the years we had lived there caused the problem). Then, dependent on the conclusions of these studies, the Insurance Company would make a final decision as to what degree of responsibility may or may not be held by themselves, with regard to our claim.

That seemed fair enough to us.

Then we came to the reason that required such careful measuring of the property with those impressive tape measures. This was all to do with the rebuild amount stated in our policy documents.

Please understand that I struggled to follow a lot of what was said here, but it would appear that we did not have a sufficient rebuild amount stated in the insurance policy documents for the whole property to be rebuilt. Apparently, even though we were only looking at a partial repair, they do the maths from your total rebuild insurance figure and work out some relative proportional amount for a partial repair, and then decide if you have enough cover. Yet another minor detail not mentioned when I took out the policy.

Generally, most people establish this figure over the phone just as I had done when enquiring about insurance. I hadn't realised how important this figure would be when it actually came to a claim.

This was going to be a big problem for us as it was the old section of our house that was in trouble, and older properties cost so much more to rebuild, putting a disproportionally large figure on a potential partial repair. You could happily build a much bigger property than ours, from scratch on the site using modern materials, from the figure quoted so I felt that we could reasonably have expected to be covered. But it doesn't work like that. The existing property was not modern and, therefore, this insured rebuild sum was not enough. There's always a slight snag isn't there?

Another major problem was that in the event that they decided that we were covered, any help they might consider giving to us could only ever amount to a 'like for like' compensation, which was, in fact, a technical impossibility as they could not give us back a historic, old building. No matter how hard they tried.

They were not allowed to give us anything that amounted to a 'material gain', and modern building methods and materials constituted exactly that. As our cottage was not a listed building and, therefore, was not exempt from building regulations, we would have no choice but to comply with modern building standards; the associated value of which in rebuild terms, the Insurance Company were implying, we were not entitled to as they would constitute a distinct material gain. Hmm, rock versus hard place!

The silly thing with all this was that while building in modern materials would be faster and more economical than trying to rebuild in cob, nevertheless in terms of pure value, the repaired building had the potential to be ultimately worth more in modern materials.

Confused? Me too!

Basically, if independent assessments agreed that we were looking at storm damage, and that was a very big 'if', then they would only able to possibly consider authorising putting us back where we were, originally.

That would be absolutely fine with us but, unfortunately, putting us back where we were was literally not possible.

Everything was still very much under dispute. Given the massive costs involved, I am not really surprised. I had no idea that these things were so complicated. All in all, we were not really very much further forward, but at least they were communicating with us and considering authorising (and paying for) the necessary reports. This was relatively good news, but you could be forgiven for thinking that I had started to buy into Beloved Husband's glass-half-empty persona by the sluggish way I was responding. Having had so little sleep in recent weeks, I was incredibly tired and found following the proceedings extremely hard. The truth of the matter was that a large elephant could have jumped up and started tap dancing, while simultaneously playing the trombone at that point, and I would have struggled to formulate an appropriate response.

Not so the Barbarians. It was evident from the pointed looks passing between them that they were monitoring everything and commenting to each other via their electronic devices. Small had shuffled right up to Chaos and they were muttering to each other, as she no doubt explained what was going on to him.

In the meantime, however, back with the adults at the table, the fact remained that it would be quite some time before a decision could be reached. Nevertheless, the Professional Gentleman accepted that we were in an untenable position with regard to the continuity of our family life. The tent, the mud, the scattered piles of belongings and the huge holes in the wall had all been duly noted and, while the company was not accepting any liability, they were open to considering our needs as a family during the time that the question of liability was being established.

Unfortunately, after much discussion, the general consensus was that there were very few options for alternative accommodation available locally in which to re-establish our family life at another location. By this I basically understood that hotels and rented houses were off the cards due mainly perhaps to the holiday season but also potentially because of long term costs that might ensue should the company determine that they were not liable to assist us after all.

I noticed at this point rather a lot of twitching coming from our teenage audience and a flurry of muted, electronic 'pings'. I concluded that there was an intense Messenger communication going on between the Barbarians as the subject of accommodation was being discussed. Then I realised that Logic was trying to gain my attention.

Employing the rather basic British Sign Language skills she had acquired whilst helping out at the after-school club that term, she was frantically trying to communicate with me. Having only a very rudimentary knowledge myself, I was finding it hard to understand her. I kept thinking she was saying "Remember Cornwall" but couldn't for the life of me think what she might mean.

Eventually, raising her eyes to heaven (teens do that so well, there must be an A-level in it!), she squeezed past the table, marched over to the sofa, grabbed the iPad off her sister and shoved it pointedly under my nose before sweetly asking the visitors if they would like refills for their hot drinks.

While additional hospitality requirements were being met, I quickly glanced at the website on the iPad screen and instantly comprehended what the girls were suggesting. Nudging Beloved Husband, I showed him, and had the satisfaction of watching enlightenment dawn there too.

Our eyes met with suppressed hope.

Such a simple solution.

If only we could get our kind visitors to play ball.

"How would you feel about a static caravan?" enquired my Beloved Husband after clearing his throat. "It would enable the family to stay together on site, protecting the remaining cottage area, prevent any danger of burglary or squatting and facilitate supervision of any repair works that might, or might not, be agreed." Two could play at the non-specifics game.

The Professional Gentleman looked at Loss Adjuster Number 2 and a discreet nod passed between them.

Just like that!

It was agreed that the Insurance Company would consider covering a one-off cost to buy and site a static caravan in our garden while the liability question of our claim could be more formally established.

Beloved Husband was to visit such a caravan emporium later that day to identify an appropriate vehicle and discern costs for purchase, siting and installation. This would be communicated back to the company in writing and if the costs were agreeable, then a cheque would be forthcoming to cover it. In the meantime, the Professional Gentleman also agreed that the Insurance Company would cover the costs of the independent reports required to establish ultimate liability on our overall claim.

It would appear that, even though no final decision had been made, we might have reached a temporary compromise.

Regardless of the final outcome of the claim, I do not believe the Professional Gentlemen will ever fully appreciate just what he did for our little family that day.

Part 4

There are dark shadows on the earth, but its lights are stronger in the contrast

Charles Dickens
1812 – 1870

17: Salvation

Definition: Preservation or deliverance from destruction, difficulty or evil.

Back in the present day….

It was during that period of time, when I was splattering acrylics left, right and centre in my little artist's cubby, that I began to realise that perhaps all wasn't as black and white as I had subconsciously painted it.

Admittedly, I had made a disastrous mistake, but to be completely fair it could also be suggested that perhaps the house insurance's initial response to us was a genuine error too, not a malicious attempt to wriggle out of their responsibilities. After all, once we had eventually managed to get someone to listen to us, it became obvious that this was much more of a 'shades of grey' type of situation. (No! Not that sort of shades of grey! Behave!!)

350-year-old houses generally don't collapse every day, or no one would ever buy one. (I must confess here that I certainly won't ever buy one again!) I am sure people can't possibly put themselves in this sort of situation for fun. Although, come to think of it, there are some very odd people around.

Thinking back, I remembered the additional pressure of knowing that we only had two more weeks left to the school holidays. Crunch time was coming.

Without a significant improvement on our current tented

accommodation, Beloved Husband and I would genuinely have had to start making the necessary arrangements for the disintegration and dispersal of our beloved Barbarian band around the countryside; sending them away from us, and each other, to live with relatives in proper houses before the school term started, with no real knowledge of when we might be able to bring them home again. It was a nightmare prospect for any parent, and dominated our every waking moment, making it impossible to think.

Prior to that first big meeting at the house, I realised that Beloved Husband and I had been totally in the dark about the right way to move forward. It is important to acknowledge that after that point in time, we were no longer trying to work out a solution to the overwhelming dilemma before us on our own.

The situation in which we found ourselves was vastly more complicated than we could ever have imagined, but at least there were now other people wrestling with the conundrum too, and they were not unsympathetic to our circumstances, even if they didn't yet know how things were going to play out either.

That one critical decision on the part of the Professional Gentleman to offer us a helping hand in the form of more acceptable accommodation, actually onsite at our beleaguered home, was of paramount importance because it gave us time and breathing space to think. Our beloved Barbarians were safe and, as long as we could stay together as a family unit, we could figure out the rest.

***

Up until now I seem to have been yacking on a bit about how that whole awful event was affecting me.

I do apologise. So selfish!

You could be forgiven for thinking that I wasn't too bothered about how it was affecting my Barbarians. Nothing could be further from the truth. On the whole they gave every appearance of having the time of their lives. As I mentioned previously, it was the school holidays and the lack of any formal routine meant they were in heaven, late nights, non-stop snacks, energetic games followed by uninterrupted, nag free, teen-slobbing time.

One could say that undergoing extremely high-pressure events can be character building, but I think you would get short shrift from my Barbarians if you dared to mention that. I believe they would comment that their characters had been sufficiently developed for the time being, thank you very much, and chilling out was definitely on the cards.

Nevertheless, Beloved Husband and I did notice there were a lot of quick hugs flying around though. I don't mean that they were hugging each other you understand, don't be ridiculous! They had the normal, healthy antipathy most siblings have for close proximity to, or physical contact with, each other.

You know the kind of thing I am on about. It generally works along the lines of 'that's my sibling, I can be rude to him/her and act like I hate him/her but you're not family so you can't!' (It works for cousins too!)

So, no, don't worry, things were not so bad that the Barbarians were going around indulging in group hugs. Nevertheless, they were behaving in an unusually polite and civilised manner towards each other and the number of times I would have to step in and mediate had diminished to zero, which would have been astonishing had I the wit to notice. On the other hand, they were flinging rather a lot of hugs in my general direction which was rather gratifying. Even Quiet, who, as with speech, generally doesn't do physical contact either, would sidle up to me from time to time and give me an awkward one-armed squeeze to the shoulders. That *seriously* never ever happens.

Initially I thought that this was an indicator of how stressed they all were and so kept repeating my rather fraudulent mantra to them that everything would be alright. Looking back though I think it was rather more of an indicator of how stressed they realised that I was and it was their way of demonstrating support and attempting to prop us up.

These Barbarians of ours and their hugs were helping us to hold on when there was genuinely nothing left in us.

18: Reclamation

Definition: the process of taking something back, or reasserting a claim or a right.

Returning to the past…

Static caravans come in all shapes and sizes as we were to learn, and moving them around the country in order to site them involves a whole host of fun and games.

Up until that point in time, the presence of static caravans on the road represented a total nuisance to me, causing disrupted traffic flow and delayed journeys. Now, however, I feel rather differently when I see one. Although the majority are probably being relocated for enjoyable purposes such as holiday homes for example, I cannot help but wonder if in fact the caravan being transported is going to save someone from rather more desperate circumstances, as ours was when it finally arrived outside our house on a humungous flatbed lorry, blocking the country lane entirely for quite a lengthy period.

The gentlemen delivering it looked exhausted as they pulled up, and looking at the size of their load I couldn't help marvel. How on earth had they got it through the ford down the road, around the sharp, wiggly bends or even under all the low hanging trees? This latter issue might well have been solved by the young man sat astride the roof of the caravan with a hacksaw. Obviously, the health and safety elf was on holiday that day (it was August after all) and, as the day progressed, it really became just as well he was.

I had visions of lopped-off tree branches being discarded all along their route. The local estate manager was not going to be pleased, but perhaps he wouldn't realise it was us.

Then we came to the rather problematic issue of actually siting our new accommodation in the grounds of our property. When it came down to it we had several basic engineering issues before us. Not least of which was the fact that in order to site the caravan, we were going to have to remove the props holding up the wonky, wobbly walls and pass it right alongside them.

Ooops!

Risky?

Just a bit!

The only safe space on the property that was big enough for the caravan to be parked long-term was in the back garden, and the only route to that space was the opening between the cottage and the garage; an area that was currently stuffed full of supportive metal scaffolding poles.

Added to that, during the manoeuvre, there would be only a maximum distance of one inch to spare on either side of the caravan as it passed through the gap meaning that extreme precision was essential. To assist the move, all guttering and external fittings had to be removed from both the side and roof of the garage and the caravan itself, before we even started, and a large section of our front hedge needed to disappear. Cue our new friend with his handy hacksaw.

Finally, as if we didn't have enough to contend with, should the worst happen and the walls actually fall onto the caravan (and hopefully not any people), then we would have to contend with the mains electricity wire also plummeting earthwards and all the associated mayhem that might ensue. Heck!

Fortunately, our team of lorry driver delivery men were definitely not a bunch of faint-hearted wimps. They were bred from the type of toughies who eat ten shredded wheat for breakfast followed by a Full English and a cup of tea strong enough to stand a spoon up in.

These tall, muscular, confident chaps were not going to let a little thing like potential death and destruction stop them from siting this caravan successfully, in spite of the obstacles in their way.

Unfortunately, leaving the caravan in the road for the next indefinable period of time and living in it there simply wasn't an option, as demonstrated by the significant tailback of cars that was building up. It just goes to show that even though there are very few houses along this little lane, lots of people use it as a rat run to avoid traffic on the main thoroughfares.

The other interesting thing was that the colourfully expressive language the thwarted drivers were using when they got out of their cars to remonstrate with our lovely lorry driver about the blocking of the road, tailed off very quickly when they realised the sheer extent of the experimental engineering that was actually in progress. Very few drivers got back in their cars to turn around and find an alternative route. Most stuck around to watch the novelty unfold and some even pitched in to help. A wealth of community spirit was propagated amongst complete strangers who all inevitably had their two-penneth of advice to toss in to the mix.

We British do love a good crisis, don't we?

So down came the props and the caravan was slowly and painfully inched through the gap with everyone watching the weak and wonky walls, with bated breath, for the slightest sign of movement. Given our luck so far that summer I didn't have high hopes but was grateful to be proved wrong, as eventually our new accommodation was coaxed into place with no casualties, other than my Beloved Husband's cherished hedge. What is it with men and hedges?

A round of applause rose from our audience with much cheering, shaking of hands and clapping of each other on the back.

Perhaps we missed a trick here and should have sent the Barbarians around with an upturned hat for contributions towards the missing £200,000. Had we realised in advance that our little crisis was going to attract such a crowd of onlookers, we could have sold tickets or at least put out some tables and chairs and flogged extortionately priced cream teas. Failing that, an impromptu car boot sale on the drive might have cleared some of our remaining junk at least.

It's amazing what could have been achieved with a little foresight.

Eventually, though, after re-establishing the wibbly, wobbly wall support system with relief and then reattaching all the fittings removed from the caravan and garage, our new friends the lorry drivers and the young man with the handy hacksaw departed, allowing our captive audience to melt away and we were left to investigate our new home in peace.

19: Comfort

Definition: The easing or erasing of a person's feelings of pain or upset.

Back in the here and now….

It was at that juncture, painting away in the present, briefly emerging from my entrancement with my recollections of the past, that I realised my artwork was definitely starting to look brighter. The distinctly disturbing demonic edge to my paintings was easing and, with my co-operation, might successfully be urged to depart on a more permanent basis.

Studying my most recently finished piece, I could see an underwater scene looking up from the depths of the sea. Oil paint in dark blues and greens at the edges of the canvas blended inwards to lighter turquoise, pale blues and white at the centre. The main feature of this painting was a shoal of silver fish spiralling in and up towards the light filtering in from the surface of the water. An altogether more positive image I felt. Progress!

After all, we cannot wallow in self-pity forever, can we? It doesn't half get boring after a while, and I did think I was beginning to feel a bit better about the whole fiasco. The radio on the windowsill was playing a track about wounds healing and the need to forgive oneself. I was beginning to think that this was a jolly good point. We should give ourselves a break from time to time and not be so harsh with ourselves.

We are only human after all and life is scattered with potential pot holes to trip us up, no matter how careful we are.

Thus, after chomping my way through the sizeable piece of chocolate fridge cake that had magically appeared on my desk with the omnipresent cup of tea, I made an important decision. If my little painted fish could swim towards the light then so could I.

There had been enough self-indulgent scourging over past events. What was done was done. I had faced my demons and acknowledged my crime. It was time to move forward. The prevalence of dark dismal shades in my work should be encouraged to give way to a sunnier and altogether more hopeful parade of happier hues. Moving the still wet canvas from the easel to the mantelpiece, from which vantage point the little silvery fish could inspire me while the oil dried, I got stuck in sorting out my work space.

Soon, a not insignificant stack of murky canvasses lurked out of sight behind me, banished along with my tubes of matt black, burnt umber and Prussian blue. Ahead of me sat a whole pile of bright, white sheets of thick paper, hopefully awaiting the studious application of the remainder of the rainbow.

Starting as I meant to go on, I selected a tube of exceptionally cheerful cadmium yellow and let my mind drift back....

***

It was around about the time of our new mobile home's arrival two years previously, that I became aware of a rather unusual phenomenon. Somehow small plates of edible comfort were appearing at regular intervals in my general vicinity. This started with things like the aforementioned chocolate chip cookies, and the repertoire expanded over time to include chocolate fridge cake, chocolate crispy cakes, chocolate fudge cake and more.

Note if you will the preponderance of chocolate, but please understand that this was balanced out with regular offerings of fruit too. There could be only one or two culprits. It would appear that certain people felt I needed feeding up.

Now it is very true to say that I started this whole debacle in a far more (how shall I put it?) well-upholstered-condition, which was probably a good thing as my appetite was one of the first things to desert me along with the stability of my habitation. Followed almost immediately by my sound mind, which beat a hasty retreat, flapping both arms and screaming loudly!

As I was in a general state of perpetual stress, I had been burning through my carefully laid down stores of fat at a remarkable rate of knots. Whilst not exactly enormous to begin with, (I prefer the term 'comfortably rounded'), I had quickly started to look rather scrawny over the ensuing weeks, which is really a very unfortunate look on me. How do all these models do it? They look slim, energetic and youthful, radiating supreme health whilst at the same time being stick thin. Whereas the skinnier version of me simply looked old, tired, haggard and very much in need of being put to sleep sometime very soon.

My darling daughters had obviously decided between them that I needed fattening up and the result was that they were cooking up suitably fat-store-inducing recipes. Quite literally! As Chaos was still finding being on her feet for any length of time rather tiring, she formed the research part of the catering team and was responsible for looking up suitably comforting and calorific recipes online, whilst Logic accomplished the development role by whipping up delicious treats in my fortuitously still fully-functional kitchen. Then, small bite sized portions were being left in suitably convenient locations in my general vicinity in the hope that I would absentmindedly notice them, gobble them up and instantaneously ingest over 1000 calories in one fell swoop.

Yum, I liked this theory. What intelligent daughters I have. The presence of comfort food on tap with virtually no effort involved on my part was definitely a dream come true for me. Add to that the fact that I had the convenient excuse that I was 'far too thin' and 'needed to eat'. Never in all my born days had I ever heard those phrases applied to me before and probably won't again. Yet it was true, I needed the energy to keep going, so each delicious mouthful was consumed gratefully and held no guilt whatsoever.

There were several other rather lucky knock-on effects from all this baking too. Ultimately, Chaos and Logic were actually learning to work very effectively together in their little enterprise, and extremely chilled out they were too. After all who doesn't find baking relaxing? In addition to this, they had the boy Barbarians totally in their thrall with this ready supply of previously unheard-of sophisticated delicacies requiring conveniently available stomachs, so their co-operation on many less exciting, more physical jobs was guaranteed.

Another positive side effect was that when they ran out of ingredients, Chaos worked out how to set up an online shopping delivery for more and thoughtfully included a basic food, veg and essentials content too. After all, if the poor delivery driver was going to have to trek all the way out to the middle of nowhere to find us, he might as well bring us shed-loads of milk and bog roll too. This, happily, meant that I could be relieved of my more arduous supermarket sweep duties and was therefore able to concentrate on more immediate home-salvaging tasks. As they say, necessity is the mother of invention. Prior to our little adventure, I am not sure that any of them really bothered to think where the family food supply came from.

20: Bedroom

Definition: A room specifically designed and kept for sleeping in.

Returning to the past and the newly-delivered caravan…

Scrambling indelicately up into our beautiful, green, static caravan (yes, they are quite high off the ground and yes, we had forgotten to order a set of appropriate steps, but never mind), we looked around us with reverence.

This was a typical six bed caravan as you would find located on any holiday camp site all over the United Kingdom. We had stayed in identical ones in Cornwall for quite a few summer holidays over the years, which is what had given the Barbarians the idea for such garden accommodation in the first place.

You would never believe just how excited we all were. After weeks of doom, gloom and wet canvas, here was a bit of pure exhilaration. No more nights in the tent. No more bending double to get under the tent flap, zipping reluctant canvas sheets closed, crawling under damp duvets to wriggle into cold sleeping bags before trying to roll or squirm into place on the mattress, huffing and puffing with exertion.

In fact, the tent had been completely removed in order to make room for the caravan. It was now suspended from the rafters of the garage in a vain attempt to dry it out before returning it to its kind owner. The poles and guy ropes had all been accounted for and the mud wiped from the pegs. The only thing bothering me about the tent was how to actually get it back into the bag it came in, but that was an issue for another time. There's only so much you can stress about in one go.

No longer would we have to put a huge amount of effort into the action of simply lying down to rest. We could merely walk into a caravan bedroom and flop onto a bed. Yay! Such sophistication!

For nearly two months now, every night had been preceded with the whole palaver of either settling into the tent with sufficient warm layers to see us through the night, having remembered to go to the loo first, or alternatively hauling mattresses off stacks in the lounge to place them on the floor as we carefully stoked the fire so that it was hot enough to burn for several hours but not spitting dangerous embers out at us while we slept.

On occasion, a single night might involve the deployment of both options if, once settled in the tent, an electrical storm started up out of the blue, resulting in a hasty and often soggy retreat from the tent to the house. In fact, storms aside, some nights it simply rained so heavily that sleeping in the tent was like trying to sleep under a drum kit whilst it was being played, so the house was often the better option and we would snooze curled up like a litter of puppies before the fire.

No more!

We had been thrown a life belt, or more accurately a life raft. Like the Owl and the Pussycat, we were about to set off in our own beautiful caravan-shaped pea-green boat to destinations unknown. Unlike them we had neither honey nor money, but we did have each other.

Now we had safe, warm civilised sleeping accommodation. Who knows perhaps we might manage to actually get some sleep. Our immediate future was settled. Regardless of the outcome of the claim, I was willing to bet that the Insurance Company wouldn't whip this caravan away from us while we needed it so desperately. It wouldn't be worth the adverse publicity to them to make a family homeless in these circumstances, and I certainly wouldn't have kept quiet about it. It was a fairly dubious notion that we would ever get it out of the garden again anyway, such a tight squeeze had it been to get it in.

This caravan had all the mod cons; electric lighting, running water and, more importantly, bedrooms! There was a master bedroom right up the far end, for Beloved Husband and I, with a small double bed (emphasis on the 'small' here – it really is just as well we like each other - the sheets from our old bed went around this mattress twice, how cute!) and a dinky little en-suite toilet. It was useful that I had lost that bit of weight I mentioned, because it soon became obvious that only stick insects go to the loo in these caravans. I must admit the term 'master suite' was far too grandiose for the space allocated but we really were not feeling fussy. Beggars not being choosers and all that!

Next to the master bedroom was the first of two twin rooms which could only be described as extremely snug. (Weren't we lucky that the Barbarians were getting on so well?) This twin room was marginally larger than the other and it was decided that the two boys would occupy it for several reasons. Firstly, they were the smallest two members of the tribe and thus the obvious contenders for sharing a small twin room. Secondly it was their habit to stay outside playing sport until the very last minute before falling into bed and dropping off to sleep almost as soon as their heads touched the pillow, so really they would spend very little time actually conscious in this tiny room anyway. Hence it was decided that their close proximity to each other wouldn't be too much of a major problem.

The other twin room presented us with a bigger issue though, as it was really very small indeed. One wonders whether it was in fact designed for twin guinea pigs rather than two humans. Nevertheless, as I said before, we were not complaining. We had become the most resourceful of individuals over the previous few weeks and as such immediately put our minds to identifying a suitable answer. Difficult situations really do inspire ingenious solutions.

Thus, it was decided that Logic should take ownership of the second twin room as Beloved Husband would drag her own small double mattress from its current position in the stack in the lounge and wedge it into the teeny tiny room on top of the two miniature single beds that were already there thus turning the whole room entirely into one bed. She merely needed to open the door and hurl herself bodily inwards at bedtime to spend the most comfortable of nights in what was effectively her own cosy little cupboard. (Just like a certain famous young wizard but with nicer family ties.)

Then we had only one more sleeping space to find.

I was keen that Chaos should not remain sleeping in the house on her own. We were a team and, as such, should stick together. Added to that, I knew I would only spend a significant amount of time trotting between house and caravan in paranoid circles to check on her so, from a purely selfish point of view, I insisted we find a way to accommodate her in the caravan as well. Thus, we investigated our new habitation for potential options.

It transpired that the caravan had a dinky little bathroom (small toilet, mini sink and a shower of upright coffin-like proportions), as well as a kitchen-dining-living area of compact yet functional design. As our own kitchen-dining-living area in the main house was still very much accessible, operational and significantly larger, it was decided that we would continue to use that space during daytime hours, unless it became absolutely necessary to retreat during future building repairs. As any such repairs were way off in the very dim and distant future at that point, we decided not to worry about them just then. One thing at a time!

However, the single most exciting innovation that the kitchen-dining-living area in the caravan had to offer us was the discovery that the incredibly uncomfortable looking sofa actually pulled out to form a small double bed. It should be noted that the pitifully thin mattress would not be an immense source of great luxury in the longer term, so Beloved Husband applied the same inspiration as before (he was definitely in an impressively inventive mood) and hauled the other small double mattress from the lounge and wedged it on top of the pull-out sofa bed.

Chaos could then rest in regal comfort in this section of the caravan. Once we were ensconced in our new bedtime locations with the doors shut, all would be able access bathrooms for night-time trips without disturbing each other and everyone was happy with the new improved sleeping arrangements.

The result was that we all had a relatively comfortable and private space which belonged to each of us. The tiny bedrooms had miniscule wardrobes and/or cupboards and we were all keen to commence marking our individual territories like cats, although we used boxes of reclaimed belongings rather than actually spraying foul scented substances. (Not so sure about the boys though, but I just decided to leave them to it.)

How lovely it would be to be able to hang clothes in wardrobes again, even if the judicious use of a crow bar were needed to get them in and out, so tightly would they be crammed in.

The only remaining issue with the caravan was one of access. We needed a set of steps. Beloved Husband disappeared off at that point to be original and imaginative in the garage, with parts of an old railway sleeper that he had unearthed from a shed at the bottom of the garden during our enforced clear out several weeks earlier, and I put the kettle on for a nice cup of tea.

Under normal circumstances, my Beloved Husband would be utterly devastated if you dumped a 30-foot mobile home on his beautifully manicured lawn. Fellas are just as funny about grass as they are hedges in my experience. However, our new arrival, which was immediately christened Hattie by the Barbarians, (No I don't know why, I didn't ask, I was too busy, but everything gets a nickname in this house) was greeted with open arms and must have triggered Beloved Husband's latent nesting instincts. No sooner had the lorry drivers disappeared over the horizon, than there he was making plans to lift up some old broken paving slabs and lay a path, crazy paving style, from the patio to the caravan door, complete with flowering pot plants on each side and a two-seater bench halfway along.

Was it so far from the house to the caravan that he thought we might need a quick sit down on the way? Although on second thoughts, given Chaos' mobility issues, this was to prove quite a good idea.

Then all that was left to do was to finish moving in properly, so we set about once again rearranging boxes and carting belongings around the garden.

21: Gossip

Definition: Casual chatting, generally about other people, usually including details that are not necessarily true.

Back to the artist, frantically painting away in the present…

I was going to have to accept the inevitable and stop painting for a while. I had selfishly dabbled away for several days now and was delighted to see the emergence of more positive pieces. Currently on the easel in front of me was a part-finished acrylic image of a saxophone, all bright, hopeful colours, dancing in the sunlight that was pouring through the window onto the page.

Noting the absence of a comforting titbit and restorative cup of tea at my elbow, I surmised that Logic must be otherwise engaged. No doubt there was some taxing A-level Physics conundrum tying up her energies somewhere. While I have no illusion with regard to my own intellectual limitations, all bias aside, I appear to have produced some surprisingly academic offspring. Although, to be fair, Beloved Husband did have something to do with that.

I supposed I should really re-engage with my beautiful band of Barbarians rather than spend my whole life daubing away at dubious musical instruments.

Still, it was a very nice saxophone!

Nevertheless, while two weeks off work sounded great, it didn't mean two weeks off running this family home so, putting my brushes to one side, I thought I had better do a quick Barbarian head count. Chaos was away at university learning about all things highly intelligent so I didn't need to track her down. As predicted, Logic was tussling with the mathematical principles of some physics experiment in her room and was best left undisturbed. So, after peeping in at her, I set forth to pin down the boys' whereabouts.

Not a difficult task as it happened. I located them easily, in the kitchen. It was obviously snack time because Quiet was energetically engaged in stuffing the entire contents of the fridge into a baguette (yes, a whole one), ably assisted by his sous-chef Small. No doubt the 'snack' would eventually be sawn in half and consumed at lightning speed along with the recently opened family size pack of crisps I spotted by the bread bin. Just as well it was only another hour and a half until tea-time, there was a real danger that they could starve without that little sarnie to keep them going!

Averting my eyes from the scene of devastation (In the interests of full disclosure, I should admit that it wasn't exactly tidy before they started.) I decided to leave the discussion about people clearing up after themselves until later on. I had learned the hard way that coming between a teenage boy and his food was an extremely reckless thing to do. Expecting any sort of a positive response at all to verbal communication was best achieved after nourishment had been consumed and not before. All that sugar in the bloodstream has a very useful calming effect on any growling, growing-boy hormones. Choosing which battles to fight had been one of the excellent pieces of parenting advice the A.P.s had given me.

Instead, I congratulated myself on having two such co-operative young men who obviously enjoyed each other's company, even if the collaboration was more driven by the fact that two of them were able to carry far more food away from the scene of a fridge raid than one, rather than from any real brotherly affection.

So, that was all of my Barbarians' locations effectively established! Jolly successfully too. They were all still alive. Job done!

Carnage in the kitchen aside, I braced myself and ventured bravely towards that space which is grandly referred to by all as the utility room. This is actually little more than a large walk-in cupboard located next to the kitchen which contains a battered old washing machine and the boiler. As I suspected, the laundry pile had been engaged in rapid reproductive activity in recent days and was now starting to overflow out of the utility room onto the kitchen floor. We were in imminent danger of disappearing under our own dirty washing. (Better than disappearing under someone else's I suppose, but still preferably avoided.) Dragging it all out and roughly sorting it into mountains of lights and darks, I shoved the first load into the machine and switched it on.

Then I turned my attention to the dry washing festooned around the conservatory on drying racks. I defy anyone from a large family to say they actually use their conservatory for sitting in. For seventy five percent of the year, ours is definitely engaged in intense laundry related duties only, and as such is always full of washing at various stages of drying. Where else are we supposed to put it when it's either always raining or too cold to dry clothes outside?

The only time our conservatory is free of laundry is if there are visitors coming and I have had sufficient notice to stuff it all out of sight, and hide the wire racks so that we can actually get to the wicker chairs in order to plant our bums on them.

While sorting through the dry clothes and allocating them into appropriate piles for each Barbarian, I was humming a little tune contentedly.

Well that was a change!

I sounded almost happy.

Considering what I had been forcing myself to think about recently, I was mildly surprised. Usually such deep reflection leaves me stomping around and snarling for hours. The Barbarians don't have a monopoly on uncivilised behaviour in this household, you know. Equal opportunities and all that! Nevertheless, thinking back, it was true that with the arrival of the wonderful Hattie and the removal of the camping component of our existence, we had moved into a far more stable way of life and a certain degree of contentment was achieved relatively quickly. We still had no idea how we were going to fix our home, or indeed how long such a thing might take, but the family unit was safe and a form of normality could be resumed.

We were winning.

In the face of seemingly insurmountable odds, we were doing alright!

It is not surprising then, when you remember how difficult achieving anything was back then, that nowadays I was quite content folding up the never-ending piles of laundry for my Barbarians, whilst simultaneously appreciating the nice, safe, warm and dry home environment around me with its agreeably sturdy structure.

In fact, so content was I that I started to remember some of the more entertaining things that had happened back then too. One such occurrence had happened totally out of the blue during a quick trip into the village one day, just after we had finished moving into the caravan.

Now, it should be remembered that we were living in the country where not a lot ever happens. Therefore, as I believe I have mentioned before, anything that does take place locally is always up for grabs entertainment-wise, especially when it comes to rumour, gossip and scandal. The best source of such hearsay is always to be found when standing in the queue at the village store. On one particularly hot day when the Barbarians had worked extremely hard moving boxes and furniture around to help me get everything sorted, I had decided to pay the local store a visit for some ice creams and lemonade. A reward for their uncomplaining hard work, if you will!

Standing in the queue and minding my own business (everyone says that but it isn't true), I couldn't help but overhear (they always say that too) what the two rather substantial ladies in front of me were saying in the hushed yet still quite strident tones of the true gossipmonger.

Apparently, there were these dreadful incomers (i.e. recent arrivals, not true country folk) who had deliberated knocked down their Grade 2 listed (i.e. very old and extremely precious) property in order to get around the rigid local planning laws so they could force the planners to grant them permission to build some modern metal and glass monstrosity.

I tried not to snort at the stupidity of such an action. After all I, myself, as a local, had frequently communicated with the planners with regard to the subtle improvements we had made at our own place and I knew how careful you had to be not to fall foul of the very strict but, on the whole, necessary rules. Intrigued, I shuffled a bit closer in order to hear more. This sounded very juicy indeed.

They say that eavesdroppers never hear any good about themselves and so it proved true, as the blabbermouth before me continued with her tittle-tattle, because of course now she was regaling her friend with the fact that these dreadful people had moved lock, stock and barrel into an expensive, luxury hotel and now had the gall to install a huge sixty-foot green mobile office in their garden for the workmen! The delivery lorry had blocked the road for two whole days by all accounts.

Would you ever believe it?

No, I blinking well wouldn't!

You guessed it, the bloated bigmouth before me was talking about us. Well a fantasy version of us anyway. I was completely flabbergasted. It was rather regrettable, or alternatively quite fortuitous depending on your point of view, that an extra member of staff opened up an additional till in the shop at that point and the queue was dealt with much faster. As a result, I was never to find out what else the old trout had to regale us with, but you could say that I had probably heard enough. Paying for my goods I quickly left the shop and scurried back to my house, the one that I had apparently deliberately and illegally knocked down.

Well, what did you expect? I was hardly going to bash her over the head with a baguette and swear colourfully until the police carted me off to the cells.

For heaven's sake, this isn't EastEnders!

In any case, on reflection, I wasn't sure that I didn't prefer her fantastic version of events. In that world it sounded like we had lots of money and got to live in a luxury hotel!

Excellent! Bring it on, I say!

Chuckling away to myself whilst sorting underpants in my conservatory in the present, it wasn't long before I realised I had run out of washing to fold, so I dumped the piles in the appropriate bedrooms in the vain hope that the Barbarians might actually put them away, and then moved on to throwing bleach around in the bathroom for a bit. The smell of bleach always gives the illusion that a bathroom has recently been cleaned, even if the opposite is true.

Content that I had at least tried to do a bit of housework, I subsequently gave myself permission to disappear back into my little art room and pick up my paint brushes again.

Part 5

You do not truly know how strong you can be, until being strong is the only option you have left.

Alice May

22: Investigate

Definition: the process of systematically enquiring into facts in order to find out the truth.

So, back to the crumbling cottage once more...

It was probably fortunate that we had plenty to keep ourselves occupied, settling into the caravan, as the required surveys of the house that had been requested by the Insurance Company were going to take some time to organise. We merely got on with establishing our cosy little home environment and the new school term was well underway by the time the next appraisal of the cottage took place, this time by someone who knew rather a lot about old cob buildings. Thank goodness.

Early one Monday morning, our Genuine Old Building Expert arrived on the property, exactly when he had said he would when he had politely telephoned the Friday before. An extremely kind and reliable sort of traditional English gentleman, he had a calming and reassuringly trustworthy manner to him and seemed truly distressed to see the state that our poor old cottage was in.

Having now satisfied ourselves that our family was out of the immediate danger of being dispersed to temporary homes around the country, Beloved Husband and I had also had time to ponder the degree of damage done to the cob and to mourn the demise of such a beautiful old building with so much history.

The cottage first appeared on maps in the early 1700s and so had been built in the aftermath of the English Civil War. That was a truly long time ago and it would have stood throughout the entire agricultural revolution, the reign of the early Hanoverian kings and Bonnie Prince Charlie landing in Scotland to unsuccessfully attempt to re-claim the British throne from them in 1745. The Seven Years war between Britain and France, the outlaw of slavery, the American War of Independence and much, much more, and that's only what happened in the 1700's. Better not to get me started on the rest.

Even though all those events didn't actually happen right here, our little cottage still represented a significant connection with the past. We felt responsible for it and could not believe it was disintegrating on our watch. Contrary to what the gossiping goon in the village shop had suggested we loved this sweet, old cottage and had very much wanted to live in it. No modern, metal monstrosities for us. It was time to find out what sort of repair was potentially possible.

Having spent a very long time examining the cottage in detail, Genuine Old Buildings Expert consumed several cups of tea and a large slice of chocolate fudge cake before departing laden with copious measurements and information. There wasn't a nook or cranny, from loft to ground floor, that hadn't been thoroughly evaluated. A detailed report would be produced in the coming weeks and we had only to wait for all to be made clear as to why this disaster had befallen our lovely home.

***

Again, we were left in limbo to wait for the results of the investigation.

In the meantime, there were so many enchanting quirks to life in a caravan that I feel I should share some of them with you here, otherwise you risk missing out on the bewitching truth of life on wheels. I know we didn't actually go anywhere in it, Hattie being of the static variety, but this caravan still had teeny tiny wheels and we were definitely on a journey of sorts, so I think the analogy applies.

The delightfully early dawn chorus as heard from a caravan was only slightly diminished from that audible in the tent. However, in the caravan it was also accompanied by the fascinating addition of a tap-dancing element, as the birds scuttled into formation on top of the metal roof above us.

The gentle fall of rain on the caravan roof was rhythmic and soothing. Wait a minute! When do we ever get gentle rain in this country? In truth, it was like living under a jack hammer (in use), but modern ear plugs were marvellously helpful, such a wonderful invention.

The charmingly mild rocking action that ensued whenever anyone moved in the caravan was vastly entertaining, as long as no one suffered particularly from motion sickness. This movement was significantly enhanced with any sudden action resulting, for example, in all occupants of the caravan being very much aware if any one of the other inhabitants turned over in bed or staggered to the toilet in the middle of the night.

I also found out that, yes, it was possible to get stuck in the caravan en-suite toilet. I learned the hard way that you had to open the door and reverse in carefully to avoid this scenario, as escape proved difficult otherwise. Space was at a premium in that little room, trying to turn around was really not necessary with a little forethought, nor was it very advisable. Beloved Husband avoided accidentally being entombed in the loo by paying brief nocturnal visits outside as only men can and was only spooked a couple of times by the horses in the field next door wandering over to investigate what he was up to.

Caravan living required an extremely petite lifestyle which can mean many advantages to the busy working parent. After all, there was so little floor space, why on earth would I think to hoover it? And with such tiny rooms, the Barbarians couldn't possibly keep them tidy so there was no point in nagging! Plus, you always had a ready excuse for being late, scruffy, and/or tired, not to mention never being able to find anything, so it was an ideal win-win situation.

Furthermore, it brought the whole family so much closer together. Quite literally!

One of the beauties of having immensely small bedrooms was that I could hear if the boys were mucking about in the next room and simply had to stick an arm out of bed and knock on the dividing wall to remind them that there were witnesses within earshot. It worked if they were snoring at night, too. In Hattie there was no need to get out of bed and walk down the corridor to go and nudge them to shift into to a less snore-inducing position, a mere hammering of a fist on the wall and the noise would disturb them sufficiently that they grumbled and turned over.

OK, everyone else would grumble too but you can't have everything.

You have to take the positive where you can find them. You might suggest that were we not in such close proximity, I wouldn't hear my boys snoring, but I would say that you have no concept of just how loud a Barbarian snore can be. I am deadly serious. My boys could win an Olympic gold medal in snoring. It is all their dad's fault, of course!

It just goes to show that one can make good use of many situations. We found it was even possible to test Small on his spellings without getting out of bed, in the cold early mornings before school, by simply calling the words through the wall and awaiting the correct sequence of appropriate letters to come back in response.

There were many idiosyncrasies of long-term static caravan life too, that had to be experienced to be fully appreciated. For example, you might think how useful it was to have a bathroom in the caravan. I will grant you that the toilets were extremely useful, particularly at night, but I would suggest that the term bathroom is far too grand for the stick-insect sized shower facility that actually existed in dear old Hattie.

With even more diminutive dimensions than the tiny en-suite toilet off the main bedroom, the communal shower unit required serious mental athletics before attempting to insert your physical being into its confines. By that I mean it was necessary to decide which part of your body you were attempting to wash before actually getting in and then you had to work out how you were going to achieve it. For example, if you wished to wash your hair, then you needed to turn on the water before getting into the cubicle with your hands already raised above your head with shampoo at the ready, because once inside there was no chance of actually bending your elbows sufficiently to bring your arms back down to your sides.

Similarly, you needed to decide whether you wished to be scalded or frozen during your shower, as at no point was the water ever at a comfortable temperature, regardless of how much one fussed with the controls. This initially led to several creative invectives in the first few early mornings after Hattie's arrival, before we all decided to give up on the caravan shower and leg it across the garden into the house to use the bathroom there.

Thanks to the general spirit of enhanced camaraderie that had sprung up amongst our little band, there were no arguments over the restrictive bathroom schedule. The Barbarians simply started to check with each other the day before with regard to who was going to shower when and all progressed with surprisingly smooth civility.

Do remember though that when you have rearranged your entire worldly goods under emergency circumstances and then rearranged them all several more times between a variety of ad hoc locations including the house, shed, tent, then house again and finally caravan, you cannot ever truly expect to locate things ever again. I guarantee that whatever it was that you wanted would not be in the same place that you ever found yourself searching.

This occasionally proved understandably frustrating if, for example, you needed to leave the caravan during a torrential rainstorm and you realised that all the coats and umbrellas were currently residing quite happily in the house. This factor definitely promoted rather more forethought than our previous existence had required, so some handy new skills were being learned by all during this period.

The early morning treks through the garden to the house for breakfast were demonstrably refreshing, especially in winter, when a brutal icy blast of morning air proved far more effective at waking you up than splashing cold water on your face from the sink in a nice warm bathroom.

Having to go outside to go to bed in the evening certainly made it easier to remember to complete our primary school-aged Barbarian's science homework to chart the waxing and waning of the moon over a three-week period. (Yes, I admit I am rather grasping at straws here in my attempt to find silver linings.) Nevertheless, the moon was right there in front of us, lighting our way, except for when it was cloudy of course, or raining.

Joking aside, those evening and early morning walks up and down the garden were actually quite relaxing when the weather was dry. The fields around the house would frequently be bathed either in moon or dawn light and took on a magical quality, the beauty of which would never be fully appreciated from inside the house.

We were fortunate that the weather was generally kind to us that year and, even though there were thunderstorms, we were spared the truly tempestuous downpours of the year before. In contrast, the fresh crispness of frosty mornings was quite delightful once you learned to layer your clothes sufficiently, prior to sticking your nose out of doors. We invested in some salt to grit the path between Hattie and the house to ensure no slippage during the really icy spells as autumn gave way to true winter.

But I am rushing ahead with my story now. We still have the ongoing debate about the house repair to discuss. There were yet more investigations to be carried out.

What fun!

***

Several weeks after our encounter with the delightful Genuine Old Buildings Expert, we opened our house to yet another independent evaluator. I would like to say we opened our doors to him, but he used the hole in the wall like everyone else. We were going to have to do something about that cavity soon because the weather was definitely closing in and autumn was well established, even though it wasn't too wet yet.

You may well ask why we were dawdling. Why not shove a whole lot of plywood and polythene over the gap and seal it all up as best we could? Please understand that we really wanted to do this, but due process had to be allowed to take place before any action could be instigated. Had we made any changes at all in the intervening time, other than the necessary propping agreed, then a true evaluation of events could not be carried out and we had been advised that there was a real risk that the Insurance Company would quite legitimately refuse all liability based on lack of evidence. They were a business after all, not a bottomless pit of money (shame!) and therefore needed to justify any release of finance with regard to settlement of claims.

So regardless of how damp and dismal it was living in the remainder of the house during the day with a socking great hole in the wall, we had little choice but to comply. It was only fair to everyone involved to establish the true facts of the matter once and for all. Believe me when I say that such a statement is a lot easier to say with hindsight. At the time, watching my damaged home rot before my eyes, I can assure you that I was not nearly as sanguine about the whole situation.

Fundamentally, these two specific evaluations were an essential part of establishing a way forward. The first was to identify conclusively what had caused the collapse and the second was to establish whether any of the building work that we had had done at the house over the years could have been a contributory factor.

These two analyses were as independent as possible. They were paid for by the Insurance Company but they were commissioned on our behalf after a long exhaustive search for appropriately qualified people. Believe me there are not that many people highly experienced in dealing with cob.

It was hoped that the results would fairly ascertain what degree of liability lay where so that a plan to move forward could be formulated to everyone's satisfaction.

It was also to be hoped that the copious cups of tea and enormous slices of cake Chaos, Logic and I were dishing out to all and sundry did not count as bribery.

23: Protective

Definition: guaranteeing preservation from injury or harm.

Back in the present…

Later in the evening, my blissful painting experience was rather marred by Logic bustling in. As I returned to reality in a somewhat dazed condition, I tried to listen carefully as she proceeded to tell me she was off out to a party. It wouldn't be late, she wouldn't be drinking and I could pick her up at midnight.

Oh! Could I?

Goody!

Also, where, when, who with and how?

Only a few of the many questions that immediately sprang to mind, followed by "Does your Dad know?"

'Aha!' I hear you say, 'so she is a normal teen after all! In spite of all that useful baking of cakes and making of cups of tea for you. She can still make you suffer like the rest of the population just as a true teenage daughter should!' I never said she was a saint!

Even though, out of all my Barbarians, this particular one was especially sensible and can be relied upon to be careful, it doesn't reduce the worry potential. Nevertheless, I had learned over the years that there was a very fine line indeed between being a supportive parent and an overprotective, paranoid wreck.

The practical part of me (admittedly this doesn't command an impressively large percentage of my overall make up) believes wholeheartedly in the process of learning from one's mistakes. The paranoid wreck within me just cannot bear yet another trip to casualty, so will you please listen to me and stop doing that NOW!!!!

For someone who really hates hospitals, the sheer number of trips to medical establishments over nineteen years with four children has resulted in a truly staggering number of hours waited, miles driven, car parking tickets paid for and grey hairs generated. I believe I should be awarded a long service medal, possibly my own hospital car park space or, more pertinently, my own personal, little, white straightjacket and a padded cell where I could recover in peace.

Please?

I do recognise that the Paranoid Parent element of my complex personality cannot be allowed full reign and that, on the whole, I should just relax and let life happen; enjoying the peace and tranquillity of not worrying about what might go wrong. Nevertheless, we should add in my overall luck factor, or rather my lack of luck. Hopefully, without indicating an overbearing sense of self-importance, Murphy's Law could have been written just for me.

If it can go wrong, it will.

Butter side down.

While other parents are cheerfully enjoying social events, chatting to other happy, relaxed parents, their offspring engaged in meaningful but safe activities, I will always be the one with a child stuck up a tree, hanging on by their fingertips, or about to throw themselves in a river just for the sheer fun of it. Or, on one memorable occasion, both perilous activities at once! (Excellent multi-tasking skills demonstrated by that particular child.)

Why?

It's not fair.

If I take my eye off the safety ball, you can bet your bottom dollar that casualty is the very next stop for us. (Do not pass GO. Do not collect £200,000.)

Generally, at all events requiring a Supportive Parent type, there will inevitably be a fair percentage of the Paranoid Parent sort pitching up too. In my case, I feel that both parental forms arrive within the one body and tussle throughout the event for supreme command.

For example, I would dutifully attend every school rugby match and lend my boys silent support from the side-lines, watching with interest as other parents jumped up and down yelled things like "Go on, tackle him!" Whilst I did agree with the general sentiment behind such encouraging vocal utterances (after all we wanted to win, didn't we?), inside my head a small voice would be muttering "Do be careful, son! Don't get stomped into the ground again!" and "How on earth am I going to get all that mud out?" whilst simultaneously calculating the fastest route to the nearest casualty department, just in case.

When my Paranoid Parent personality has full control, I have been known to go to events with bags of frozen peas packed in cool boxes with ice blocks in the back of my car in anticipation of multiple soft tissue injuries being sustained. I have frequently been amazed at how long it can take the staff at any sporting facility to produce ice if you need it, especially once you have explained that you don't want it floating around in a large vat of fizzy drink.

On the whole though, Supportive Parent generally wins the internal power struggle and at the end of each the match, I would smile and chat with the other parents as we trotted off for a nice thawing cup of caffeine whilst the bedraggled, mud spattered team straggled off to shower, change and then demolish twice their body weight in refreshments to replace the energy expended on the pitch.

Back to this instance in particular, though, considering how hard Logic had been working for her A-levels, I realised that she was due a bit of fun. All work and no play and all that! So, I decided to let Supportive Parent win and agreed that she could go to the party, settling in for an evening of hovering by my mobile phone and checking that I still had signal, just in case she needed rescuing and texted me asking for help.

A parent's job is never an easy one!

After all, if she never went out, I'd be worrying that she was anti-social and didn't have any friends, wouldn't I?

24: Stoicism

Definition: the suffering of pain or difficulty without showing feelings or complaining.

Back in the past, waiting for the independent assessment reports...

As with all professional reports, the latest required reading took quite some time to materialise, but we were busy enduring our cramped caravan existence and getting on with the business of everyday life, including the school term and our jobs. Several weeks later, two things happened; the October half term arrived and so did two reports.

The first concluded that which I had suspected, in that the old walls had become damaged by the action of driving rain under the influence of high winds during a series of unusually significant storm events in quick succession. The result being that the footings of the walls had become washed out, leaving little or no support for the weight above. Hence storm damage was officially confirmed as the cause of our wibbly, wobbly walls.

So far so good, you might say!

The second report concluded that the previous building work at the property had all been carried out in an acceptable manner and, therefore, did not constitute a contributory factor to the cob collapsing. This was excellent news, and you could be forgiven for thinking that all our problems were over, that knights in shining armour would now swoop in and fix our house for us in record time, and it would all be over like a bad dream. If we lived in a Disney movie you would be right, that would probably be precisely what would happen.

Sadly no!

Unfortunately, that is not how these things work.

Nevertheless, you are right, this did constitute a big step forward. Through the conclusions of these two reports, the cause of the collapse had been irrefutably established and was confirmed in writing in a charming email from Loss Adjuster Number 2.

Accidental Damage was now a thing of the past. A dim and distant memory, thank goodness. Sadly, however, this was only a tiny baby step in the grand scheme of things to come. We had successfully opened a whole new can of worms. Now that Storm Damage was on the table, it was necessary to establish to what degree our claim might potentially be settled. Apparently, that wasn't going to be straight forward and required yet more reports to be done.

Yes, of course it did!

Great!

Why would we expect anything else? After all, there were still more trees left on the planet to cut down to make the paper for these reports, therefore they needed to be written. (Sorry I am ranting, I will try to stop that, I promise!) There were a number of questions which would need to be answered and another meeting with Loss Adjuster Number 2 was scheduled. This took place at the end of the half-term holiday and a number of issues were discussed at length.

I should point out at this juncture that the girl Barbarians still didn't think that their parents could be trusted to handle a meeting with the Loss Adjuster without them. As a result, they had both taken up creative culinary posts in the kitchen from which they could eavesdrop with impunity. Logic, standing at the breakfast bar, was beating the stuffing out of something white in a clear Pyrex bowl; an icing sugar dust halo hovering gently over her head. Next to her was Chaos who, having chosen a more savoury option, was perched on a stool attempting to first blanche and then peel thousands of cherry tomatoes to make some sort of sophisticated soup.

The boys had decided their talents were best put to use charging around the garden like maniacs. That left Beloved Husband and I to sit at the dining table in the conservatory with Loss Adjuster Number 2 trying to get our heads around the next stage of the procedure.

As I mentioned before, should a rebuild/repair be authorised, we were only theoretically entitled to 'like for like' in our policy, which in this case would mean rebuilding in cob and this proved to be the first in a whole series of sticking points that were slowing up the decision-making process.

Modern cob building methods are not necessarily the same as ancient cob building methods. I would be surprised if anyone really knew precisely how it was done hundreds of years ago, but they no doubt have some very interesting theories. Nevertheless, whatever cob reconstruction method might be employed, it would definitely be fiendishly expensive and the Insurance Company were understandably not keen on this, unless it was absolutely essential, which as the house was not listed it wasn't.

Secondly, to rebuild in cob would take a very long time to accomplish, as work could only take place in the dry months of the year and therefore the rebuild might have to take place over several successive summers. I think you can understand why neither we nor the Insurance Company were keen on this particular option.

As a result, we were immediately moving away from 'like for like' territory which was inevitably going to make things difficult. It might be thought that as a cob rebuild was so expensive then, surely, we could simply be allocated that amount of money and spend it how we liked on a general cottage rebuild. Any leftover finances could be used for a long foreign holiday in the sun somewhere to get over the shock of it all, couldn't they? Obviously, I am joking! I am not the brightest bunny in the hutch, but even I knew that wasn't going to happen.

Any money released to us for any rebuilding work was going to need to be fully justified, understandably, and the work would need to be confirmed as having been completed appropriately by an independent third party. This would protect all involved and should ensure that any repairs were carried out to an appropriately professional level, and the Insurance Company could then be confident in continuing to insure the building into the future.

Putting a cob rebuild aside, modern building methods now needed to be considered. Not surprisingly we had rather gone off the quaintness of cob over the last few months and were quite keen on a bit of concrete. These modern methods had the advantage of being considerably cheaper and faster but the disadvantage was they would potentially result in greater overall value being added to the finished building which couldn't be permitted under the terms of the insurance policy. Thus, we have sticking point number 3.

I should explain why Beloved Husband and I were feeling so very jaded at this particular meeting, especially as it was really not helping our general comprehension of the complicated proceedings.

You might think that this weary outlook was purely due to the whole 'falling down house' related stress and 'living in a caravan in the garden' issue. You would be right to a point, but what you don't know is that we had foolishly added to our sleep deprivation problems recently by agreeing that the Barbarians could have a Halloween party two days before. After all, what better setting than a real-life, ancient, falling down, wonky house for that extra spooky feel?

Given the state of the place, we didn't even really have to make any additional Halloween decorations, but that didn't stop us. My particular favourite was the scarily realistic, life-sized skeleton covered in fake gore that Beloved Husband had left slumped up against the old cottage door. (Don't ask me where he got it from. I really don't want to know.)

In fact, Skelly, as he was immediately christened, was so effective that we decided to keep him long after Halloween was over. He proved a great deterrent to discourage people from ducking under the lines of red warning tape around the house and trespassing too close to the wobbly walls.

Beloved Husband had a habit of moving him periodically, purely for his own amusement. I would frequently come home from work to find Skelly engaged in any number of activities from dangling half out of one of the holes in the wall, doing chin-ups from an upstairs window ledge, or apparently climbing through the crack between the wall and the roof, waving maniacally. I was relieved to see that his sense of humour hadn't completely deserted him, and the Barbarians found it hilarious.

It should be remembered that there was absolutely no electricity available to the front of the house at all, due to the damage, and no street lighting either, due to the deepest, darkest country location. Fortunately for the party, Halloween fell on an eerily clear moonlight night that showed the damaged walls off extremely effectively with the help of a few pumpkin lanterns littered around the place. Possibly a bit too effectively, if I am completely honest, as almost all parents refused to let their kids get out of the car until they had rung us on their mobiles to check that they really were in the right place.

In our defence, we had warned them all on the invitation what to expect, but I wasn't surprised that they had assumed we were exaggerating. Beloved Husband gallantly acted as an escort (with a high-powered torch) to assist our guests around to the back garden and the patio doors into the house and the party was a huge success, involving several tonnes of pizza, many hours of silly games triggering raucous laughter and some extremely loud music. (My apologies are offered once again to our lovely neighbours! We thank you for your continued patience.)

Beloved Husband and I eventually escaped to the caravan for a rest, leaving the Barbarians and their friends to their fun. Sometime later on we were called upon to accompany waves of guests back past the crumbly cottage walls to their parents' cars.

All in all, a very successful party, but, my goodness, we were still tired two days later so concentrating on what Loss Adjuster Number 2 had to say was not easy.

I rubbed my eyes and tried to focus on what was being discussed.

A fourth (and definitely not the final) issue with regard to repair/rebuild was precisely how much of the cob would need to be removed and rebuilt, and how would the rebuilt section be tied-in to the remaining cob. After all, the cottage originally had four cob walls, only two of which were damaged. There are arguments that cob requires a ring structure in order to remain strong, in other words, all four walls built at the same time in a ring-like formation. There are no such things as truly straight lines or ninety-degree angles in cob, only a vague approximation. Potentially, leaving two walls in-situ and not four constituted a ticking time bomb as they would eventually fail as well.

However, as the two remaining walls were not currently crumbling they did not signify as 'needing repair', therefore, the insurance repair job would only extend to the presently damaged walls. If carried out using modern materials, these would need to 'tie-in' to the old cob in such a manner that would make all four walls stable. Sticking point number 5. I stopped counting after this, before my brain exploded with too much information. Why was it all so complicated?

An experienced 'old and new building' structural engineer was going to be required. Thankfully, we already had one of those in the form of Genuine Old Buildings Expert. Phew!

Sat at the table in the conservatory listening to Loss Adjuster number 2 explaining, at length, yet more reasons why this situation was so complicated, I have to confess that my mind was really struggling to keep up. I found myself absently watching my boy Barbarians practicing their rugby conversions at the bottom of the garden. In the absence of a set of rugby posts, the boys were using the branch of one of the oak trees as a marker for the height of the necessary kick. All progressed as you might expect, until I noticed that the smaller Barbarian appeared to be attempting to murder the larger one.

Clearing my throat in a meaningful manner, I caught Logic's eye in the kitchen and nodded towards the garden. She was just taking a batch of fresh cookies out of the oven. Glancing out in the direction of the boys, she grinned in comprehension before leaning over and casually ringing the ship's bell that hangs near the sink. Just once. A short, sharp ding!

I should probably explain the bell. A significant number of years earlier, I had determined that actively calling four Barbarians to the table at meal times before the food went cold was an impossible task, given the size of both the house and the garden. The A.P.s had solved the problem by donating a ship's bell to the household which meant that, in one 'ding', the message that a meal was served could be heard loud and clear by all, without me going hoarse in the process. It soon became the most effective method of gaining the whole family's attention for all sorts of reasons if needed, as all would come running immediately. In a family as big as this one, you need to be quick if you are going to get your fair share of any snacks.

Impressively, in a response worthy of Pavlov's dog, the instant that the bell rang out, both boy's heads shot up and the bad behaviour in the garden ceased. Within seconds, they were both on their feet and charging for the kitchen, slowing up only long enough to slip off muddy shoes and carefully skirt around the meeting taking place at the table. Once in the kitchen, Logic allowed the boys to devour still warm cookies whilst muttering quietly to them that they cease and desist in their efforts to commit fratricide while there was an independent witness present in the form of Loss Adjuster Number 2.

I am sure training your children to respond to a bell does not appear in any of the good parenting manuals, but in my defence the adults in the family answer the call too. In fact, at that very meeting, when Logic rang the bell for the boys, I could see Beloved Husband's involuntary response quite clearly, as his attention was diverted from what Loss Adjuster Number 2 was saying and he immediately looked towards the kitchen.

Logic took pity on him and brought a plate of fresh cookies over to the table for us too.

Anyway, the result of our discussions with Loss Adjuster Number 2 was that another report needed to be done. What a surprise! This one was to establish what potential options were available for a repair at the property. It was to focus on the bare minimum that needed to be put into place to effectively make the property habitable. I do not mean luxuries like carpets, curtains and decorating, even though all of that had been damaged by the initial collapse event. The bare minimum meant the repair of the basic structure, i.e. the two crumbly walls and nothing else. It was to consider both rebuilding in cob and also modern materials as options.

Once this report was available it was to be sent out to five different building companies for them to come to assess the proposed work identified for the cottage and work out quotes for what the various options would cost. Then the Insurance Company would decide if they were going to get involved and to what degree.

It was decided that Genuine Old Buildings Expert was suitably qualified to carry out the required report and he was to be commissioned to return to the cottage, as soon as possible, to assess the potential repair options.

Does your head hurt after reading all that? I am sorry.

I have to admit that I am only explaining these events to the level that I understood them myself. I cannot claim that I had a full grasp of what was actually going on. After this latest meeting, I needed to crawl away and have a long lie down to process everything. It didn't really matter though, there would be plenty of time to recover because all those additional reports and assessments were going to take us well into December before any more decisions could be made. What would happen after that was anyone's guess.

I decided that I had better buy more ingredients for my dear Chaos and Logic. We were going to be requiring considerably more edibles.

25: Galvanise

Definition: to stimulate a person into taking some action.

In the past, winter really gets underway ...

With the approach of December, we realised that we were going to be spending Christmas in Hattie. That isn't to say that we didn't receive plenty of offers from other members of the wider family to feed and house us all over the Christmas Holidays. However, the Barbarians, Beloved Husband and I agreed that we wanted to spend the time together just the six of us, and we didn't want to leave our broken home empty and vulnerable to potential intruders by going away. Hence, we started to plan exactly what little things we each wanted to do in order to make a crumbly cottage and caravan-based Christmas special.

Inevitably, most of our plans centred around food.

The onset of winter galvanised me to try to contact Loss Adjuster Number 2 yet again, to explain how the weather was penetrating the cottage through the damaged walls. I requested permission to take some sort of action to make the useable parts of the house more watertight. The smell of damp from the old section of the house was getting really unpleasant, no matter how long we kept the fire lit and, I couldn't swear to it, but I did wonder if we hadn't gained some little scurrying, furry friends that had made the most of the easy access points available through the walls.

No, I don't mean rats, or I sincerely hoped I didn't!

The spiders had certainly been coming in out of the cold for a while now, and I had found several little piles of mouse droppings. I am, of course, not really keen on either spiders or mice living with us, but at the time there wasn't much that could be done. I couldn't spend my whole life standing on stools and screaming, it didn't really go with the strong independent image I wanted to project to my Barbarians. After all, if they spot a weakness, then believe me you have had it. Just to clarify, I am talking about the Barbarians spotting a weakness here, not the other wildlife!

Permission was granted for polythene sheeting to be layered down and around the outside of the damaged walls, to prevent much more of the wet weather entering the property. This was really going to annoy the young postman who delivered our mail to us on a Saturday. I had noticed that he had taken to driving by at speed and just lobbing our parcels through the hole in the wall. If we sealed up the hole, he was in danger of having to actually park his van and walk round to the back door to deliver the post like his more mature colleague did during the week. Perhaps I should arrange a basketball net style drop box by the gate for him. It seemed a shame to spoil his fun.

At the same time as wrapping the cottage in polythene, the plan included building a small stud wall between the old section of the house and the new with insulation included so that we would effectively be able to heat the useable parts of the house. The central heating pipework in the damaged walls was to be isolated so that we were not pouring money down the drain trying to heat the great outdoors, whilst simultaneously reducing the chance that exposed pipes would freeze in the coming cold weather and then burst.

Following on from this small victory I also mentioned (yet again) that the oil pipe which supplied our central heating boiler was still vulnerable to damage from any falling debris should the crumbly cob collapse any further. I politely reminded Loss Adjuster Number 2 that I had raised this issue previously because I was afraid that there would be significant environmental damage done if the pipeline broke and oil leaked into the ground. It turned out that this meant yet another assessment would need to be carried out with regard to what could or should be done.

Oh, goody! Just what we needed, another report!

I wondered if I dare mention the mains electricity supply that was still dangling precariously from the damaged gable. No doubt that needed a report too, or it would be feeling ever so left out, and we couldn't have that.

With all the reports that were being generated on our behalf, I did wonder which forest was being cut down to provide all the paper. I hoped it was a sustainable one. After all, there was no guarantee that there would be any actual money left to repair the house at the end of all this; any possible budget could potentially get used up paying all these people to write down their opinions. I supposed that we could always screw up all the paper used in these accounts, make spit balls and then cram those into the cracks in the walls. They always proved quite hard for the caretakers to dislodge from the ceilings at school, when I was a child (it wasn't me, honest). I am sure the Barbarians would be glad to help out. Anything for a good cause! Might it count as recycling perhaps?

In the meantime, while all these lovely written commentaries were being created, we simply had to cross our fingers and hope either of the two damaged walls didn't fall any further. Oh! Wait! We were already doing that. Can you cross already crossed fingers? Is it any wonder that I couldn't sleep? Every day that passed I would pretend to be coping well, brushing off expressions of concern from kind friends with jokey comments, yet at the same time I was desperately worried that something even worse was around the corner.

I must confess though, that while I was definitely driven by altruistic motives to protect both the environment and my beloved Barbarians' lives, I was also rather petrified of the cold showers and chilly rooms that would result if the oil pipeline was damaged and our boiler ceased to function. Self-centred of me I know, but it was already cold enough dashing from Hattie to the house without following it up with an icy cold drenching. Added to that, it would only give my boy Barbarians yet another reason to avoid taking a bath, and the olfactory essence of their room in Hattie was taking on a personality all of its own already without adding to it unnecessarily.

On the other hand, if the pipeline broke and the electricity mains came down at the same time, the resultant incendiary combination might be really quite spectacular. That was one way to get warm I suppose! One for the diary anyway, or at least YouTube, so I made a note to keep a video camera on standby, just in case. Looking on the bright side, I wondered how many hits such a video would get….

***

While inevitably exhausting, each of these small steps was definitely taking us in the right direction. Even though it felt like every decision had to be written about in triplicate and then discussed by a large committee before anything could actually materialise, at least things were happening. It might seem that very little ground had been covered in more than six months, but every baby step was actually a major victory.

The acknowledgement by the Insurance Company that we might possibly have a legitimate claim, had another fortuitous knock-on effect. Even though there was no guaranteed repair offer on the table, the fact that they were in communication with us meant that Beloved Husband was able to justifiably approach the mortgage company with regard to releasing some additional funds for us to put towards 'home improvements' that might take place whilst any repair work was going on.

A modest sum was agreed which we could use to contribute towards whatever work might be needed. As a result, both Beloved Husband and I felt as though we had a little bit more control over the painfully slow proceedings. We didn't, of course, (it's not as if it was our house or anything like that, heaven forbid that ownership should come into this!), but it was nice to pretend we did.

I would be dishonest if I didn't confess at this point that it seemed to me that everyone else involved in our situation was making quite a tidy living out of it. It is probably not remotely true but from our perspective it appeared to be a nice little earner for all concerned apart from us, so you can understand my frustration as yet more delays for assessments and reports appeared at every turn.

I just wanted to scream "For goodness' sake! It fell down!! It needs fixing!!! Please can we just get ON WITH IT???!!!!"

Immensely frustrating, yes, but progress was being made.

26: Oblivion

Definition: A state of total unawareness.

Returning to the family in the present…

I was floating in a blissful cloud of colour, beautiful rainbow shades swirling in a cascading waterfall as I became aware of another sensation. Instead of visual, this one was auditory but was just as lovely. The sound of gentle piano playing penetrated my painting fog. It was a sound I recognised, it was truly lovely and made me smile but, drifting back to full consciousness, I was aware that something about the music didn't make sense.

Both of my beautiful Barbarian girls play the piano, but they each have their own very distinctive style and musical preference. This particular piece did not fit with the acknowledged female Barbarian that was currently in residence at home, and thus required me to mount an investigation. After all, the boys don't play the piano. What a ridiculous suggestion! It requires far too much concentration and focus when there are snacks to be unearthed, brothers to wrestle to the ground for no reason and random balls to be chased!

Hurriedly washing off my paintbrush in the jar of murky water on the desk, I dumped it on the scrap of towel beside the jar and went to delve into the apparent mystery. For once, the radio wasn't playing and the cat had abandoned her sunny windowsill. There was definitely something afoot.

Stepping into the hall, I could see that I was right. Tinkling away on the ivories of the old upright by the stairs was Chaos, playing her signature tune. She had written it herself during the caravan years. It sounds like a joyfully flowing stream, skipping down a mountainside and it brings tears of happiness to my eyes every time I hear it now. Possibly my all-time favourite piece and the reason I had known for certain that Logic was not playing. (Not that I'm saying she doesn't play beautifully too, of course!)

Torn between delight at seeing her, yet also wondering what on earth she was doing here and confused as to how she had managed to get home from university without parental assistance, I watched her finish the piece with a flourish. She turned to me, bounced off the piano stool and gave me a quick hug.

"Hey Ma, you look happy!" she said. "Don't worry! Lectures are cancelled today and tomorrow. It's because the January exams are over. It gives the lecturers time to mark everything. We start back Monday, so that gives me four days at home."

I nodded absorbing the rapid-fire information stream and hugged her back. I couldn't help smiling.

"One of the guys in my Halls was driving home for the weekend so I persuaded him to make a slight detour to drop me off. He's coming back Sunday to pick me up, I said you'd feed him a huge Sunday lunch in place of petrol money. You don't mind, do you?"

Turning to go into the kitchen to put on the kettle, I hid a huge grin. Chaos' powers of persuasion are legendary in this family, so the poor fella from her Halls hadn't stood a chance. I imagine that her 'slight detour' was probably quite considerable as we do live in the back of beyond. There's no doubt he would truly deserve a nice dinner when he got here on Sunday, if, indeed, he ever found us again. Besides, when you are cooking for a horde this big, one more mouth to feed is never a problem.

"Anyway," she continued without an answer (she is also notorious for not necessarily needing any verbal feedback to carry on a conversation), "I thought I would take the opportunity to check out your new paintings."

"And possibly get your washing done?" I asked innocently, having just spotted the huge rucksack quietly steaming away by the utility door.

"Yeah, the laundrette at my Halls is out of order. Sorry!" She didn't sound remotely sorry but it didn't matter in the slightest.

"Be my guest," I said, setting down two cups of tea on the counter top. "Just remember the forty-five-minute, thirty degrees setting is the only one that actually still works."

Sipping my tea, I watched through the open utility door as she upended her rucksack spilling the rather rancid contents onto the stone floor and started shoving armfuls into my poor, beleaguered washing machine. It really should have been given a long service medal and copious amounts of danger money coming to work in this house. It had slowly given up all hope of operating any of its fancy, sophisticated, higher wash functions, settling for the basic fast-wash facility on an extremely regular basis. There was never any time for anything else. Even that one working setting was a bit hit-and-miss, but there was no money for a new machine and anyway, I felt rather attached to this one. It had come through the caravan years with us, and I felt we could put up with its little foibles.

Nevertheless, looking at the festering contents of Chaos' rucksack, I wondered if this might just be the final straw for my poor machine and couldn't help but speculate on how on earth I would cope if it decided to go on strike permanently. My conjecture was interrupted by the shrill tones of the landline. Picking it up, I listened carefully to the caller, before agreeing several times, saying goodbye and then disconnecting the call.

Inveterately nosey, Chaos was out of the utility room like a shot, wanting to know what was going on.

"What was that?" she asked as I sat staring at the handset with a bemused expression on my face.

I looked at her for several seconds before I found my voice. "Apparently, I've sold a painting!"

"Really? That's great! Which one? I didn't think there were any left from the old lot."

"I'm not really sure," I said. "I lent several to a friend, quite a few years ago. She was setting up her own business and wanted some art on the office walls. She didn't have a huge budget and I had a few pieces available. There was no point them staying in the shed when someone was offering them wall space, so I let her borrow them if she would agree to put a price tag on them. I had forgotten all about them to be honest."

"Wow, that's great, how much?" asked the eternally poverty-stricken student.

"Enough to replace that washing machine if you kill it with your rucksack of rankness!" I said with some degree of satisfaction. It might be the end of the line for the whining, wheezing washer but not for the rest of us just yet.

As we were all probably going to live, a little bit longer at least, I thought I had better turn my mind to planning and shopping for a suitably stimulating Sunday lunch to restore Chaos' friend if he did eventually successfully locate us. Once again, my cupboards were looking worryingly sparse. How does that happen?

Please understand that I would never claim to be a Michelin Starred Chef. (Beloved Husband would die laughing if I tried and we wouldn't want that, would we? Hmmm…) Nevertheless, the one thing I can do really well is a Sunday Roast.

In truth, I must credit Delia with the overall continued survival of my brood of Barbarians. My entrenched position as chief cook and bottle washer for this tribe has not been easily earned. They would not have endured half as well as they have, were it not for Delia Smith's Complete Illustrated Cookery Course which resides on my kitchen shelf in dilapidated splendour, wearing just a splash (if not considerably more) of virtually every dish I have ever attempted to make.

My heartfelt thanks must go to my cousin and his lovely wife who gifted the book to us as a wedding present. Beloved Husband was in no danger of dying of starvation when we first got married because of the plentiful variety of excellent takeaway establishments within easy reach of our first home. That was our original home with good solid foundations and nice, strong, concrete walls! Why on earth did we sell it? However, once the Barbarians started arriving and we moved to the deepest, darkest depths of the countryside, he had to survive on my culinary skills alone even though they could more accurately be referred to as my incineration skills?

It's just as well for all of us that in the intervening years I have learned to cook. This happened in the same rapidly exponential manner that the Barbarians learned to eat and I now have no qualms about throwing together vast banquets of edible shenanigans. Nothing fancy mind you, just good, honest, wholesome, nourishing food.

With regard to that good, honest, wholesome, nourishing food, it was time yet again to raid an appropriate establishment for ingredients.

27: Resilience

Definition: the ability to survive in spite of change or misfortune.

Returning to the crumbly cottage conundrum in the past…

We were being visited by yet more experts. This time our visitors were construction experts (a.k.a. builders), a whole series of them, arriving one after another, all ostensibly coming to quote for the potential work ahead. Although some I felt were really just there to be nosey as our house was now notorious far and wide. I told you we should have been selling tickets.

Who cares? At last, after nearly six months we had builders at the property. Yay, result!!!

Builders, hooray, I hear you shout! Do calm down, please!

It was not really a cause for mass celebration. They weren't staying long enough to actually rebuild the place. They were simply assessing the potential cost of a series of rebuild scenarios determined by one of the many previously generated engineering reports from Genuine Old Buildings Expert.

Nevertheless, it was yet another baby step forward. When is this baby going to learn to run? Can't we skip walking, we really don't have time?

Of course, as with everything else in this whole messy scenario, it wasn't actually easy to show builders inside a tumble-down property.

This was especially so, now that the huge crack in the wall had been sealed over with thick black polythene. Believe me, there was no way I was going to let anyone cut a route through that if I could help it. It was the middle of winter and the polythene was one of the few things keeping the true extent of the miserable, wet, cold weather from joining us on the inside of the house.

The original front door of the cottage was wedged shut, not intentionally so, but rather more due to the sheer weight of the damaged wall suspended over it, pressing down under the influence of gravity. Added to that complication, the only internal access from the back section of the house had been boarded up with more plastic sheeting, plywood and thick insulation materials. Again, I wasn't having that dismantled in a hurry either. Gaining entry for inspections to be carried out was not going to be a walk in the park.

Luckily, we had anticipated that access might be an issue, and had left a downstairs window in the undamaged side wall unlocked for this very purpose. Unusually for a cottage, it was a rather large window and lifted upwards from about mid-thigh height, allowing our callers to scramble over the sill and enter the ground floor. I have to admit, I had never in my life thought we would be encouraging guests to clamber into our home through a window, but it just goes to show that anything is possible given the right set of circumstances.

Understandably, with the majority of the front section of the house encased in black plastic and the fried electrical circuits turned off, it was rather dark inside the old cottage, necessitating the deployment of independent light sources. Each group tended to look rather like a bunch of miners about to descend to the bowels of the earth, with head torches attached to hard hats. The only missing equipment was the traditional pickaxe.

Once inside the cottage, it was quite evident to both Beloved Husband and me, even by torchlight, that very gradual, incremental movement was still merrily underway. The previously charming, characteristically low cottage ceilings were now distinctly more low-slung, meaning that everyone (even short people like me) had to bend over to walk towards the stairwell at the far end of the room to prevent banging heads on the straining beams. Large chunks of internal plasterwork littered the floor, and the smell of damp and mould was overpowering. Derelict and depressed, our dear old cottage was definitely dying before our eyes.

Needless to say, these internal examinations got more and more brief with each subsequent arrival, mainly due to the sheer impracticalities involved. Nevertheless, each new builder arriving to assess the situation insisted on attempting to take internal photographs, even though we warned them that the last lot of builders' photographic attempts were useless due to the poor lighting conditions.

Beloved Husband and I eventually become rather used to not existing to these people. It was as if we were an encumbrance to be endured, a nuisance, and so we gave up accompanying them inside the derelict ruin of our home, and resorted to just counting them in through the window and then out again afterwards.

The contractors wanted the work but seemed to know that we were irrelevant in the decision-making process and hence they were focussed entirely on communicating with Genuine Old Buildings Expert and, through him, the Insurance Company.

Even Genuine Old Buildings Expert, who was, in theory, supposed to have been engaged as a neutral third party to communicate between the Insurance Company and us with regard to the project, was still actually paid by the Insurance Company. As a result, while he was an extremely nice chap with the very best of intentions, he seemed unable to involve us in any decisions. Communication was kept to the bare minimum. We were simply informed what was going to happen once decisions had already taken place.

This was actually quite unfortunate, if you ask me (and nobody was asking me – we've established that), because the Insurance Company were still adamant that they were only potentially considering accepting liability for the bare minimum repair on the cottage. Yet it should be remembered that critical decisions made at this point were going to affect the amount of actual work that needed to take place and would significantly affect the final repair bill, which ultimately would be down to us to pay.

All the delays in decision making were allowing the cottage to fall in to even greater disrepair, leading to an exponentially increasing ultimate invoice which again would inevitably be presented to us to settle.

In short, we couldn't help but feel marginalised by the system, which fitted very well with the other helpless, hopeless and totally powerless feelings overwhelming us. We were like a cork bobbing in the ocean being blown this way and that by the winds over the surface of the water whilst simultaneously tugged at from below by the currents; defenceless and vulnerable.

"Do you think they actually see us?" I muttered to Beloved Husband one day after holding the window up for yet another set of contractors to scramble through.

He just shrugged and raised his eyebrows. I closed the window and sat on the low wall nearby, waiting for this latest bunch of builders to knock and ask to be let out again. He sat next to me and we rested, shoulder to shoulder, in companionable silence, watching our breath generate frost clouds in the air before us, until eventually he gently shoved my shoulder with his and said in a remarkably cheerful tone, "I guess lots of builders is better than none."

"Hmmm," I agreed, thinking distractedly that his comment was an indication that Beloved Husband was, perhaps, trying to see things in a glass-half-full capacity, just as I was tipping into glass-half-empty territory. Looking back on that horrible time, it is interesting to observe how the dynamics between the two of us fluctuated. How, on the whole, one of us would carry the other at different times. Although both of us had been brought very low by the whole ordeal, whichever of us was feeling slightly brighter would instinctively try to bolster up the other.

Thankfully, there were very few moments when we were both reaching complete and utter despair at the same time, and at those points our lovely Barbarians were instrumental in keeping us both going. Whether their more comical antics were deliberately designed to revitalise us, I will never know, but somehow our little team managed to sustain itself, each protecting and encouraging the other.

Quite shockingly, one of the very last builders to visit the site at that time actually spoke to us! He asked us what we thought should be done. We were pathetically grateful to be consulted about the future of our own property, and he seemed genuinely interested in our opinions, which was quite a contrast to those who had come before! Such a shame we probably weren't going to get a choice as to which builder would get the job in the end because, with that one simple conversation, he just beat all the others hands down, as far as we were concerned.

Eventually the steady stream of visiting builders dried up and we were left in peace to wait for a few more weeks while they went away and compiled their reports for submission as tenders for the potential repair work.

***

When I say we were left in peace, I am lying of course.

What I mean is that we were abandoned yet again to worry about how things were going to unfold. Sleepless nights were standard. I spent hours lying awake in the dark pretending to sleep so that I wouldn't disturb anyone else. All that time, collapsing-building-related disaster movies were playing on a loop in my head to visibly demonstrate to me just how much worse our present situation could potentially get. (I have an excellent imagination and have already admitted to a hefty dose of paranoia!)

I rather think that my obsession with imminent catastrophe was rather justifiable considering preceding events. After all, there are certain disasters in life that one can mitigate for. For example, if one fears a home fire then it is reasonable to take the time to turn off electrical items after use, especially before leaving the house for any length of time.

Obviously turning electrical products off doesn't give 100% protection from a home fire but it certainly improves your odds of such an event not happening.

It would stand to reason when buying a house that, if you have had a full structural survey which indicates that all is in good order, and you carry out all appropriate standard building maintenance and repairs in good time and to a high standard, you don't usually spend time worrying about your house collapsing. This is a fundamentally rock-solid basis for your personal sense of home security.

Until one day, it does actually fall down.

Then, believe me, any potential disaster is up for grabs.

Therefore, I don't think I was really that mad to be a touch obsessed about the oil pipe. Especially as every single one of the builders who had visited the site to inspect the damaged walls had said to me cheerfully and, I felt, rather patronisingly, "You want to watch that oil pipe, love," as they trotted past it. (I was trying to get it watched but no one was listening!)

It eventually struck me during one of those painfully long, dark, sleepless nights that we were approaching the situation from the wrong angle. The oil pipe was admittedly in danger. There was no doubt about that. I had warned the Insurance Company about it yet they were fairly non-committal and I now realised why.

They didn't see that it was their problem.

You see! I said I wasn't that bright. It can often take me a while but I do get there in the end.

Now, I have already admitted to significant sleep deprivation by this point, so I do not actually know if the following is factually correct. Nevertheless, it occurred to me that the pipe hadn't actually been damaged yet, and as I had foreseen that it might get damaged and informed them of this, then they could very easily turn around to me in the event that it was ultimately severed by further slippage and ask me why I hadn't taken preventative action to sort it out.

Catch 22 perhaps?

I would argue that the damage was caused by the falling wall. They would no doubt respond that I could have (in fact I already had) predicted the damage and, therefore, should have done something to prevent it. I could argue that they should have listened to me, advising me what action to take, but they could counter that it wasn't their problem until it actually happened, and even though I did have oil spill cover in my policy, because I didn't have accidental damage or some other such cover I was probably not protected.

In short, I didn't really expect them to help.

Paranoid? Me?

Not at all, I am now a realist.

Or is that a fatalist?

Hmmm…! Not sure! Anyway, do you blame me?

Still, let's not get side tracked. While I don't actually know if this is what would really happen, it was entirely possible that we could ultimately argue until we were blue in the face with oil pouring into the ground and the Environment Agency issuing a big fat fine.

I was still pretty certain that that bill would land on our door mat, too. They do say that misery loves company and we were pretty miserable.

I wasn't prepared to go there, as I simply didn't have the energy.

Oil is always a fairly slippery subject, but in all of the years that we lived in the country, we found that it was the simplest, most economical and efficient way to heat our home, regardless of which fuel crisis the government was bleating on about at the time.

I have to confess when we first moved to this remote location, I was concerned about not being on mains gas. I wondered just how we were going to maintain a constant supply of fuel. Surely, we would run out just when we needed it the most? After all, knowing our luck (as by now you should), it would have to be the coldest day in the darkest winter, just as all our pipes were in danger of freezing instantly if the heating wasn't on, that our oil supply would give up the ghost.

Yes, I know, my pessimistic streak is showing again. Sorry! I will try and put it away.

As it happens, most tanks can be fitted with a very clever device which comes free from the oil supplier, giving them an electronic reading on the level of oil in your tank at all times so that as soon as the fuel level drops below a certain amount, they send a nice chap with a tanker load and fill it up for you. You pay a monthly amount, just as you would to a gas company, and everyone is happy, and more importantly warm!

The location of your oil tank is generally very carefully considered. There are quite a few rules to govern where they can go even though many properties struggle to conform to all of them, mainly because they are quite contradictory, as all truly efficient guidelines should be.

It's no fun otherwise.

As a result, our tank site was to the far side of our property, away from the cottage, the thatch, the garage and all of the sheds. It was not too close to the flammable wooden fencing and there were no overhanging trees or wood stores nearby. An excellent location you might think, apart from the fact that it was also quite a long way away from our actual boiler, the bathrooms and the mains water supply.

Not a problem! That's why we have an oil pipeline. If laid with sufficient fall, then gravity can enable an uninterrupted supply of oil to flow from the tank along a substantial length of pipe to the boiler. Usually this pipe would be laid close to major structures such as the base of a house, or even partly buried underground to give it some protection from inadvertent damage; and so it came to be, that our pipeline ran along the base of the cottage wall, around the corner to the boiler. In our precarious house-falling-down situation, the oil pipe was in the prime location for maximum potential damage should either or both walls succumb to gravity.

The last thing we needed right then (apart from obviously not wanting to be the source of any environmental damage) were yet more financial threats in the form of potential fines looming over us. I am sure you can understand just how concerned we were about the situation. It felt like there was the Sword of Damocles hanging over us, or at least hanging over our oil pipe, and we needed to get it sorted.

The final straw, as it always seemed to, came after yet another windy night. You would be forgiven for thinking that we lived in a hurricane alley or something, the number of storms I keep wittering on about. I assure you we don't; it is just that those couple of winters were very volatile. That night of the final straw, some of the black sheeting that encased the damaged cottage walls had come loose at one end and flapped like an untethered sail all night while the caravan rocked alarmingly. We spent the night wondering what would happen first; either the house would take off or Hattie would, to be found half a mile away in the morning messing up someone's duck pond.

Yet, as before, a sleepless and stormy night resulted in a morning of action. Beloved Husband and I decided to take matters into our own hands. The laptop was redeployed and a further email sent to the Insurance Company telling them that, in the absence of any response from them, we were going to make our own arrangements to prevent an oil spill on the property. This was followed by a bit of research and the purchase of a new oil tank.

You might wonder why a new tank was necessary. Surely we were overreacting! Could we not move the one we had?

Now that would be far too easy.

Haven't you been listening?

We don't do easy here.

The answer to your very rational question is no, and there were several reasons for this. The principle one being that the rules wouldn't allow us to. Our tank was not of the most recent design. Whilst made of the appropriately thick plastic material required and in excellent condition, it was not what is referred to as 'bunded'. This means that it should effectively be two tanks, one inside the other so that if the inner wall fails for whatever reason, there is a second wall to prevent oil egress. How you tell if your inner wall has failed I don't know, but I assume there is a clever bit of electronic kit that will inform you.

Fundamentally though, our tank simply didn't comply with the latest regulations. While it remained in situ it was perfectly OK to continue using it. However, if it was to be moved, then we were obliged by those pesky government imperatives to install the latest acceptable design. Hence a new tank was unavoidable as we were planning to move both tank and pipeline, temporarily, around to the other side of the property so that they were no longer at risk.

Your next question, if you are paying attention and haven't got bored and wandered off to make a cup of tea, might be why move the tank at all? Why not simply reroute the pipeline away from the damaged walls?

Excellent suggestion! Well done, you are still awake after all that, aren't you? I am impressed.

Sadly, we had already considered this and had a quote as to whether this might be possible. It wasn't. The distance around the back of the house was simply too far and did not permit sufficient fall or drop to allow the oil to flow efficiently as far as the boiler. Shame really, as this would have been a nice cheap and easy, temporary solution. From a purely practical point of view, the presence of a second tank made the move far easier as it meant that the new tank could be installed before the old tank was decommissioned, allowing all the oil to be decanted across from one to the other; although there was an awful lot of oil to move.

Having made the decision to act, we were able to order a new tank within minutes, thanks to the internet. It would be delivered in four days' time and could be plumbed in two days after that, which would leave us the weekend to spend decanting oil from one tank to the other. We had elected to do this fun job ourselves as it would keep the bill to a minimum and the pennies were definitely not in plentiful supply.

Exactly eight days later, our potential oil spill disaster had been averted. The new tank was installed and fully operational. The old tank was retained in the hope that it could be used for the whole process to be repeated in reverse, should we ever successfully repair the house and be able to move the new tank back around to the original tank's location, after which we planned for the old one to be appropriately recycled as per the Local Authority's regulations. Beloved Husband and I made use of our still functioning boiler to generate copious quantities of hot water for several lengthy showers because (take my word for it) oil does not wash off easily. There is a certain odious quality that lingers long after contact and generates some very odd looks in the queue for the village post office on a Monday morning, or so I found.

Part 6

A wise individual does not allow their future to be stolen by the events of the past.

Alice May

28: Teamwork

Definition: the collective action of a group of people operating collaboratively towards a mutual goal.

Once again, back in the present…

Dabbing away at a wet canvas in my little hidey-hole, I became aware of a peaceful quiet within the house around me.

This sounded a dim warning bell.

Early life with the Barbarians had led me to be highly suspicious of silence. It usually meant that mischief was underway. Even now that they were growing up into surprisingly civilised individuals, I couldn't suppress an instinctive distrust of tranquillity. In addition to the stillness, I noted the conspicuous absence of my usual sugary sustenance, which was also rather peculiar and definitely required investigation.

Just to be on the safe side, I sidled over to the door, brush in hand, and peered along the corridor towards the kitchen.

Aha! Interesting!

Logic had obviously welcomed the temporary return of Chaos to the family home and they were both contentedly coating my kitchen surfaces with a variety of sticky, sugar-related substances as they slipped back into their customary roles of culinary creation. That would explain the absence of my mid-morning snack. It was probably still in the oven.

The peace and quiet was due to the fact that each Barbarian was plugged into a separate iPod and silently nodding along to their individual choice of auditory entertainment, obviously content to be together but not necessarily requiring any form of verbal exchange. They always did seem to read each other's minds, which is quite an achievement for two such unique personalities.

Smiling, I retreated back to my canvas where some bright summer flowers were in full bloom.

If the girls were content, I could safely assume the boys were suitably occupied. I knew from past experience that Chaos and Logic would be very quick to stomp loudly on any outrageous Barbarian boy behaviour, and the boys wouldn't dream of stepping out of line if there were freshly baked cookies in the offing. Rather than interfere, I returned to enthusiastically splodging a selection of scarlet snapdragons across my colourful canvas, all the while contemplating how lovely it was to see my beautiful daughters enjoying each other's company once again. They had missed each other.

Our little family unit was changing, with one Barbarian already having left home and the second soon to follow. This was a gradual modification. Our team was adapting to the change naturally and not being brutally and prematurely ripped apart like it had so nearly been two years previously. This change was a healthy one and we were handling it well so far. Thinking back over our time in the caravan, I marvelled at what situations you can adapt to if you are willing to put your mind to it. Once what had previously passed for 'normal life' had been thrown out of the window, our Barbarians were very quick to start pulling together as a team.

In the early days of our little family's creation, as with all sibling groups, there were inevitable tussles and power struggles. Brothers and sisters never fully appreciate each other's finer points until they start to grow up a bit. However, living through the disastrous loss of our home and the potential destruction of our family life, as well as surviving the close confines of caravan life for an extended period of time, seemed to have brought a significant maturity to their overall approach to life that any parent would be proud of.

It had been fascinating to watch them thinking up ways to make our new garden-based existence generally easier for all. For example, astonishing levels of collaboration went into things like establishing a boosted internet connection that would reach Hattie from the house enabling them to each engage in electronic endeavours without having to trot back to the house to gain a connection.

They also seemed to pay far more attention to what was going on around them, although this was in all probability due to the fact that when you are living with five other people in a 35 ft by 12 ft metal box, you can't really ignore anything, or anyone, effectively.

Nevertheless, they obviously noticed which general day-to-day jobs were so much harder to achieve during that instalment of our life, and I was always grateful to accept any offers of help that came my way. They were all suddenly quite content to carry things to and from Hattie and the house for me, when it would never previously have occurred to the Barbarians to offer to carry anything anywhere, be it taking clean washing upstairs or lifting the vacuum cleaner downstairs, without me first employing a verbal three-line whip. (OK, I really mean 'indulging in a hissy fit'!)

On occasion, Beloved Husband I had even observed them co-operating to help each other carry necessary paraphernalia back and forth.

So, all in all, life in Hattie did have its good points. Not that I am recommending it to anyone, you understand.

***

Anyway, returning to the student and the wet washing in the present…. Later that day, following the consumption of the most delicious still-warm chocolate brownies, I was helping Chaos to distribute her wet undergarments along the radiators in the conservatory, listening to her chattering away about university life. As usual, she didn't really require a verbal response from me and I was just enjoying having her at home for a fleeting visit regardless of the significant increase in damp laundry that now festooned the house. She was telling me about how she and some friends had recently signed a contract to rent a house for their second year and was describing the property to me in detail. One comment in particular caught my attention.

Whilst telling me that the house was a fairly new property, with double glazing, five double bed rooms, no obvious damp etc, she said earnestly, "It does seem stable enough!"

I experienced a quick flash of pity for the rental estate agent. I bet they had never come across a student like Chaos before. Most young people probably stressed about who was going to get the biggest bedroom, how many bathrooms were available or if bills were included in the rental price. Whereas Chaos had probably demanded to see a recent full structural survey and asked if there was any evidence of subsidence in the area. I wouldn't have put it past her to check if the garden was large enough to accommodate a static caravan too, just in case.

Our home collapse had no doubt had a lasting effect, both positive and negative, on all of our beloved Barbarians.

Yet hopefully, at the same time, perhaps they had gained true knowledge about their strength of self and the value of teamwork to overcome significant odds; along with basics things like learning to always check the small print on your insurance documents.

29: Conclusion

Definition: A decision based on reasoning.

Back to the messy situation in the past…

We eventually settled into an unusual but comforting domestic routine. We were getting rather used to our unconventional existence with its cosy and companionable evenings around the fire in the house before making a chilly bedtime dash to the caravan, armed with hot water bottles, fleecy dressing gowns and waterproofs, just in case. Interestingly, for the first time in their lives the Barbarians were discovering the point of the slippers I have always bought them, especially now that the patio flagstones more often than not sported a thin layer of ice, courtesy of Jack Frost, in both the evenings and the early mornings.

Although we were very grateful for the protection that Hattie's arrival had afforded the family unit, prolonged periods of time spent in the caravan rooms felt immensely claustrophobic, especially now that winter was on us and all doors and windows had to remain closed to retain any available heat. It had become our habit to stay together in the house by the fire until the last possible moment, then to go to bed and hopefully straight to sleep.

The result was actually very pleasant as we would sit together, sometimes watching TV as a group or at other times each engaged in our own individual tasks thanks to judicious use of headphones, laptops and iPads etc. As a result, A-level studies and last-minute homework could take place alongside cartoons, rom-coms or televised sporting events. It proved to be a very companionable and cosy way for a large group of mixed ages to spend the evenings.

The boys soon learned to take advantage of the almost permanently lit open fire to work out what snacks could be warmed, toasted or occasionally incinerated over it. Having unearthed an old-fashioned toasting fork during the main house clearance, they started out with simple things like scorching marshmallows and progressed through cremating slices of bread to transforming chipolata sausages into charcoal sticks. Then the real fun began as they moved on to making actual filled toasties in a homemade contraption they had devised themselves out of two broken, metal sieves stolen from my kitchen. (I have my suspicions that my sieves weren't actually broken prior to the Barbarians getting their hands on them but learned a long time ago not to ask questions that I probably didn't want the answers to. This was one of those occasions.)

Having assembled the complicated contents of their sandwiches they would clamp them between the flattened metal netting sections of the sieves and, using an extended handle, they would hold the whole contrivance over the fire for the bread to brown, first on one side and then the other.

It took several goes to get it right at first but eventually their offerings were really very edible indeed. The contents of the toasties would melt into a pleasing and warming evening delicacy that the rest of the family were queuing up to consume. Even some of the more outlandish combinations of flavours that Quiet created were willingly ingested.

This certainly kept the boys well occupied throughout the chilly winter evenings and meant that any form of formal supper was not really necessary, as someone had to eat the results of each experimental phase. There was even a scoring system based firstly on how successfully the snack stayed together during the toasting phase and then on the overall taste. Points were lost for partial disintegration or complete loss of snack to the flames below. Who needs reality TV? We had 'come toast with me', an altogether far more brilliant and explorative form of untried TV viewing. It was amazing just how inventive the evening culinary exploits became. Move over Jamie Oliver, the Barbarian Boys have arrived!

It was during such an evening as this, a few days before Christmas, that I noticed Beloved Husband suddenly freeze with a fairly mundane cheese, ham, pepperoni, mayonnaise and pickle toastie half way to his mouth. His eyes were staring fixedly at his laptop screen. Concerned that he might either be choking or actually having a seizure, I abandoned my own plate, hurriedly extracted myself from the pile of floor cushions near the fire (the best location in my opinion to simultaneously stay warm and get first refusal on the most successful looking snacks), and crossed over to the sofa to see what the problem might be.

Having ascertained that he was indeed breathing just fine and also fully conscious, I realised that something in his email had caught his attention. Nosy as always, I read it over his shoulder and gave a squeak. He turned his head and we looked at each other with eyebrows raised in surprise.

Obviously, in a family like ours, this odd behaviour wasn't going to go unnoticed for long.

"Well?" demanded Logic, having extracted her headphones from both ears.

Beloved Husband looked questioningly at me and I shrugged.

"It's an email from the house Insurance Company," he said.

"OK, what reports do they want to do now? Surely there's nothing left they can possibly assess, or do they want second opinions on everything next?" Chaos said dryly.

"No, far from it, it would seem that they have finally made a decision," he said.

"And?" said Quiet.

"It doesn't say. Apparently, we have to wait. The Professional Gentleman is going to telephone us to let us know."

"So, their second refusal won't be in writing, I suppose," Chaos huffed. "That won't stop us going to the Financial Ombudsman though."

"Does it give you any idea when he might phone you?" Logic asked. "Is it likely to be before Christmas?"

"I shouldn't think so!" I said.

There was silence, apart from some significant hissing and spitting from a forgotten cheese sandwich in the fire, as we all looked at each other apprehensively.

Suddenly the telephone rang.

All six of us jumped and then leapt for the handset at once with Beloved Husband winning by a country mile. (Longer legs you see. He is such a cheat!) From the tangled heap on the floor where the rest of us had landed, after he shoved us all aside in his haste to get to the handset first, we listened transfixed to his side of the conversation, which was extremely uninformative and went something like this.

"Hello."

Pause.

"Yes."

Pause.

"O.K."

Pause.

"Uh huh."

Pause.

"OK."

I'll stop there. It went on like that for quite a while but I am sure you get the general picture; on the whole, not very illuminating.

It was rather a shame that he was not using the speaker phone, but I suppose he was trying to spare the Barbarians from, what was very probably, bad news. Although from the hissed exchange passing between the two girls, they had already assumed it was bad anyway, as had I.

After a few more "yes"s and another couple of "OK"s there was a "bye" and Beloved Husband lowered the phone and stood stock still in absolute silence.

Ah! He was looking rather shocked and didn't make any attempt to speak although his mouth did open and close a few times. Unfortunately, he seemed unable to summon any sound at all. (Please don't tell me that we were returning to the days of living with a verbally challenged ostrich, I really don't think I could cope with that again.)

"It's OK!" I said encouragingly, jumping to my feet and stepping over a few Barbarians to reach him. "Don't worry! We knew they would probably refuse to help us."

"No!" he managed to mutter shaking his head in disbelief. Surely he couldn't really have thought that there was much chance that they were going to help us.

"Don't worry, Dad," chimed in Logic scrambling out from under Small.

"Get them to put their refusal in writing and we can appeal," I said standing right in front of him. "It's wicked to do it over the phone so we can't appeal."

"No!" he said urgently, looking at me with a wild expression in his eyes.

'Oh heck,' I thought, 'he's really lost it this time.' With Beloved Husband struggling to form more than that one word (obviously complete sentences were out of the question), it must be incredibly bad news.

"It's alright, Dad!" Chaos added. "The letter to the Financial Ombudsman is already written. We finished it last week."

"Yes," I said, "It's just waiting for the details of the second refusal and then we can send it straight away."

"No!" he said grabbing hold of my shoulders, "Stop!" That was another word. Progress! Excellent!

"Stop what?" I asked confused.

"Stop talking!" he said, giving me a gentle shake. "Let me think!"

"OK" I said, "but would you mind hurrying up, please?"

After a few seconds he took a deep breath and said "It's going to be OK!"

"I know! That's what I said! If you can…." I tailed off when he gave me a look. (Ooops, I was still talking.) I shrugged mutely back at him, apologetically.

We all stood looking at him in total silence for a few seconds before he took a deep breath and smiled (the first real smile I had seen from him in more than six months).

"It's going to be OK," he said, "because the Insurance Company has agreed to the basic repair! The builders start in January!"

30: Hero

Definition: A person who, in the opinion of others, has heroic qualities.

Two years after that momentous telephone call and we are back in the present day.

I was surprised to find myself humming along to the radio while doing a happy little jig whilst applying relaxed, paint-loaded brush strokes to my latest canvas. While I am not allowed to name the song due to copyright laws, if you think of the happiest song to grace our airwaves in recent years then you can probably guess what I was listening to.

My goodness! What a change! Here I was practically dancing.

Looking about me, I had to admit that I really couldn't refer to this particular room as anything other than a studio now, no matter how hard I tried. It was not a study or a cubby hole or a spare room anymore. The filing cabinet, a shelving unit and two chairs had been evicted and the space was now stacked full of finished canvases. I had to accept that my painting was back to stay, so an 'art studio' it was!

I was mentally contemplating the vast amount of artwork that I had generated in the last few weeks. There was more than enough here for an exhibition, if I ever felt like putting physical evidence of my desperate climb back up from the depths of complete emotional disintegration on public display. Perhaps not! Demonic daffodils and suchlike are not everyone's cup of tea. However, I felt my silver fish, swimming determinedly upwards from the deep oceanic abyss were quite optimistic, even rather inspiring. This particular image marked a very positive turning point in my recovery and I had painted several different variations on that theme in the end, as they were so enjoyably relaxing to create.

The musical paintings definitely had potential, too, especially if they were framed up as a pretty and colourful orchestral series. The bright, vibrancy practically danced off the canvases with joy, even though I do say so myself.

A small sound and the appearance of a steaming cup and a plate of cake by my elbow made me turn. Expecting my intruder to be Logic, I was pleasantly surprised to see Beloved Husband standing next to me. Ah! It had never occurred to me that he might be the source of any of the sustaining snacks that kept mysteriously appearing recently? Was he the one who had been looking after me all this time that I had been mentally wandering through the past?

My own personal superhero brandishing fresh cake and a hot cuppa, what more could a girl want? White knights on powerful steads are all very well but I've always thought that the armour and horse hair, not to mention the ego, would get in the way?

I met his eyes enquiringly. "You've been busy!" he commented casually.

"Hmmm!" I agreed.

"Are you feeling any better yet?" he asked.

I regarded him steadily, but didn't reply.

"You seem better," he continued carefully, "happier? Have you managed to work some things out?"

I nodded, looking down at the paintings spread all around me and smiled.

"Dare we hope that you have finally forgiven yourself then?" he said.

Startled, I looked up at him but quickly looked away again in confusion. I don't know why I was so surprised really. He has always had this peculiar ability to know what was on my mind. (No, he is not literally reading my mind word for word, but he pays far more attention than you would think, and he's probably the only person on the planet who actually remotely understands me. Poor chap!) I had been quite grumpy, so it probably wasn't that difficult to put two and two together.

"You do know that none of us have ever blamed you for what happened, don't you?" he persevered. "We've all said so. Many times, but you won't listen. You just keep on holding yourself accountable, way more than anyone else would or even could."

There was a moment of silence as I gathered my wits, before I gave a deep sigh and spoke. "If I had not made that mistake with the insurance right at the start, things would have been so different."

"Not necessarily," he said. "You don't know that, none of us do. I have a feeling that everyone has a bit of a battle on their hands with any big insurance claim. It's inevitable that you have to justify any sizeable application for funds, and this was a pretty big claim. It's different if it's just a broken TV or a window pane. Anyway, it wasn't accidental damage in the end was it? That definition was irrelevant. Whether the insurance latched onto that as a bit of a smokescreen to try to wriggle out of a big pay out, or whether it was a genuine mistake, I don't think we'll ever know. The only thing that matters is that they came good in the end. Eventually!"

"Relatively speaking," I said darkly.

"True," he agreed. "They only covered part of the work, but at least it got us started so that we could then help ourselves back onto our own feet."

"I suppose so." I nodded slowly. He was right, he had said it before. Perhaps now, having finally managed to process all that had happened, I was ready to listen.

"Even if we had had the accidental damage cover, I bet it would have still been a long old haul to prove we qualified for that, simply because of the scope and complexity of the situation." He moved over to the desk as he spoke and leaned against it with his arms crossed, before continuing.

"The mistake we made, and please note I said WE, was to buy an old house. Not because it fell down, although that obviously wasn't ideal let's face it, but because it was never going to fit into any of the standard definitions available when taking out house insurance policies."

"But..." I interrupted, then stopped when he shook his head at me.

"I know! We took great care to choose a company that understands old properties. However, we were very naive to think that we were going to be fully covered against all eventualities. That was an unintentional miscalculation but we made it years before the actual cob collapse happened. Think about it! Elements of the house were very, very old, but bits of it were not quite so old and some of it was really new. We had part cob construction, part wood, some brick and glass, and then finally some concrete, all mixed in. It was thatched but also tiled with a section of conservatory roof too. It had an old chimney and also a second more modern chimney. I challenge anyone to find me one Insurance Company tick box form that will cover all of that, especially over the telephone."

"I should have tried harder." I insisted. "I should have thought of that. There must have been something I could have done to either stop it or fix it."

"Don't be ridiculous! Stop being such a control freak! I know you like to organise everything but sometimes it's just not possible. It was a disaster waiting to happen from the moment we bought the house. Accidental damage or not, the house was a ticking time bomb waiting for that one final winter when the biggest storms on record for 250 years simply blew it up."

"I guess," I conceded.

"Remember, it could just as easily have been me that made the phone call to set up the insurance when we moved in. The result would have been the same."

"Really?"

He sighed, "I have said all this to you before, you know, and I will keep on saying it if I have to. Are you ready to listen to me now? Or are you going to carry on blaming yourself? You're so stressed all the time now. Worrying about everything and scared of your own shadow. I have been really worried about you. You are constantly convinced that the worst is about to happen and keep trying to work out ways to avoid potential disasters. It's an impossible task. You cannot micro-manage everything. You'll make yourself ill. Don't forget that you risk damaging the rest of us as much as yourself by refusing to let it go."

He stepped over to me and slid his arms around me. "Please let it go?" he asked. I turned to face him, resting my cheek on his chest. "I feel just as guilty as you, you know," he continued after a moment.

"Why?"

He sighed.

"For loads of reasons. For not being able to afford to immediately move us all into a hotel or rent another property straight away. I should have been able to provide for the family. I should have worked harder, made better arrangements for emergencies."

"But you were working so hard already," I said, "and you did take on extra when you could. The house insurance we were paying was supposed to cover emergencies! It was costing us enough, for goodness' sake!"

"There you go, see? It's not just you that can play the unreasonable blame game. We have to relax. Carrying it with us will give it a power it doesn't deserve. It's over, let's move on without it. All of us. Together."

"OK." I leaned happily into a warm hug and smiled.

"I just have one question though," he said.

"What?" I asked suspiciously.

"Where the hell are we going to put all these paintings?"

Epilogue

Definition: A comment or conclusion from the author at the end of a book.

That, I think, is an appropriate place to leave our heroine wrapped as she is in the arms of her own personal superhero. They have both reached a place of understanding, acceptance and forgiveness (however necessary or not – let's not start debating that one again), and are content to move forward into the future, if not completely whole, then as a partially repaired 'work-in-progress'.

After all, who among us do not bear the scars of our past?

***

Now, a brief footnote on those we have abandoned in a crumbly cottage in the past.

Don't worry! The younger versions of our hero and heroine and their intrepid, happy, little band of Barbarian campers are going to be OK too!

It's Christmas and who needs more of a reason to celebrate?

There are fairy lights strung along the crazy paving to light the pathway from Hattie to the house. Skelly has been brought around from the front of the house and is now ensconced comfortably in a deck chair on the patio next to a Christmas tree in a pot. He is currently sporting a warm red cloak and a battered old top hat from a charity shop with some tinsel around the brim, whilst holding an empty beer can in celebration of the festive season.

It is time to draw this little tale to a close as the family contemplate their small success. They don't yet realise what a dangerous and rocky mountain road they still have to climb in their quest to rebuild their home and become their future selves, but that is another story. The Insurance Company have agreed a rudimentary package of help for them and this is the helping hand up that they so desperately need to start repairs. All the rest can be worked out in time. One step at a time!

It would be a shame to upset them, with knowledge of what is to come. So, for now, let us allow them to look forward to their cosy little Christmas. A Christmas that would admittedly be rather light on actual presents but heavily weighted towards family fun and festive food!

They are not yet out of the woods but, at this moment in time, it does not matter. Should they have fought harder and not accepted the Insurance Company's bare minimum offer? Some would say yes. It could be suggested that they should have pushed for more comprehensive assistance, but each delay would no doubt mean additional months and even potentially years in limbo, probably with yet further assessments being carried out and reports being written but no restorative action taken.

It should be remembered that, in all decisions, our beleaguered couple have been motivated entirely by damage limitation, choosing the option that ensured that their beloved Barbarians would suffer the least. Any choice that would speed up the repair process and enable them to resume normal life had to be made, regardless of who was liable or responsible for the monetary bottom line.

So, we shall leave the family there, dear reader, as they are about to celebrate what was an unexpectedly wonderful crumbly-cottage-and-caravan-based family Christmas together.

The promised start date of the rebuild was set for the 2nd January. A New Year filled with fresh possibilities (and no doubt more disasters knowing them but let us hush for now!).

Everything will be alright in the end.

May you always have walls for the winds, a roof for the rain, tea beside the fire, laughter to cheer you and those you love near you…

Irish Blessing
Anon

BOOK 2

RESTORATION

More tales from the house that sat down.

For
Gill and Nigel, Granma and Papa, Mum and Dad,
so many names for two very special people!

Also:
For Guinevere,
the little girl on the swing.

Restoration

Definition:
The process or act of returning something to its previous condition, to rebuild or repair

Part 1

The (wo)man who moves a mountain begins by carrying away small stones

Confucius
551BC 479BC

Preamble

Definition: A word from the author to set the scene…

With hindsight, it would appear that my tale is not over.

Welcome back my dear friends. It has been some time since last we spoke. I had intended to leave my story where it ended in Accidental Damage, but so many people have asked me 'What happened next?' that I have taken to my trusty, old keyboard again.

If you had told our heroine at 7am this morning that she would be on her knees, cradling a human head in the centre of the local town's high street by 9.09am, she wouldn't have believed you. She had no idea that it was going to be one of *those* days!

As you know, we last saw her in the arms of her beloved husband when he finally persuaded her to stop blaming herself for her part in the disaster that had befallen their home and had nearly torn their family apart. One might be forgiven for thinking that this was the end of the story, but it would seem not. There are some unforeseen consequences to those previous events, which are starting to make their presence felt and our heroine has her work cut out in order to deal with them. We are soon to re-join her in both the present, approximately six months after we left her in Accidental Damage, and also in the past as the family struggle with the practicalities of rebuilding their home.

Let us begin with the present day because, as you can see from the above introductory statement, she is back in the thick of drama once again. Had she had any inkling of what fate had in store for her on that particular morning she would (quite understandably) have gone back to bed to wait for tomorrow. As it was, that morning started much like any other, as she sleepily listened to the radio whilst scraping three day old, concreted-on, Weetabix from a cereal bowl excavated from beneath her teenage son's bed.

'Cradling a human head?' you say. 'Why on earth is she doing that?' Well I am glad you asked because I can assure you that she is not doing it for fun. I'll let her tell you all about it now....

1: Re-evaluate

Definition: to consider something for a second time in order to judge value, quality or importance.

Present day once again…

It was quite unbelievable just how much my knees were hurting.

I tried unobtrusively to shift the weight on them without disturbing the head that I had clutched in my sweaty hands. The head was encased in a motorcycle helmet; a nice, black, shiny one. No doubt shiny, black helmets are very cool but they are also rather slippery. Don't panic though, the head was fully attached to the motorcyclist's body and that body did appear to still be breathing. (I don't do gratuitous gore and there's no need in this instance anyway, as the feared injuries turned out to be relatively minor in the end, but nobody knew that just then.)

I must confess that the reason I was coping with the scenario so well was the fact that I had my suspicions that the aforementioned motorcyclist was not particularly badly hurt, although I was certainly not going to say so out loud, as I could have been wrong. It has been known to happen.

Nevertheless, I had been afforded a ringside view of the motorbike rider overtaking the car in front of me as I sat stationary in my little purple car at the traffic lights. The handlebars of the bike had unfortunately clipped the car wing mirror as it passed, setting the rider off on a somewhat wobbly and erratic course. All valiant attempts to bring the bike back under control ended in it rising up onto the back wheel to perform a slow and lazy pirouette, while dumping the rider on the ground before the machine bounded through a gap in the oncoming traffic and collided with a parked car on the other side of the road.

Ooops!

We all make mistakes, but this one was a spectacularly messy one, leaving bits of motorbike scattered everywhere, so I had immense sympathy with the rider on the ground before me. He had single-handedly caused all movement to come to an abrupt standstill on the high street at a critical point in the Monday morning rush hour. This was the only route through our busy market town, and as both sides of the road were now completely compromised, absolutely no one here would be getting to work or school on time.

If I were in his leathers, I think I would lie still and keep very quiet too.

I could hear multiple sirens heading our way indicating that the confident sounding gentleman, who had rushed out of the flower shop on hearing the sound of a collision and insisted on me holding the rider's head still, had successfully alerted the authorities. Excellent news!

Fortunately, just as I was thinking that I wasn't sure quite how much more my knees could take, I was distracted by the arrival of two enormously handsome paramedics. It's an ill wind that blows no-one any good. I smiled up at them when they cheerfully introduced themselves before realising they were talking to the head in my hands and not the old woman holding it. I relinquished my hold on the helmet when asked to do so, brushed the ingrained grit and tarmac out of my kneecaps, and sat back to appreciate the much-improved scenery, listening to the paramedics at work. They had opened the visor of the helmet (it hadn't occurred to me to do that, although in my defence I don't have three hands) and were speaking gently to the casualty.

I was surprised to note two things. The rider was a very pretty, very young *she*, not a *he* at all. That'll teach me to make assumptions! I also noted, with some fascination, that she was in possession of very trendy black eyebrows (the sort that look like they've been drawn on using a marker pen) and the most abundant forest of fake eyelash extensions, complete with gemstone embellishments. It was quite impressive that she had managed to open her eyes at all under the sheer weight of these adornments, but fortunately she was managing to flutter them at the paramedics quite successfully, which suggested to me that she was probably OK. Relieved to see this, I excused myself and went to find a policeman to give my name and address to in case they needed a statement.

Give them their due, when they swing into action, the British Traffic Police are very good at keeping things moving and it wasn't that long before we were all on our way again as soon as the lady with the eyelashes had been carted off in an ambulance.

I pulled away from the high street, leaving the hustle and bustle of the town behind me, to head along empty country lanes in the direction of home. My plan for the morning had been to go to a local gallery and ask if they had any exhibition space but the drama of the last hour had rather put me off that idea. It was no great loss, I wasn't really sure I wanted to get back into exhibiting anyway. I just wanted to get on with the next painting, not faff around selling the last one. However, my Beloved Husband obviously felt entirely differently about the matter and had been making some very pointed comments recently, suggesting that we might end up buried under finished canvases if we're (he means 'I'm') not careful. I don't know what he's on about. They are all carefully stored away in my little studio.

Ok and the shed (it's a small one) and part of the garage (not a small one). I suppose there are a few behind the sofa, and there's a really big one stuffed down the side of the freezer too. Hmm! Maybe he has a point. I will have to get it sorted out, but not today.

Twenty minutes later I pulled onto the drive back at the cottage and was rather shocked to see a 'For Sale' sign emerging from our front hedge. Wow! That hadn't been there when I left, although I shouldn't really be surprised, as we had discussed putting the house on the market. Nevertheless, I wasn't quite prepared for the reality of it. I guess it's a bit like the difference between the suspicion that the mobile speed camera probably caught you and the actual police enforcement notice landing on your doormat.

It would seem that we were now the proud clients of an extremely enthusiastic and efficient estate agent. This was a very new development but one which Beloved Husband and I had always suspected might be the final price to pay for the events of three years ago. You might say that the writing had been on the crumbly cottage walls all along in spite of everything we had done to try to prevent it.

Now, I don't know about you, but I hate it when I am reading a sequel and the author spends at least two chapters bringing me up to date with what happened in the first book. It's a waste of time, paper and ink, in my opinion, so if you haven't read Accidental Damage, I would politely suggest that you probably should before continuing with this book.

Having said that though, there is something I didn't mention previously, about those early days after the cottage started to crumble, that you do need to know for the continuation of my tale, and so I'll explain that here. I'll be quick, I promise!

You already know that a large part of our 350-year-old cob cottage started to disintegrate one day leaving the vast majority of our home uninhabitable and forcing us to move into a tent in the garden while we tried to work out what to do about it. You also know that we spent quite some time trying to salvage our possessions from the wibbly, wobbly part of the house and that we continued to use a ground floor kitchen/lounge/conservatory extension built at the back of the property, even though we didn't know if it was entirely stable.

What you don't know is that there was one small bedroom that was built over part of that extension. Now going on the theory that the kitchen/lounge/conservatory might be stable and therefore safe to use, there was a chance that this bedroom was too. Both had been built more recently than the cob section of the house and we hoped the old bit falling wouldn't pull the newer part down as well. Unfortunately, we were unable to access this bedroom as to get there you had to go through the crumbling cob section and climb the collapsing staircase. Not really advisable under the circumstances.

In a moment of madness back then, we had considered cutting a hole up into this room from the kitchen ceiling below and using a ladder to reach it at night, we were so desperate for more civilised sleeping accommodation than the tent. Fortunately, reason returned before we did this, as smashing holes in the bit of the house that was still standing was never going to be a terribly inspired idea at the best of times, but let's face it, we weren't really thinking clearly back then.

You will no doubt remember that, in the initial aftermath of the cob collapse, we had systematically (and some would say foolishly) stripped the damaged section of the house of all our belongings using a slowly disintegrating staircase that behaved rather like the enchanted staircases at Hogwarts. The treads moved underfoot and the whole stairwell seemed determined to reconfigure itself as we passed, with chunks of masonry falling at random just to spice things up a bit.

Accepting that it wouldn't be long before someone was injured or killed en route, we made one final trip upstairs, during which my Beloved Husband and I hauled anything left (apart from a really heavy wardrobe in our son Quiet's room that we had to abandon where it was) through into that little back bedroom and stacked it up as neatly as possible. These were items that we hoped we would be able to manage without for an indefinite period of time, as once the door was sealed off (using insulating board and thick layers of industrial tape to keep the worst of the weather and the dust out), there would be no way back in until the house had been repaired.

One such abandoned item sat in the sunshine on the windowsill of that sealed room; a half-completed oil painting of a little girl on a swing, my creation of which had been rudely interrupted by the collapse of the house. Over the next year, the little girl would stand guard in suspended animation over the entombed contents of that room, the partially completed oily brush strokes of her face hardening off and drying in the sunshine, a colourful testimony to the suddenness with which our contented, ordinary life had ceased that day.

***

Sat in my car on the drive staring at the brand new Estate Agent board, I could remember quite clearly sealing up that little back bedroom and recalled how, at that moment, I hadn't been entirely sure that a time would ever come when I would be able to enter it again. There were a lot of hard decisions and plenty of tears to get through before such an event could come about, with no guarantee of success.

I sighed heavily. It was no good! The collision earlier that morning had certainly unsettled me but the arrival of this For Sale sign, such visual evidence of our failure to save the house, compounded things. I was going to have to paint while I sorted things out in my head. Opening the car door and stepping out, I noticed a small white feather lying on the ground at my feet. Absent-mindedly I reached down to pick it up, but as I rose I noticed a sudden light-headed feeling and an odd fluttery sensation in my chest. 'Silly woman,' I thought to myself, 'you stood up too quickly. Pull yourself together!'

Taking a couple of deep breaths and shaking my head to clear it, I slammed the car door and headed into the empty house, my footsteps echoing in the hallway as I marched directly to my little art studio next to the stairs. Putting the feather on the window sill in the sunshine where the cat used to sleep, I turned on the radio and started pulling out brushes and tubes of paint.

2: Transmute

Definition: to change something from one form to another, or to be changed in this way

Staying in the present....

It wasn't long before I was settled in front of my easel with a canvas primed and loaded brush poised. I could already feel myself beginning to relax a bit.

You might ask why I found myself in such a contemplative mood. It's only a For Sale sign, after all! It's not quite that simple though; things never are, are they? We had fought so hard to keep our Barbarians together when the house fell down and we had succeeded against the odds. But things change and now the oldest ones were starting to leave us of their own accord. Even though I don't like it, I do have to accept it. After all, that is life! It is time for them to move forwards, and it's not fair to make them do it whilst dragging their mother kicking and screaming behind them.

Don't get me wrong, I was pleased that our two girls, Chaos and Logic, were going to university, but simultaneously I missed them. How dare they leave me, but didn't they do well? A contrary little Yin and Yang to keep me endlessly entertained!

It needs to be appreciated that the absence of two girls changes the balance in a home significantly. I found myself abandoned in a very a male dominated environment consisting of Beloved Husband and our two boy Barbarians, (significantly-less) Quiet and (not-quite-so) Small.

Now that Chaos and Logic were not around talking all the time, Quiet seemed to have found his voice, albeit a voice that operated in an entirely different register than it had before, (When did that happen?). He was now in sole charge of a dangerously deep vocal instrument and took great delight in creeping up behind me and making sudden loud sounds that reverberated in a booming bass register, for no other apparent reason than to see me jump out of my skin before he ambled off grinning contentedly to himself. Bless!!

Whereas Small just kept on growing! No doubt this had something to do with the colossal amount of food he managed to eat every single day. I had noticed recently though that, at the same time as continuously consuming calories, he seemed to need to incessantly ingest information. He was always asking questions. Intelligent ones! Most of which I didn't know the answers to. Sometimes I suspected that the little smart Alec realised that and was only asking so that he could watch me squirm. For goodness' sake, he wasn't even out of primary school yet! Thank heaven for Google, is all I can say on that one!

For so many years it seemed that our home was knee high with toddlers complete with the associated noise, exhaustion, mess, mayhem and fun that all that involved. Yet now, all too soon, the eldest two had grown and flown. It required serious adjustment, especially for a control freak like me! Even my cat had abandoned me in the most ultimate way possible and I found that I missed the disdainful looks she used to give me, and her smug attitude way more than I had ever expected to.

Don't get me wrong, the house was still filled with commotion and noise, the boy Barbarians saw to that, but there was something missing. It was hard to put a finger on it. In the blink of an eye, there were simply not enough people in this cottage anymore and I didn't like it one little bit.

Nevertheless, it is the natural order of things and I had to adjust. After all, if they didn't leave home at all then I would be grumbling about that, wouldn't I?

I know!

There's just no pleasing me.

***

A little later on, when I had worked up quite a thirst throwing paint at the canvas, I started to run out of steam. Looking round for sustenance, I realised that I was going to have to shift for myself if I wanted a cup of tea.

Ten minutes after that, having investigated all kitchen cupboards while the kettle boiled and failed to unearth anything remotely sugar based, I wandered out into the front garden to sit on my little wrought iron bench in the sunshine clutching a steaming mug of tea.

I couldn't help thinking of another time when I had sat here, over three years previously, bundled up against the cold in almost every layer of clothing I possessed and clutching a cup of tea, while I nervously awaited the arrival of the promised builders to begin the rebuild process of our beautiful but wobbly cottage.

We had been assured that the building team would arrive at 9am on January 2nd, almost six months from the day that the walls had fallen. I remembered sitting in this exact same spot on that day waiting for them and how I couldn't quite believe that it would actually happen.

At that time, the front and side walls of the main damaged section of what was the oldest part of the cottage were encased in thick sheets of black plastic and were propped up with a random selection of scaffolding poles, wedges and strong-boys, some inside and some outside. These props were attempting to prevent any further slippage, but I was pretty certain that incremental movement was still merrily underway. Amazingly, the beautiful thatched roof appeared totally unaffected by the almost complete lack of support from two of the walls beneath it.

As I had sat there waiting for my promised builders, I had found myself wondering exactly what sort of state the house would be in, under all that plastic, having been abandoned for so long through the cold wet months of the autumn and early winter. The smell emanating from beneath the protective covering was a disturbing one of overpowering damp and rot.

The black sheeting effectively hid the extent of the damage to the casual observer, but beneath all the plastic were two huge cracks, one in each of two main supporting walls, that ran the full height of the building from the ground to the roof. One of the cracks, when I had last set eyes on it before the plastic encased it, was large enough for a fully-grown person to walk straight into the house (followed closely by a friendly dog of unknown origin). Windows hung at odd angles or had fallen out completely, old lathe and plaster internal walls were destroyed, and ceilings had come down. Hidden in the all-encompassing darkness created by the plastic sheeting, over in the far right-hand corner of the ground floor were the remaining treads of that magically morphing staircase I mentioned.

We took huge risks in continuing to use the potentially unstable single storey extension, with its little bathroom, right at the back of the house during the months of negotiations that took place with our house insurance company to decide who was liable for the cost of the repair. In effect, a very real game of Russian roulette was played on a daily basis. The whole 'home collapse' scenario had successfully redefined what constituted sensible behaviour for all of us and we quickly became fairly blasé about spending time in what was effectively part of an old ruin that might come tumbling down around our ears at any moment. We grew to be quite comfortable living with one eye constantly on the nearest exit, ready to escape in seconds if needed. A habit which, I can assure you, never really leaves you once it is learned!

During all those months of living in a sort of suspended animation, not knowing if an agreement would ever be reached with the insurance company that might enable us to move the situation forward, we became almost philosophical in our defiance of danger. My though processes often ran along the lines of 'I'm cold and I'm tired. The house is not actually falling down right at this particular minute and I want a hot shower. Therefore, I'm going to have a hot shower. If I get squashed, then I get squashed. So be it!'

But all that was about to change! An agreement had been reached. That cold, fresh January day was one of positivity. It was a massive turning point. There would be no more marking time, stagnating and waiting for progress to start. That day we would start to rebuild our home and move forward with our lives.

Assuming the builders ever turned up of course!

Let us go back to that time in the past and see what happened next…

3: Genesis

Definition: beginning, origin or mode of creation of something.

Back in the past: Day 1 of the long-awaited house repair job

In the beginning, it was so very cold.

I had been waiting on the driveway since 8.40am, alternately hopeful for a start to the rebuild and already despairing that the promised builders genuinely might not turn up. Nothing else in this whole fiasco had gone smoothly so far, so I felt I could be forgiven for being a bit mistrustful.

The Barbarians were all slumbering peacefully (I lie, they were all snoring loudly!) away in their various cosy nests in the caravan that we had eventually had installed in the garden after spending many weeks in a tent. However, I had been up horribly early, as usual. I had carefully applied multiple layers of clothing and then sneaked out of the caravan, trying not to wake the slumbering snoozers, before scuttling barefoot across the icy cold paving slabs to the patio, wishing I had remembered to take my slippers out to the caravan with me the night before.

Skirting around Skelly, (a fake – at least I hope so - skeleton which had arrived for the Barbarians' Halloween party last November and never really left), who was sitting in a deckchair next to our potted outdoor Christmas tree outside the conservatory, I noted absently that someone had thoughtfully supplied him with a hat, a blanket and *my* slippers!

So that's where they were! I bent down to retrieve my pilfered footwear before my frozen feet actually fell off, and then hastened through the French doors into the back section of the house. Once inside I shivered violently as I speedily stuffed ten icy toes into my slippers and waited impatiently for the kettle to boil, hopping painfully from one frozen appendage to the other in the hope that the action would restore circulation. This activity was interrupted by the cat reluctantly peeling herself away from the stone hearth and any dwindling residual heat from yesterday's fire to loudly demand sustenance.

Having dealt with the famished feline, I scouted around the accessible bit of the house for any other items of attire that I could put on, including a padded body warmer that was the perfect size to allow me to shove a mini heart-shaped hot water bottle just inside the front zipper at chest height. This had the double advantage of keeping me warm and made me look like I had had a significant bust augmentation.

Eventually I had to stop putting on clothes because, firstly, I ran out of them, and secondly, I was about to lose the ability to bend and/or breathe if I added any more. This getting dressed lark wasn't a random process, by the way. I had had months to perfect the precise sequence of layers of clothes that enabled me to get the most on, promoted the maximum body-heat retention whilst maintaining a basic efficiency of physical movement. I could write a detailed article on it for some science journal, if I had the time, assuming anyone was remotely interested, of course. After all, I do have a science degree, you know, I am not just the slightly mad, art-obsessed owner of a crumbly cottage in the country.

So anyway, half an hour later there I was, sat on my little wrought iron bench by the garage, with a cup of tea waiting nervously for someone to turn up.

Anyone!

Fortunately, I didn't have to wait that long. I could hear the gunning of a straining engine long before a white van swung speedily onto our drive and ground to a halt, churning up a bow wave of pea-shingle before it. An interesting start, I thought to myself, struggling to my feet.

The van door swung open forcibly and a man got out.

At first glance, I could tell he was a very cross and grumpy man.

"Do you have any idea how long it's taken me to find you?" Grumpy Van Man shouted accusingly at me, without so much as an attempt at 'hello,' or even 'good morning.'

"Um! No?" I swallowed nervously, taking a small step back, rather wishing he hadn't found me. This was not a promising development.

"Why does anyone want to live way out here for? It's the middle of nowhere!" he continued.

I refrained from pointing out that, usually, living way out here meant I didn't have to deal with people like him. Instead I bit my tongue. Hard! Some of us were brought up with good manners.

He opened the back door of his van and rummaged noisily around in it for a few moments. As I watched him nervously, I was distracted by something brushing past my face very gently. Looking down quickly, I saw a small white feather had landed on my augmented bust-line. Carefully picking it off, I examined it absently.

"So!" barked Grumpy. "Where are these solar panels you want installed then?"

What? I shoved the little feather into my pocket and looked at him startled. Then I registered what he'd actually said.

Thank goodness!

I don't think many people smile at Grumpy, which is not really surprising given his attitude, because he looked most disconcerted when I beamed at him in response to his rude question. But the sheer relief that he obviously wasn't my much-awaited builders was almost impossible to hide.

"I'm sorry but I think you are in the wrong place," I said, whilst probably not looking remotely apologetic.

"I am not in the wrong place!" he replied forcefully, "my satnav says the solar farm is here." He jabbed his right forefinger firmly toward the ground at his feet.

"It might well say that," I agreed, looking from him to the wobbly walls of my house. "But can you actually see a solar farm here?"

"It must be here somewhere," he said belligerently, while looking suspiciously around him at the driveway and then at me as if I was playing some kind of trick on him. I ask you! Seriously! Where on earth would I hide a solar farm? And more importantly, why? I didn't have time for silly games with grumpy strangers. I just wanted some builders to fix my house, hopefully nice ones and preferably today.

"You're on the right road," I said encouragingly, "only you're a few miles out. It's that way!" I pointed helpfully along the lane.

He looked as if he wanted to argue with me but I wasn't planning on sticking around to listen. I hadn't had enough caffeine yet to deal with this, so it was best to abandon him before I said something I shouldn't.

"By all means stick around if you want to. Feel free to search for hidden solar farms, but you won't find any," I called over my shoulder as I headed around to the back of the house to put the kettle on again. "But stay away from the wobbly walls, they're dangerous. I'd hate for you to get squashed!"

With that, I put him from my mind and stalked back indoors to recharge my cup and my hidden hot water bottle.

4: Juggernaut

Definition: Huge powerful, overwhelming force or large heavy vehicle, especially an articulated lorry.

Still in the past…

Ten minutes later I was back on the drive with more tea, relieved to find that Grumpy Van Man was gone. No sooner had I settled back on my little bench seat than I registered an unusual noise; quite a loud noise and one that was getting louder all the time. In all honesty, I could actually feel this particular noise too. The very ground under my feet started to tremble and so did the bench beneath my bottom. I looked nervously at my wobbly cottage walls as the intensely vibrating noise got closer and closer.

'What next?' I asked myself. For a quiet country lane, it was all 'go, go, go!' that morning. I was about to struggle to my feet again, to investigate the disturbance (with that many clothes on, any sudden movement was considerably impaired) but before I could do so, a large vehicle hove into sight at the entrance to the drive. It was enormous. I wasn't sure exactly what was going on, but it would appear that the largest lorry on the planet had just arrived outside my house.

I wondered several things simultaneously. Things like: Had the driver seriously not spotted the two clear 'not appropriate for heavy goods vehicles' signs at the turning onto this lane? And 'How on earth had they actually made it through the ford at the far end of the road?'

There were other questions that sprang to mind, but the one I was most interested in was this, how exactly was he planning to get that humungous thing out again? After all he couldn't very well leave it parked outside my house now, could he? If that were an option, then believe me our static caravan would be located right there and not in our garden so that Beloved Husband would not have had to mourn the loss of such a large section of his hedge last year. He still hasn't got over it!

Guessing correctly that this probably wasn't our much longed for building team either, I stood up as quickly as my multiple layers would allow and wandered over casually, as the colossal cabin door swung open. A small shaggy-looking male figure emerged. His face was bug-eyed with tiredness. The stale, rumpled air of someone who had been driving for far too many hours without a break, hung off him like a badly-fitting coat.

Between you and me, he looked far too young to be in charge of such an enormous piece of equipment (no dodgy metaphor intended). But then everyone looks too young to me these days; paramedics, policemen and now juggernaut drivers. Not that I had ever seen one of the latter before. I had always assumed that such people were somewhat similarly proportioned to the vehicles they drive.

It would seem not.

I watched as the slender, dishevelled young man slithered to the ground and sat on the footplate looking dazed and exhausted. Maybe the shock of trying to negotiate the icy ford followed by a hairpin bend in such an outsized mode of transport will do that to a fella. Who am I to say? I find it hard enough in a Citroen C3. Proof that size isn't everything, if we ever needed it.

Anyway, the driver and I eyed each other for quite some time. At least he wasn't shouting at me like the last chap so that was an improvement.

I smiled tentatively and raised my eyebrows inquiringly at him. He nodded, sighed and shrugged.

Ok, so he was one of those. The silent type!

No matter! I had a wealth of experience of communicating with verbally-challenged young men (Yes, I am thinking of my previously silent, older son, Quiet) so I fixed this new arrival with one of my 'no-

nonsense' looks.

"Hello," I said clearly. "Are you OK?"'

He shook his head sadly and sighed again.

I can't help it, the mothering instinct kicked in without me really being aware of it. He looked so exhausted, lost and young. It made me feel like inviting him in and feeding him before ringing his mother to tell her he was safe. You will be pleased to know I resisted the impulse. I had more than enough people to look after as it was without adopting any old (or young) lame duck who happened to park his lorry outside my house.

"Are you lost?" I tried again.

He rubbed the back of his neck, and then the rather grimy stubble on his chin with a very shaky hand. Even though this really wasn't going terribly well, I persevered.

"Can I help you?" I asked. There was more head shaking.

I did wonder if I should just hop up into the cab and attempt to move the monster vehicle far enough down the lane so my missing builders could get past it and onto my drive, (if they ever turned up that is). Then again, I thought that perhaps I should just leave this rather odd chap to sit in the road in peace and quiet for as long as he wanted to.

All of a sudden, he reached into his back pocket and fished out a mobile phone.

'Great!' I thought, 'typical youngster, can't communicate with an actual person and would far rather be on some social media site than engage with a real human being.' However, contrary to appearances, it became clear that he wasn't on Facebook or Snapchatting with his mates about the strange lady he had just found standing next to a crumbling old cottage in the deepest darkest countryside. He started speaking into the handset in rapid … um… well I didn't actually know what it was. All I knew was that I definitely didn't understand a word he said.

Then, to my alarm, he handed the phone to me.

I looked at it as if he was trying to hand me a grenade.

I should point out here that I have always had a lifelong issue with telephones. I absolutely hate them. Texting I can do. Even e-mailing is fine, but talking on a telephone? Not so much. It's got something to do with not being able to see the other person's face. I find I turn into my older son, Quiet, on the phone and start shrugging, which isn't terribly useful. I never say the right thing and I always feel that I am missing the main gist of the conversation; all potentially relevant verbal responses fall straight out of the back of my head, never to be heard of again.

Looking at the handset in horror, I tentatively reached out for it, almost as if I expected it to bite me at any moment. I put it to my ear wondering what hope I had of successful communication with a complete stranger in an unidentified foreign language.

"Hello?" I said cautiously.

"Allo," crackled a cheerful voice from what seemed like a thousand miles away.

OK, that was a good start! I felt ridiculously emboldened by this minor success. We had greeted each other in spite of the potential pitfalls of my telephone phobia, an undisclosed distance and an unidentified language. I didn't know who I was talking to, where they were or even why I was talking to them. Nevertheless, I was rather intrigued as to what would happen next.

"Wayit pliz!" Cheerful said.

OK, I thought, I could wait. I looked at the lorry driver but he merely shrugged again before inspecting his tatty trainers.

I could hear some sort of a scratchy conversation going on in the background of wherever my new telephone pal was and then all of a sudden, he was back. "Ewe spik German?" he demanded.

I contemplated my thirty-year-old German GCSE result for a second before answering "No!" very firmly indeed. Even though I had successfully scraped through that particular language exam, I was pretty certain that the extensive German vocabulary I had swotted up on to describe what I did on my holiday in 1985 was not going to be terribly useful for any 'moving a lost juggernaut on a country lane' issues three decades plus later.

"OK. Wayit…." there was another pause before he continued hopefully, "Polish?"

"No chance."

"Russian?" Cheerful's voice was gaining a slightly impatient edge now.

Seriously?

Was this just some big hoax to make me feel linguistically inferior?

Employing the entirety of my Russian language repertoire, I replied "Nyet" very clearly.

There was a sigh from the other end of the phone as if Cheerful thought I was being most inconsiderate and unhelpful.

As we seemed to be playing some sort of language one-upmanship here, I felt like suggesting Welsh or Icelandic as options. I had spent 15 years in Wales as a child and acquired not only the ability to put on a strong Valleys accent but also an extensive collection of colourful expletives. I had also learned how to ask, politely, where the nearest toilet was in slightly imperfect Welsh. None of which would be terribly helpful here but, still, it was another language to throw into the pot!

Added to that there was the 'learn-to-speak Icelandic' tape I remembered my dad listening to nearly four decades before, but, as I didn't think that would prove particularly constructive either, I kept quiet.

There was more muted discussion in the background. The sleepy-looking lorry driver continued to contemplate his feet, although I was beginning to wonder if he had actually nodded off.

Feeling fairly inadequate now, I ambled down the (not inconsiderable) length of the vehicle as I waited to find out what other languages they would like to know that I didn't speak. Come to think of it, it was a fairly extensive list. Chinese, Mandarin, Urdu? And many, many more… We could be here all day!

"Français?" Cheerful asked with a certain amount of disgust in his tone. Obviously, he was not keen on French as a method of communication.

"Mais, bien sûr, Monsieur!" I answered him with studied nonchalance. At last! A language I stood half a chance of blagging my way through. I continued, very casually, "Je parle français, pas de problème!" I didn't want to let on that I hadn't used my French language skills since I'd burned my A-level notes twenty-seven years previously, following a mortifying U in the French literature paper that brought my overall grade down from a comfortable B to an extremely embarrassing D. Especially as that particular paper had been the only one written and answered entirely in English! But let's not go there! Some things are best forgotten.

As I could be fairly certain that Cheerful wasn't about to launch into a detailed discussion on the literary merits of Le Comte de Monte-Cristo versus Les Liaisons Dangereuses over the telephone, I felt it was pretty safe for me to resurrect my dubious French language skills.

It turned out Cheerful wasn't a French expert either. In fact, I wouldn't be exaggerating if I said that my French was vastly superior to his, although this really wasn't much of an achievement. In the meantime, I had been wandering along looking at the sides of the huge vehicle while we spoke, and I thought I knew where my tired truck driver was trying to go.

Cheerful murdered several sentences in French which proved entertainingly incomprehensible. Nevertheless, I replied "Oui!" encouragingly a number of times before the jumble of mashed phrases he used included two words in particular "ferme" (farm) and "solaire" (solar). Putting these clues together with the pictures on the side of the lorry, I concluded that my lorry driver was attempting to get to the very same solar farm as my earlier visitor Grumpy Van Man. No doubt this mega-transporter was carrying the very solar panels that Grumpy had been enlisted to install. So, he was right all along, I did have his solar panels – ho hum!

Thank goodness the juggernaut was facing the right way so there would be no need to try to turn him around. His route from here on would be simple, if I could only persuade him to get back in the cab and start the engine.

"OK!" I interrupted Cheerful's tidal wave of 'almost' French. "C'est simple. Vous allez tout droit pour trois kilomètres," I said firmly, if not entirely correctly. "Bien, vous êtez arrivés a la ferme solaire." (Basically, as I've already mentioned, I told him that the solar farm was a bit further down the road.)

I handed the phone back to its owner, who took it reluctantly and listened to Cheerful translate my directions from French into whatever language he understood. There was a fairly lengthy, unintelligible argument between the two, but I rather felt I had done my bit, so I waited patiently for him to accept the inevitable and go away.

The tired lorry driver looked at me suspiciously several times, but I simply smiled and nodded encouragingly, whilst pointing down the road. Then he sighed heavily before shoving the phone back in his pocket. He hauled himself up into the drivers' cab and starting the engine; without so much as a nod of thanks my way, he slammed the door shut and eased his huge vehicle off in the direction of the solar farm. There's gratitude for you!

Quite frankly, Tired and Grumpy were welcome to each other.

I sat back down on my bench before concluding that it had been a long morning already and it was definitely time for me to find some breakfast.

5: Alchemy

Definition: medieval chemistry based on attempts to transform base metals into gold.

Returning to the present 'me' sitting on the bench on the drive, over two years later…

Having finished my cup of tea, whilst contemplating the past, I realised that I still really needed a sugar hit. Chaos and Logic's goodie-baking habits were proving to have been far more addictive than I had ever realised. Having freshly baked cookies and cake on tap all the time is a hard thing to learn to do without. It's almost as bad as the girls leaving home in the first place, followed by me belatedly realising that I was the only female left behind.

It had taken a while to sink in, but now it was official! The family's two resident bakers had both left home. I was completely bemused as to who was going to sustain our not insignificant sugar habit and tried to brush off the seriousness of the situation. 'It'll do us good to go without so many sweet things in our diet,' I had thought initially, 'we'll be fine.'

Ha!

Wrong!

It only took ten days for me to realise my mistake! Ten days of the sulks (yes, me, not the boys!); I blamed my bad behaviour on a combination of low blood sugar and seeing Facebook and Snapchat photos of the cakes and cookies that were now being made for new student-flat friends. Traitors!

In desperation, two weeks after my girls left home, I had decided to try and dust off my dormant biscuit-making skills.

"It can't be that hard," I told myself, "I used to do this all the time. Anyway, who on earth taught them to bake in the first place?"

We should note here that I was conveniently forgetting that it was my mother-in-law and also my mother who had both been quite active in educating my darling daughters in the fine art of baking. I am generally way better at savouries than sweets.

You can take my word for it. Baking is not at all like riding a bike. It is entirely possible to forget how to do it, and it soon became apparent that I had successfully done just that. What followed was a series of batches of slightly soggy shortbread and several dangerously depressed cakes, but on the whole the flapjacks looked quite good. At least, they did until I tried to take them out of the tin. Fortunately, the boys didn't seem to mind, they demolished all my seriously, sub-standard offerings with impressive speed. It's all sugar after all, isn't it?

Eventually I had given in and started buying in biscuits and cakes but they weren't the same. Fresh home-baked produce is far more satisfying than the highly preserved packet variety on sale in most supermarkets. A small portion of one of my girls' lovely fresh cakes was a treat that filled me up, whereas shop bought cake just left me feeling unsatisfied and looking round for more sugar.

Unfortunately, while I was quite capable of throwing together hearty and healthy savoury dishes, my baking skills left a lot to be desired. As my mum always says, practice makes perfect. Hmm, quite a lot more practice was needed it would seem, but never mind.

No time like the present then...

'Right,' I thought pulling myself together and heading for the kitchen, 'I am a strong independent woman! I can bake, it's easy.'

However, as I dived into the kitchen cupboards in search of ingredients, successfully emerging sometime later with a scraggy bag of sugar, some ancient oats and some long-forgotten raisins, I knew that the skill required to transform these basic ingredients into something of significantly more edible value might well be beyond me. It looked like flapjacks might potentially be on the horizon if only I could locate some butter somewhere.

While I was amassing useful baking related paraphernalia, like scales, bowls and wooden spoons, the iPad on the kitchen surface started to bleep at me indicating an incoming Skype call.

One positive aspect that had come from my girl Barbarians leaving was that it had forced me to be a bit more technologically minded. Chaos had set me up a profile on Facebook with a group chat so that we could stay in touch and Logic had demonstrated some of the finer points of Skype, which meant that I was able to accept incoming calls from both girls at the same time and we could all chat together. Get me! Just call me a tech queen!

Flipping the iPad open, I accepted the call and couldn't help but smile when I saw Logic grinning back at me.

"Hi there! Hang on just a mo, Chaos should be joining us any minute now!" she said, "Hey, are you baking?"

Before I could answer her, the screen flickered ominously and I thought I was going to lose the connection. An incoming call registered and I accepted it; then all of a sudden, the picture split and Chaos appeared.

"Hiya!" she said, "wow, are you baking?"

"I can bake you know," I said defensively, suddenly tempted to turn my iPad camera off so they couldn't see what I was doing.

There was an almost infinitesimal pause before Logic said soothingly, "Of course you can!"

"We know that!" insisted Chaos, rather too firmly.

There was another pause.

"So!" She continued, "What are you making?"

I looked at the sorry looking pile of random ingredients. Casting around quickly I spotted the tail end of some butter lurking by the bread bin, obviously waiting for someone to clear it away after breakfast (like that was ever going to happen) and grabbed it quickly.

"Flapjacks!" I said triumphantly.

"That's cool," replied Logic. "Have you remembered to put the oven on to warm up?"

"I know what I am doing," I said, although I hadn't remembered of course, but there was no way she could know that for certain. "So, how's university going then?"

They both tumbled over each other to tell me what was going on in their lives and I smiled contentedly as I listened and measured out my ingredients. It wasn't perfect, but it was almost like having them back at home with me, sat around the breakfast bar like we used to, with a cuppa having a chat.

I heard all about their lectures and flatmates, as well as the cute guy Logic had met the day before at the university sports hall. Chaos updated me on the latest book she was writing and promised to send me a draft to read through. During all that time she had spent in hospital recovering from that emergency operation, just before the house fell down, she had started writing teen fiction. The stories were full of attitude, action and adventure, so I could see why she now had a growing following of adoring teen/tween fans all clamouring for the next book to be published.

It was just like old times, chatting away to them both and I soon forgot how lonely and lost I had been feeling.

Unfortunately, it couldn't last and real life eventually interrupted our glorious gossiping session. Chaos had to go to a lecture and signed off, followed a few minutes later by Logic.

"Bye," she said, "and remember, put the oven on." With a cheeky wave she was gone too. Both girls had dived back into their exciting new lives leaving me standing alone in an empty, echoing house. I stood and looked at the blank screen for a few minutes before going over to switch the oven on ready for my flapjacks.

I usually find that baking is a bit like painting, although for me the paintings generally have a much greater success rate these days. Regardless of the outcome I find both activities very relaxing. So, as I slung oats, sugar and butter together in the present, grateful to have reconnected, however briefly, with my two gorgeous girls, my mind drifted back to the arrival of our superhero builders in the past

Part 2

A journey of a thousand miles begins with a single step.

Lao Tsu
(604 BC – 531 BC)

6: Synthesis

Definition: the process of mixing constituent elements or different things into a single/cohesive object.

Back to the past, waiting on the drive ....

Having successfully raided the biscuit tin in the kitchen, I had returned to the driveway yet again just as my third lot of visitors of the morning arrived. At precisely 9.25am, a battered, blue van coasted onto the drive and three laughing men spilled out. A more disparate group you couldn't hope to meet but I wasn't complaining. After my earlier two arrivals, I took the fact that this lot were smiling as a very positive sign.

The driver sauntered over to me and I noticed that the closer he got, the further up I had to look. He was immensely tall. "Sorry we're late," he rumbled down at me from an impressively lofty height, as he jerked his head in the direction of one of his companions. "He forgot his hammer so we had to go back for it."

A more medium-sized gentleman, beautifully sun-tanned, sporting a full beard and long blonde hair held back from his face with a red bandana, stepped forward swinging a large sledgehammer from fist to fist in a surprisingly unthreatening way. (That takes some skill.) This Thor-wannabe smiled and said "Good morning." The third gentleman was tiny, probably a junior apprentice or maybe a work experience student. He was very young and hung back behind Thor. I think he was shy. Nevertheless, he nodded perfectly politely at me. Another verbally challenged young man it would seem – what is it with the youth of today? (Oh dear, now I sound like my grandmother.)

"So!" continued Lofty, looking around hopefully. "Is The Boss here yet?"

"The Boss?" I queried.

It must be remembered that Beloved Husband and I had had absolutely no control over which building firm had been awarded the contract for the repair. That decision had been entirely made by the Insurance Company and communicated to us via Loss Adjuster Number Two. He was the professional representing the house insurance company and had liaised with Genuine Old Buildings Expert, who was the appointed structural engineer for the project, in establishing what work would be done. Between them they had determined which building firm was appointed.

Not surprisingly the Insurance Company had awarded the contract for the work to the firm that submitted the cheapest quote, but Genuine Old Buildings Expert had assured me that they were a very professional firm and were definitely qualified for this sort of complicated job. Nevertheless, Beloved Husband and I only had a very vague idea as to who was actually going to pitch up today, although the owner of the firm (The Boss) had kindly telephoned us and introduced himself after the decision on the contract was announced.

"Don't worry! He'll be here with the structural engineer to get us off to a good start. It's important that we approach these sorts of projects in the right way," continued Lofty.

The decision, made by the insurance company, had been to not demolish the whole cob section of the cottage and rebuild it, but to prop up the roof and simply repair the two disintegrating cob walls by taking them down in stages and then rebuilding from the ground up. Now you won't be able to persuade me that supporting a massively heavy thatched roof on a few steel poles and then knocking down the walls beneath and rebuilding them is a normal 'everyday' job for anyone. Or even that it is terribly safe but as I said, I wasn't the one making the decisions round here. I was also not going to be hanging around under the propped-up roof for any length of time.

I planned on staying a safe distance away. Someone had to be alive to dial 999 for an ambulance if it all came crashing down, didn't they?

The structural engineering team had checked the roof very carefully only recently and concluded that it had not been adversely affected by the disintegration of the two supporting walls beneath it. Genuine Old Buildings Expert had assured me that the remaining solid wall structures plus some very key industrial props were sharing the weight of the roof extremely effectively. He had personally devised the proposed repair programme about to be implemented and assured me that it would effectively fix the problem. I had no choice but to bow to his superior knowledge as he really did seem to know what he was talking about.

Nevertheless, I was rather glad when The Boss and Genuine Old Buildings Expert arrived to oversee the start of the job. Genuine Old Buildings Expert always made me feel that he was completely in control of things and it was a very pleasant surprise indeed, to realise that I recognised 'The Boss'. Wrapped up against the cold in an expensive long woollen coat, thick scarf and leather gloves, smart trousers and shoes, he looked very different from the last time I had seen him, dressed as he was then, in a grubby boiler suit and yellow hard hat with accompanying head torch, as he was about to scramble into my damaged home through a side window.

He happened to be the only builder who had actually acknowledged that Beloved Husband and I existed during the whole depressing 'quoting-for-the-rebuild-job phase' of this riveting tale. The really nice one! The one who seemed to sympathise with our situation and asked us what we would like to do with the house if we got the chance. All the other prospective building firms had ignored us completely and concentrated on communicating directly with the insurance company.

You will probably agree, in the light of this development, that we were off to a rather good start. I could feel myself starting to believe that this just might work after all. So, having greeted these two new arrivals with genuine delight, I set off for the kitchen to make the first of a great many rounds of tea while they all had a pow-wow about where to start.

Shortly afterwards, The Boss came around to the patio door and said, 'We have a slight problem.'

My heart sank.

Already? They've only been here twenty minutes!

"Don't worry!" he continued, "we can sort it out, but would you like to come and see, and I'll explain what needs to be done and why?"

Wow! Inclusion, with information! Yes, I would definitely like to come and see.

It seems that the insurance's rebuild plan, which relied so heavily on the roof being propped up, had also relied on there being a solid concrete floor for the propping equipment to rest on. Unfortunately, our 350- year-old cottage didn't have a concrete floor of any description, solid or otherwise, which was something that hadn't come to light until just now, when our new builders dug a small exploratory hole to check.

It would seem that we had been living here for nearly fourteen years not knowing that our beautiful 1970's wooden parquet flooring was laid directly on to compacted earth. It was in remarkably good condition under the circumstances – well, apart from the sections that had been damaged by the collapsing walls, oh and the bits that had got wet near the cracks where the rain had got in - but other than that it was fine. Unfortunately, it wasn't going to be strong enough to support the weight of the first floor and the roof as planned.

"There's quite an easy solution really," said The Boss smoothly, "we're going to have to bring in some large steel girders to lie across the floor in place of the concrete slab that was supposed to be here. Then the propping plan can go ahead as before. It's just going to take a little time to get them here. There's a bit of prep work we can do in the meantime, but we can't really get going till the steels are in place. Sorry!"

'Please don't say you are leaving?' I screamed silently in my head.

I genuinely thought I might cry!

"We can get them here late this afternoon with any luck. Is that ok?" he asked.

Phew! The tearful deluge was averted.

"Sure," I said trying not to sound too relieved. With our luck I had thought they were going to say they would be back in six weeks! We'd been waiting so long, another half day I could cope with, but I don't think I could bear to see them leave at this point. So late this afternoon was good!

7: Infusion

Definition: a remedy or solution created by soaking the leaves of a plant or herb in a liquid

Returning to the present...

Having thoroughly mixed up the flapjack ingredients while I thought back over that first day of building work, I now shoved the tray of oats, sugar and butter into the oven to cook and started back to my studio to carry on with my abandoned painting. On the way there though, my attention was caught by another canvas. Unusually, this particular piece of work hadn't been hastily stuffed out of the way as was my normal habit with finished canvases.

Beloved Husband had taken a bit of a shine to it and had appropriated it before I could shove it in one of the sheds. As a result, it now adorned the wall in the hallway near the front door. The Barbarians seemed to be quite fond of it too, which surprised me as I had been going through a very dark phase of guilt when I'd painted it last year, so in some ways it is quite menacing. It had a deep, Prussian blue acrylic base that was applied in a frantic rush using a roller from the DIY store. Over that I had used silver to pick out the highlights of a lone lady surfer riding a massive curling and crashing wave.

Looking at it now, I supposed that it really represented the resilience of human beings overcoming the immense power of nature and surviving in spite of the danger around them, which could probably be considered very meaningful given what had happened to us. Anyway, I shrugged the thought away and carried on to my studio and my new canvas.

This was also going to be a fairly big painting. I had found a large, old canvas board lurking at the back of my wardrobe. I had no idea what it was doing there. Perhaps I had bought it and then felt guilty at the expense (the big ones can be quite pricey) so hidden it for a bit and then forgotten about it.

It's a bit like when you buy a new dress or shoes but don't like to admit you've spent quite so much, so you put them in your wardrobe for a few weeks before actually wearing them in public. Then when your Beloved Husband says "Is that new?" you can legitimately say dismissively "What, this old thing? It's been in the wardrobe for *ages*!"

The sensible husband makes no comment at that point, other than to say, "You look lovely, dear." He knows what you are doing, and you know he knows, but honour is satisfied. Or at least an unpleasant disagreement is avoided, which is just as important. It's also far too late by then to return the items for a refund so you have to keep them.

Devious? Not at all. Merely practical!

Anyway, I had liberated the rediscovered canvas board and made use of it. As always when stressed, I reverted to painting fish. These paintings are all different, but still have the same innate message of hope and positivity as the fish spiral up out of the deep dark depths of the ocean towards the light, breaking through the surface of the water.

Usually, I found the process of painting my little silver fish immensely soothing although Quiet had taken to commenting tactfully (or not!), "Why on earth are you painting more fish? Are you obsessed or something?" I generally ignored these remarks. For a mild-mannered chap, he'd been a bit irritable lately. I put it down either to hormones or the fact that he was actually missing his sisters. Not that he'd admit to either factor of course.

I don't know what he was worried about though. These paintings were really popular. The imagery was representative of 'the light at the end of the tunnel' and was very uplifting. People were always asking to buy them from me to give as gifts which made me confident that they would sell well if I ever got around to exhibiting them. So it wasn't as if we were collecting a huge pile of useless fish paintings or anything – well

- apart from the fact that I hadn't arranged an exhibition recently so the pile was growing steadily.

OK, maybe he had a point!

Probably due to my agitation after the road accident that morning and then the arrival of the 'For Sale' sign, this new piece of work was a rather more energetic painting than previous versions. Done in traditional oil paints, I had applied paint in fat lines directly onto the canvas board straight from the tube and then blended using a large rounded palette knife. Thick swirls of Prussian green morphed upwards from the bottom left corner, through phthalo turquoise, French ultramarine to cerulean blue and on into sparkling titanium white at the top right-hand corner. Such fun! Messy but so exhilarating to paint! The oils were going to take a very long time to dry completely but I didn't care about that. I never did when I was immersed in a piece of work. I also didn't mind that I was wearing rather a lot of paint too. It was almost as if I had become part of the canvas for a time.

Now the ocean component of the piece was complete it was time to add the fish. Payne's Grey and silver smoothed into the thick shades of green and blue using a smaller palette knife to create each shape. This critical phase required absolute concentration and precision to get the right effect. The larger fish at the base of the painting weren't a problem but when it came to the smaller ones further up, I started to struggle.

The canvas was quite big, so I looked around for a small stool to stand on. My thinking was that if I could reach the upper section more easily, then perhaps all would be fine.

Unfortunately, it wasn't that simple.

I lost count of the number of times I approached the canvas with my sharp knife loaded with silver paint, ready for the quick sweeping action that would bring my little fish to life in the rippling water, only to have to stop short because I couldn't control the distinct tremor in my hands.

You would be forgiven for thinking that I was in some sort of delayed shock given the eventful morning I had experienced. In a way you would be right, but it was unfortunately more profound than that. This was happening more and more these days. I had tried to ignore it, but it wasn't going away. It would seem that I had developed a significant and uncontrollable trembling of the hands for no apparent reason.

I didn't think there was anything physically wrong with me. I actually felt fine – well, it's all relative, isn't it? Let me put it this way, I didn't feel as rubbish as I had previously when I had been consumed with guilt over not being able to protect the Barbarians from the house falling down. I was much better than I had been then, but this persistent shaking was concerning. Beloved Husband had tentatively suggested a number of times that I ought to consider going to see my GP about it. It wasn't that bad though, I was sure it would settle down in time. No need to waste the good doctor's time, or my own, come to think of it.

I tried one more time to complete the smaller fish, but it was no good. Bizarrely, I found that concentrating hard on keeping my hands steady made the tremor seem even more pronounced. Finally, snarling in frustration, I flung the knife down, heedless of the silver oil paint splattering everywhere, turned on my heels and left the room.

I headed straight for the kettle. Switching it on forcefully, I lifted my prized teapot off the shelf and reached for the caddy of real tealeaves, hoping that the action of making proper tea in a proper pot would calm me down.

As the kettle came to the boil, I noticed the smoke coming from the oven. Sighing heavily, I swiftly extracted the cremated flapjacks, dumping them on the draining board, before concentrating on warming the pot thoroughly and then making my tea. With a loaded tray containing the teapot, a cup (with saucer – let's do this properly), and a milk jug, I headed back outside to sit on my bench on the drive, hoping to calm down in the beautiful sunshine.

The next twenty minutes saw me work my way through at least four cups of tea. At the same time, I let the warm sunshine wash over me, soothing my nerves and calming me down. I was pretty certain that the tremor was probably just an annoying legacy from the most bizarre period of my life, the physical manifestation of delayed stress. Perhaps an over-reaction of my fight or flight response, no doubt brought on as a result of living under the immense anxiety associated with having a falling-down-house for such a long period of time.

There had been other more cosmetic consequences too. I have heard it suggested that the lines on your face can tell the story of your life and that one should be proud of them, not try to conceal them. By that measure, I should be full to the brim with pride! Believe me, I am not particularly. In my case, I felt that every second of the time that we lived in our garden had been chiselled into my face in bold italics and underlined twice for good measure.

Not to mention the striking silver (ok, grey) streak that now adorned my head for all to see. I am not joking. I woke up one morning, soon after we had moved back into our home, to find that the minor sprinkling of grey hairs that I had been kidding myself were little blond highlights, had migrated overnight to congregate in one place, just above my right temple, forming a wide grey streak that no amount of home dye could hide.

No matter how much I tried to laugh about all these changes, I couldn't ignore the fact that my shaking hands were seriously starting to interfere with my art and things would only go downhill if I couldn't paint.

Sitting there in the warm sunshine and trying to relax, I became aware of that sensation of light-headedness again. It was quite bizarre. I could hear the blood rushing in my ears and feel my heartbeat thumping loudly in my head. Then, all of a sudden, the thumping seemed to stop.

I know we are not normally aware of our own heartbeat, but there was a long pause in which I definitely knew that my heart wasn't beating at all. Something similar had happened several times over recent weeks but those previous episodes had passed relatively quickly.

This time it wasn't passing quickly at all.

Time seemed to slow right down as I gasped for breath.

What on earth was happening?

All of a sudden, the thumping resumed as my heart seemed to crash back into play but this time the systematic rhythm was all wrong. It felt off-kilter, as if it was missing beats out or trying to beat on something that wasn't there.

I blinked rapidly as I tried to stay calm, not really succeeding. A panic attack right now really wasn't going to help things. I tried to think what to do but my mind went blank. All I could hear was my own rapid, gasping breathing as the seconds dragged by. Was I having a heart attack?

Was I going to die?

Sat outside my cottage in the middle of nowhere?

On my own?

I had rather pinned my hopes on a moving, yet peaceful, deathbed scene in my late nineties, surrounded by my children and hundreds of grand and great grandchildren. With that in mind, dying now, on the driveway, without an audience, would be somewhat disappointing!

Just as my brain formulated that irreverent thought, I became aware of the fact that my funny heartbeat had returned to normal. The rushing sound in my ears subsided. The light-headedness started to clear, and I could once again hear the birds singing in the hedgerow and the drone of a passing bumble bee.

My breathing started to ease and my shoulders relaxed.

What on earth had happened? I don't know how long I sat there feeling dizzy and faintly nauseous but, eventually, I came to the galling conclusion that Beloved Husband was probably right. How annoying! I was going to have to pay a visit to the doctor.

When I was certain that all of the weird sensations had stopped, I slowly gathered up the tea things, including a large white feather that had somehow found its way onto the tray, headed back inside and reached for the telephone. A short while later I found myself in proud possession of an appointment to see my doctor the next day, which was nothing short of a minor miracle. Normally, the doctors at the local surgery are so overworked that you have to wait ages to see anyone at all. So, getting an appointment with the one specific doctor you would prefer within twenty-four hours is unheard of. Apparently, I was in luck and there had been a cancellation just minutes before I telephoned.

Still feeling somewhat dazed and shaky, I rummaged under the sink to find a cloth so I could clean up the dramatic spray of silver oil paint in the studio before it became a permanent feature on my nice new wooden flooring and beautifully rebuilt cottage walls.

***

The next afternoon, I found myself being called into the doctor's consulting room after a surprisingly short interval in the hot and stuffy waiting room. There was some sort of children's clinic on at the same time, so lots of mothers had brought their darling offspring along to share bugs and scrap over the sparse, grubby and somewhat battered, old

Fisher Price toys provided. A mere ten minutes in that overcrowded space with so many small children gave me a fairly stark reminder of what it was like to live with toddlers again and I could feel myself beginning to re-evaluate quite how much I missed that period of my life!

Gratefully leaving the scene of mayhem behind me, I shuffled nervously into the consulting room, closed the door and sat gingerly on the edge of the chair provided. I don't really know why I was nervous because my GP is lovely, even though she was looking decidedly tired and harassed. I didn't blame her. I'd seen what was in the waiting room and that was probably only a small snippet of what she had on her plate to sort out that day. I was beginning to wish I hadn't bothered her.

Now I am sure I have mentioned my opinion of people discussing their health issues before. It is a subject that has the potential to be very boring and I don't intend to start banging on about my own problems here. Suffice to say it is unfortunately a necessary part of this storyline and therefore I will sum up what went on in the doctor's consulting room as concisely as possible.

Obviously, I mentioned the funny turns I'd experienced and my history of persistent trembling. The doctor, stifling a yawn, pulled a blood test form out of a drawer and started to fill it in while asking about any recent stresses. I briefly mentioned that the house had fallen down and that we had spent over a year living in the garden with the children while we rebuilt it and that the house was now on the market. This information certainly got her attention and she looked significantly more interested. I didn't mention my almost permanent headache or the recurrent nightmare I was having that featured the staircase disintegrating beneath me and an awful sensation of falling. I felt that the psychiatrists would have a field day with that one, hence it was best avoided. Some things just don't need sharing.

Inevitably the question of low mood and anxiety came up and a prescription was offered and politely refused. Whether this was a wise decision or not on my part I couldn't possibly say, I just know I hate taking tablets. I agreed with the doctor that I had probably been depressed the year before but that had since improved; it was merely the recent development of physical symptoms which worried me. What followed was quite an enlightening discussion on the fact that ongoing stress and high anxiety can manifest in some very real physical symptoms, so whilst my mood had lifted the rest of me was struggling to follow. The pressure of living under such difficult circumstances had potentially left me with a physical legacy that my body was trying to recover from and it was up to me to give it the best chance of doing that by looking after myself. It certainly seemed logical the way she explained it.

The upshot of the whole consultation was that I was to have some tests on my heart to rule out any major problems, but she didn't anticipate any being identified. Then she gave me a gentle but firm lecture on self-care; recommended that I give up caffeine, reduce my refined sugar intake, avoid too much alcohol because it interferes with both mood and sleep patterns and finally, I was to get some exercise.

No major surprises there then.

"You might also consider making sure you socialise a bit more. If you miss your daughters so much, go and join some ladies' groups. Get some female company that way. There are plenty around; book groups, lunch clubs, the Women's Institute. Take your pick." She grinned and handed me the blood test form as she said this.

"So, will all this get rid of the shaking so I can paint?" I asked, getting to the root of what I was really worrying about. (I know; I am obsessed.)

"Well, art can be a very powerful therapy and you must definitely keep painting if you find it so helpful. I'm sure you can adapt the way you paint to work around the tremor if you put your mind to it. But the really important thing is that you start to put your general health higher up on your priority list. I know you're a busy mum and that you have a job as well. But that's no excuse for not taking care of yourself. If *you* don't do it, no-one else will." She said, rather bluntly, and then muttered, "We mothers are allowed to put ourselves first occasionally, you know!"

Whether she was talking to me or herself at that point I wasn't too sure. Either way, she made a good point.

Gathering up my blood form and bag, I smiled, said goodbye and retreated back out into the corridor trying not to trip over any toddlers as I crossed the waiting room. Tiptoeing around a two-year-old indulging in an epic tantrum, I thanked the receptionist and headed off to visit the vampires at the local hospital to get those blood tests done.

8: Amalgamation

Definition: uniting, the bringing together of associated items that work well together or combining to create a whole.

Back to the reconstruction site in the past…

The steels arrived, just as The Boss said they would, late that afternoon. This was almost unbelievable. It seemed that we had fallen on our feet at last. After so many months of waiting, enforced inactivity and uncertainty, I was going to have to re-learn that some people are reliable and that it was possible to make forward progress.

Some time ago I received a fortune cookie that, when opened, revealed the following wise words: *you don't have to see the whole staircase to take the first step*. Under the circumstances this was good advice on two levels because, theoretically speaking, I had no idea how our home was actually going to be fixed and, practically speaking, we didn't have an operational staircase at all just then.

The majority of the old, damaged staircase had been cleared out that morning by Thor with his trusty sledgehammer. The rubble had been replaced with a sturdy wooden ladder so that the construction crew could reach the first floor safely.

I watched with some satisfaction as our team of builders busied themselves installing the steels in carefully selected locations overseen by Genuine Old Building Expert. Then I observed the assembling of an intricate system of props initially lifting the weight of the first floor onto the steels laid down on the ground floor and then establishing a second series of props upstairs to take the weight of the roof on the now stabilised first floor joists.

There was much bustling around and calling out to each other and readjusting of props as they carefully ensured that what was left of our house wasn't going to move any further when they were eventually ready to go about the tricky business of taking down the remnants of the two damaged walls in order to rebuild them.

This all took place very smoothly, in spite of the fact that the whole of the front of the property had previously been encased in black plastic sheets to try and keep out the worst of the weather. These sheets had been left in place for the time being with a large, upright split cut for access level with the largest crack in the front wall of the house. The builders were using this crack as a door, because the actual door had been wedged shut by the weight of the disintegrating wall above it. The team had come fully prepared with large industrial lights and long extension cables to light up the inside of the property so that they could see what they were doing.

The Boss arrived back on site just as the team were packing up to go for the day. He checked everything over thoroughly and then turned to me with a grin.

"It's an unusual remit, of course," he said. "But the structural engineers have got everything in hand. We've worked with them on several very complicated jobs and they really do know their stuff. You're in good hands, I promise. They're the geniuses behind this operation and they've worked out exactly how to do this so you don't need to worry. We're going to follow their instructions to the letter and if we hit any snags, we'll just call them out to advise us. The property is all completely stable now, so we can start taking the first wall down tomorrow."

"Are you sure it's safe?" I asked, regarding him sceptically.

"Completely! Believe me! I wouldn't put my team at risk, or you and your family. Relax. Now that all this is in place, this project can officially start. As of tomorrow, we're going to begin fixing your home."

I really wanted to believe him but my faith in things being OK had been stretched rather thin over the last six months.

I think he realised how twitchy I was feeling so he continued reassuringly "Just think, you'll have proper foundations too, when we've finished. These new walls won't be going anywhere. I promise!" He turned to go but then remembered something and said, "By the way, they're going to be delivering a Portaloo for the team to use while we're here. It should arrive sometime this evening. Would you mind telling them to site it over there please?" He waved vaguely in the direction of the garage before nodding to me and heading off for the day.

A Portaloo? Good idea. While the team were welcome to use the loo in the house, it wasn't easily accessible for them and the one in the caravan would be tricky. I decided not to wonder where they had done their business that day. Some things you just don't need to know.

It was reassuring to know that our team of genius engineers and super-talented builders had thought of everything even down to the most basic essentials. Brilliance and common sense together in the same package! This I felt boded well for the job to come.

I understand the concept of genius. Not that I am a genius myself, of course, far from it, but I know a few people who are pretty darn smart. As a result, I am well acquainted with the fact that true genius doesn't always come hand in hand with common sense.

I came across one of my favourite genii not five minutes after I had waved goodbye to my lovely building team for the evening. When I had left Chaos earlier, to watch the fascinating propping process take place and then to chat briefly to The Boss, she had been sat at her books at the breakfast bar and was muttering to herself about the electron density distribution of multi-hetroatomic molecules. (No, I really don't know what that is. I had to get her to write it down so I could type it in here.)

I returned to the kitchen in time to see she had relocated to the other side of the room, by the dustbin, and that she was apparently having a major physical issue with something.

Small was leaning against the oven eating ice cream directly from the carton, like they do in American sitcoms. (Please note that it's against my house rules to eat anything straight from the carton, but it would seem that he had conveniently forgotten this fact and I couldn't summon the energy to enforce it at that particular moment. The chances were that he would eat the whole thing in one sitting anyway, so I decided to focus on the fact that there would be less washing up and let the issue slide.)

He was observing his sister's unusual behaviour with mild interest but no obvious sign of alarm.

He looked across at me as I approached, momentarily distracted from his sibling's antics, and grinned rather messily around a large mouthful of mint choc chip. I raised an enquiring eyebrow at him, but he merely shrugged and resumed watching the live show unfolding before us.

Chaos hastily brushed some long blonde hair out of her eyes and shook the item in her hand even more violently. She gave a dramatic sigh before saying crossly, "Why do they design them like this? It's ridiculous!"

I edged a little closer to see what it was that she had in her hands. Having correctly identified the object, I began to understand what was going on. Looking accusingly at Small, I sighed heavily before saying, "OK, are you going to tell her, or am I?"

"Tell her what?" he said, looking confused. He clearly had no idea what was going on and wasn't going to be much help.

I approached the frustrated genius myself, held out my hand and said calmly, "Give!"

"It's jammed!" she said. "They're great for a while and then they always get jammed and you can't get the stuff out. Someone should design them a bit better. I've got all this work to do," she gestured at the paperwork spread all over the kitchen counter, "I haven't got time for this." She thrust it at me and huffed.

I looked her directly in the eye and said; "Watch this!"

Then I turned the item over and carefully peeled off the plastic base allowing the compacted bits of unwanted paper to fall easily into the bin.

"Oh!" she said entranced, "Is that a thing? That's really clever." I replaced the plastic base and gave it back to her and she examined it really closely. "Brilliant! That's so simple. Thanks Mum."

My little genius had been trying to empty her hole punch by shaking the bits of paper back out the way they had gone in. So much incredible scientific intellect in one brain that there is no room to spare for small practical details. I tried not to smile. She understands multi–hetroatomic molecules. Someone has to. I'm glad it's not me. I understand hole punches.

We all have our parts to play in life. I decided then and there that I was going to have to trust my clever structural engineers and their team of superhero builders. They seemed confident that they knew what they were doing. I didn't have a clue, so I was going to stick to what I do know and keep them well supplied with tea.

9: Tincture

Definition: a drug made using a slight trace of something

Returning to the present again…

I was barely back in the house after my appointment with the GP and my subsequent encounter with the vampires, when the iPad alerted me to an incoming Skype call. Fumbling around with it clumsily I eventually managed to accept the call and put the kettle on at the same time.

"We're worried about you! What's this we hear about you going to see the doctor? What's wrong?" Chaos' dulcet tones filled the kitchen as a second incoming call registered. A digital image of Logic, in her pyjamas eating a slice of buttered toast, nudged Chaos' concerned expression across to one side of the screen.

"Hang on a minute! How on earth did you two know I was going to the doctors?" I asked.

"We know everything," Logic said ominously and then spoiled the effect by confessing, "Small saw a note about the appointment next to your handbag this morning. He told Quiet, and then Quiet texted us. So, what did the doctor say?"

I took a second to absorb the fact that my youngest child was now colluding with his brother to rat on me to both of their older sisters. This probably meant that the boys were a bit concerned about me, so I said reassuringly, "There's nothing to worry about. I just had a funny turn. I've got a bit of a wonky blood sugar. Apparently, I need to cut out caffeine and refined sugar and get out a bit more, meet some people, do some exercise. That's all. I'm fine." I crossed my fingers, not admitting to the upcoming hospital tests. There was no way they knew about those and I would make sure I didn't leave the appointment letters lying around when they arrived so that my resident Sherlock Holmes and Dr Watson couldn't snitch on me.

"I'm not surprised your blood sugar is shot to bits if you're eating that rubbish!" said Logic with a sniff. I followed her gaze and realised that she had spotted half a packet of shop bought biscuits on the kitchen counter. "Cutting those out for a start will make you feel much better."

Damn! I'd forgotten that they could see what I was doing.

"So, are you going to do as you are told?" Chaos prompted.

I hadn't really decided to be honest, I was still trying to process everything the doctor had said, but I wasn't daft enough to let my girls know that.

"Of course!" I said, grabbing the offending packet, sweeping it into the bin, just as the kettle clicked off with a noisy 'ping' indicating that it had finished boiling.

"OK, that's good!" Chaos continued, "So is that a decaf tea you're making now?"

"Ummm! Not exactly, I've only just got back from the doctors and I'm gasping for a cuppa. I haven't had a chance to go shopping yet." Truth be told, I wasn't keen on the whole decaf option. I had vaguely been thinking of just cutting back a bit and perhaps not having quite as many strong cups of coffee and tea a day.

"Mum!" the girls' amplified joint reaction informed me that I clearly wasn't going to be allowed to get away with that.

"But I am going shopping this afternoon. I will buy some decaf tea and coffee then. I promise. OK?"

"OK! Good." Chaos smiled and nodded, so I foolishly thought I was off the hook for a second. Oh no! She simply took a deep breath and then continued. "Now the other thing we wanted to talk to you about is that Quiet said you haven't really been eating proper meals lately. He says that even though you cook supper as usual, you never sit down to eat with them in the evenings these days. Why?"

"Oh, I'm just not very hungry." I replied vaguely. I could hardly tell my girls the truth, which was that I couldn't bear to look at their empty chairs at the table during meal times; the spaces where they used to sit. It was a bit pathetic really, and I genuinely hadn't realised that the boys had noticed that I wasn't joining them. They always seem in such a hurry to get back to whatever computer game supper had inadvertently interrupted.

"That's not a good thing Mum," said Chaos. "Promise us you'll try to look after yourself a bit better. It's supposed to be us developing poor eating habits because we're students, not the parent left behind. We can't concentrate on our studies if we're worrying about you. So, you have to sort yourself out OK? Otherwise we're going to have to come back and look after you."

"There's no need for that," I replied. "I will behave, I promise."

After a little more insistent nagging from both girls, I finally got them to sign off and head for their lectures so that I could make myself that cup of tea.

Funnily enough though, I had rather gone off it by then, so I ended up sitting and looking at it for a while, thinking back over the conversation with the girls. Eventually, I concluded that they were right. Enough was enough. I was going to have to accept that, regardless of any test results, I wasn't actually very well and it was beginning to affect the people I loved, including those that weren't living at home anymore. I couldn't have that. I was going to have to pull myself together and start looking after myself, which meant following the doctor's advice.

Tipping that last cup of caffeinated tea, in its entirety, down the kitchen sink and setting the cup on the draining board, I caught sight of the dining table in the conservatory with its six matching chairs. Scooping off the pile of junk mail adorning it, I yanked and pulled at the mechanism until I had removed the central leaf and contracted the table-top to a smaller configuration. Then I picked up two of the chairs and put them out of sight, one in each of the girls' bedrooms. Eventually I was left with a dining table suitable for a family of four and hoped that this evening I would be able to eat a meal with my husband and two sons without focussing on how much I missed the people who were not there. I was being silly! I couldn't have my boys worrying about me, and I shouldn't miss out on mealtimes with them just because their sisters weren't home.

Enough wallowing! It was time for things to change.

On that decisive note, I grabbed my bag of shopping carriers, picked up my wallet and keys, and headed for the door. It was well past time to raid the supermarket for decaf coffee, herbal teas and some healthy snack options. As I stepped out of the house I nearly tripped over a basket left on the doorstep. It was stuffed with fresh seasonal vegetables still wearing a cosy coating of warm earth. It would seem that my lovely neighbour had been around to leave an offering from her amazingly prolific vegetable garden. She was very well acquainted with my inability to grow any sort of plant successfully, and is incredibly generous with her own produce. Perhaps she had decided I needed looking after too when I bumped into her at the village shop the previous day. I was going to have to give in to the inevitable and start taking care of myself so that no-one else felt obliged to.

I strongly believe that there is nothing better for you than fresh organic veggies straight out of the ground so, gathering up this kind gift, I decided that I would make some healthy soup that afternoon and ensure I ate a large bowl of it to get my new self-care plan off to a good start.

But first, the supermarket was calling!

***

I had expected a lengthy wait for an appointment at the hospital after the doctor had referred me, but I was actually seen within ten days. It just goes to show that we can grumble all we like about the NHS, but when it works, it does so absolutely brilliantly.

After sitting in another packed waiting room for about twenty minutes up at the local hospital, this time surrounded by a large number of very elderly people in wheelchairs with accompanying oxygen tanks, I was called in to have my heart scan. Following that appointment, I was swept off to be fitted with a series of wires stuck to my chest. They were attached to a small box that I was instructed to wear clipped to my belt. The technician explained quite firmly that there were to be no showers for 24 hours, so I was going to pong a bit, but as I had no major plans that day it didn't really matter. I returned the next day for the whole thing to be removed and then dashed home to hit the bathroom.

Approximately a week later, I received a telephone call from my GP to confirm that thankfully the tests showed nothing to be concerned about. She reassured me that I had probably been experiencing episodes of palpitations which might happen again and that, while these could be quite alarming, they weren't anything to worry about. She encouraged me to follow all the advice she had given me before and asked to see me again in a couple of months so that she could check how I was getting on.

After hanging up the telephone I reached for the brochure for the local leisure centre that was pinned to the notice board by the bread bin.

In my opinion, it is a very brave man who gives his wife a membership to the gym for her birthday. If I were of a more suspicious mind I could, for example, think that he might be trying to tell me that I was FAT!!! Only it should be remembered that it wasn't so long ago that he was telling me I was too skinny. The pain of having to potentially send the adored Barbarians away to live with relatives, rather than live indefinitely in a tent in the garden with us, had robbed me of the ability to swallow and even speak let alone eat anything.

Therefore, I felt it was necessary to give him the benefit of the doubt as it was much more likely that he had realised I had a birthday coming up and he had no idea what to buy me as a gift. Thus, after my first appointment with the G.P., when I had given him the news that I was probably not going mad or suffering from some disastrous heart defect, merely stressed and in need of more fresh air, exercise and significantly less, sugar, caffeine and alcohol, he had dashed out and bought me a year's membership to the local leisure centre, a bottle of sugar-free lemonade and a large box of decaffeinated teabags.

I had understood the doctor's advice to mean a brisk walk and some deep breathing exercises by the sea every morning after the school run, rather than a personal return to the Green Goddess movement of the 1980's. I had done keep fit classes before and wasn't that keen to revisit them. However, I guess it's the thought that counts. So, I had decided to accept the gift graciously and give it my best shot, after all I did want to feel better, I just didn't want to die of exhaustion on the way.

Carefully scanning the list of available exercise classes to identify those that looked like they wouldn't be too strenuous, I found myself mentally avoiding sessions called INSANITY (do people willingly go to these things?) and BODY ATTACK (seriously?) that were listed in the 'calorie burning' column and opted instead for classes entitled Slow Stretch and Body Balance from the low impact list instead.

There was one class called 'Play', but I wasn't fooled. It looked highly suspicious as it was held in the gym with all the weights and resistance equipment. That was surely just a soft title to lure you into a high intensity interval training workout.

Over the previous few weeks I had dutifully been going to a couple of random classes a week, as well as taking those brisk walks along the beach in the mornings before going to work. Unfortunately, I had yet to find a class that I wanted to stick to. I had proved that I didn't really have much rhythm or co-ordination in the Zumba class and that I lacked the basic core stability required for the Body Balance class. I don't even want to mention what happened at the 'Begin to Spin' class. Some things need to be forgotten. Yet, in spite of this less than successful beginning, I planned to persevere.

Yoga sounded interesting but there were so many different types that I hadn't a clue where to start. Ashtang, Bikram, Hatha and Moksha to name but a few, then there were modified versions such as Power Yoga and Yoga Fusion, the list seemed endless. Nevertheless, it was listed as a 'relax and re-energise' class rather than an 'Endurance' one so that was probably worth a go. I decided to try one of them out that evening and on my way to do the school run, that afternoon, I bought a yoga mat from the charity shop in the village, in anticipation. This just might be the exercise class for me.

Lots of serenity and calmness! Bring it on!

10: Re-energise

Definition: to give renewed vitality and enthusiasm.

Staying with the stressed-out mother in the present...

That evening, as soon as I had collected the boy Barbarians from school and given them their tea, I changed into my gym kit determined not to back out of my plan to try Yoga.

I must confess that I did fuss about a bit first before leaving. I told Quiet that he was in charge until Beloved Husband got home from work in half an hour and then reminded him twice to make sure that if anything bad happened, like the house falling down again, he and Small were just to get outside to safety as quickly as they could and then to phone me ASAP.

I do not deny that I am still paranoid! Lightening can strike twice you know. I am just rather hoping it won't.

Eventually, Quiet said, in his not-so-quiet-now voice, "For goodness sake mother, just go, will you?" Or words to that effect! He's a teenage boy, so I have no idea what he actually said, but I got his general meaning and therefore sped off in my muddy, little, purple car towards the gym and my very first yoga class.

On reflection, I probably should have taken the time to check that I had been looking at an up-to-date class timetable. But I hadn't. Had I done so, my evening would no doubt have been very different.

A warning bell potentially could have rung when the receptionist breezily told me that the yoga class time had changed but there was something very similar on instead that was very popular. Apparently, I was in luck because there was one space left and the bouncy, young receptionist was sure that I would love it. She swiftly swiped my membership card and I naively took the ticket she returned with the card, before heading to the loos for a last minute, precautionary, pre-exercise class wee. Let's face it, after four babies one's pelvic floor isn't what it was, regardless of how conscientiously one did those exercises recommended by the health visitor all those years ago.

Having completed my visit to the ladies I came out of the swing door to experience a total assault on my visual senses. A figure encased almost entirely in luminous orange, green and yellow leopard print erupted from the gents' toilets at speed and almost mowed me down.

The Luminous Leopard flung his lower arms up from the elbow in horror, wrists flicked back, as he trilled "Oops! Sorry!" ever so cheerfully. Turning sideways he shimmied past me flashing me the sweetest smile as he went. I smiled back, involuntarily, reeling just a bit with shock at the contrast his bright white teeth made with the deep fake tan of his skin.

'There goes a supremely confident individual,' I thought to myself, as I watched him sashay off down the corridor in his tight leggings. Pulling myself together I shuffled off towards Studio One and what used to be yoga but was now something else.

I probably should have been concerned by the sheer number of people waiting outside the studio for the class, or the fact that they were all at least half my age and dressed (or rather more accurately, not very dressed at all) in teeny tiny bits of tight, bright Lycra. However, I was tired and not really paying enough attention. Anyway, if this new class was similar to yoga then it couldn't be too bad, surely?

When the studio doors opened and the sorts of ladies I was expecting to attend a yoga class, all carrying yoga mats a bit like mine, poured *out* of the room and all the very young men and women that I was standing with poured in, I began to get cold feet. Nevertheless, the sheer volume of the crowd surging into the studio simply carried me along helplessly. Once inside, standing at the edge of the room in shock and clutching my yoga mat for dear life, I looked around in bemusement.

What on earth was going on?

My luminous friend from the loos, in all his leopard print glory, sauntered up to me with one of those microphone headsets on, and patted me on the shoulder. "How lovely to see someone new today," he squealed delightedly. He grabbed my yoga mat and flung it to the side of the room. "You won't need that dear, have a couple of these instead." Thrusting two small plastic sticks from a bright blue bucket he had hanging from one elbow, into my empty hands, he continued, "Now don't worry if you can't follow everything, just go with the flow. OK? Enjoy! You'll feel like a new woman after this."

Without waiting for a response, he bounced off like an over-excitable puppy, handing out plastic sticks to everyone else and after that bounded over to the door to the studio, closed it and *switched off the light!*

What?!?

I will admit that, up until that point, I had been considering quietly trying to sidle off towards the door and leaving unobtrusively, but I realised my chances of finding the door successfully were significantly reduced in the dark.

That was when the music started, really loud music with a heavy beat. I had no idea what band was playing, or even what genre of music it was other than *very modern*, but they were belting it out with impressive enthusiasm. Following that, a machine was turned on that sent a glitter-ball effect of tiny pinpricks of light dancing around the room.

Weirder and weirder!

I have to confess that I wasn't feeling terribly de-stressed right then.

The Luminous Leopard started to talk (ok, I really mean shout) over the music into his microphone headset "Right everybody, let's get moving and have some fun. Put your hands in the air!"

I noticed that suddenly there were a lot of bright lights being waved about in the air around me and realised that what I had been handed earlier was a pair of glow sticks. Fidgeting around at the bases of these I found a couple of switches and turned them on.

"Here we go!" Luminous Leopard started to talk the class through a series of complicated dance routines that I hadn't got a hope in hell of following, even if I could see what he was doing, but I did my best. Eventually I realised that if I couldn't actually see anyone else in the room apart from their glow sticks, then they probably couldn't see me either. I concentrated on just making my glow sticks do what everyone else's glow sticks were doing whilst shuffling about from side to side. After a while I started to pick up some of the basic routine which, beneath all of the fancy flourishes, turns and kicks that the Luminous Leopard was banging on about through his microphone, was actually quite simple and very repetitive.

I have heard it said that you don't have to dance to the same tune as everyone else, and I certainly wasn't this evening. (Well, strictly speaking, the tune was the same but my dancing was definitely unique.)

I was surprised to find that this whole 'exercising in the dark' lark was really very liberating because I could just enjoy it without wondering if anyone could see my flabby bits wobbling around. In fact, in the dark no-one can see you at all, let alone your flabby bits, so all I had to do was just chill and go with the flow as the Luminous Leopard had so wisely advised.

I am quite sure that I got everything wrong. After all, I am very aware that I have little to no co-ordination, but I just didn't care. It was like being in a protected little bubble, away from the rest of the world and all my worries. All I focussed on were the glow sticks and the beat of the music. (And not bumping into the person next to me in the dark, of course!) By the end of the fifty-five minute class I was drenched in sweat, but I found that I had really enjoyed myself.

Never in a million years would I have willingly chosen to go to a 'Clubercise' class (it is part of the scary, high intensity bit of the class timetable and therefore automatically on my 'definitely-do-not-do-list') but I was seriously considering doing it again. It was great fun!

I whizzed off home in an exhausted cloud of euphoria, leaving all the barely dressed young things in Lycra to trot off to the bar and flirt outrageously with each other. A short while later I skipped into the house past Beloved Husband and the Barbarians humming happily to myself.

"Do I take it that the yoga was a success?" asked Beloved Husband.

"In a way!" I said with a mysterious smile as I headed for the shower. There's no way I was telling him or the boys what I'd really been up to, they might die laughing and I wouldn't want that.

Part 3

On ne saurait faire d'omelette sans casser des œufs…
One cannot make an omelette without breaking eggs…

François de Charette
1763 -1796

11: Deconstruction

Definition: to take apart

Back with the construction project in the past…

It is often a factor that things need to get worse before they can get better. In the case of the cottage, it was necessary for a degree of demolition to take place before any useful construction could be achieved.

Interestingly, it would appear that someone had felt that Skelly would enjoy watching the rebuild project, as he had migrated from his position on the back patio and was present on the driveway. Wearing a fluorescent yellow jacket, he was comfortably ensconced on my little bench, which had been relocated next to the side of the garage in order to facilitate a prime view of proceedings.

Fortunately, the builders didn't bat an eyelid at their unusual audience and carried on regardless. They've probably seen it all before, although I am pretty certain most normal families keep their skeletons locked up in dark cupboards rather than openly flaunting them in the front garden for all to see; then again, you probably know by now that we are not normal.

By 9.30am on the second day of the rebuild project, everyone had already had a very busy morning indeed.

After many fruitless phone-calls on my part over the previous months to the electricity company and also the telephone company to ask them to come and make the mains electrics and telephone lines that were dangling precariously from the damage gable wall safe, I had given up. However, it would appear that my builders had more influence than I because, all of a sudden, two engineers, one from each of the electricity and telephone companies, had arrived that morning at 8.30am. Their brief was to remove the hazardous mains electrics cable and the telephone line from the top of the crumbling cob wall under the thatch and reattach them to a section of more stable wall under the slate roof to the rear of the house.

After a bit of "you first", "no, no, you first" to-ing and fro-ing from these two engineers, I finally solved their polite procrastination by firmly suggesting that the safest option for everyone was to sort out the mains electricity first, so that the telephone engineer couldn't possibly be accidentally electrocuted as he moved the telephone line. Once that was established my nice builders peeled off the black plastic sheeting that had enshrined the cottage for so many months and the engineers got to work.

Shortly thereafter, 'death by falling electricity cable' had been removed from the morning's agenda and the telephone line was also reattached to a more stable part of the house. The visiting engineers disappeared as suddenly as they had arrived and our builders could at last get on with taking down the damaged wall.

The plan for the next few weeks was to remove the crumbling gable wall first (leaving the damaged front wall) in situ, then digging a foundation trench and filling it with concrete. When the concrete was set, a new gable wall would be constructed over it, using cement block work with a cavity, in accordance with appropriate modern building methods. As soon as that reached roof height and had set, it would be able to take the weight of the roof; then the same process would be done for the damaged cob wall at the front of the house. Steel rods would be run through the two sets of foundations in order to bond them together and the block work of the two walls would be interlinked, retrospectively, for additional strength. The new walls would then be tied in to the remaining two undamaged cob walls using steel bars.

But that was for a later date. For now, the first damaged wall had to be deconstructed.

The Boss had assured me that this would be done in a carefully controlled manner. However, after watching this particular stage, I was beginning to think that The Boss and his building team had very different definitions of both the word 'careful' and the word 'controlled'.

Five minutes after The Boss had left the property, the builders' radio was cranked up to full volume and Thor was dancing around on top of the thatched roof above the damaged gable. (How on earth had he got up there so quickly?) He was wellying the chimney rhythmically with his sledgehammer, whilst singing Queen's 'Bohemian Rhapsody' at the top of his voice. (My dear neighbours, please forgive me.)

Occasionally he would get a bit distracted during his accompanying dance routine and start smacking the other chimney too.

When this happened, Lofty would quickly stand up from where he was putting together a scaffolding tower with Shy Guy and yell at him, "Wrong one, mate! That one is staying! And be careful!" Thor would pause, shrug and skip back along the ridge to the right chimney and resume his whacking with renewed enthusiasm.

From my perch next to Skelly on the bench by the garage, I began to suspect that Thor might have some ADHD issues.

Although the chimney stack over the damaged gable did put up a valiant fight, it eventually conceded to the demands of the sledgehammer. Then, once the weight of the stack was gone, it was time to start on the removal of the cob wall.

Never in my entire life had I thought I would ever willingly allow someone to take a pneumatic drill to the side of my house. Yet there I was, shivering in the January wind, watching in fascination as huge holes were repeatedly drilled into the side of my home.

You might ask why the drill was necessary after all. If they just took the external supporting props away, surely it would just fall down, wouldn't it? That was the point though. The cob was already cracked and disintegrating, but the wall needed to be brought down in a controlled manner so that no additional damage was done and nobody injured. Hopefully this meant a significantly more controlled manner than the chimney dismantling operation I had just witnessed.

Thus, Lofty and Shy Guy stood at the top of the newly-erected scaffolding tower, and were drilling into the damaged wall with grim determination. Beginning at the peak of the damaged gable wall they cut the cob into manageable sized chunks that could be lowered safely to the ground and put into a waiting skip. It was slow, heavy work and I found it surprisingly exhausting to watch.

Controlled and safe it might be, but the amount of dust generated was unbelievable. It went everywhere.

It is a most surreal experience to watch from the outside while one of the rooms of your home is being revealed inch by inch from the ceiling down, as the side of your house is taken apart. Eventually, I couldn't take it anymore and went back round to the kitchen to put the kettle on and try to calm down.

After several hours, I returned to the work site laden with refreshments for the builders. By then it was possible to see directly into the first floor of the house and what had formerly been Quiet's bedroom. You could still see his big, old wardrobe standing where the corner of the room used to be, the door wide open, as if he were up there, in the middle of choosing an outfit for the day.

It felt so wrong.

I became aware of a warm presence next to me and turned my head to see Quiet, standing beside me, his hands deep in his pockets, staring up into his old room with an unfathomable look on his face.

"You OK?" I asked.

He shrugged and sighed heavily, all the while his gaze was locked on his former bedroom. Wondering what was going through his mind, I tucked my hand through his arm, squeezed it comfortingly and we just stood there watching for a while in silence before we retreated to the relative warmth of the back of the house.

Logic had got the fire going in the grate earlier on and it was doing its best to successfully counter the January chill. Deciding that comfort food was needed to cheer us all up and help keep us warm, I rummaged through the fridge for ingredients and set about making bangers and mash with peas and gravy for lunch.

It was the last day of the school Christmas holidays, so the afternoon was spent trying to encourage the Barbarians to check their school bags and finish any remaining homework, as well as locating their clean uniform and sports kits so that the school run the next day could take place in an organised fashion. There was little hope of actually achieving any degree of true efficiency, considering the circumstances under which we were living, but I felt I had to try.

Later that afternoon, I popped round to the front of the house to see what progress had been made. As the early darkness of winter was falling, work had to stop and the plastic sheets were being wrapped back around the cottage walls. Only now almost the entire gable side of the house was missing. It looked as if someone had sliced into a Battenberg cake revealing the coloured layers inside. From the road and driveway, you could see right into the side of our home on three storeys, the loft at the top, then the bedrooms upstairs, the remainder of the stairwell and study downstairs, as well as all the layers of the damaged floors, ceilings and joists in between.

I could see lightshades dangling in the middle of the ceilings, carefully chosen wallpaper and much-loved posters still adorning what was left of the internal walls. Random, abandoned bits of furniture that we hadn't been able to remove stood exactly where we had left them. It was our home but at the same time it wasn't.

How peculiar!

It was like looking at a memory that didn't quite fit with what we thought we remembered, or a previously treasured photograph that was now battered and faded with age.

If I stood on my tiptoes, I could even see the door of the sealed off bedroom where the little girl on the swing was waiting for me.

I was glad that it was all hidden again behind the black plastic by the time Beloved Husband came home. The missing wall was concealed and the cottage looked normal again. Well, as normal as a cottage wrapped in black plastic can look, I suppose. Only Quiet and I had seen our home so exposed, as all the other Barbarians had quite sensibly stayed inside in the warm all day. I figured that there was no need for anyone else in the family to feel so unsettled unless it was unavoidable.

As usual, Quiet wasn't talking but I couldn't tell if this was his normal sort of 'teenage boy' not talking or whether it was a new more sinister 'definitely upset' kind of not talking. I resolved to keep a close eye on him as I rustled up supper that evening.

12: Practice

Definition: to perform an action repeatedly in order to acquire a degree of skill

Back to the present…

Surprisingly enough, I woke up the morning after my Clubercise class feeling pretty good in spite of several previously unknown (and now rather sore) muscles that I must have identified with all that strenuous 'dancing'. I realised that I had slept right through the night with no nightmares disturbing me. Result!

Even the school run and a rather tedious morning at work didn't dent my enthusiasm for the day so, as soon as I made it home just after lunch, I shot into my little studio and started to rummage around in my boxes of art supplies intending to start a new painting.

After my visit to the GP, I had finally finished my wobbly silver fish painting by following her advice to adapt my painting technique. Letting the thick paint dry, I was then able to let my hand rest directly on the canvas to steady it while I marked in the final little fish. Just because this wasn't how I usually did things didn't mean it shouldn't be done. The result was remarkably successful and any inadvertent wobbling in the new layer of paint I felt could be attributed to an attempt to create the illusion of movement in the water.

Buoyed up by this triumph, I had started to look into other painting techniques and spent rather a long time on YouTube researching new ideas and then experimenting. I particularly liked the concept of mixed media pieces and had started to adapt my ideas to incorporate the use of textured canvases and other layering and staged techniques. Some of these experiments worked and some didn't, either way it was exciting and really rather fun. Change really wasn't such a bad thing.

While I was digging into a large box of equipment that sits under my desk next to the easel, my fingers brushed against a bubble wrapped package stuffed right at the back. I'd always known it was there but had been studiously ignoring it. It was about the size of an A4 piece of paper and as thick as a pack of cards. I gently withdrew the package and thoughtfully turned it over in my hands.

My musings were interrupted by the noise of a Skype call on the iPad. Instantly, my mothering instincts were on red alert. I had already spoken to the girls briefly that morning and no-one else Skypes me, so why were they calling again? Placing the package on the windowsill next to the desk, where I could ignore it for a bit longer, I flicked the iPad on to accept a call from Logic.

"Are you OK?" I asked.

She frowned, "Yes, I'm fine. Calm down! You're supposed to be trying to be less stressed remember, not more. I just forgot to mention something earlier."

"Oh!" I relaxed, "What was that then?"

"I wanted to know how you were finding the whole decaf tea thing."

"Umm. Not so good actually," I confessed, looking at the barely touched cup of decaf tea in front of me. "I don't really like it so it's a bit of a struggle. I am trying though. It's been three weeks now since I had a cup of the real stuff, but I have to admit I really want one."

"Well there's this guy on my course who told me that there are still traces of caffeine in decaf tea and coffee," she said.

"Really?" I asked. "Are you sure?"

"Yeah. There's this other girl too, who agreed with him. She's a bit of a hippy type and lives down the hall from me. She's really into all that new-age stuff. Apparently, she's trying to 'find' herself. I don't understand why though, she's eighteen! Surely she should have worked out who she is by now?" said Logic with the absolute confidence of one who has never had any doubt with regard to her own personal identity. "Anyway, she said that you needed to be drinking herbal teas and stuff like that to be truly off caffeine."

"Ugh!"

"Yeah, I know! But she says that it's easier to do if you are completely caffeine-free. I don't know if it's true or not, but it might be worth a try. Have you thought about hot water with fresh lemon juice in it? It's quite nice, especially if you add honey rather than sugar, then it's a bit healthier. Try it and let me know what you think. Anyway, it was only a quick call to ask if you wanted me to see if she knows any really good herbal teas or coffee substitutes that she'd recommend. There might be one you actually like."

"I doubt it," I responded gloomily. "But OK, thanks."

"Sure, call you later then. Bye!" She was gone again. It was nice that she was trying to help me. I decided that I'd better make sure I stayed on the no caffeine wagon and try to help myself too. Next step, perhaps a real yoga class or something similar tonight. Maybe with inner peace I would also find a liking for herbal teas, especially if Logic's hippy friend could recommend some that didn't taste of cat's pee.

Smiling at the thought, I reminded myself that shaky hands and a few nightmares weren't the end of the world. My heart was fine. The six of us were still a family, even though our girls had left home. This was just a different phase in our lives together. We had each other. We were going to be OK.

I turned to a small canvas board and started to work on a blue and white seascape scene reminiscent of the end of a long sunny day on a Cornish beach holiday, all sparkling water and silhouettes. Before long, I had created the outline of a small boy running into the picture towards the sea and chasing seagulls to make them take off into the air. It was a very free and easy piece with not too much fine detail, so my tremor hadn't particularly interfered with what I was trying to achieve. The doctor was quite correct when she had said that there were ways of adapting my art to fit my abilities and I ought to put my mind to exploring more of that.

It did occur to me to wonder if an element of the shaky painting hands might also be down to lack of practice. In the past I had painted prolifically. Every day I had worked on finely detailed pieces. It was very true that I hadn't completed anything that required that sort of precision for a very long time, but I hadn't really wanted to. The pieces I worked on now were generally large, colourful, energetic pieces that didn't need too much detail. They were pleasing to the eye, really fun to paint and helped me relax.

It could be argued that I should probably put in some fine brushwork practice and see if that bore any fruit. There was only one way to find out, so I dug out a new blank sheet of canvas paper, as well as a series of small brushes, and set about putting my right hand muscles through a whole series of painting exercises that required precise movements and fine brush control. The results were total rubbish if I am completely honest but, no matter how disheartening this was, I resolved to do the exercises every day, without fail, to see if things improved.

After all, it has to be said, that the only true failure in life is a failure to try.

The brush manipulation exercises were not as immediately successful as I had hoped they would be, and this rather underlined just quite how bad my fine motor control had become. The tremor was still very pronounced which I found depressing. I thought I had hidden my feelings quite well, but it was brought to my attention later that week that I might have been rather grumpy, when the fellas in the family joined forces to try and persuade me to go out for the evening on my own.

Now there was a time many years ago when Beloved Husband had been somewhat nervous about being left alone with the children, given their rather uncivilised behaviour. (Hence their affectionate nickname 'The Barbarians'.)

I was reminded of one particular Saturday morning when Supreme-Parent-in-Charge duties fell to Beloved Husband. He was to escort Quiet to a party. All suggestions on my part, that it would be prudent to keep our mild-mannered, four-year-old Barbarian away from a specific brand of small, round, highly coloured, chewy sweets, were brushed aside. He could cope, he said confidently. Did I not trust him? I wisely invoked the Fifth Amendment at that point. In all fairness, I should point out that, although I had witnessed several occasions when our calm and contented, silent third child had achieved a transformation similar to that of Bruce Banner becoming The Hulk, following the consumption of that particular brand of sweets, my Beloved Husband had not.

Long story short, an hour later he was obliged to use super-human effort to contain the uncontainable, in order to extract Quiet from the party and return him home in one piece. Pulling onto the drive looking grey, sweaty and exhausted, Beloved Husband uttered these immortal words: "You were right," before falling out of the car and dragging himself into the house. Under the circumstances I didn't feel that the words "I told you so" would be terribly well received, but that didn't stop me thinking them! I merely smiled and leaned into the back of the car to release the Incredible Hulk from his car seat, although, on reflection, it might have been wiser to leave him there until his Bruce Banner persona had reappeared!

Over the years the Barbarians had become far more civilised and they were now fully equipped with all the necessary social graces. Hence Beloved Husband felt fully confident about making a concerted effort to get rid of me for the evening. No doubt there was some sports match on the telly that he and the boys wanted to slob-out in front of, eating junk food and yelling "Foul!" at regular intervals whilst exclaiming loudly at the referee. It appeared that the boys agreed with him that their grumpy mother would just get in the way. (Obviously none of them was particularly hungry at that point.)

Small sweetly suggested that I might like to go to another Yoga class as I had seemed to enjoy the last one so much. Beloved Husband agreed that this might be a good plan and hinted that he would give me a lift, probably so that he could be sure that I went.

Quiet joined in then, peeling his eyes off his iPod screen and running them down the list of gym classes on the noticeboard on the wall next to him. "There's one of those Tai thingy classes you were on about the other day at 8 o'clock in Studio 3." He said encouragingly, and after a brief, closer inspection, he continued. "It says it's for seniors so you'll fit right in!"

"Thank you very much!" I exclaimed "I'm not that old! I'll have you know that I am only in my mid-forties." Cheeky beggar!

"I was only saying what it says here, but if you think it'll be too much for you, don't go." He shrugged and returned his attention to his social media mates.

"It's not going to be too much for me!" I insisted adamantly.

"Fine, go then," he said, as if it made no difference to him either way, which, let's face it, it probably didn't.

"OK, I will," I said.

"Great," said Beloved Husband, relieved that a decision had been made. "Go get changed and I'll drop you off. I can come back for you after the football is finished."

Aha, so I was right, there was a match on and the boys did want to get shot of the grumpy girl in the house.

The thought of a gentle Tai Chi class for senior citizens did sound rather relaxing. Not that I know anything about Tai Chi you understand. Or senior citizens either, for that matter. They could be a really energetic bunch. Either way, it had to be a major improvement on listening to the boys shouting at the TV all evening.

13: Quandary

Definition: being in a state of perplexity over a troublesome decision between two or more equally undesirable alternatives

Back to the repair job in the past…

The first school run of the January term took place the next morning with no real disasters. Well, I say that, but I really mean no disasters that I didn't manage to solve.

I felt we did extremely well in our leaving-the-caravan-and-escaping-to-school-and-work routine. All Barbarians had got up, showered and dressed with minimal grumbling. Breakfast had happened and all necessary elements of educational paraphernalia were appropriated. So off we had set to the various schools in fairly good time.

Now ordinarily I would advocate that the older Barbarians should use the school bus. After all, if there is a splendidly civilised service like that available in the country, then we should make use of it. Use it or lose it. Plus, it makes my life so much easier. Nevertheless, they do have to walk quite a long way to get to the bus stop (a glorified term for the corner of a muddy field, a bit closer to civilisation than our house) as we do live in the middle of nowhere. Added to that minor inconvenience, the bus always arrived at a disgustingly early hour in the morning as there were quite a few other remote hamlets for it to grace with its presence before it could return to the sophistication of the urban environment and the school gates.

I take my hat off to the brave bus driver who does venture out this far, as he has to stop at every little lay-by and crossroads on his tortuous route; if he's out here with a bus, then he might as well fill it. However, he does run the risk of getting stuck behind slow moving tractors and being forced to suddenly avoid any number of random breed of livestock wandering across the road unexpectedly. This includes anything from ducks and chickens to wild ponies ambling into his path; to say nothing of cats, rats, or slinky wild ferrets moving at speed. Then there were the herds of cows, udders heavy with milk, ponderously crossing from the fields to the milking parlour at regular intervals.

Our gallant bus driver has also been known to rescue the odd motorist stuck in the water-logged ditches. These fiendish traps lurked in the undergrowth at the side of the road, ready to trap those impatient drivers that attempted to squeeze past the slow-moving bus on the narrow, single-track country lanes. These persons had no idea they were taking their lives in their hands by driving on the overgrown verges rather than reversing back to the designated passing place and waiting to let the bus pass.

Amazingly, this intrepid hero successfully drags his laden vehicle back to the metropolis and through the school gates by 9am Then, at 3pm in the afternoon, he does the whole thing again in reverse. (The route is in reverse, obviously, not the bus!)

Brave bus drivers aside, Chaos and Logic were now in the midst of the build-up to the A level and AS level exam period and, as the potential for drama and excitement on the aforementioned school bus added a certain amount of stress to the start of their day, I had taken to driving them into the sixth form to ensure they arrived in a relatively calm and collected condition.

As I triumphantly swung into a space outside the sixth form entrance and pulled on the handbrake, there was a gasp of horror from Chaos who was sat beside me. My heart sank! What had we (she) forgotten?

Looking over at her, I saw genuine alarm in her eyes.

OK! Bracing myself I raised my eyebrows at her questioningly and I watched her face crumple.

"Mum! I'm still wearing my slippers!"

"Ah!"

Both boys dissolved into a heap of unhelpful hysterical laughter in the back of the car while Chaos and I both looked tentatively down into the passenger side foot well. True enough, there on her feet were a pair of pink, fluffy, bunny rabbit slippers complete with floppy ears and whiskers. Seriously, how had we all missed them as she got into the car earlier on?

To give me my due, while my initial reaction was that the slippers did have a good sturdy sole and would probably stand up quite well to a whole day walking around the sixth form college, I did accept that her social reputation would not survive in a similarly hardened condition.

There are times as a parent when we must make extreme sacrifices. The demand comes upon us when we least expect it and solutions can require the most painful of concessions.

With a heavy sigh I knew I was going to have to pay the ultimate forfeit.

Looking down at my brand new (size five) shiny, black ankle boots I gave them a sad, mental goodbye. I had worn them for less than an hour. Closing my eyes, I slipped them off my feet and handed them over, wincing as she shoved her (size 6) feet into them gratefully.

"Mum! You are a star!" she said. "They're a bit tight but I'll be fine! Don't worry!" She gave me a relieved smile and a quick kiss of gratitude, before climbing out of the car. While I hadn't been remotely worried about her feet, I knew that my poor boots were never going to be quite the same again.

Quiet was still shaking with laughter as I watched the girls head off to their lessons.

"Are you going to get out then?" I prompted sharply. His secondary school was on the same campus as the sixth form, so this was his stop too.

Pulling himself together, he opened the rear door and stepped out, then, still sniggering, he stuck his head back in and said "You do realise you've got the primary school drop to do now, don't you?"

"Oh heck!" He was right! Sighing heavily, I accepted that I was going to have to drop Small off in the school playground whilst wearing pink bunny rabbit slippers. Funnily enough, Small immediately stopped laughing in the back of the car once the full potential horror of this particular outcome dawned on him.

After that, I was going to have to drive home and walk past all the builders, in order to get to the caravan before I could change out of the slippers into a proper pair of shoes and then go on to work.

Late.

Great!

It turned out that my luck was in that morning as I was able to palm a very subdued Small off on another mother in the school carpark, without having to set foot outside my vehicle. Not surprisingly, this was a solution that my youngest was more than happy to co-operate with, thank goodness. Phew! One problem at a time!

Arriving back at the house I squared my shoulders and decided to simply brazen it out, and walked with a confidence I didn't feel across the drive towards the caravan, braced for any comments. But the building team were too busy playing with Skelly to notice me.

On my return from the caravan, with suitable work shoes appropriated, I noted that Skelly now sported a fetching blue hard hat, a packet of Marlboro Lights stuffed into the top pocket of a fluorescent yellow jacket and a copy of The Sun tucked under one arm. I gave the boys a grin of approval for their handiwork and set off to work where a nice, warm, dust-free office full of leftover Christmas biscuits and cake awaited me.

***

When I returned from work later that afternoon, it was obvious that the work on the gable wall had cracked on at a fair pace. No sooner than the cob was down than the lads had started digging the foundation trench.

That evening the Boss kept me fully informed of what was going on, when and why, which was fascinating but, in some ways, it might have been easier not to know. I told you I was contrary. Only a few chapters back I was grumbling about not being told anything and now I am doing the same because I have too much information. Sadly, it just gives me more to worry about.

Too much information was the reason I spent the next three whole nights in a row watching the thermometer readings of the external air temperature. The Boss had explained that laying foundation concrete in cold weather wasn't ideal (I've had enough of 'not ideal' now, I want ideal!), but that as long as the temperature didn't drop below freezing, all would be well. Just for a change!

Fortunately, there are all sorts of precautions you can take to make sure your concrete sets beautifully in colder temperatures and The Boss' team had implemented them all so no problems were anticipated. Nevertheless, I latched on to the fact that it was January and pretty damn cold. Adding in my overall bad luck factor, I was convinced that it would freeze and the concrete would be ruined, hence my nocturnal obsession with the outside temperature. Noticing my concern, Chaos kindly gave me a lengthy lecture on the amount of heat produced by the chemical reaction that takes place in setting concrete and explained that this would offset the dropping external temperatures. Eventually I simply had to accept that it was all way beyond me and so tried to make myself relax.

As luck would have it, we experienced a very mild two-week period just at the critical concrete setting stage so my fears were unfounded. The new concrete block wall grew quickly upwards to meet the roof and, as soon as that was strong, the builders turned their attention to demolishing the second wall. All seemed to be going to plan and I started to think that everything was going to be ok.

Silly me!

That, of course, was a big mistake.

Huge!

Soon after the second wall started to come down, the Boss and Genuine Old Building Expert came around to the back of the house to have a little chat with us. We all sat around the table in the conservatory with hot cups of tea and the plans for the rebuild were spread out so that they could update us on the progress of the work. This was the point at which Beloved Husband asked the question that had been bothering us both for quite a while.

"How effective is the repair plan when it comes to tying the new walls into the remaining cob walls?"

The Boss and Genuine Old Building Expert exchanged a long knowing look.

We should probably have kept quiet and jollied on through life oblivious to reality, but we didn't. Having asked the question, we were going to have to deal with the answer which was basically not very effective.

The insurance company had been understandably intent on restricting their own liability on this job. As a result, we now had a repair plan which, while fit for purpose in the short term, had some serious potential flaws when it came to long term sustainability.

Genuine Old Building Expert agreed that it was definitely possible to tie the old and new walls together effectively but, that with the dissimilar material types expanding and contracting differently with temperature changes, over time there would always be every likelihood of a 'crack' of some sorts at the juncture. While this crack would not necessarily be a structural problem, it would definitely be a cosmetic one and would influence the value and potential saleability of the property.

The second issue with the plan on the table was that it left two cob walls in situ. This was potentially a big problem. Cob works most effectively as a single, solid, ring-like (or a square with rounded corners) structure. If you remove half of this then what is left is always going to fail eventually.

The insurance company were not going to replace the two walls left because they weren't failing yet. The key word in that sentence was 'yet'. The two remaining cob walls represented a ticking time bomb that would definitely fail at some point in the future.

The Boss and Genuine Old Building Expert reassured us that this was likely to be quite some time in the future and that the repair as designed on the plans before us would work in the short term, but they couldn't guarantee that we wouldn't have major problems in the future.

In short, what really needed to be done to prevent us being put back in this position again, was to take out all four cob walls and rebuild the whole cob section of the house.

Thus, to paraphrase the immortal words of Jane Austin, 'an unhappy alternative was before us.' We could allow the repair to progress as the insurance company had devised it and risk putting our children through their home collapsing again in the future. We could, of course, attempt to sell the repaired building, but we didn't fancy our chances of being able to do that, especially as any structural survey would identify the potential risk and make it impossible to sell anyway. Who would take it on?

The alternative was to extend the repair job to include the removal of the other two cob walls and to find the money to pay for it ourselves. We were already going to have to find extra finances to cover the installation of a concrete floor to meet building regulations on the repair. In addition to this, there were going to have to be significant repairs to the central ground floor ceiling/first storey floor joists and boarding, as well as the same for the loft.

A new staircase was required too, as the insurance company repair plan didn't have any contingency built into it for that aspect of the job either. Then there would be costs associated with redecorating throughout and carpeting or flooring. Apparently, all of those would count as material gain and we weren't allowed that unless we paid for it ourselves.

There was some good news though. When the first gable wall came down, Genuine Old Building Expert had been able to confirm that the back section of the house had been built entirely independently of the cob at the front. Apparently, it had been built as close to the cob wall as possible, with a gap of a few centimetres which had then been stuffed with straw and sealed over with render. This meant that the whole of the kitchen/lounge/conservatory was completely stable and unaffected by the damage at the front. Isn't hindsight a wonderful thing? It would have helped us enormously to have known that last year! Anyway, as a result of this information, we could be confident that removing the entirety of the cob would not cause any structural issues with the back of the property. Thank heaven for small mercies!

The Boss and Genuine Old Building Expert left us to think through our options. It was obviously not a fun part of their job, but it was important that they gave us a full and honest picture of the potential pitfalls of the repair in progress. Now we just had to decide on our next move.

The obvious choice was to remove all of the cob walls and do a proper complete repair job rather than the more short-term solution that the insurance company was proposing. The problem was that our finances were stretched really tight and we were looking at having to find a not insignificant amount of money for the full repair.

Beloved Husband and I sat side by side at the table for a long time after they had left, each trying to mentally work through the implications of this new information, and both with very heavy hearts. We felt we had come so close to fixing things only to have it all snatched away again. As I blinked rapidly trying to disperse the hot tears threatening to break free, I felt his hand reach for mine under the table and hold on tight.

"It'll be OK," he murmured. "We'll sort it out."

I really hoped he was right.

14: Indomitable Spirit

Definition: an unconquerable warrior, a courage or will that cannot be overcome.

Returning to the present day and the new exercise schedule…

Hence, half an hour after it was decided by the boys that I would attend a Tai Chi class, I found myself hastily dumped outside the leisure centre. Having watched the three of them speeding off back to watch the football, I turned and hurried in the direction of Studio 3.

With only moments to spare before the class started, I bumbled through the studio door and put my bag down by the side of the room before turning around. I was a bit surprised by what I saw. This was not a room full of zen-like persons of a more mature generation, instead there were at least a dozen well-put-together gentlemen in their mid-thirties and forties all wearing loose white vaguely pyjama-like outfits and looking at me with curiosity.

One of the supremely fit-looking men ambled casually over to me. (Please note, I mean sporty-looking 'fit' not the other type of 'fit'. Honestly!)

"Welcome." He smiled at me, before continuing, "We always like to see new people in class. Have you done any Taekwondo before?"

What?

Taekwondo?

Looking at the other chaps in the room, I noticed that they were all now tying impressive looking black belts around their white uniforms. I was to learn later on that these suits are called doboks.

"No, I haven't," I replied. "But I think I might have come to the wrong class. Perhaps I should come back another time?" I started thinking about whether I could subtly edge towards the door.

"Well you would probably be better off in the junior belt class with the other beginners next time, rather than this senior class," he agreed, still smiling. "That's at 7 o'clock, but you're here now, so why not give it a go? Just take it easy and enjoy."

So, senior belts not senior citizens and Taekwondo not Tai Chi. Quiet had a lot to answer for. From now on I was going to be checking that class schedule very carefully indeed. Fool me once etc…

The instructor seemed so enthusiastic and encouraging that it was impossible to grab my bag, sidle out and run for the hills. Promising myself that I could kill Quiet slowly later on if I survived, I returned his smile and said "Sure, why not?"

Addressing the whole room, he called, "Line up everyone."

All of the black belted gents lined up in rows facing the instructor. Two of them gestured for me to join them in a row at the back.

"Copy us!" one said.

"Yeah! We'll show you what to do," said the other.

I smiled gratefully and shuffled into place between them as the class came to attention, bowed and started a series of warm-up exercises.

I had expected to be massively out of my depth and to these expert Taekwondo students I probably was. Nevertheless, I was surprised to realise I was enjoying myself. The warm-up consisted mainly of exercises that I had done before; push-ups, sit-ups, squats, jogging on the spot, and stretching. Given the fact that I had been attending random exercise classes two or three times a week for at least four months, my fitness had obviously improved significantly. I found that, with some encouragement from my two back row buddies, I could just about keep up, which gave me a bit of a buzz.

Then the class moved onto kicking drills and punch combinations, moving forwards and backwards in formation in the rows that we had started in. The instructions were first given in Korean and then thankfully translated and demonstrated by the instructor. Eventually we took a break for some water and the guys all started to put on protective equipment and pair up. Apparently, the next bit of the class was for sparring (i.e. fighting matches).

Probably the largest bloke in the class came over to me and said, "We'll go together, OK?" He was huge! Made even more immense by the massive trunk protector, helmet, groin, shin and arm guards he was wearing. I wasn't going to argue with him.

"OK!" I swallowed nervously, aware that I didn't have any protective equipment and mentally renewed my vow to make Quiet pay later.

If there ever was a later, of course!

I needn't have worried though. While the rest of the class spent the next half an hour happily kicking the stuffing out of each other, my large partner patiently taught me how to kick him. He never once kicked me back.

It is a novel experience kicking a big fella who simply smiles at you, says you need to kick him harder and then shows you how to improve your technique so that you can attack him more effectively. Not surprisingly, I found it exceedingly therapeutic and, by the end of the class, I was able to thank my partner, my back-row buddies and the instructor with genuine enthusiasm.

As I made my way down the steps of the leisure centre after the class looking for Beloved Husband, my phone buzzed. A text message informed me that the football had gone into extra-time so he was going to be a bit late picking me up. There was no point hanging around in the car park, so I turned on my heel and went back into the building to head for the bar. Replying to his text I said I would get a glass of lemonade and read my Kindle and that he should come in to the leisure centre and find me when he was ready.

On entering the bar, I spotted some of the fellas from the Taekwondo class ordering a round of drinks. It is very thirsty work kicking each other after all!

I am not quite sure what Beloved Husband thought when he arrived an hour later to find me sinking a pint of shandy surrounded by my new martial arts mates. In my defence, I was actually following the doctor's orders to the letter. She told me to do some exercise and to get out and socialise. Well! There I was doing both, and very effectively too, I might add.

***

The next morning, after probably the best night's sleep I had had in over three years, I woke up feeling unusually cheerful. Admittedly I did have a slightly muzzy head, (I only had one pint!) I also had a lot of very sore muscles, but that didn't stop me from feeling great. Obviously kicking people was good for me! I was going to have to make a point of doing it again.

After dropping the boys to school, I trotted off to work quite happily and, as soon as my shift was over, I whizzed around the supermarket to restock the kitchen cupboards for the Barbarians to forage through when they got home.

Back at the house, I took the opportunity to return my lovely neighbour's (now empty) vegetable basket, as I had spotted her car in her driveway. Whilst I was there she repeated an earlier invitation for me to join her as a guest for at an upcoming Women's Institute event in the village. Given my positive mood following my brilliant night's sleep, I found myself agreeing to go along. The exercise classes were certainly proving to be fun so perhaps the Doctor's suggestion of some female company wasn't such a bad idea either, and if there's one place you can guarantee to find female company it's at the WI.

Feeling like I had made a massive step forward in my campaign to look after myself, I settled down to more brush control exercises in my little studio with renewed enthusiasm. I was determined to beat this anxiety issue. I was going to relax, get fit and stop being so grumpy. My hands were going to stop shaking. Positive thinking!

Everything was going to be OK!

After putting my brush technique through the full exercise program that I had devised for myself, I decided to do a little mixed media experiment on a small canvas in order to test my progress. Having prepared a textured canvas the previous day, using crumpled up tissue paper and PVA glue, I selected a series of bright blue, green and silver acrylic paints and soon a light, tropical ocean unfolded before me with a bright, sparkling shoal of fish spiralling through it. Tiny iridescent scales decorated the larger fish, each one created using trimmed sequins which were glued directly into the wet paint adding to the textural dimension of the piece. It was careful, fiddly work and took ages. My hands still shook but not to the extent that I couldn't function, so it was with some triumph that I sat back several hours later and looked at the finished piece.

I was so pleased with it that I didn't even mind when Quiet loomed behind me later that evening after supper and stood looking at it critically for some time.

"Hmmm!" he said in a very non-committal way. "More fish!"

"Yes," I agreed seriously, "But these are different fish. These are sparkly fish."

"Yeah," he said, sounding very unimpressed. "It's all a bit glitter and unicorns though, isn't it? I didn't think that was your sort of thing."

I looked back at my painting and tilted my head on one side. "I suppose it is a bit glittery but I don't see any unicorns. Anyway, who says it's not my sort of thing? I quite like it. I plan to do some bigger ones."

"Oh great!" he said with typical teenage disgust. "You'll be painting rainbows next."

"Oh, don't worry," I said reassuringly, "it probably won't ever get to that stage!" Crossing my fingers out of his line of sight, I surreptitiously nudged an extremely colourful canvas, depicting a rainbow patchwork toy teddy bear, with my foot and sliding it further behind the stack of large fish paintings leaning against the wall.

Small came into the studio and stood behind his brother holding an apple in one hand. Torn between wanting to marvel at the fact that he was voluntarily in close physical contact with fruit without being blackmailed into it, yet not wanting to bring undue attention to it, I just smiled at him and said, "What do you think of my fish?"

"Cool," he said, sparing the painting a brief glance before he leaned back against the wall, drew two more apples out of his pocket and started to juggle with them. "So, how did you get it to sparkle like that then?" He was totally focused on the flight path of his apples as he spoke and thus failed to register my dawning disappointment that he probably wasn't planning to eat them.

I should probably explain the apple juggling. The day before, following an unfortunate incident with both boys, two tennis balls, a football and a large glass vase, Beloved Husband had banned all balls from the house. Employing the obtuse ingenuity of the young male mind, Small had started to use the contents of the fruit bowl as ball substitutes.

At least he seemed to like my painting.

Quiet leaned over and snatched one of the apples out of the air mid-juggle and said, "Like you know anything about art, Shorty!" before running off. Small gave a loud yell and barrelled after him. I didn't give much for Quiet's chances if his brother caught up with him. He looked like he meant business and, as I have said before; he wasn't actually that small anymore.

I sighed heavily. Thank goodness I had agreed to go out that evening to the WI event. Female company was definitely in order. Even though I hated the idea of going into a room full of strangers on my own, I was going to be brave. I was a grown-up after all! Wasn't I?

***

Several hours later, I was forced to re-evaluate just how grown-up I actually was, when I found myself standing nervously outside the main door into the village hall. The WI meeting was to be held inside. My lovely neighbour had been obliged to go there early to help set up, so we hadn't travelled together, and I was now lingering in the car park trying to pluck up the courage to open the door and go in on my own. Just as I was deciding that perhaps I would simply go home instead, a group of ladies arrived, all chattering and laughing as they made their way towards me. One of them smiled brightly at me.

"Hello," she said, "are you joining us tonight?"

I shuffled my feet shyly and nodded, trying to smile back but not really doing a very good job.

"Don't be nervous, we don't bite. I promise! Come on in." She opened the door and I found myself whisked into the warm, noisy room along with the rest of their party. Before long, my name had been ticked off a list, I had located my lovely neighbour, and we were all sat down together for the rest of the meeting.

All I can say is that it wasn't at all what I had expected a WI meeting to be. There was a lot of laughter that evening, the nice sort of laughter. Everyone I met was incredibly friendly and welcoming, and I wasn't once made to feel inadequate because I don't make my own jam or knit my own socks! In fact, I enjoyed myself so much that by the end of the evening, I was considering joining. It would seem that the good doctor had been right once again.

Part 4

"Heaven knows we need never be ashamed of our tears,"

Charles Dickens
1812 – 1870
(Great Expectations 1860)

15: Integrity

Definition: being of sound morals, having ethical principles

Back to the decision about to be made about the wobbly walls in the past...

The day after that depressing conversation with The Boss and Genuine Structural Engineer Man, was a Saturday and we had no plans at all. Ordinarily we would all have liked a nice long lie in, but given the cramped conditions in the caravan, the icy cold temperatures and the sprightly starlings skipping around on the metal roof from half-past-extremely-early (whilst wearing their best hob-nailed boots), that wasn't really an option.

Beloved Husband and I had endured a seriously disturbed night, as we both tried to get our heads around the implications of that discussion. Under the circumstances, any hopes for a visit from Mr Sandman were futile and we spent the hours tossing and turning from side to side repeatedly, much to the disgust of the other caravan occupants who objected to the distinct rocking motion this set off in the whole unit. Mentally trying to sort through the dilemma before us was an exhausting nocturnal activity but, even as the sun started to come up, we each found ourselves no closer to reaching a conclusion.

We had spent rather a long part of the previous evening discussing our options on the telephone with various members of our extended family. After all, one of the main benefits of being part of such a large clan is that you can ring your parents or siblings up with really dim questions from time to time. Luckily, my brother had had some experience of working in the building trade as a student and, while he didn't have any direct knowledge of cob buildings or their associated structural engineering issues, he knew a few people who did. After making several phone calls on our behalf, he eventually came back to us and confirmed that the advice that Genuine Old Building Expert and The Boss were giving us was legitimate. The best option in structural engineering terms for the long-term future of the house was to remove the cob entirely.

So, at seven o'clock the following morning, Beloved Husband and I gave up pretending to sleep and opted to go for a long walk instead. There would be no builders on site today. We had until Monday to decide what to do. After pulling on multiple layers of thick fleece, with hats, gloves and walking boots, we opened the caravan door and stepped out into a crisp, white, beautifully frosty morning, leaving the grumbling Barbarians to snuggle down under their duvets and go back to sleep.

Startled by the caravan door closing behind us, a buzzard took off from his perch in one of the oak trees at the bottom of the garden. We watched as he then swooped almost noiselessly towards us across the lawn, his large wingspan a majestic collection of brown and white feathers creating a magnificent display against the frost-bound land. As he settled on a nearby fencepost with a noisy fluttering of wings, a single perfect feather floated to the ground by my feet. Bending down, I picked it up examining its natural beauty close up.

Crunching my way across the frozen grass to the house, I carried the feather into the kitchen and placed it on a shelf above the sink. Then Beloved Husband and I each grabbed a couple of bread rolls, stuffed them with leftover sausages from the night before and headed off into the forest for a stomp.

Having munched our snacks in thoughtful silence, we eventually started to chat through our various options again, but it wasn't until we reached the trig point out on the heathland to the north of our home that we finally came to a decision.

"I don't see that we can risk staying in that house if we only repair the two damaged walls. If there's any chance the remaining cob will fail at some point and the kids will be made homeless again……" I trailed off.

"The fundamental problem," Beloved Husband mused, "is that I don't think it would be fair to carry on with just this repair job and then sell a house with a significant potential problem on to another family."

"No!" I agreed. "That wouldn't be fair."

"We don't really have a lot of choice. We're going to have to take the structural engineer's advice and do the full 'cob-removal' option. It's the only thing to do. I don't see another way round this."

"But we can't afford it!"

"I know," he sighed. "The insurance company won't cover the cost of replacing the undamaged walls, as they're actually stable at the moment so not technically in need of repair."

"Meaning that somehow we will have to find the money for it," I said gloomily.

"It's the right thing to do. The good news is that the back bit of the property is absolutely fine and won't be affected. Now that we know the cob was built entirely separately, we can be certain that the disintegration at the front hasn't caused any damage to the rear section. So at least we know the absolute limits of this particular job. I suggest we crack on and get it done properly. Then we have options. There is a little wriggle room to extend the mortgage a bit which will cover part of the cost of the work. But after that, we'll have to juggle things. It'll be a while before the bills start to come in. You never know what will happen. We might manage to hold on to the house, but then again maybe not."

"I could take on some extra shifts at work," I offered.

"That'll help, but either way we have to accept that we will probably be forced to sell the house after the work is completed. I don't see how we can sustain a mortgage of that size for too long."

We were standing next to the trig point by then, a single concrete marker set at the highest bit of the common. I turned and stared out over the beautiful view of grey/white heathland rolling away from us down the hill towards the ancient woodland that we had just hiked through.

I didn't dare face Beloved Husband because I was ashamed of the tears that were welling up in my eyes. Whilst I was frustrated with myself for being such a watering pot, I simply couldn't cope with the thought that my poor babies were going to lose their home anyway, in spite of the brave way in which they had coped with everything so far. The

Barbarians had been amazing, pulling together as a team over the last nine months. They had put up an incredible fight in order to not be split up and sent away last summer in the wake of the house collapsing. How on earth were we going to be able to tell them that we'd eventually lose their home anyway?

I genuinely felt that my heart might break. I couldn't believe that we were back here yet again. When the insurance company had finally agreed that we had a legitimate claim, I had foolishly thought that our troubles were over. Yet it seemed that the fates had other ideas and we were to be their play things for a bit longer. I could only hope that I had the strength to survive it.

Thousands of possible consequences crowded into my head all at once. What if, after spending so much of their later teen years living in such cold and miserable conditions in the garden with two stressed out and grumpy parents, our two girls went to university and decided never to come home again? It was a bit of a leap I know but I was afraid that they would leave and never want to come back. If we sold their childhood home, then they wouldn't have any emotional ties to any new place we bought. We'd have no shared history there.

Beloved Husband wrapped his arms around me from behind and I leaned back into him and sighed. Everything was still and silent. The only movement came from the frosty clouds of our mingled breath in the air and the hot tears that spilled unchecked down my cheeks.

"I can tell you're fast forwarding to total disaster in your mind," he murmured quietly. "You do have a tendency to jump to the worst possible outcome these days."

"Hmm!" It was all I could manage around the painful lump in my throat.

"Whatever it is that you're frightened of probably won't happen you know. Selling the house won't be the end of the world. Let's just take it one day at a time, OK?"

There was a long pause.

"It's the right thing to do," he continued quietly. "Let's fix this house properly. It's the only way to move this situation forward."

We stood there in contemplative silence for several minutes before I could collect myself and answer him without my voice wobbling. "I know. You're right," I said, "I'm just really tired."

Then Beloved Husband straightened up and squared his shoulders. "OK! Decision made!" he said firmly. "Let's not tell the children yet," he continued after a moment. "There's no need to upset them unnecessarily. Who knows, we might find a way to keep the house but, if we don't, we can be happy in another one. As long as we're all together, nothing else matters."

He was right, of course, but it didn't really make me feel any better about it. Grabbing my hand, he gave it a little reassuring tug and we started back towards the house feeling lighter for having reached a decision on how to handle things.

16: Jamboree

Definition: a large gathering, or a noisy boisterous celebration.

Back in the present…

The weekend following my first encounter with the Women's Institute was a busy one. Due to the significant distances involved, not to mention the cost and basic travel times courtesy of British Rail's little foibles, visits home from university during term time were a rarity. However, this particular weekend Chaos and Logic had both managed to plan a trip home to coincide with each other, so I was in anticipatory heaven. I couldn't wait to get all my chickens back under one roof, even though it would only be for two days. Their train journeys even overlapped for the final connection to the nearby town, which meant I could pick them both up from the local station at the same time, which was useful.

I had been looking forward to the six of us being back together again so very much, but I have to confess that I hadn't calculated on quite how much dirty washing would be descending on the house at the same time, as both girls staggered off the train with a hefty rucksack and a wheeled suitcase each, stuffed to bursting point with rancid raiment.

Fortunately, I reasoned, in between cups of tea and gossiping nineteen to the dozen, that they had both become fairly self-sufficient as students and were quite capable of feeding the washing machine themselves. It wasn't long before the kitchen was full of happy chattering and bursts of loud laughter as the girls sorted through their light and dark loads. They were so grateful not to be stuck in some university launderette unable to leave the machine in case the cycle ended early and some other student emptied their clean washing onto the floor.

Knowing my daughters as I do, and hopeful that they might fill the freezer with some goodies for me, I had made sure to stock up on a good selection of potential savoury and sweet baking ingredients. As a result, it wasn't long before normal service had been resumed. The oven and radio were switched on almost the minute we arrived home from the station and soon the aroma of fresh pasties, sausage rolls, sticky cakes and fresh cookies filled the air.

I watched Quiet with interest as he chatted casually away to Chaos, whilst carefully positioning himself in the most likely location to be able to snaffle hot sausage rolls as she unloaded the first trays from the oven. Small had cunningly persuaded Logic to let him help roll out the cookie mixture, so that he could take sneaky tasters of the raw dough when she wasn't looking. I think the boys had missed their sisters, although they wouldn't ever admit it of course.

Logic had brought home some organic maple syrup from the helpful hippy's highly-recommended health food shop and was working on some alternative recipes that had a lower refined sugar content. Chaos had come supplied with a special type of cleansing green tea that she had researched for me on the internet.

It was lovely to hear my four Barbarians chatting away to each other, teasing and laughing and keen to share their news, so as soon as I was handed an acceptably non-stimulating hot drink and some fresh maple, oat and cranberry (surprisingly tasty) cookies, I snuck off to do some painting, content to have my Barbarians all home again. The house felt right. It was full, even if it was only for a couple of days, so I was happy.

In that moment, it occurred to me that the nourishment supplied from home baking is not so much to do with the end product, but with the process itself. The rich aromas of butter, flour and savoury or sweet mixes warming the air during their transformation from base ingredients to enchanting delicacy, speak so much of love and care that they create an indefinable feeling of security and companionship. It's about family, friends and sharing, which is something you don't get to quite the same degree from shop-bought equivalents. One homemade shortbread is infinitely more fulfilling than anything you can buy off the shelf because it is part of something so much more significant.

I began to realise why all those shop-bought treats had not been able to fill the huge void inside me. It was as if I had been trying to fill in a deep, dark well of emptiness using tiny pebbles, so no wonder I had eaten entire packets with no discernible results. It wasn't actually the sugar I was craving, it was the whole magical phenomenon of sharing, caring and belonging.

***

It doesn't take much to have a bit of an impromptu party when you are part of a big family. Just getting together creates a crowd. Listening to the noise of music and happy chitchat filtering into my studio from the kitchen, I knew we were all going to have a fantastic weekend together.

I hauled out the colourful rainbow canvas I had hidden from Quiet previously and checked it over. It was one of a whole series of rainbow related paintings, the detail and complexity of which had increased significantly with each piece as my dexterity improved. It wouldn't take much to finish this one off. I smiled to myself, I knew he was only teasing me when he grumbled but, if he really didn't approve of rainbows, he definitely wouldn't be very impressed with the paintings I was planning to do next. I had every intention of using glitter, unicorns and everything else besides. It was time to have some fun!

For some reason I had spent the previous few weeks obsessed with images of feathers. In fact, everywhere I turned it seemed a feather would appear. I had quite a collection of them now on windowsills and various shelves around the house. While I frequently found myself uncertain over the concept of the existence of a higher being, I did sometimes wonder about guardian angels.

It struck me that our traumatic home collapse ordeal could be looked at two ways. Obviously, on the surface of things, it was tragic and very upsetting, but I felt it was important to remember that a great deal of good had happened too. Those positive elements led me to suspect that someone had definitely been watching over us during the awful time that we lived in the garden, not knowing how we would manage to stay together and fix our home.

For example, that first day when the cottage walls actually gave way out of the blue, several massively important things should be remembered. Firstly, there was no one inside the house to be hurt or killed by flying debris and falling masonry. Had the walls fallen at 2am not 2pm, then there was every chance that we could all have been killed. A very sobering thought indeed! But they didn't and we weren't! Secondly, builders had appeared, completely unexpectedly, to pick up some equipment that they had left behind months before. They had been able to start attempting to stabilise the disintegrating structure almost immediately and the damage to the cottage was prevented from being so very much worse.

Then, weeks later, just as Beloved Husband and I were facing the fact that we would have to split up the children and send them away indefinitely, the house insurance company suddenly changed tack and agreed to supply us with a caravan so we could stay together.

In the years that have followed, all the issues arising from the rebuild have each been solved one by one, to the point that the house is now absolutely perfect. The sole remaining issue, the overwhelming debt arising from the work, would eventually be solved with the sale of the property.

In that vein, the personal health issues I had been experiencing could be overcome too. I was very lucky that it wasn't anything more serious and was already making good progress. With the help and support of the rest of the family, I had every confidence that we would beat this difficulty too. None of us could expect not to be affected by what had happened but we could take every step available to help ourselves to recover, thus limiting the hold that past events could have over us.

I was beginning to see that this was merely the next stage in our journey; just one step in a whole series of steps that we were taking in order to climb back up from rock bottom. It was definitely time to move forward. We would be fine. So, I reached for a fresh canvas and, whether Quiet approved or not, I was planning a painting with my feathers as a tribute to our Guardian Angel whoever and wherever he or she might be.

***

A couple of hours later Chaos came into the studio.

"Wow!" she said. "Quiet said you were painting what he called 'fluffy stuff'. I didn't realise he meant actual feathers but they look really good. Simple but powerful! Kind of spiritual!"

I looked at her closely to check she wasn't taking the mickey out of her old mum and realised that she was serious.

"Anyway, Logic wants you in the kitchen to try a new sort of cake out. She says the sugar content is quite low but, between you and me, I can't tell the difference."

"Oh OK!" I said, "I need to clean these brushes off anyway." I may have sounded less than keen but it was all a front, of course, because I was more than happy to try any sort of cake on any sort of occasion, low sugar or not. I headed for the kitchen but realised I had forgotten to bring my palette knife with me to wash too. Turning back into the studio, I caught Chaos taking a photo of my feather painting on her phone.

She stopped when she saw me and looked guilty.

"What are you doing?" I asked curiously.

"Sorry, I should have asked first. Do you mind if I take a photo? I really like it," she said.

"No of course I don't, take as many as you like." I grabbed my knife and headed in the direction of the cake, assuming that she would follow me, but she stayed in the studio quite a while before re-joining us.

***

A little later that evening, we all enjoyed a proper family supper, one that involved all six chairs around the expanded dining table for once. There was a great deal of joking and teasing banter. I had cooked everyone's favourite, lasagne with salad and garlic bread. We rounded off the meal by each having a generous slice from a freshly baked, lemon drizzle cake that sat on a large plate in the middle of the table surrounded by big, fat, juicy strawberries.

Eventually, as Small was working his way through his second slice of cake, Chaos looked at Logic and raised a questioning eyebrow. Logic nodded. Turning towards Beloved Husband and me, Chaos shoved her empty cake plate aside, folded her arms on the table and leaned towards us saying, "We noticed the 'For Sale' sign outside."

Beloved Husband and I exchanged a look and he said, "Yes, it is rather obvious isn't it? It's been up a couple of weeks."

"Yeah, we know," said Logic. "Quiet sent us a photo the day it went up. So, what's going on?"

The reason for this joint visit home suddenly became clear. Other than getting their washing done, I mean. It seemed that the Barbarians were staging some sort of intervention.

'This should be interesting,' I thought to myself, with a smile.

Small surreptitiously helped himself to a third slice of lemon cake elbowing his brother sharply for no reason whatsoever while he did it. Quiet grinned briefly and shoved him back hard, before looking down at his iPod and behaving as if he was totally deaf or on a different planet or possibly both. Beloved Husband reached over and neatly plucked the iPod out of Quiet's hand, putting it face down on the table in front of him.

"We did explain to both your brothers why we were going to put the house on the market, and we were planning on telling you as soon as you came back." As I listened to Beloved Husband speak, I kept my eyes down and examined the paint stains on my sleeve closely. I didn't feel I could look at the girls. I was really worried how they were going to take the news.

"Well! Here we are!" Chaos continued. "So, tell us what's going on."

"Ok, your mother and I always knew that there was a risk we might have to sell the house after the rebuild was complete because of the escalating costs that weren't covered by the house insurance policy. We didn't tell you because we were hoping that it might not be necessary. We've managed so far, and we could technically keep going if we have to, but it would take the pressure off us massively if we could sell up and move to something a bit more economical. So, we thought we would put the place on the market and see what happened."

"That makes a lot of sense," said Logic. "It's an absolutely beautiful house now the work is all finished. We should get a really good price for it."

"I can't see there being any trouble getting a buyer," agreed Chaos. "Selling's a really good idea. Would it mean you could both take a bit of time off?"

"What do you mean?" asked Beloved Husband.

"She means we know that you're always working so hard trying to pay off the additional mortgage. If we sell the house and move somewhere more economical, will you both be able to work a bit less? So that we can see more of you?" asked Logic bluntly.

I looked up hopefully at the liberal sprinkling of the word 'we' in both of their responses. Obviously both girls were thinking of moving with us. This was a good sign.

"Yes!" confirmed the love of my life. "Your mother and I should both be able to relax a bit more if things go to plan."

"Well why on earth haven't you done it before now?" exclaimed Chaos. "It's quite clear that Mum isn't well, she's been self-medicating with caffeine and rubbish sugar products for far too long, and I bet you aren't much better. You have both been under too much pressure for too long. The human body isn't designed to cope with that. If there is a way out then you should take it. We all agree." She said this with a defiant confidence that hinted at lengthy chats with her siblings on this very subject.

"It's been well over a year since the rebuild was completed." Logic chimed in. "For goodness' sake, why have you waited until now to put the house on the market? There's no point in you grinding yourselves into the ground if there's an alternative."

Quiet shrugged, "It's a no brainer, Dad!"

Small nodded and said "Yuhpm!" emphatically, unintentionally punctuating his comment by spitting a few stray crumbs out of his bulging mouth. My subconscious mind vaguely noted that, somehow, the large, decorative serving plate that contained the remaining section of lemon drizzle cake had mysteriously moved so that it now sat squarely in front of my youngest child.

Beloved Husband turned to me with his blue eyes twinkling and smiled, asking, "Are you listening to them?"

"What do you mean?" asked Logic.

"Your mother has been worried that if we sell up it will break the ties that you girls have with your home. She's afraid that you won't want to come back if we move now that you've left home for university. That's why we've hung on for so long."

"You daft woman!" exclaimed Chaos with her usual delicacy, looking directly at me with her eyebrows raised.

"Yes. Where on earth did that come from, Mum?" asked Logic.

"This is your home," I said, "it's where you grew up!"

"Yes, it is," confirmed Chaos "and it's been really lovely growing up here, wobbly walls and all. But it's people that count, Mum, not bricks and mortar. If there's one thing the whole crumbly cottage thing taught us it's that! Just because we move somewhere different, this family isn't going to fall apart. We'll still be us, just in a different house somewhere else. I know we're at uni now, and after that there'll be the potential for jobs and stuff so who knows where we'll have to go for those, but we'll still come home. You're not going to get rid of us that easily, you know. The vast majority of students move back home after college anyway. You do realise that, don't you?"

"Come on, Mum," said Logic, "you've always told us that our strength comes from family. If the last few years haven't proved that to us then nothing will. House move, or no house move!"

Quiet cleared his throat and everyone looked at him, sensing that one of his carefully thought out and meaningful statements was imminent. Then in his lovely, deep voice he said slowly, "If we can live in a tent and a caravan together for over a year then I am pretty sure moving house will be a doddle!"

"MmmmHmm!" agreed Small, chewing hard while dabbing his finger around the large (now empty) serving plate to make sure he hadn't missed any escaped cake crumbs.

"This is a gorgeous house, Mum, but it's probably time for us to give it to someone else to enjoy; perhaps a family with little kids. They'll have a fab time growing up here, just like we did but without the wobbly bit at the end. It's like magic here with the forest and the coast nearby. All the open space and fresh air. We've been so lucky."

I was quietly stunned. I had thought that they would just have bad memories. That all the good ones of the early years would be overshadowed by what had happened more recently, but it seemed that this was not the case. I am constantly amazed by the incredible resilience of youth! What amazing young people they are. It made me think that they could cope with anything life throws at them.

"Don't forget, Mum," said Chaos, "we uni students are urban dwellers now. This is an opportunity for you to consider moving back towards civilisation. It's pretty amazing! There are all sorts of sophisticated things in the city, like street lights, pavements, mains drainage, gas pipes, public transport and night clubs."

"I'm not sure the parents will be too excited about night clubs, Chaos!" said her sister, grinning at her.

"Ok, maybe not night clubs, but you know what I mean," Chaos laughed. "This could be the start of a whole new adventure. But whatever we buy and wherever we buy it, I suggest we avoid 350-year-old cob cottages. Ok?"

"Yeah!" they all chorused loudly, and fell about laughing. Quiet had to quickly start bashing Small firmly between the shoulder blades because chuckling so hard had made him choke on his last mouthful of cake.

As Beloved Husband and I listened to the mayhem around us, he smiled at me and nudged my foot under the table in a 'I told you so' kind of way. Grinning slowly back at him, I could feel something tight and knotted, way down deep inside myself, suddenly start to unravel and float free. I should have trusted my beloved Barbarians more. It seemed they had no problems with the idea of moving onto the next stage in our lives together.

17: Ramification

Definition: a consequence that directly relates to an earlier decision

Returning to the past and the on-going rebuild project...

As is often the case if you look closely at many disastrous situations, you can usually find some sort of silver lining. Even if sometimes you have to look really, really hard.

The decision to take out the entire cob component of the house, while sadly, massively increasing the cost, had the beneficial effect of simplifying the job significantly in some very practical respects. There was now no possibility of salvaging the damaged floors and ceilings as these would need to be removed entirely. This would give us the opportunity to increase the ceiling heights of the downstairs rooms, which in their original incarnation had been quite low even before the walls had started to crumble.

Thor was able to set to on Monday morning and swing his adored sledgehammer to his heart's content, smashing and bashing at the ancient lathe and plaster partitions, and wooden joists that divided up the internal space in the old cottage. He had a significantly less conservative approach to demolition than the other two builders. The main premise of his method seemed to involve randomly whacking things with all his might until they disappeared.

Destructive and very probably dangerous, he was nevertheless surprisingly effective and made short work of his clearance brief.

The roof was basically supported on three sides at this juncture as the new gable wall had set firmly by now and the undamaged second gable and back walls were still in situ. It was only the front wall that had stability issues and the builders wanted to use this time to install huge, industrial, ground to loft joist props to hold the roof more efficiently, while the other three walls were to be systematically stripped out and rebuilt over modern foundations. This would be done one at a time in the same way that the new gable had been completed.

Skelly and I spent quite a lot of time watching this process over the coming weeks, as February trundled on towards March.

Unfortunately, as February left so did Jack Frost. The beautifully crisp, fresh, cold weather was suddenly a thing of the past. You would think that we would be relieved that the true chill of winter was on its way out, but it proved to be more of an 'out of the frying pan into the fire' sort of a situation. The rain arrived with a vengeance in the first days of March and we began to realise how lucky we had been up until that point.

Hammering down in sheets with the wind adding force to the impact, the rainstorm started and simply didn't stop. A few days into the wet weather I noted that Skelly had acquired a golfing umbrella from somewhere, but Beloved Husband and the Barbarians denied all responsibility for its appearance.

The lads were working on the front of the house at this stage, having once again gone through the process of bringing down the damaged cob in careful sections.

Thank goodness for the thick plastic sheeting, that had been suspended from the roof plate to protect the walls four months previously, as the building team were able to pin the lower sections of these sheets away from the wall that was being dismantled to act as a kind of tent which enabled them to keep working, as it kept the worst of the water off them.

Once the removal of the old wall was complete, the builders must have been absolutely frozen digging the foundations for the new wall whilst standing knee deep in icy cold water. Surprisingly this didn't seem to bother them. They just turned the radio up and kept singing. I was amazed that they didn't develop trench-foot but they were an impressively hardy bunch. I suppose it probably helped that they got to go home at the end of the day to nice warm houses to dry off and thaw out.

That was a luxury that unfortunately eluded us

With all that rain, came an invasion of mould.

It wasn't too bad in the house because we kept the fire going almost permanently and the space was quite well ventilated (there was a wall missing after all). Nevertheless, in the caravan I quickly noticed the steady creep of black fungus on both windows and walls which proved virtually impossible to keep at bay.

Unfortunately, the built-in heating in the caravan didn't work at all. A friend had kindly lent us two portable oil storage radiators, the type that you plug into the mains electricity sockets. These operated independently via an internal thermostat and were quite effective at taking the chill off the air in the caravan.

However, each trip to the house and back in the never-ending rain brought water inside the caravan on coats, shoes and umbrellas which increased the damp atmosphere and eventually generated more and more condensation. Opening the window wasn't an option due to the weather, so it was a constant battle to wipe moisture from windows and walls on a daily basis in the hope that it would halt the pervasive progression of the insidious rot.

During that soggy spell we spent as much time in the house as possible, staying in the lounge area as late as we could in the evening before making a dash for the caravan in between the heaviest bursts of rain.

One evening I paused in the middle of clearing up the supper things in the kitchen and just watched my beloved Barbarians. Chaos was on her laptop, totally engrossed in whatever it was that she was typing so frantically (one of her books as it turned out), while nodding away to her music through her headphones. Logic was knitting something blue and fluffy and casting absent glances towards whatever Small was watching on TV. Quiet was engrossed in some sort of Snapchat/Messenger conversation with his school mates. All four were encased in thick fleece blankets on the sofas and the open fire was roaring away, creating a cosy warm bubble.

I smiled at the scene they created, just as a small movement caught my eye. Adjusting my glasses and focussing hard on the carpet to the left of the fireplace. I could hardly believe my eyes. There, in plain sight next to the log basket, were three little field mice basking in the flickering glow from the flames.

The cat was comfortably ensconced on the coffee table and gave me a measured look as if to say, "I wouldn't bother if I were you." It was quite plain that she'd already spotted the encroaching wildlife and had no plans to do anything about them.

I sighed heavily. The mice were getting very brazen about sharing our living space now that it was so wet outside, but there was no way to stop them unfortunately. I had tried the humane mouse catchers but no matter how often I emptied the entrapped occupants out in the field next door they were often back in the house before I was. I absolutely refused to set real traps. Alive mice were bad enough but dead ones? No thank you!

I comforted myself with the knowledge that the caravan was wildlife-free, and at least we didn't have rats. Once the house was completely rebuilt it wouldn't be hard to evict all the additional, unwanted guests. They were only mice after all and they tended to stick to the warm hearth area, not venturing into the kitchen much at all. They probably knew better than to push their luck!

Nevertheless, everything about our life at that point was made so much harder by the wet weather. For example, changing the bedding in the caravan involved a massive effort on a weekly basis. (My one concession to luxury of any sort during those months had been to send the bedding out to the laundry to be washed and, more importantly, properly dried as it was simply impossible to achieve this anywhere in the house or caravan.)

While the beds themselves were actually quite small, the caravan rooms were equally tiny, which made the manoeuvres necessary to actually change the bed sheets very difficult, if not almost impossible.

In the case of Logic's bed (which, if you remember, was little more than a small double mattress crow-barred into a cupboard of similar dimensions), I had to scramble into the space by climbing on top of the mattress and then try to change it a section at a time whilst trying not to get in my own way. This involved peeling a bit of mattress away from the wall, hooking the sheet over it somehow and then letting both flop back into place against the wall again. It was rather like wrestling with an octopus. (Not that I have ever done that, of course.) The other beds weren't much better. There just wasn't enough room to move. I suppose it did give me a good work out though, as I always needed a sit down and a strong cup of tea after the job was done.

It wasn't long though before I noticed that sheets, duvets and pillows were starting to speckle with mildew when I did the weekly change and I knew that it was definitely not good for the Barbarians' health to be sleeping in such damp conditions. All we needed at that point, to really finish us off, was someone to get ill. In fact, I was surprised to note that, so far, we seemed to have escaped the worst of the winter bugs that were floating around that year, which was a small mercy but a very welcome one.

Just as I was formulating a plan to avoid the mould by moving us all back into the lounge to sleep on the floor by the open fire in the house, as we had done before the caravan had arrived, the wet weather finally broke. The sledging rainstorms that were arriving with relentlessly regularity, one after another, suddenly stopped. It was as if someone had finally remembered to turn off a gushing tap and then the sun came out, bright, warm and so very beautiful. What a transformation it was.

At last, April had arrived, as had what was to be the warmest Easter on record for many years. If someone was watching over us they had obviously realised that we needed a break.

Everybody's spirits started to lift just a little bit higher with each day of sunshine that followed. The girls' A and AS level exam revision could now take place out on the patio, on loungers in bright beaming sunshine. At the same time the boy Barbarians could resume their lifelong quest to cause benevolent, physical damage to each other via spectacular rugby and football related tackles outside, where I didn't have to watch them while they did it. I was also grateful to note the trio of friendly field mice sneaking out of the open patio doors and heading back into the wild.

Meanwhile the builders could dry their boots off and shed their many layers of ratty jumpers. Skelly put away his brolly and acquired a pair of shades, while the repair job at the front of the house progressed ever onwards.

The extraction of the cob was a very painful thing to watch, especially once the team had moved onto the two undamaged walls. Beloved Husband and I had fallen in love with this little cottage precisely because of the beautiful mix of over three centuries of history that she represented. I felt like such a failure that the original seventeenth century walls were being removed on our watch. It seemed somehow sacrilegious to be dismantling something that had stood for so long. Yet what choice did we have?

It became obvious that the people who had built her all those years ago had used pretty much anything that came their way in the creation of those old walls. Lofty and Shy Guy, who continued with their carefully systematic carving up of the cob into manageable chunks with the pneumatic drill, frequently presented me with their finds. A chipped pottery jug, some blunt and useless, abandoned tools and a broken, wooden broom handle were all found entombed within the cob as it came apart. Shy Guy took great delight in each new discovery and spent so much time carefully extracting them that he could have been auditioning for a part on Time Team.

It was such a shame we didn't come across a chest of lost jewels or other such valuable hidden treasure that might cover some of the cost of the bills to come, but never mind. Such a discovery would no doubt slow things down and cause complications anyway. The last thing we needed was to have a visit from the County Archaeologist forced on us by the Council to delay things, especially if we were then made to donate any such discovery to the British Museum rather than auction it off to the highest bidder. Yes, I am not ashamed to admit to a few mercenary tendencies! I am only human, after all!

With the advent of the lovely dry, sunny weather, it wasn't long before the main structure of the new front wall was in place and ready to take a share of the weight of the roof while the second gable wall was taken down. This gable consisted of a massive inglenook fireplace and the associated chimney breast with its ancient foot and hand holds that stretched right up inside.

Work on this wall had to take place on the inside of the cottage as the other side of the second cob gable wall was yet another small, single story extension. This structure, like the back section of the house that was now part of the kitchen, had been built in the 1900's. We were hoping that, like the back section, it had been built independently too, with a small gap between the two structures meaning that the cob could be removed without causing any problems.

I found it absolutely heart-breaking to watch this part of the cob being taken apart, as the large, inglenook fireplace was my absolute favourite feature of the whole house. Nevertheless, as it came down it was to reveal a hidden secret.

As Lofty and Shy Guy were systematically cutting up this section of cob, there was a thunderous crash followed by sudden shouts of fear and the two of them came haring out of the cottage as if Beelzebub and all the hounds of Hell were chasing them.

Startled, I leapt up from my spot in the sunshine on the bench next to Skelly and ran towards them. "What is it?" I asked.

Both were panting heavily and wide eyed with shock. Lofty pointed back towards the house and said "It's huge! I only had seconds to recognise what it was. I've seen one before but never that big… and then we just ran, but none of them…. well…..I don't think any of them are alive… its…horrible…" he tailed off with a shudder, bending over and putting his hands on his knees as he tried to slow his breathing.

Thor and I looked at each other intrigued. How interesting! Had we stumbled across some dead bodies? Please don't tell me there had been a murder and we needed to call the Coroner! Not wanting to sound unsympathetic here, of course, but that really would chuck a spanner in the works and delay things massively.

All the noise and yelling had alerted the Barbarians to a potential disaster and soon Logic was sprinting round from the back of the house armed with a first aid kit, although what use she thought it would be if any of our builders had actually been crushed to death I wasn't too sure. I admired her optimism that an antibacterial wipe, a few sticky plasters and a sling might be all we needed.

Chaos followed in her wake, very sensibly clutching a mobile phone (presumably in case we needed to call an ambulance) and an ice pack. Even the boys had peeled themselves away from the PlayStation and wandered round to see what the kerfuffle was all about.

Anyway, back to the dead bodies…

Gesturing for the Barbarians to stay well back I moved cautiously towards the house and peered through the gap where the door would eventually go and looked at what was left of the old fireplace.

Wow!

It took me a few moments to work out what it was that I was looking at, but when we did… well! Forget the Coroner! I rather thought we ought to be ringing David Attenborough!

Behind the chimney breast, between the old cob and the wall of the 1900's extension, there was approximately a five centimetre gap from ground to roof. A large section of cob had fallen away, which had revealed an enormous wasps' nest filling the entirety of this gap. It was absolutely huge!

No doubt it had proven to be a fabulously warm and protected location behind the almost constantly operational fireplace. Lofty and Shy Guy had been quite right to run. Had this been an active nest they would no doubt have been on the receiving end of a mammoth angry swarm. No wonder they looked alarmed. My little bottle of Piriton wouldn't have been much help against a million or more wasp stings.

Fortunately for us all, this nest was an abandoned one, apart from a few desiccated corpses. Even so, it was unexpectedly beautiful close up, if a bit creepy. A most impressive structure indeed, but I am glad I hadn't known it was there in all the years we had lived in the cottage. Ignorance is bliss in these circumstances, I feel.

Given the shaky state of two of my poor builders, we rather felt it was time for some tea and biscuits. Logic took the (thankfully not needed) first aid kit back to the kitchen and filled the kettle. I didn't really think that any of the builders should be back in charge of the pneumatic drill until they had calmed down. So Lofty and Shy Guy sat down next to Skelly on the bench to wait for refreshments whilst Thor went back to what was left of the inglenook fireplace to do what he does best. He bashed and smashed about with his sledgehammer removing all traces of the wasps' nest so that his comrades could carry on with their demolition job when they were ready. After a restorative cup of tea and large plate of chocolate cookies, they both felt much better and the rest of the wall came down with no further drama.

For now, anyway…

18: Perseverance

Definition: the determination to keep doing something even though it proves hard or difficult. Not giving up in the face of failure.

Returning to the present day …

A few days after the girls had returned to their temporary university homes, I was thinking about my unplanned Taekwondo taster session and then my enjoyable evening with the local WI ladies. It occurred to me that I had experienced several more good nights' sleep in a row. It was getting quite addictive, this restful sleep lark, I rather enjoyed it. I found myself completing my daily fine motor skills exercises with a smile on my face. The radio warbled away to itself in the corner and I occasionally sipped at my hot water and lemon juice without noticing the absence of caffeine. Important progress, I felt, added to which I was pleased to see some not insignificant improvement in my fine brush control.

In view of how much fun my unexpected introduction to martial arts had been, I had decided not to do Quiet any actual bodily harm. He had unwittingly done me a favour, but I wasn't going to give him too much credit for it because he would never let me forget it. Even so, I had decided to go to the junior Taekwondo session later on that week.

To my surprise, Beloved Husband was not keen on my choice of preferred exercise class and kept suggesting alternatives. It would seem that he was ok with the idea of a wife who does yoga but not so much ok with one who does martial arts. An interesting position, but not one I planned to pay any attention to.

Once we had firmly established that I was going to go back to Taekwondo whether he liked it or not, he decided to come with me, saying that he was worried I might get hurt. I think it is possible that he had clocked just how many fit (yes, I do mean *that* sort of 'fit' this time) fellas there were at the class and felt a teeny, tiny bit insecure. Although it is probably more likely that he merely liked the idea of a couple of pints in the bar afterwards! Either way, I was pleased he was coming too. It would be fun to do something together.

Spurred on by their father's resolution, or possibly the thought of being allowed to legitimately kick each other in public without being told off, both boys declared an interest too, so there were going to be quite a few more novices in the junior class that week. I smiled, looking forward to it, which in itself was a measure of how significantly less anxious I was.

Why wasn't I worrying about the boys getting injured? Or even my Beloved Husband?

Maybe I was finally getting the hang of chilling out.

In the meantime, there had been a couple of telephone calls for me but I had missed them. Quiet had taken messages for me and muttered something about exhibitions. He had scribbled a telephone number and a name down on the back of an old envelope. He kept nagging me to call the lady back, but I never seemed to have the time. He was right though, but don't tell him I said so, it was time to sell some of my used canvas collection. I just wasn't sure that I wanted to get back into the world of exhibiting. So much effort went into each show, but I wasn't entirely sure that it was worth it.

Nevertheless, there was no doubt that if I agreed to do an exhibition it would cheer Beloved Husband up no end because he could have one or two of his sheds back. It would also stop Quiet making sly little digs about my fish painting 'obsession'. Philistine!

I heard the clang of the letterbox, signalling that the postman had been. Today was obviously one of the random two days a week that we were a scheduled part of his route. You don't get post every day when you live at the back of beyond. That was something that would change if we successfully sold the house and returned to civilisation.

I shoved that whole exhibition issue from my mind and went to pick up the sealed and stamped envelopes that now littered the floor just inside the front door, spotting immediately that there was an intriguing little parcel for me. Smiling contentedly to myself, I ambled into the kitchen and tore open my package to find that Logic had sent me a little plastic bag containing a muslin pouch full of what looked like very suspicious herbs. Hmmm!?!

My heart flipped over as my brain immediately leapt to entirely the wrong conclusion! Please don't tell me my smart mathematician daughter had fallen into the wrong crowd and started experimenting with dodgy substances? She's only been a student five minutes! (OK, six months to be exact, so plenty of time really.) More to the point, why on earth was she sending this stuff to me? I know we are lucky enough to have a very close mother-daughter relationship, but she must realise that sending me illegal drugs through the post was pushing the boundaries a bit surely? Not to mention quite risky. I know how nosy people can get in the queue for the village Post Office now that you have to say exactly what's in your parcel at the counter. Admittedly, I'm as bad as anyone else, you just can't help earwigging when you're standing waiting in line. Every time I want to send a package now, and I have to declare what's in it, I am tempted to make up something outrageous just to entertain the person behind me; but I don't think it would ever occur to me to suggest I might be posting marijuana. Hmmm!

Quickly scanning the little note included with a card from Logic tucked inside the parcel, I soon gave a sigh of relief. Apparently, the little muslin twist was a type of herbal tea bag, a gift from her friend the Hippy down the hall. Now, I appreciate that this doesn't completely rule out suspicious substances but, from what Logic has told me about this new friend, she is a vegan and treats her body like a temple. Something I should really consider doing one day when I have the time. Not that I could ever be bothered with all that faddy 'clean eating' the newspapers have been banging on about, which is just as well because they seem to have backtracked lately and are now saying it's not good for you at all. I am glad I didn't waste my time.

Logic wrote that when she had told her friend that I was trying to go completely caffeine-free but hated herbal teas, the Helpful Hippy had insisted that I was obviously drinking the wrong type and was no doubt making it the wrong way too. The little note she had enclosed was a detailed list of written instructions from the Hippy on just how to make a good cup of herbal tea. By the time the kettle had boiled, I had educated myself appropriately and made my first cup of surprisingly pleasant-smelling blackcurrant and vanilla herbal tea. Perhaps she might be right after all.

Unfortunately, the Hippy ended her missive with the advice that if I really wanted to go caffeine-free, I was going to have to give up chocolate completely and kindly suggested several alternatives that were available from most health food shops.

Like that was ever going to happen! Anyway, I was starting to feel better already so there was no need to go completely overboard.

While I drank my herbal tea, I rattled off an email to Logic to thank her friend for the tea bag and the advice and, mentally crossing my fingers behind my back, I promised I would think about giving up chocolate. Then, tea break over, I headed upstairs to change the beds.

Part 5

Every new beginning comes from some other beginning's end.

Seneca
54 AD

19: Resurgence

Definition: a significant increase in activity after a period of reduced action.

Back to the crumbly cottage and a disgustingly early morning in the past…

I rubbed my eyes and stared at the wall of green boxes in front of me. I seriously hadn't had enough sleep for this.

I couldn't really blame Beloved Husband for the fact that we had woken up ridiculously early again. Now that the weather was improving and the mornings were getting lighter earlier, the dawn chorus was starting to crank up in the really small hours again and the dance routine of the sprightly sparrows on the metal caravan roof was getting more adventurous. You would think that we would have become accustomed to the noise by now, but the random nature of the scratchy, hoppity skips and jumps proved impossible to tune out. Not so for the Barbarians it would seem, as they usually managed to slumber on determinedly until lunchtime, given half a chance.

Nevertheless, I could (and did) blame Beloved Husband for dragging me out of bed and off to a garden centre on the first Saturday morning that it wasn't teaming down with rain. Seriously, I didn't even know they opened this early. I could have been having a nice, cosy lie in with a cup of tea and a book, yet here I was looking at …. well…. surely not? I rubbed my eyes yet again and scrutinised the shelving unit before me in disbelief.

Then I gave Beloved Husband what can only be described as a 'speaking look'. It was saying quite a lot to him, along the lines of: 'Are you seriously asking me what type of grass seed to buy?' Among other less polite things, if you get my drift.

Obviously, as a method of communication, this look was fairly effective because he gave a sheepish grin, shrugged, grabbed the nearest box and said, "OK, fair enough, I'll just get this one then....or maybe...um..." Looking at me again, he hastily exchanged his selection for another almost identical box, and declared, "This is the one we need. It's perfect!" At last! He had chosen a huge box of grass seed from the wall of indistinguishable alternatives and then we set off for the plant department.

Now it should be noted here that I don't *do* gardens. Don't get me wrong, I like them, but I don't *garden* if I can help it. Fortunately, Beloved Husband does and it was rather nice to see him so cheerful after the last few months of doom and gloom. Now that the sun had returned he was no longer obsessing about the building site at the front of our house because he could focus on the wilderness at the back. Admittedly it was getting a touch untidy. The emergent growth of the new spring would soon over run us if he didn't exert a little control, but I loved the bright succession of natural beauty that was unfolding with the new season. It began with snowdrops and was rapidly followed by daffodils, bluebells, buttercups and daisies; a promise of the coming summer which filled me with so much hope. Although I did have a little sympathy for Beloved Husband as I could see he was itching to get going with lawn mower and hedge trimmer.

This morning's little trip was to find grass seed to repair the huge tracts of damaged lawn in the back garden created during the installation of the static caravan the previous September. He hadn't had the heart to do anything about the damage at the time which just goes to show how devastated he was by the whole house falling down fiasco. So, it was nice to see a bit more of a spring in his step. (No seasonal pun intended!) Although I personally felt we should leave the damaged area well alone because the caravan was going to have to go back out the way it came in, eventually. No doubt causing just as much damage as it passed. I didn't mention that though, I didn't want to think just how long it would be until that might happen. If Beloved Husband wanted to plant grass seed, then grass seed he could plant. Who was I to get in his way?

It has become quite apparent over the last 21 years that my Beloved Husband and I have wildly different approaches to the garden. He usually launches himself enthusiastically into the great outdoors intending to assert his dominance over nature, with the help of various petrol driven implements such as the chain saw and the leaf blower. It's an obsession; there's always some new device that needs road-testing, although he hasn't bought a ride-on lawn mower yet, much to my surprise.

I, on the other hand, always enter the garden with the sole purpose of sitting down, preferably with a cup of tea and a jolly good book! So, I am not really sure why he seemed to think I even wanted to go to the garden centre with him that morning. But there I was and, having selected the chosen grass seed, we were apparently then off to buy some sort of flowering stuff.

Later that day, it became patently obvious to me that the cup of tea/book option still wasn't on the agenda. As I was approaching my favourite rattan patio chair, Beloved Husband waltzed past purposefully on his way to select his weapon of choice from the garage. Pausing dramatically, he nodded disdainfully at the patio planters and suggested in a polite but firm voice that I might like to 'do' something about them.

Hmmmmm!!!! Really?? Would I?

Let me think......

'Nope, not really' was the immediate response that sprang to mind, but I could tell from the expression on his face that such a retort wasn't going to be received terribly well. So, for a quiet life, I rolled up my sleeves and got stuck in. It's amazing what you can achieve in a short period of time when you really put your mind to it. I made quick work of dealing with the dismal-looking and very dead whatever-it-was he planted last year, and instead installed the delightfully dainty dahlias we had selected from the garden centre that morning.

When Beloved Husband returned an hour later (having beaten the early spring growth of grass into submission), the pots looked beautiful as I serenely turned the pages of my book and sipped nonchalantly from my mug of coffee. I have to confess that I had my fingers crossed that the dahlias would survive, as I had been somewhat brusque with them. I don't really have a good gardening track record. So far, the only things I've managed to nurture with any success in my life are my four Barbarians and they seem to be surviving in spite of me, not because of me. They grow like weeds, especially the boy ones. Perhaps I should plant weeds!

Narrowing his eyes suspiciously at the speed with which I had achieved my allotted task, Beloved Husband obviously came to the conclusion that letting sleeping dogs lie (or rather leaving reading wives alone to get on with it) was probably his best approach at that moment in time. He is a wise man on occasion. Shaking his head in exasperation he headed off, no doubt to find a sharp and dangerous toy to play with.

As I sat there sipping my coffee, my attention wandered from my book and I couldn't help but remember some of the fun times we'd had in this garden with the Barbarians as they had grown up. There was one particular summer when they had discovered Lara Croft and the Tomb Raider films and, as a result, Beloved Husband was over the moon. At last Disney had been banished and the Barbarians were starting to watch the sort of films he enjoyed too. Soon it would be Lethal Weapon and Die Hard!

Having watched all three Tomb Raider movies in one weekend, he and the Barbarians let their imaginations roam free as they developed their own version of the story in the back garden with loaded water pistols and holsters strapped to each thigh. In addition, a serious, homemade assault course was constructed in the garden as part of the adventure.

With hindsight, the combination of a rope swing, a tractor tyre tunnel, a wobbly balance beam, a rusty climbing frame and an overexcited nearly forty-year-old is obviously an accident waiting to happen. Fortunately, the inevitable ensuing trip to casualty, with Beloved Husband's ankle encased in frozen peas, proved to be just as entertaining for our hardy horde of Barbarians, because we were there for quite some time. Thankfully I was able to persuade them that shooting the other patients with their water pistols wouldn't be very sporting, so they just concentrated on 'poor Daddy'!

Heaven only knows what the casualty officer thought we had been up to though. I did try to brush everyone down before we went in, but when you've been fighting enemy Tomb Raiders all morning you don't generally look terribly presentable. All those commando rolls and fighting your way through hedges etc... There were streaks of mud and twigs in all sorts of random places.

Eventually we returned home with our wounded hero even though he had significant difficulty in believing that the ankle wasn't actually broken. It hurt! The x-ray must have missed something!

Having installed him on the sofa and administered a hefty dose of painkillers and some fresh cool packs, we decided to feed him a lot of ice cream to cheer him up and then watched all the films again just to make sure we hadn't missed anything important the first time around. The Barbarians and I kindly helped him to eat the ice cream while we were watching.

***

Now, while all the messing around (sorry, gardening) at the back of the house was going on, the building team at the front were making amazing progress. It wasn't long before we had four solid walls, all built to modern specifications. Only four short weeks after the sunshine arrived, so did the Easter holidays and by then we were all able to safely stand inside the front section of our home and stare in awe right up to the inside of the roof ridge.

Genuine Old Building Expert had checked the work over extremely thoroughly that morning and given us a massive 'thumbs up' with a huge smile on his face. Master Roofer had also popped by to give the roof a once over and concluded that it was still in excellent condition in spite of all the shenanigans that had gone on beneath it.

There was no longer any need for steels and props to hold the roof up. Incredible! Our new walls with their fabulous foundations were perfectly capable of doing the job themselves. We still had a long way to go, as there were no internal walls, joists or ceilings and no floor, first storey, staircase, windows, lights, heating, or front door to speak of yet, but we had walls. Progress! Yay!

No more nights lying awake worrying that there would be a colossal crash telling us that the roof had given way to gravity at last, or had even been blown clean off in the wind. We could lie awake worrying about other stuff, but not that, which was a massive load off our minds.

The Boss made one of his visits to apprise us of the next stage of the project and to warn us of the likely costs that would ensue. We had to swallow hard at the figures but had no choice other than to agree that the cottage needed a floor. We couldn't continue to live over bare earth now that we knew that it was there. Building regulations wouldn't sign the job off if we didn't put in a modern standard floor. It wasn't The Boss' fault that he had to be the bearer of bad news in the form of costings, and he obviously took no delight in it. Nevertheless, his advice was sound so we braced ourselves and agreed to the work needed for the floor.

Two days later we watched together as the building team took delivery of the dinkiest, little, hired mini digger we had ever seen. This machine was so tiny that it could be driven through the gap left in the front wall where a porch (with a front door) would eventually be built. As this new section of the house didn't have a first floor in place yet, the lads could use the digger to quickly remove the earth floor down to a suitable depth to lay a modern, insulated, damp proofed, concrete floor.

It goes without saying that everyone wanted a turn operating the little digger. Especially Small!

I came home from work later that day, after the lads had gone home, to find Skelly firmly ensconced at the controls with a crook lock jammed through both the steering wheel and his lower rib cage. Apparently Beloved Husband felt that he would act as a deterrent to stop anyone wandering down the lane from the nearby village pub and having a go on the dinky digger after closing time.

Not a bad call! I was quite tempted to have a go myself…

20: Transfiguration

Definition: a total change in form or look to a more enhanced or spiritual condition.

Let's return to the present where things are definitely looking brighter for our heroine....

Now that I was sleeping regularly, I was starting to wake up with more energy. I sometimes willingly sprang out of bed at 6am ready to get on with my day, much to Beloved Husband's utter disgust. That morning, having taken a sneaky degree of pleasure in *accidentally* waking him up even if it was only momentarily before he dropped back off to sleep, I scurried downstairs in his dressing gown (it's warmer than mine) and dived into my studio. I found I had been dreaming of the beautiful spring flowers that had grown around the caravan while we had been living in the garden, and I had awoken with a new painting planned out in my mind. I wanted to get a start on it before I had to go to work.

This was going to be quite an ambitious piece and would involve some of the new techniques I had been working on as a result of the good doctor's suggestion that I adapt the way I work. I knew exactly how I want to approach this painting because I had dreamt about the process over and over all night.

Dragging a large, square, stretched canvas out of the studio and into the kitchen, I laid it on the stone floor on top of some newspaper. I knew that I was about to annoy the entire family because what I did next was going to mean they would all have to tiptoe carefully past this wet canvas, whilst trying to find breakfast and get ready for school. However, that didn't stop me, they know what I am like and I really needed a wide flat surface that could be wiped down afterwards. The kitchen floor was perfect.

I armed myself with paint, PVA glue, a four-inch brush and loads of tissue paper. Switching on the kettle first so that a hot cup of something wasn't long away, I opened the pot of PVA and poured it all over the bottom third of the canvas, smearing it around with the big brush to get complete coverage. Scrunching up the tissue paper I then layered it over the glue base and moved it around gently. Tweaking and pushing, sometimes tearing the fragile fabric, I made what would eventually be an intentionally textured surface when the glue finally dried. Then, mixing more PVA with generous quantities of dark green acrylic paint I slathered this all over the top of the tissue paper, making sure that every single speck of canvas was covered. Just as I was standing up having completed my mission, Beloved Husband stumbled down the stairs and ground to a halt when he saw what I was up to.

"Seriously?" he asked with a rumpled grin. "This is why you bounced out of bed so early? What are you on?"

I smiled happily and leaned over the wet canvas to pass him a cup of tea before pouring hot water on my own herbal tea bag. "Well, not caffeine anymore!" I declared. "I feel great. This is going to take all day to dry before I can do the next stage, so I thought it made sense to get it done first thing. I'll be able to work on it upright in the studio after that."

"Hmmm! Of course! That makes perfect sense," he muttered, a touch sarcastically before asking, "Have you got paint on my dressing gown again?"

I quickly rolled up the cuff and smiled brightly, "No! Of course not!" It'll wash out. Hopefully.

He stepped back towards the stairs and yelled up them, "Boys! Be careful when you come into the kitchen, your mother is at it again."

There were several dramatic groans from upstairs, but I ignored them. I had just realised that I had literally painted myself into a bit of a corner and would have to go out of the conservatory doors and walk round to the front of the house in my dressing gown to come back in the front door to reach the stairs and my bedroom to get dressed for work. Oh, how I suffer for my art! Beaming cheerfully at Beloved Husband as he wrestled with the bread bin and the toaster, which were fortunately on his side of the huge wet canvas, I set off with my brush and paint pots intending to wash them out using the tap by the garage on my trip round to the front of the house.

Eventually, after depositing clean painting equipment back in my little studio, I headed up to take a quick shower when I bumped into Quiet as he came out of his bedroom stifling a yawn.

"So!" he said with a long-suffering sigh, "what are you painting this time? No! Let me guess, more...."

"Nope!" I answered triumphantly. "No fish. You'll see."

"Can't wait!" he murmured sarcastically under his breath as he stumbled down the stairs in search of a cereal fix.

***

A short while later, while on the way to work, having delivered the boy Barbarians to school, my phone sprang into life. Luckily, Beloved Husband had set up the hands-free gadget in my car for me so that I could safely answer it. If he hadn't, I would have spent the whole journey worrying which of the Barbarians had met with some catastrophic accident and needed me, but obviously not daring to pick up the phone and answer it while driving in case I caused a catastrophic accident of my own.

Luckily there was a supermarket car park just ahead where I could pull in and park up so I could concentrate. Pressing the button on the steering wheel to answer the call, I was both concerned to register Chaos' voice but simultaneously relieved to hear that she sounded fine. "Are you alright?" I asked. I was puzzled as to why she might be ringing me this early. It was only half past eight in the morning. Surely, she should either be dashing to a lecture or fast asleep like any normal student.

"Of course I am!" she replied indignantly.

"Good!" I said and waited.

There was a crackly silence.

"Was there something you wanted?" I asked eventually.

"Just checking you are OK," she said, somewhat defensively.

"Chaos!" I said sternly, "What is this about? I'm on my way to work and I am going to be late. You are going to have to be more specific!"

There was a pause and then, "I had a message from Quiet....and....well... actually he's a bit worried about you."

"Really, why?"

"He said you're painting dark stuff again."

"Yes, I was this morning," I agreed. "What's the problem?"

"He thinks he's upset you. Apparently, he said something to you about your last painting. Um...rainbows or unicorns or something? Anyway, he says he didn't mean it, he was only teasing you but now he says you're painting in really dark colours again. A big canvas. Like last time, when you were... you know..." she trailed off uncertainly.

I laughed, "Ha! He thinks he's tipped me back into a major depression with his jokey comments, doesn't he? Serves him right! He shouldn't tease his poor old mum. Text him back and tell him I'm fine. Never better in fact."

"OK, are you sure?"

"Absolutely!" I replied, "I feel fine! Don't worry about me." I didn't like to mention the minor episode of palpitations I had experienced whilst in the shower that morning. It was only a small one and passed relatively quickly. Other than that, I really did feel fine.

"That's great!" she said with enthusiasm before continuing, "and the dark canvas?"

"Don't worry, it's only a base for something. I plan to cheer it up significantly this evening if it's dry."

"OK good. Well you certainly sound much better to me. I'll tell him not to worry."

"You do that. Now I've got to get to work OK? I'd better go. Let's chat tonight."

"Sure! OK! Take care! Bye!"

The phone connection dropped off and the radio came back on as I pulled out of the car park and headed for work. I hummed cheerfully along to it as I threaded my way through the morning traffic. Ten minutes later, I neatly squeezed my little purple car into the last parking space outside the office before heading inside to pick my way through the pile of paperwork on my desk.

21: Evolution

Definition: the gradual change of something from simple to more complex.

Back at the building site in the past…

I admit it! I talk to myself. Many people would think that suggests I might be a little bit mad.

I don't know if you are the same but, as a multi-tasking mother, I often feel that no one is listening to me, and by talking to myself I am at least guaranteed one attentive audience member.

Hence, there I was one day, in the kitchen, chatting away to myself when I spotted the most enormous spider. You know, the sort with hairy legs and wearing big, black boots. Now, I am not a fan of spiders it must be said but, with the sheer number sharing our crumbly residence at that time, I had had no choice than to get used to them popping up all over the place. Rather than continue talking to myself, I often started talking to my eight-legged companions instead. Usually I was asking them politely if they minded just staying where they were and not scurrying around in that jerky, jumpy spider-like way they have.

Usually those conversations ran along the following sorts of lines:

"Oh! Hello nice Mr Spider, you gave me a shock! I didn't see you there. Tell you what, you just stay still over there where I can see you … and I'll carry on doing what I am doing over here …. and we won't have a problem……OK?"

You get the general idea I'm sure.

On that particular morning I was muttering away to Sammy, (yes, I gave them all names too – it helped make them more approachable, along with the assumption that they understood English!) when I heard a gentle cough coming from the direction of the patio doors. Taking my eyes of my amiable arachnid for a split second or two, I saw that Thor had trotted around from the building site at the front of the house with a tray of empty tea cups. From the puppy-dog look on his face, he was obviously after more caffeine. He had thoughtfully taken off his muddy boots and was shuffling across the stone floor in his (not very clean) socks to deposit the tray by the sink for me.

Now that the rain had stopped, it was a really hot, sunny day outside and I noticed that Thor had taken off his shirt. (Settle down! He is far too young for me and I am a married woman!) From a purely artistic point of view, I couldn't help but take benign note of his bulging biceps and impressive six-pack, as well as the intricately decorative tattoos he had on display. It suddenly dawned on me why so many of Chaos and Logic's friends from Sixth Form were making the effort to walk, cycle and sometimes even hitch lifts over to our house to do their A-level revision.

Their earnest claims that it was so quiet and peaceful for revision out here in the country hadn't really rung terribly true, but I hadn't pursued the matter. After all, this place is not much more than a construction site with the radio blaring full volume and three beefy builders singing their hearts out (with varying degrees of accuracy) all day!

But I digress... back to Thor and the, now, confused look on his face as he realised I was talking to someone that he couldn't see.

"Hi!" I said brightly.

"Hi!" he replied, smiling cautiously and looking round to see who else was there. "Sorry to interrupt, I thought you took the kids to school."

"I did!" I confirmed.

"Who are you talking to then?" he asked.

I nodded towards Sammy. "Him!"

Thor's eyes followed my gaze up to the corner of the kitchen ceiling.

"Ah!" he said nodding slowly. Then after a pause he looked back at me and said, "Why?"

"Because he might stay where he is if I do." I replied sheepishly, realising how daft this sounded. "I don't really like spiders, I can cope with smaller ones but he is a bit too big for me."

Thor considered this for a minute, then nodded as if this were a perfectly reasonable response. Then flicking his long blonde hair over his shoulder, manfully, he nodded at Sammy and said, "Want me to get rid of it for you?"

"Yes, but please don't kill him," I said hastily, having visions of Thor fetching his sledge hammer. "I don't want to hurt him; I would just prefer he was somewhere else."

"Fair enough!" he replied with a nod and he reached up, cupped his hands around the huge spider and gently carried him outside, walking right over to the garden boundary in his socks, before leaning down and tipping Sammy into the long grass of the field beyond the fence.

Coming back into the kitchen he seemed deep in thought for a moment before eventually looking at me and saying carefully, "You do realise he'll probably be back, don't you?"

"Oh, I know, but I'll worry about that tomorrow. There's quite a lot of additional wildlife in this house now because of all the months we have spent with broken walls. I'm getting used to it, but I am looking forward to when we can sort all that out, after the rebuild is finished. It won't be a problem for ever. Now, how about I bring you guys round a tray of fresh tea as a thank you for rescuing me?"

He smiled and nodded his thanks "That would be great, thanks. The concrete for the new floor is down now. It just needs to set. We're going to finish off the porch walls next and then that'll be our bit of the job over and we'll leave you in peace. The chippies will be starting as soon as the floor is dry enough to walk on."

I hadn't realised that the team would be changing but I suppose it was obvious really. These guys specialised in concrete and brick work and the next stage would require skilled wood workers. It was a fantastic step forward. They would start to reconstruct the inside of our home and put in ceilings, stud walls and stairs. We were making amazing progress, but as I watched Thor shuffling back across the stone floor to the doors and slipping his boots back on, I realised I would be sorry to see them go.

While the kettle came to the boil, I dug in the tins to find the latest batch of chocolate chip cookies the girls had whipped up the previous night. Knights in shining armour deserved cookies after rescuing damsels in distress from big fat spiders I felt, so I put some on the tray and headed round to deliver the refreshments and check out my new concrete floor.

Handing out the drinks and cookies, I noticed Thor scrabbling around on the floor just inside the half-finished porch. He spotted me and gesturing at the floor he said "Look! It's a present from us to you to say thank you for all the tea!"

I went over and looked down at a cartoon of a smiling spider with long legs and big boots carefully carved into the semi-wet cement of the new floor.

"This one will stay right here and not move a muscle, I promise!" said Thor with a chuckle. "Even when the carpenters lay that wooden floor you've chosen over him, you'll know exactly where he is. Standing guard!"

I couldn't help grinning back at him and asked, "Will he tell all the other spiders to stay away?"

"Absolutely!"

I laughed, I was definitely going to miss these guys.

22: Purgatory

Definition: a place of extreme suffering where one expiates one's sins

Back to the mother juggling jobs in the present…

Fortunately, the work day passed quickly, and it wasn't long before I was picking my boy Barbarians up from their schools and dropping them at their chosen after-school activities. I just had time to pop home and check on the progress of my drying canvas before I had to go back and retrieve them.

It was gratifying to see that the gluey, dark green base was almost dry, so it wouldn't be long before I could start the next stage of my painting. Noting in passing that there didn't seem to be much in the way of any edible items in either the fridge or the cupboards, I headed straight back out to raid the supermarket on my way to the school.

Once home again, laden with basic food supplies, I was able to pick up the canvas and lean it against the wall near the patio doors so that it was out of the way while I unpacked the shopping and started to cook dinner. I couldn't wait to get on with painting, but I made myself mentally run through all the practical things I would have to get sorted out first, like feeding the hungry horde, sorting out some washing before it spilled out of the utility room and buried us all alive and…. oh no! A sixth sense made me check the family calendar…. parent's evening! Oh heck, I'd forgotten about that!

Heart sinking, I realised that I wasn't going to be able to paint that evening at all. It would be too late by the time I got back, the light would be all wrong. I could feel my spirits dropping down into my boots with the disappointment. Damn! If it wasn't bad enough that I had all this washing to do, I was now going to have to attend the scrum that the local primary school called parent's evening as well.

Going on the experience of previous years, this would generally involve all the parents for a particular year group being herded into the centre of the main school hall, with all the tired looking teachers sitting behind desks set out around the edge. I was never quite sure if this particular arrangement was so that the teachers could get a better view of the parents as they politely pushed, delicately elbowed and sometimes actively flailed fists to get past each other, in order to be first to park their bums on one of the two seats set out in front of their preferred teacher, so that they could discuss 'Little Johnny's' progress.

It was a very educational experience in more ways than one, even though it was utter torture for both parents and teachers. I found it quite amazing that there were always some parents with such an inflated sense of self-importance who refused to pay any attention to the list of appointment times which had all been carefully booked up in the preceding week. These parents would simply barge their way to the front of any vaguely polite queue that the other (more reasonable) parents were trying to stick to.

It should be remembered that there were over 100 pupils in each primary school year. One must also keep in mind the fact that the staff had already done a full day's work keeping all those pupils alive, under control and hopefully educating them at the same time. Given that fact, I would be very surprised if any of the teachers I managed to get near that evening could remember their own name, let alone that of their students. In fact, one year I was so exhausted by the time I got to the teacher that I didn't notice for the first three minutes that she was talking about someone else's child. As that other child was handing in their homework on time and generally doing very well, I decided that was good enough for me. I didn't have the energy to correct the mistake.

Nevertheless, no matter how much I hated these evenings, if I wished to consider myself a good parent and didn't want the school to note my absence and inevitably draw unflattering conclusions, I was going to have to attend.

Checking the communal diary on my phone I was not surprised to see that Beloved Husband conveniently had a late meeting at work scheduled in for that evening. I couldn't help but surmise that he had clocked the date of parent's evening well before I had, and made sure he had a reason not to be available! A very small part of me applauded his ingenuity.

Considering the hell that I now realised I was facing for the evening, I wondered if I was brave enough to suggest that it was time the boys learned how to use the washing machine. This might mean that I didn't have to do all that washing by myself, but I decided that I couldn't quite bring myself to unleash that particular monster. My poor machine was only hanging on by the merest thread as it was, so letting the boys loose on it might send it over the edge and then where would we be? If I had to do parent's evening by myself and then came home to a broken washing machine, I might just go on strike.

Shoving a load of whites into the machine and switching it on while the potatoes merrily boiled over in the kitchen, I warned the boys that they would be on hanging-out-the-wet-washing-in-the-conservatory duty after supper while I was up at the school. Surely they couldn't get into too much mischief doing that?

Hmmm! No comment.

23: Headway

Definition: moving forwards or making progress in spite of conditions which slow you down.

Let us return to the reconstruction project in the past again....

It came to pass that I was sat on my drive again, waiting for the arrival of more workmen. The chippies, (sadly I had learned that is short for a team of carpenters not the Chippendales!), were on their way to begin the next stage of our crumbly cottage reconstruction project.

Fortunately, there was none of the nonsense that had marked my previous vigil for builders and the new team turned up on time with The Boss in attendance once again. I was a bit concerned at this latter development as I had learned the hard way that The Boss' appearances generally coincided with the news that there was a 'slight problem', which usually meant we needed to find more money. There wasn't any more money, we were up to our eyeballs and beyond in debt, but I didn't think that was going to stop him. It wasn't his fault, I did realise that, but the job was a complicated one.

It turned out that I was right, unfortunately, and, once he had introduced his new team and set them to work, he asked if he might have a word in private. Deciding that I couldn't hear this without some form of sustenance, I invited him around to the kitchen and put the kettle on (yes, again!). Armed with a plate of cookies, I drifted over to the table and invited him to sit down and tell me what the problem was.

Apparently, the issue was with the staircase. Previously we had been the proud owners of an extremely ancient set of rickety stairs that were full of charm and character, if not terribly safe or practical. As is often the way in old cottages, the original set of stairs had been constructed in a fairly ad-hoc manner and squeezed into a ridiculously small area which in no way conformed to modern building regulations. The new staircase would have to abide by the up-to-date rules. Today's conundrum was that a modern staircase would not fit where the old one had been.

There were two interconnecting issues associated with this situation. Firstly, the current rules meant that each step on a staircase had to be even and regular, which is perfectly reasonable and completely unlike that which we had had before. I had no problem with this rule whatsoever. So many people had fallen down the old set of stairs over the years that a nice, new, safe set of treads sounded like a jolly good idea to me. The problem was going to be how to get a whole flight of them into the designated area.

The second issue related to the ceiling height for the ground floor. Modern building regulations also had rules with regard to the minimum height (floor to ceiling) that was acceptable in a room; this figure definitely didn't match with how low our old ceilings used to be. Again, I had no problem with this. I was fed up with people banging their heads on low beams all the time. (Not that I had experienced a problem myself, having stopped growing at just over five foot, but people don't half grumble when they walk slap bang into stray chunks of wood innocently hanging around the place.)

Now, on the whole, this wasn't going to be a problem as we could steal the extra height out of the roof space. It would just mean a smaller loft and slightly more sloped ceilings upstairs. As I've mentioned, I don't do lofts, so I didn't care what size it was. (Unless smaller lofts mean smaller spiders of course, but I don't think it works like that.) Therefore, ceiling height was only an issue when it came to the actual staircase.

Unfortunately, a higher ceiling downstairs translated into a need for a bigger staircase, and we were struggling to fit our original staircase length back in, so increasing the size would be a significant problem. We were going to have to pay extra (what a surprise) for a custom-made staircase which would make things a bit easier to fit on a practical level, but it would still need to have a set number of stairs at regular intervals within a certain distance to conform to the rules.

As The Boss and I were pouring over a plan of the ground floor considering our options, Logic stumbled sleepily in from the caravan to locate a late breakfast. The Sixth Form were on an inset day and she and her sister had been making full use of the extra revision time this afforded them by having a nice long lie-in.

Having loaded the toaster and made a couple of cups of tea to take back out to the caravan on a tray when the toast was ready, she eventually came over to have a nose at what was occupying us at the table.

The phrase 'you can't see for looking' is quite true sometimes. We had been staring at the plans until we were going cross- eyed, but once we had explained to Logic what our little enigma was, she immediately said "I assume you've tried the obvious, haven't you?"

I should explain here that Logic is a puzzle freak. She loves spending hours doing impossible jigsaws, so she can usually see how things fit together very quickly. I don't mean the standard 1,000-piece jigsaws. I mean three dimensional ones, and the type that have an impossible and almost identical picture printed on *both* sides so that you don't know which side relates to which puzzle. I don't understand how she does them. She can't see any difficulty.

She even likes constructing flat-packed furniture too! A skill that would come in very handy when we eventually moved back in; after all, we had half a house-worth of dismantled furniture piled up in the garage waiting for her.

Anyway, back to the staircase riddle.

Quite clearly, Logic could tell from our blank expressions that we had no idea what she was talking about. At the same time, I could tell from her face that we had missed something pretty fundamental.

"Well, it is tricky, but…," there was a moment's pause before she sat down next to me and pulled a pencil from the knot of long dark hair she had piled loosely on top of her head.

"May I?" she asked politely, whilst firmly sliding the plans out from under The Boss' reluctant fingers. For a minute or two she looked closely at the dimensions outlined and then started to quickly jot down a systematic series of numbers in the margin of the plan.

The Boss tried to object and pull his plans back across the table out of her reach, but she merely held on tighter, shushed him and carried on writing.

I watched both her actions and The Boss' reaction with amusement. Logic is a gifted mathematician, and I had seen her enthralled by numbers many times before, but The Boss had not and the alternating annoyed and suspicious looks he was casting her way were extremely entertaining. I could tell he wasn't terribly happy about this small, sleepy, seventeen-year-old girl scribbling all over his plans. He kept looking at me as if waiting for me to step in and tell her to stop, but I merely raised my eyebrows in return and smiled serenely. It wasn't as if she was a toddler with a wax crayon. If there was a solution I was completely confident that Logic would find it.

Eventually her calculations ground to a halt and she replaced the pencil in her topknot and nudged the plans back towards him.

"There you go," she said with a yawn. "That'll give you the direction and angle, with the height, and length of the run including measurements for the sizes and regularity of the treads. I assume it'll be a custom-made job. If you use those figures, then it'll fit!"

Fresh eyes on a conundrum always help, especially if they don't come with any pre-conceived ideas (and they belong to someone who is really good at maths, of course). We had been trying to fit the new staircase into the footprint of the old one. An impossible task in fact, but if you turned the whole thing ninety degrees and moved it over a bit towards the new porch then it worked. Easy!

It would mean that the entire layout of the inside of the property would have to be rejigged on the plan but they hadn't started constructing it yet so that wouldn't be a problem. Logic had kindly included altered figures there too. The Boss looked at it for a long moment in silence before nodding briefly. "That does look as though it might work," he conceded reluctantly. "I'll just run that by the structural engineer to double check the numbers are correct, and then run off a new plan for building control."

He was so busy rolling up his plans that he didn't spot Logic raising a single eyebrow at me, and me grimacing back sympathetically. Her numbers were always correct, I knew that from experience, but The Boss didn't. I subtly shook my head at her. We had to let the project leader do his job. He would find out soon enough that she was right.

"I'll let the boys know that the dimensions are probably changing. They'll need to order a staircase to the new figures once they've been confirmed and then we'll be off and running with the next stage," he said as he stood up. "They can build the porch roof for you while we are waiting for the finalised figures for the new internal layout. With any luck we'll have some electricians and plumbers on site too by the end of the week." With an emphatic tap of his rolled-up plans on the table, he turned and headed for the door.

***

It turned out that Logic was right (I told you so!), the staircase was going to fit in the new location and the rejigged internal layout would work as well. The Boss was right too, as we had both electricians and plumbers on site by the end of the week as well as the carpenters. As a result, the construction related noise levels from the front of the house increased massively.

Over the course of the next week, now that the dinky digger had gone back from whence it came, Skelly resumed his supervisory role from his perch on the bench by the garage. The chippies weren't quite sure what to make of this and gave him quite a wide berth to begin with, but they soon relaxed and the work cracked on a pace. Beams went in, stud walls went up, and wires and pipes were laid in all directions. It was quite staggering just how quickly the inside of the cottage was coming together. One morning in particular my phone was constantly going off at work. Each time it was a different question about light fittings, radiators and doorways etc. There was so much progress being made in such a short time. It was all positive and so very exciting but simultaneously exhausting.

There was a continuous cacophony of sawing, shouting, and banging with the ever-present radio playing in the back ground, but I didn't mind. The house was beginning to look like a house again. It was possible to start thinking that we might actually get to move back in properly and live a normal life. Well, as normal as life ever gets with us.

Several days later, I was contentedly chopping up vegetables in the kitchen listening to the sounds of building work through the temporary stud wall between the kitchen and the front section of the house, when I heard one of the chippies say loudly, "Hang on a minute, where's Tiny gone?"

It took a moment to register what had been said, and just as I was starting to wonder what or who Tiny was, I heard the cat start to hiss and spit behind me. Turning towards the open patio doors I froze. There was the most enormous Great Dane standing in the conservatory staring at me, with a long drool-covered bone sticking out either side of its jaws. He took a tentative step towards me and the cat shot off the flagstone floor and scrambled up the outside of my trouser leg, then on over my t-shirt to my shoulders where she hid under my hair and growled menacingly. The big toughie! I was actually quite impressed. She was getting on a bit now and I hadn't seen her move so fast for years. Unfortunately for me, my skin was now lacerated with hundreds of little puncture marks, physical evidence of her newly-rediscovered speed and agility, because her claws had gone right through my clothes and skewered me multiple times.

The massive dog merely put its head on one side curiously and continued to drool.

Now I believe I have already mentioned the fact that we had a lot of extras living in the house with us at that time, in the form of spiders and mice, but I draw the line at letting random dogs just walk in too. (Been there, done that, bought the T-shirt!) If I did, I might as well invite the horses in from the field next door and be done with trying to run a civilised household.

Standing stock still, I raised my voice to carry through the wooden partition to the workmen and I said, "I think you'll find that Tiny is round here!"

"Oh heck!" (No, he actually said something much fruitier than that in reality.) "Hang on I'll be round in a sec!" came an anxious voice.

Within a minute, Tiny was joined by an apologetic carpenter. A compact, wiry man who was covered, head to toe, in sawdust burst through the patio doors and tried to persuade Tiny to follow him out of the kitchen.

Tiny really didn't want to leave. He was eyeing my cowardly cat with extremely intense interest.

"I'm so sorry," said Dusty. "He's only a puppy. My wife's gone away to look after her mother. I can't leave him at home alone. I thought he was asleep in the car, but he must have woken up and gone for a wander. I'll try to keep him round the front if it's OK with you." He looked so worried that I had to smile.

"No harm done, I just wasn't expecting him, that's all," I said, attempting to carefully unpeel the reluctant cat from around my neck without losing too much skin in the process. "He's perfectly welcome outside, as long as he doesn't eat my cat, of course. She really wouldn't appreciate it. Can I suggest that it would probably be a good idea to keep him on a longish leash round the front though? Some of the cars that come along the lane are ever so fast. I'd hate for him to get squashed."

Dusty sighed with relief and nodded. "OK, thanks I will."

"One thing though," I said as he turned to go. "Do you think you could persuade him to give my skeleton back his leg, please?

Part 6

"It is not in the stars to hold our destiny but in ourselves."

William Shakespeare

24: Exacting

Definition: making significant demands on one's skills, resources and ability

Coming forward to the present day once again…

It was at least three days before I was able to return to my big dark green canvas and spend any time on it because, parents' evening aside, so much of life seemed to conspire to keep us apart. However, I finally made it into my studio, shut the door firmly behind me and then the paint literally started to fly. It was as if I had painted this so many times already in my head that my fingers knew what to do without being told. In fact, that was exactly what had happened. Over the last three days the actions that I needed to take to complete this piece had been rehearsed over and over on a separate loop in my head, whilst in reality I was getting on with going to work, doing the washing, the shopping and cooking dinners.

Several hours later I stepped back from the canvas utterly exhausted. It was finished. In the same way that the blackest of nights eventually ends with the glimmer of the new day dawning, so the bleakest of winters is beaten with the arrival of the first new shoots of spring. This latest painting was alive with new spring growth. Buttercups, bluebells and daisies all vied for space amongst deep green leaves on the canvas. Bright, energetic and colourful, it was a massively pivotal piece for me that I felt was indicative of just how much better I was getting.

I staggered out of my little studio and collapsed in an exhausted heap onto the sofa by the fireplace. Several minutes passed as I sat there not moving, and then the telephone rang. Fortunately, it was on the coffee table right next to me, as no-one ever remembers to put it back on the base to charge. I reached over and picked it up, certain that it would be one of those silent electronically-generated cold calls. We get a lot of those. Only it wasn't. A very refined female voice was asking to speak to me.

I sat up a bit and confirmed that it was me answering the phone.

"Oh, that's great!" the lady enthused, "I keep leaving messages for you, but I'm sure you've been very busy."

I vaguely remembered Quiet giving me several messages in the last few days that I hadn't really listened to.

"Yes, sorry, I have." I agreed sheepishly.

"Oh, don't worry about that," she said breezily. "I know what you creative types are like. Anyway, I just wanted to let you know that I have a space coming up for a two-week exhibition if you'd like it. It's not for a couple of months so there's no great panic, but we've been let down by another artist who is taking her work to a big gallery in New York. While I'm very excited for her, it means that I'm looking for something fresh and new to fill the space and I think your work would fit the bill nicely. We'd need about twenty canvasses, medium to large."

"Um, how do you know my work is what you want?" I asked, feeling like I was missing something fairly vital. My foggy brain was struggling to keep up. As far as I was aware she hadn't seen any of my paintings.

"Well I'm looking at the jpegs your agent sent through on my laptop now. I particularly like the fish, very positive and motivating, especially the message behind it; the whole looking up from the depths of the ocean and moving towards the light. Your agent tells me there's an art therapy story behind the work which sounds interesting too. And everyone likes fish," she said.

'Quiet doesn't' I mentally muttered to myself, but at the same time I was also thinking 'What agent?'

"I like the feathers too. I think they will prove very popular. So spiritual. People have a thing about Guardian Angels, don't they?"

The jpeg comment helped some pieces of the puzzle to slot into place. I remembered the weekend that Chaos and Logic had both come back from university together. This must be what Chaos had been plotting when I had caught her taking photos in my studio. She never actually said what she wanted the photos for, but she was quite capable of sending jpegs out to galleries without me knowing about it. She'd also make a pretty good agent, come to think of it. I wondered vaguely who else she'd contacted.

"Really?" I said faintly. "My agent, how very enterprising of her."

If I remembered correctly, this lady was from a prominent gallery in the nearby town. It wasn't the usual sort of run-of-the-mill pretentious place that was stuffed with weird creations but a gorgeous old building housing genuinely beautiful and uniquely stunning artwork. The owner had an excellent reputation locally for promoting home-grown artists and was a successful artist herself, having exhibited all over the world. She also ran all sorts of inspiring workshops to encourage people to try creative art-related activities themselves. Exhibitions in these sorts of places don't get handed out to just anyone. I'm not sure I would ever have had the courage to approach her. Not that such a thing would ever stop Chaos. This was quite an opportunity.

"Yes, she's really keen on your work. She says you have quite a few completed canvasses available."

"That's true," I admitted, thinking of the huge stacks lurking in random locations around the house and garden.

"Well that all sounds very promising. Tell you what, I'll pencil you in for those two weeks and perhaps I can pop over sometime next week and take a look in person? Does that sound OK?"

I paused and then said, "Yes, alright. You do that." I didn't see what choice I had. Even though exhibitions are very draining, and require massive amounts of hard work, it seemed that I was going to be doing this one.

I am pretty certain that Chaos would have killed me if I hadn't.

25: Emergent

Definition: in the process of developing or coming into existence.

Back in the past again…

Now that Thor had left the site, we weren't quite so inundated by love-struck teenagers hoping to catch a glimpse of him with his top off. Nevertheless, the repair job was moving on at a cracking pace and we still had a reasonably high turnover of adolescent visitors. The dreaded A level and AS level exams were looming ever more closely, so the amount of revision needed was getting pretty serious and they all needed to concentrate. As a result, the level of noise from the communal study sessions on the patio was significantly less these days. However, I wasn't used to complete silence.

My well-oiled parenting radar is still going strong after all these years and I have learned to my cost that silence nearly always means trouble. So, you can understand my concern when I realised that there was absolutely no chatting whatsoever coming from the teens one afternoon. There wasn't even the distant echo of the two boy Barbarians tackling each other to the ground for possession of some form of inflated, roughly-spherical bag of wind.

Creeping over to the conservatory, I could see that every one of the random students that had arrived at the house that day were all stood staring out over the grass and concentrating intently. They all seemed completely mesmerised, apart from Logic who was attempting to use her

British Sign Language skills to signal something to me from behind her back whilst she looked out into the garden at the same time. I couldn't really understand her, but it looked a bit like she was trying to say 'come over here, slowly and quietly'.

I tiptoed up behind her and stared over her shoulder into the garden. "What are we looking at?" I murmured after a minute had passed and I couldn't see anything of interest. Perhaps they had all gone a bit mad. Too much studying in all this beautiful sunshine can do that.

"Look!" she whispered, pointing very slowly, "under the caravan." I followed the direction of her finger and was immediately transfixed by the sight of a small round bundle of fluff peeping out from behind the caravan steps. Thank heavens I had my glasses on or I would never have spotted it.

As I watched, another one appeared, and then another.

My goodness!

It would seem that Hattie the helpful caravan had been sheltering more than just us in recent months. I had been congratulating myself that the inside of the caravan was a wildlife-free zone, but obviously underneath it was a different matter entirely. An expectant, wild rabbit, probably from the warren two fields over, had decided to make a nest for her babies under our caravan. This was a bizarre decision to my mind, given the noise we must have been making and the associated activity on our building site house, but it is quite common apparently for them to do something like this. An excellent example of hiding in plain sight with the theory being that a predator (like a fox) would be less likely to venture near to the caravan so the nest would be safer.

Quite clearly the mother rabbit's logic had been correct, but I really hoped that Dusty was genuinely keeping the delightful Tiny on a lead now. It would be a shame to traumatise all these spellbound students by letting them watch a 'puppy' massacre these sweet, little bouncing baby bunnies as they were enjoying their first outing in the sunshine.

Eventually the mother rabbit appeared, after we had counted at least six cute little bundles of brown fluff, and started to marshal them off out of the garden and towards the nearby warren.

The students gave a heartfelt group sigh as the little cotton tails disappeared from sight and then immediately fell to chattering about how cute they were. I took this as my cue to disappear back into the kitchen. It was getting late in the afternoon and there was no way I was going to be able to shake off any of the additional teenagers without feeding them first. I figured that half a dozen pizzas were probably in order and set about making up the dough for them and chopping up a selection of toppings.

***

A short while later, with the oven stuffed to the brim with bread, tomato sauce, ham and melting cheese, I left Chaos and Logic loading up the next batch of pizzas with toppings, while I filled a tray with fresh cups of tea and took a brief trip around to see how the builders were getting on.

On the way, I trotted past Skelly who was reading a copy of The Financial Times. I observed with interest that his femur had been fully restored and that Tiny had taken up residence at his feet. The huge dog was apparently asleep in the sunshine, but I couldn't help notice that he occasionally stuck out his enormous tongue and gave the skeleton's lower leg a quick lick when he thought no one was looking. I made a mental note to check that Skelly had all his associated parts later that evening after Tiny had gone home.

The chippies were looking very pleased with themselves when I stepped through the gap in the wall that was the front porch entrance, and so they should be. The inside of the cottage was really taking shape. Dusty enthusiastically invited me to inspect all the work they had done that day which involved using a ladder (still no staircase yet) and admiring the upstairs rooms. The team were so intent on proudly showing off the new layout complete with ceilings, floor and doors that they failed to spot that I was totally terrified about how on earth I was going to get back down to ground level again. Ladders and I do not have a good relationship. Up is OK, but down? Not so much! Thank goodness I was wearing trousers not a skirt; otherwise things could have got rather undignified.

It was a bizarre feeling to be able to walk around upstairs again after ten months or more, but lovely at the same time to see that the children's bedrooms were starting to take shape, if only as a very basic framework. I could really see how our home was slowly being restored to us which made me feel quite emotional.

Nevertheless, Dusty was keen to discuss a few technical issues with me that might hold proceedings up. There's always something, isn't there? Apparently, the main problem of the moment was with the upstairs windows. Due to the fact that we had raised the ceiling heights downstairs, the windows on the first floor were going to be quite low down in proportion to the floor, with the windowsills at approximately knee height. They couldn't be moved up as the windows needed to be able to open outwards beneath the overhang of the beautiful original thatched roof. That wasn't a problem in my mind as the low windows looked completely in keeping with the whole slightly quirky, rustic cottage ambiance. Unfortunately, the health and safety elf didn't agree. It would seem that we had to have bars on these low windows to stop us accidentally throwing ourselves out of them. The rebuild would not be able to be signed-off by building control otherwise.

However, in contrast to this directive, the fire department were saying that we were not allowed to have bars on the windows in case there was a fire and we actually did want to throw ourselves out deliberately in order to escape the flames and couldn't. So, we were rather caught between two different, completely contradictory, aspects of the health and safety system.

Dusty had a cunning plan to get around this by designing some removable bars for the windows which would hopefully mean we could comply with both requirements. As he was enthusiastically explaining his ingenious invention in the minutest of exhaustive details, I could feel my attention beginning to wander.

Casting an eye towards the door to the bedroom that had been sealed up so many months ago, I was pleased to see that the tape around the insulating board looked like it was still holding. Hopefully it would keep out all the dust from the construction work for a little bit longer. I wondered how the little girl on the swing had fared through the cold and wet of the winter. It wouldn't be very much longer before we could open up the partition and find out.

Eventually, Dusty ground to a halt and looked expectantly at me. Having not heard a word he'd said in at least the last five minutes, I smiled and nodded at him and said "I think that sounds ingenious. Well done!" Which was obviously the right response as he grinned, looking very pleased with himself.

With a lot of well-meant, but not very practical, encouragement from the carpentry team, I successfully made it back down the ladder without disgracing myself and returned to the kitchen, just in time to rescue the second batch of pizzas from the oven before they burned. Only a few moments after that I was ferrying them out to the teenagers on the patio who fell on them ravenously as if they hadn't demolished four already. It looked like we were going to be requiring considerably more pizza at this rate!

26: Culmination

Definition: to start to bring something to a close or to reach a climactic point.

Remaining in the past....

As with many building projects, things can seem to take forever before one sees any progress and then, all of a sudden, everything starts to come together. This is the stage that we were now at with the rebuild of our beautiful cottage.

At long last the new staircase went in, the walls were plastered, and the space started to feel almost useable again, instead of some noisy old barn stuffed to the brim with busy builders. I took such great delight in walking up and down the brand new, modern, safe set of stairs that I think poor old Dusty thought I had finally lost the plot. I was so pleased with it that I even went to get the Barbarians from the caravan to come and try it out too.

The Barbarians completely understood my fascination with the new stairs. We had spent so many years with the old rickety 350-year-old cottage staircase that it was a complete novelty to have a full set of even, steady treads complete with a handrail! Fancy that! Marvellous! All five of us spent a merry half-an-hour testing the new flight out, and then going into each of the newly rebuilt bedrooms and generally getting in the way of the bemused workforce. Then I took lots of photos of the four Barbarians on the stairs with Skelly and sent the images to Beloved Husband at work to cheer him up.

Eventually, having been physically prevented from trying to get poor Skelly to slide down the new, unpainted bannister, Small changed the subject and nodded towards the sealed up back bedroom door, saying bluntly, "So when are you going to open that up then?" He was only trying to distract me. I knew he'd already made his mind up to try the banister sliding thing later when I wasn't looking, but I had to agree that he had a point about the little bedroom.

The bulk of the really dusty work had been completed. The carpentry, the plastering and the electrics were almost finished bar a few minor details. We even had a front door! Amazing! A beautiful forest green one with a little glass window in it and sleek, black fittings. We were now able to actually secure our property after nearly fourteen months with a gaping hole in the wall direct to the outside world. Wonders would never cease. Such a small detail but so important to a family's sense of security and one that signalled that yet another significant change was on its way.

It really wouldn't be long before we could start to move back into the house and begin to live like normal people once more. It all needed painting and then carpets of course, but that would not take long. The funny thing was that we were all getting a bit nervous about it. Had you told us last year that we'd get twitchy about moving back in, I would have told you not to be so daft; but now that the time was approaching, none of us felt ready. Maybe it had something to do with not trusting the house not to fall down again – I simply don't know! To distract myself, I had been focussing on mentally organising all the various jobs that would need to be done to achieve complete resettlement in our home, but it seemed that the Barbarians had other more fundamental issues on their minds.

Quiet was standing in the doorway to his new/old bedroom. It was a new door in a slightly different place to the old one due to the altered staircase layout, but the room was generally where his old bedroom used to be, it was just a different shape to how it was before. He had a pensive expression on his face.

"What's wrong?" I asked.

There was a pause before he answered doubtfully, "It's a bit big, isn't it?"

"Yeah!" said Logic uncertainly, "Mine is too! What on earth are we supposed to do with all this space?"

I looked at them both in total surprise. Were they joking?

It would seem not. They both had genuinely perturbed looks on their faces. This was not a reaction that I had expected.

It should be borne in mind that cob walls tend to be at least three-foot deep. In contrast, modern walls are nowhere near that thick, so they were quite correct that both bedrooms were significantly bigger than they had been before, even though the external dimensions of the house hadn't changed.

I had thought they would be delighted but they had been living an existence of complete uncertainty, in a very confined space, for such a long period of time. They had spent over a year with next-to-no elbow room. Their accommodation in the caravan was extremely snug and they had all coped incredibly well with being crammed into such a small area, their personal belongings thinned down to the absolute bare minimum. This new change, even though it was what we had all been working towards for so long, was obviously going to take some adapting to.

"I'm sure you'll get used to it!" I said encouragingly. "We can't move back in just yet, but when we can, you should take your time. Remember, it'll look far more like home with paint on the walls, some curtains and carpets. Maybe try it out for a night or two and see how you feel. We won't be able to remove the caravan terribly quickly anyway, so there'll still be space outside if you prefer to stay there for a bit. We'll need time to put together all your furniture again and then you'll be able to get all your clothes and books and other things out of the boxes in the sheds, which will be nice."

Quiet nodded and shrugged. Logic chewed on the inside of her cheek and stayed silent.

"I can't wait!" said Chaos cheerfully. It was nice to know her enthusiasm for throwing herself headfirst into things without looking too carefully hadn't been dimmed by events. There's a lot to be said for not overthinking things. "Now, answer the question, when are you going to open up that room?"

"Well!" I said, "I guess there's no time like the present!"

Dusty, who was probably desperate to get us out of the new bedrooms so he and the electricians could finish up for the afternoon, handed me a Stanley knife and I stepped up to the sealed-off door. Running the knife blade through the tape, I cut the plastic sheeting and insulation board free from the door frame and eased them out of the gap. Quiet lifted them from me as if they weighed nothing and then passed them back to the builders.

Reaching for the handle, I turned it slowly and opened the door. Light flooded the room from the open curtains and lit up thousands of little dust mites suspended in the air above all the boxes and furniture that filled the space.

Across the packed room I met the eyes of the little girl on the swing.

She seemed pleased to see me.

The Barbarians crowded into the small space behind me, silently looking around the once-familiar room. It was a very surreal experience seeing all these old belongings in what was effectively a time capsule of our lives before the collapse. We probably could have stood there for ages just looking but Dusty was keen to move things along and called through the doorway, "Do you want us to take the temporary partition downstairs apart now too, so you can come through from the kitchen? Then you won't have to walk all the way round the outside anymore to bring us tea."

"Oh!" I exclaimed, "Is it time to do that already?"

"I don't see why not!" he said. "Now the porch is finished and the front door is on, everything is secure. There's no real need to keep the front and back separated off. I've got a set of front door keys for you downstairs too." The thought of having a door key again was really quite exciting. I hadn't realised how much I had missed having an operational front door, let alone a key. How civilised!

The boys had perked up at the idea of watching the partition coming down. They were no doubt envisaging sledgehammers and other destructive action, but I rather thought that they would be disappointed as Thor wasn't here anymore. Dusty was significantly more cautious in nature and likely to take very good care of the new plasterwork nearby.

"Sure, OK!" I agreed, quickly leaning over the piles of boxes and reaching to lift down the little painting before turning to follow everyone else down the stairs. Our house was about to start becoming a functioning home again.

Dismantling the partition really wasn't that exciting, but it was a massively significant moment nonetheless. Beloved Husband made it home from work just as the initial sections of hardboard were being removed and he and the Barbarians thoroughly enjoyed walking through the archway several times just for the sheer novelty of it, after Dusty had finished. Yet more photos had to be taken and dispatched onto social media to prove that we had a whole house again; then we decided that a celebratory piece of cake and a round of hot chocolates in the kitchen was a fitting way to mark the occasions.

I carefully wrapped the half-painted little girl in bubble wrap and tucked her away safely before joining the rest of the family.

27: Perseverance

Definition: steadfast determination to achieve something regardless of obstacles in the way.

Now for some positive progress in the present....

Having committed myself to meeting with the Gallery owner the next week, I went into my studio and started to think about what this might actually mean.

The bubble-wrapped package on the window sill next to the radio caught my eye. Then I held out my right hand and watched it carefully for several minutes observing the tremor. It was definitely less pronounced than it had been. Perhaps it was time for this one last challenge. Picking up the parcel I started to break the seal.

Unwrapping it quickly I stared at the small, half-finished canvas as the plastic bubbles fell to the floor. The little girl on the swing had waited a very long time for me to get back to her, yet here she was as bright and cheerful as the day I had liberated her from her incarceration.

At that point in time, the day we regained our whole house back again, I hadn't ever planned on painting again. I probably would have destroyed this unfinished work then and there, had I not promised Beloved Husband that I would never again burn my work as I had done after the cottage initially collapsed. That awful destruction had come about as a result of our need to find sufficient space to accommodate the Barbarians more comfortably, and to store all essential items that had been rescued from the disintegrating house, but it had also been a personal punishment. One I had inflicted on myself due to my feelings of guilt and helplessness at not being able to protect my children from what was happening.

In some respects, Beloved Husband had been more distressed than I at the sight of all my paintings burning. Not because he liked the paintings particularly, although he didn't have anything against them either, but more due to his concern that I would regret my destructive impulse. My determination never to paint again had been unsustainable and he had known that I would eventually need to return to what I loved.

He was right. I had missed my work. Not all of it, some of the burned canvases were utter rubbish, but some good pieces had been lost as well and I did miss them. I wish things could have been different. But that sort of thinking doesn't get us anywhere, does it?

In order to keep Beloved Husband happy, this little half-completed painting didn't end up in the bin or on the bonfire, but had been hiding away, wrapped carefully in bubble wrap, and tucked in the box of painting paraphernalia that I had then stored for a very long time at the back of my brand-new under-stair cupboard in our beautifully restored home. This retrieved canvas was small, about the size of an A4 piece of paper and easily tucked out of sight where I could pretend she didn't exist. Even when I had eventually started to paint again, I had never dared to unwrap her, until now.

I had been too afraid that there would never come a time when I would be able to finish her. I had known that I was damaged and that successfully completing this particular piece of work would only be possible if I actually managed to finally heal myself both mentally and physically. In my mind, she had been a half-acknowledged goal to aim for in my attempts to put the pieces of my heart and soul back together.

I wondered if maybe it was now time to try finishing her.

There were a number of problems that this particular challenge presented me with, in addition to my dubious dexterity difficulties.

The fact of the matter was that it was well over three years since I had started this painting. At the time that I had been interrupted by the house falling down so long ago, I'd had every intention of returning within hours, or a day at the most, to finish her, but events had taken over and more pressing matters had resulted in her being abandoned.

Back then I had been working in traditional oils, using a wet in wet method. Traditional oils take quite a long time to dry, and in this case the (now completely dry) paint was quite thick in places. Both of these factors would mean that as she was completely dry, restarting the painting process was going to raise some problems. Any fresh work was going to have to be done very carefully so that there would be no future cracks developing between the old paint and the new.

It would no doubt be easier to simply start again on a fresh canvas but, to me, completing this little girl represented my journey as I came full circle from the artist I used to be to the artist I was now. She was important. I might never attempt a piece of work like this one ever again, but, to my mind, finishing this painting would be like putting a triumphant full stop at the end of the tragic tale of the house that sat down; and I was determined to do so.

Arming myself with a selection of brushes and a jar of linseed oil, I sat down to rummage through my box of oil paints, picking out the exact same tubes I had used before. Setting the little canvas on the easel before me I reached over to flick the radio on and set to work.

28: Realisation

Definition: The achievement of something long-awaited.

Finally, the day dawned in the past when we could move back in....

In spite of the incredible progress and the fact that we now had a functioning house, it took a while for us to get used to this new development. It felt really strange walking from back to front and vice-versa without heading outside first.

There were still a million tiny things that needed to be done in order for us to be able to start moving back in and resume anything remotely resembling a normal life in a normal house. Firstly, we needed carpets before we could practically start repopulating the bedrooms. We didn't want to move all the furniture back in and then have to move it all out again, so the carpets could be fitted, but there was a minor problem as usual. The carpets had been measured and ordered and delivered to the shop, but no-one had thought to book a fitting date. Oops! So near and yet so far! There was a very long waiting list for carpet fitters apparently and we were at the back of it. It would seem that we might have to stay in the caravan for another couple of months which was very frustrating.

Just as we adjusted to this idea, there was a phone call out of the blue from the carpet company, telling us that there had been a cancellation and the fitters could potentially come the next day which was fantastic news, but we hadn't yet finished painting the walls because we thought we would have more time. Beloved Husband accepted the booking for the next day. After he had hung up the handset, he looked at me and said, "OK! We have 5 rooms and a double height hallway, walls, ceiling and woodwork to paint in less than twenty-four hours. Are you up for the challenge?" Just as I was about to firmly tell him I could do anything he could do, there was a muffled knock on the door. ('Need to get a door knocker' immediately went on my 'to do' list.)

Opening our lovely new front door, we were confronted by the Godfather. No, not Robert De Niro; the real one. The Barbarians' Godfather was standing on the drive and smiling broadly at us as he said "I've got the day off. Need a hand with anything?"

On closer inspection we noted that he was wearing well-used painting overalls and carried a bag, out of which were sticking several paint brush handles. A most timely intervention! He probably wasn't expecting to have to help us complete quite such a big job in such a short timescale, but he didn't complain, he just got stuck in beside us. The Barbarians pitched in too when they got home from school and by the next morning, totally exhausted and covered in paint from head to toe, we opened the front door again to welcome the carpet fitters.

Carpets aside, there were a few snagging issues to sort out but, considering the size of the job, not many. I did have to spend quite some time persuading our lovely, but rather OCD, electrician that I didn't mind that the socket heights in all the rooms weren't quite the same. I hadn't even noticed that they were fractionally out to be honest, but he had and he wasn't happy about it. Apparently, one of his colleagues had done the measuring and hadn't been precise enough. I was just glad to have sockets, but it was only by spinning some nonsense about how I felt it was important for there to be some rustic variation, so that the long sense of history of the house was preserved, that I managed to persuade him not to rip them all out and start again. That would have put us back weeks and no doubt cost even more to fix, so I was relieved when I finally managed to convince him that a sleepy, stressed out mother in a recently rebuilt cottage could cope with minorly mismatching socket heights.

Once the painting and carpets, final electrical work and other snags were completed, it was time to start sorting out what furniture was to be brought back into which rooms. So lengthy debates with regard to which legs went with which table and which doors went on which wardrobe etcetera began. Eventually, after what felt like a hellish week of constantly putting together flat pack furniture, without the assistance of the usual unhelpful instructions, definitely not the right pieces and apparently none of the correct screws (even though I had been so careful to keep them all together in little bags and taped them to part of what they came from), we finally managed to reassemble most of the bedroom furniture.

At last we could spend our first night back in our newly rebuilt home.

29: Apotheosis

Definition: The topmost point in the development of something.

Now we have the Final Act in the present…

I couldn't believe just how busy the room was for the opening of the exhibition. Everywhere I looked I could see people mingling, drinking glasses of wine and chatting. Somewhere off to my left came the repetitive flash from a photographer who was recording the event for the local paper. Now, I hate crowded rooms at the best of times and I particularly hate having my photograph taken, so these circumstances would normally have me running for the hills. However, this time I couldn't because all of these people were here for me, including the photographer. Not actually me specifically, of course, but my paintings and as the featured artist I had been told in no uncertain terms by the Gallery Owner that I needed to be here to generally mingle and network.

Fortunately, the regular exercise sessions I had recently indulged in had not only improved my general fitness but also trimmed my figure down significantly, which gave me far more confidence than usual. The outfit I was wearing was my favourite. It had been consigned to the back of the wardrobe ages ago due to the fact that it had become far too snug. Not so anymore! I was definitely all on the inside of this gorgeous dress and feeling pretty amazing with it.

Interestingly enough, I hadn't had any episodes of palpitations in recent weeks either, so I was beginning to feel very much better, no doubt a direct result of my new regime of self-care. Sharing regular, nutritious meals with Beloved Husband and our boys was something I looked forward to, without constantly dwelling on the absent members of the family. I had come to terms with the sale of the house and no longer feared that moving would tear the family apart. As a direct consequence of that, I no longer had that deep gnawing emptiness inside me. I still missed our girls but wasn't obsessed about it anymore. They had bright futures ahead and I was so very proud of them.

I was adapting, morphing into a stronger, better me. The aching hollows in my heart, that I had been attempting to pack with junk food in a subconscious and futile attempt to fill them in, were now healing properly. Like our beautiful, restored cottage I was beginning to feel whole again for the first time since the old walls had crumbled.

On a lighter note, I also found, to my delight, that I was able to occasionally treat myself to a cup of real tea or coffee, as long as I didn't overdo it. Added to that, a good friend of mine (who also happens to be the most talented hairdresser on the planet, in my opinion) had kindly done something magical to my hair, blending colours and adding subtle highlights so that my grey streak now looked like a deliberate, quirky fashion statement. Therefore, if there had to be a photographer around for this event, at least I knew I had managed to scrub-up relatively ok.

The last few weeks had flown by on a tidal wave of finalising all the necessary details for the gallery exhibition, making sure I had sufficient pieces of the right dimensions to work together on the beautifully smooth white walls. Then ensuring all of the paintings were suitably framed, had the correct hanging attachments and were marked up and catalogued with the titles, descriptions and prices. After that came the on-line marketing and advertising campaign to bring in this crowd of interested people for the opening night. The crowd that were making me increasingly nervous, although when I looked closer, I spotted several of the ladies from the WI and a few of the other students from the Taekwondo class, all chatting happily with each other while checking out my paintings.

"Stop looking at the door, dear, I'm not going to let you run away you know!" said my glamorous new friend, the Gallery Owner. She was a tall, slim striking woman dressed in a chic, black, layered ensemble with the most impressively high-heeled zebra print statement shoes. I had no idea how she was managing to walk in them, but she seemed perfectly poised and in complete control. I had liked her from the moment I met her when she came to the cottage to see my canvasses. An artist herself, she was an incredibly knowledgeable, inspiring and energetic person. She had immediately insisted I double my prices and suggested that I introduce a line of cards and framed prints for the gallery, in addition to the original canvasses to be exhibited.

"You need to be here for this," she continued. "As I predicted, it is a tremendous success! Well done! Have you seen how many have sold already? We've only been open an hour and quite a few have already been reserved. I told you those feathers of yours would fly off the walls, not to mention the colourful animal paintings."

I had never intended to display many of these pieces, especially as some of the earlier ones had been fuelled by some very deep and painful emotions. Nevertheless, now I could see the entire collection exhibited together, they depicted a spectacular journey out of the darkness and into the light, especially when seen in the context of the very human story behind the work.

In a unique addition to the opening evening, the Gallery Owner had persuaded me to give a short presentation to introduce my paintings and tell a little bit about the events behind their creation. I was terrified of standing up in front of all these people but if I could survive my house falling down then I wasn't going to let something like this beat me.

"It's OK," I answered, smiling "I'm not trying to escape, honestly. I'm just looking for my husband and my boys. They said they would be here….Ah" I trailed off in relief as the door opened at that point and in walked Beloved Husband and the boy Barbarians looking very smart indeed.

"They're here!" I explained and then exclaimed "Oh!"

Behind the boys I spotted Chaos and Logic looking extremely elegant as they made their way through the throng towards me.

"I didn't know you were coming!" I exclaimed in delight, giving each of the girls a gentle but heartfelt hug, taking great care not to rumple their gorgeous outfits. Of course, I wouldn't dream of hugging the boys in public, their street cred wouldn't stand for it, so I just smiled and settled for patting them each, briefly, on the arm in welcome. All six of us together again. How wonderful!

"Sorry we're late," said Beloved Husband, grabbing two glasses of sparkling wine from a passing waiter and handing me one. "Their train was late, but we made it in the end. You must have thought we weren't coming. The girls made me promise not to tell you they were planning to be here. They wanted to surprise you."

"Well they certainly did that!" I said, still grinning like a Cheshire cat. "I'm so glad you're here." I took his free hand and squeezed it. "Thank you," I said quietly.

He winked at me. "Anytime!"

"If you think your agent was going to miss this, then you've got another think coming!" Chaos said sternly, but with a broad smile on her face.

"Yes!" I exclaimed, turning towards her again, "about that..."

"You know you'd never have got around to it," interrupted Logic, grinning at her sister. "In fact, I rather think you owe her one! Me too, for distracting you with cake so she could take the photos."

By then, Small had completed a quick circuit of the room and briefly examined each of the canvasses on the wall before coming back, having blatantly pilfered an entire bowl of 'posh' crisps from the elegant buffet table at the end of the room.

"What do the red dots mean?" he piped up from around a crunchy mouthful.

"When someone wants to buy a painting, the gallery put a red dot on the information card on the wall next to it to show that the original is no longer available for sale to anyone else. Then when the exhibition is over the painting can be taken away."

"You've sold some then!" he said triumphantly.

"I have!" I said with a grin, looking pointedly at Quiet. "You won't believe this but quite a few of the guardian angel paintings have gone and several of the fish ones too."

"There's no accounting for taste," he said solemnly before flashing me a quick sideways grin.

"No!" I agreed, smiling back at him. "There isn't is there?"

"Right!" said Logic, tucking one of her arms through mine and one through Chaos'. "Let's have a look round at these paintings then. It's so nice to see them on display and not just chucked in the shed. Come on!" Leaving the boys to raid the food supplies, we set off on a tour of the room together. The girls exclaimed how well the canvasses looked in the space with all the sophisticated lighting. Eventually we made it to what I felt was the most important painting, the centrepiece of the whole exhibition, the small canvas of a little girl on a swing.

"You finished her!" said Chaos.

"Yes, I did. It took me long enough!"

"She's beautiful!" said Logic. "Well done!"

The rest of the open evening passed in a happy blur. Now that I had my rocks around me to steady my nerves I could deal with the crowds of people and even enjoy circulating and chatting with everyone.

It was really interesting to hear the various discussions about the paintings too. Especially the comments that arose about the fully dressed skeleton reading a tabloid newspaper, sitting on a wrought iron bench in the corner of the gallery sporting a complete builder's outfit including hard hat, reinforced, muddy boots, concrete encrusted trousers, a faded flannel shirt and luminous waistcoat (all cast-offs kindly donated by our fabulous building team when they left us).

Anything goes in art apparently and, while I had merely not wanted to leave Skelly out on my big night, most of the guests seemed to think that he was actually a deliberate and very thought provoking 'installation' piece. People were even sitting next to him on the bench and taking selfies. He was so popular in fact that the boys had to put their own red dot next to him to make sure that he wasn't accidentally sold.

In a brief lull later on I dared to ask the girls how long they were back for.

"I've got to go back for my results next week and then I will be home for the summer," said Chaos.

"Really? That's wonderful news," I said, trying to contain my delight.

"Yeah!" said Logic, "University is great fun. I've enjoyed every minute of it and I'm looking forward to going back next year, but you're stuck with me from now until September because I've already finished. I got my old job back in town for the summer, starting Monday."

"You should see how much washing she's brought back," teased Chaos. "It's all in the back of Dad's car."

"Oh great!" I exclaimed and rolled my eyes, pretending exasperation, "my poor washing machine!" Leaning over I gave Logic a quick hug. "Only joking! Welcome back!"

It seemed that my fears that my babies would not want to come back to live with their parents, who had been so stressed and anxious and who were now selling their childhood home, were totally unfounded. They might only be here for the summer, but it didn't matter. They had chosen to come back to us and that was what was most important.

Beloved Husband slung his arm around my shoulders and gave me a squeeze. The boys trailed after him, each with a large plate of food in hand. "Happy now?" he asked.

"Oh yes!" I said, beaming broadly at everyone and thinking how lucky I was to have these amazing people in my life!

"Really happy!"

Epilogue

Definition: the final word from the author – for now.

There, my dear friends, is an appropriate place to draw an end to this part of my tale.

Our heroine is once again surrounded by those she loves; the people who have helped her to stick the broken parts of herself back together. She is wrapped in the warm, double embrace of both their unfailing support and the unexpected success of her work; the many paintings that have been such a key part of her recovery as she climbed slowly and steadily out of the terrifying abyss of complete mental and physical exhaustion.

I think it is possible to spend far too long searching for meaning in events. One can frequently hear people saying that things occur for a reason. In many cases they do, but I believe that sometimes things just happen and then it is essential to focus on simply surviving. Afterwards, as the phoenix rises from the ashes, it is possible to emerge stronger and (hopefully) wiser than before.

With her Beloved Husband and the adored Barbarian Horde around her, our heroine is going to be absolutely fine; and therefore, we'll leave her for now with her bright, creative future in front of her as she uses her newly forged strength to move on from the disasters of the past.

BOOK 3

REDEMPTION

Moving on from the house that sat down.

For

Patricia Naomi
Grandmother, Artist and Inspiration

Thank you for giving a six-year old child a dream.
Who knew it would take me forty years to realise it?

Yet here I am!

Redemption

Definition:
The action of regaining something that was lost.

Part 1

"No matter how hard the past, you can always begin again."

Buddha

Preamble

Definition: A quick word from the author to establish a time frame

Welcome back, one final time, my dear friends. No-one could be more surprised than I was to find myself thumping away at my keyboard for a third time. It would seem that there is yet more to my tale, as the house that sat down has had a surprising legacy.

When you last heard from our heroine she seemed to be sorting herself out. She had enjoyed a successful solo art exhibition at a local gallery, having come to terms with the difficult decision to let the family home go. It is my intention to continue my tale in the past from that point as the family reluctantly attempt to sell their beautifully rebuilt cottage. Unfortunately, certain political shenanigans at the time have caused the market to stagnate and they haven't had much luck finding a buyer, but they are not letting that get them down.

However, I will also be telling you what is happening in the present, approximately 6 months after the big art exhibition you read about in Restoration finished, because some interesting things have developed. I shall attempt to weave the past and present time frames together so that we can arrive at a final conclusion. Our leading lady has been on an incredible journey, the direction of which she could not possibly have imagined the day she stood on her drive and watched the walls of her cottage crumble before her eyes.

But enough of such story spoilers for the moment. All will be revealed in time. Right at this moment she is rolling around on the dusty old floorboards of the stage at the local village hall, wiggling her legs in the air in a most unseemly fashion. In front of an audience!

"Oh dear!" I hear you say. "That is most unlike her." You could be forgiven for asking yourself whether she has finally lost the plot.

Hmmm…quite possibly! What on earth has she got herself into this time?

It's a long story. I'll let her start telling you all about it now.

1: Volunteer

Definition: To freely offer to take part in a task, or assist in the undertaking of an event

Let us kick this tale off in the present day…

I could not believe I was doing this! What on earth had possessed me? I was prancing around on stage. In full view of not only people I knew, but also quite a few that I didn't know! This was not normal; I simply don't do this sort of thing. Ever!

Let me give you the full picture just for the record, I was wearing a wetsuit (one of the 'shorty' variety), a luminous pink shower cap with white spots on it, goggles and I had a piece of tinsel tied round each of my ankles. It was fortunate that this was a man-free zone. I was not a pretty sight.

Just as I was beginning to think I had completely taken leave of my senses the sound of laughter reached my ears. It would seem that the ladies in the audience were enjoying the show, which made me smile in spite of my reservations.

Please remind me, the next time I decide to volunteer for something, that I really should find out precisely what is entailed before signing on the dotted line. When a clipboard and pen had been shoved under my nose at the end of a Women's Institute meeting six weeks ago and I was asked if I would like to be in the Christmas show, all I thought was that it was nice to be asked to join in. I didn't like to say no. I thought that it might be quite fun to be in a little nativity play. While I have never really liked being the centre of attention, I don't like to be a spoilsport either. It's a tricky line to tread. As I scrawled my name on the list, I thought that perhaps I could be a silent shepherd lurking at the back of the stage disguised by a fake beard and a tea towel on my head. Or failing that, I was certain I would make a superlatively self-effacing sheep or perhaps some other variety of bashful barnyard beast. In my mind that would be perfect. I could take part without being too obvious.

Silly me! (Note to self: Always read the small print and never make assumptions, especially where the Women's Institute is concerned!)

About a week later, I turned up to the first rehearsal clutching a suitably stripy tea towel, to find myself part of a small but very glamorous group of ladies who had no intention of doing any form of 'traditional' Christmas entertainment. There was to be no nativity at all! No shy shepherd, no coy cow, not even a diffident donkey. That would be far too boring. I don't know whose bright idea it was (well I do really, though I am naming no names) but several weeks of arduous rehearsals later, here we were at the Christmas Party doing a synchronised swimming routine.

On stage!

Minus a swimming pool!

I know! Totally mad!!

In fact, if I'm honest, we were lacking a fair degree of synchronisation too but no one seemed to be too worried about that; if the chuckles, giggles and downright belly laughs from the audience were anything to go by.

There is one thing I've learned recently and it is that the ladies of the WI don't let minor difficulties get in their way. I have yet to meet a more spirited bunch of women. These zany females are a very determined lot! Much could be learned from them.

With a sheet of blue plastic draped over a rope, stretched across the lower third of the stage to indicate the water, our 'swimming' routine was taking place behind it, with either our upper half on display or, alternatively, just our legs poking up whilst we lay on our backs out of sight. The middle section of the routine involved some rather tortuous floor positions in order to achieve the desired effect, but I am sure you can use your imagination so I won't go into any more detail other than to say think of a rather intense Pilates class and you will be halfway there. It was generating an awful lot of hilarity, from the ladies on stage as well as the audience, which was obviously the point. Contrary to what I had expected, I was actually quite enjoying myself. Who knew making a fool of oneself in public would be so much fun?

Eventually our time in the spotlight came to a close as the music, the Blue Danube, ended and each swimmer did a flourishing 'dive' into (i.e. behind) the plastic water - not an easy feat when you consider our average age and the advanced arthritis afflicting some of our 'athletes'. We all landed in a somewhat undignified, tangled heap on the floor behind the plastic sheet and hurriedly sorted ourselves out to lie in a row on our tummies, chins propped up on our palms, facing the audience as the 'water' came down and loud applause rang out.

What followed was quite a lot of indelicate scrambling as we got to our feet. In our defence, it's really not very easy to move around in a wetsuit on dry land, as they are rather restrictive. I liked to think that I had a small advantage over the others, having had had plenty of practice moving about in thick layers of clothing when we were living the garden the year before last, after the house fell down, but it probably wasn't true. Nevertheless, we eventually managed to form a ragged line and took a bow to what was a standing ovation, before those talented ladies who were nominated as Artistic Director, Choreographer, and Musical Director stepped forward to take a well-deserved additional bow.

There was a rather hurriedly cobbled together encore - we hadn't expected to be asked to do one and therefore hadn't choreographed one, so it was a bit random. Eventually, we were relieved to see the curtain come down for the final time. There are only so many times you can throw yourselves to the floor in a pretend 'dive' in one evening and get away with it. I had my suspicions that we were all going to be sporting some rather impressive bruises the next day.

Hastily stripping off sweaty wetsuits behind the curtains on stage with the rest of the troupe and slipping into something a bit more glam for the rest of the party, it was soon time to join everyone out in the main hall. After our exertions, we were definitely all set to tuck into a large glass of wine and some of the gorgeous gourmet delights displayed on groaning tables. I was surprised how quickly the time flew by because it wasn't long before it was time to help clear away, then scoop up my wetsuit and scuttle outside in a merry festive haze of goodbye hugs to find Beloved Husband waiting in the car outside ready to give me a lift home.

***

I won't lie to you, getting up the next morning was a bit of a struggle. The combination of bruises and a few strained muscles from the 'swimming' routine, coupled with a bit of a muzzy head from the wine (I only had 2 glasses and they were small ones, honest!) plus the cold, dark December mornings all made me consider giving up on the idea of getting up at all. If only I could simply choose to hibernate for the rest of the winter. Wouldn't that be nice?

Beloved Husband was already up and gone. Facing a long early morning commute to his first meeting of the day, he had battled his way out from under the duvet at 6am with all the finesse of a very rumpled, grumpy lion. I valiantly ignored his growling about how unfair it was that he had to get up so early, and the fact that he insisted on putting the light on so that he could make sure he was wearing matching socks. Personally, I always think wearing odd socks is much easier and far more interesting but he cannot bring himself to do it.

However, when he started muttering that his shirt hadn't been ironed, I simply pulled the duvet over my head and tuned him out completely. He is nearly fifty years old and should know by now that there is no such thing as an ironing fairy. Not in this house anyway. If he wants something ironed he should do it himself, or give me three weeks advanced notice. Even then there'd be no guarantee I'd actually do it, unless he bribes me of course. I wasn't too worried about his griping though because I knew he'd cheer up soon enough. He's usually a fairly happy chap. He just doesn't do mornings terribly well. Or ironing, for that matter, although I have wondered if, like the washing up, he does it deliberately badly so that some unsuspecting female (i.e. me) will step in and say "Oh for goodness sake, you're making a right pig's ear of that, let me do it." Happily, I am wise to such tactics which is just as well because there are only the four of us at home now; three fellas and me. I could be ironing and washing up all day if I fell for such obvious ploys. But enough of such mundane matters!

He eventually stomped off down the stairs to ransack the kitchen before leaving the house, so I switched the light back off and I snuggled down to enjoy an extra half an hour in my lovely, warm bed. One of the things I really appreciated these days was my bed. Having had to go without it for so long after the house collapsed, I cannot tell you how much I cherished the simple act of going to bed every evening, falling asleep in warm, safe comfort and then waking up the next morning fully rested and ready to take on the hectic pace of daily life in this mad house.

I was very tempted to stay right where I was that morning, regardless of the fact that it was a Wednesday and I had the school run to do, which would be followed by a lengthy to-do list including both a shift at work and then lots of house-related tasks. For just a little while I pretended that I could 'accidentally' sleep in and stay in my cosy nest indefinitely.

As if it could ever be that simple.

Only a blink of an eye later and our youngest Barbarian, Small, knocked noisily on the bedroom door before poking his head around it and rudely interrupting my daydream.

"Mum!' He whispered loudly, "Are you awake?"

There was a pause while I checked if I was willing to admit that I was awake.

"No!" I answered eventually.

"Oh!" Sounding a bit confused by my answer, he obviously decided that I was joking and pushed the door open a bit more so he could slip in to the room, before sitting heavily on the side of the bed next to me and continuing, "I brought you a cup of tea."

Now that did get my attention. He never makes me tea. Something must be up. Rubbing my eyes briefly, I struggled into a more upright position, which is not easy when someone is sitting on top of the duvet next to you and effectively pinning you in place. Extricating enough of my upper self to be able to lean back against the headboard and switch the light back on, I quickly took hold of the wobbly cup of tea that was being waved in my general direction.

As I mentioned, we call our youngest Barbarian Small. It seemed appropriate at the time. Of course, ironically, he is now nearly twelve years old and is already taller than me, so it is a bit of a misnomer. Admittedly I am rather short, but he is genuinely quite tall for a boy his age.

"I didn't know you could make tea," I said, looking somewhat suspiciously into the cup.

"I can't," he admitted. "Quiet made it!"

"OK!" I said, wondering what his big brother was up to. I never get given tea in bed, not even on my birthday. I didn't have long to ponder this as the sound of a rather heavy tread came up the stairs. A moment later the bedroom door crashed right back on its hinges and Quiet appeared, brandishing a plate of toast and Marmite. As you can probably work out from my older son's name, just as Small isn't actually small any more, Quiet can no longer be described as being even remotely quiet. He has grown so much in recent months that I don't think he's remotely adjusted to his new proportions; hence he keeps accidentally bashing into things. He's not enormous, just quite a bit bigger than he used to be, and as a result significantly noisier.

Leaning over, he shoved the plate of toast under my nose and asked, "How was the show?"

Goodness me; tea, toast and polite conversation, all before 7.05 in the morning! I looked at the alarm clock to check. He was remarkably awake, organised and cheerful. Something was definitely afoot.

"Fine, thank you," I replied, trying to keep suspicion from colouring my tone.

"Good." He gave me a quick grin, shoved his shoulder away from the door frame and disappeared. As I listened to his heavy tread thumping back down the stairs, I looked at Small.

"That's strange," I said casually, "what's he up to?"

"Dunno," came the unhelpful reply from my youngest child, who then nodded at me gravely before levering himself off the bed and stomping after his brother.

I sighed. This was going to require some investigation but, in the meantime, I planned to enjoy the unexpected treat of tea and toast in bed for five minutes. As I sat back with my surprise breakfast, I recalled the fun of the evening before. It had gone really rather well considering my previous experiences with Christmas shows.

The village hall had had been the location of a number of productions over the years, some more memorable than others. I could vividly recall the girls' first nativity in which they both appeared as angels sporting tinsel halos on springs attached to their heads via a nineteen-eighty's 'deely-bopper' style hairband arrangement. Unfortunately, mid-performance, Chaos discovered that if she nodded her head firmly enough she could get her halo to bounce down from above her head to gently bash her nose and found this most entertaining. Distracted from the song that the Archangel Gabriel and his gang were supposed to be singing at that point, she did this repeatedly to growing sniggers from the audience, while I watched helplessly with mounting mortification.

Unaware that all eyes were on her, Chaos then decided to demonstrate her newfound skill to Logic who was standing next to her. Sadly, in her enthusiasm, she misjudged the distance between them and accidentally head-butted her poor sister instead. Surprised by this unprovoked attack, Logic was thrown off balance and staggered backwards with her arms outstretched to try to stop falling off the stage. Unfortunately, she didn't achieve this objective and, as my younger daughter tumbled, she managed to haul the entire heavenly host with her in a flurry of white cotton smocks with rustling tinsel trims. It was certainly a very dramatic finale to the whole production, if not quite that which had been rehearsed. The entire audience leapt to their feet as one body, but obviously not to applaud. Instead we all began extracting small children from the jumbled pile, assured ourselves that there were no bones broken and then calmed them all down with hugs and kisses followed by squash and biscuits.

It was with some trepidation, therefore, that I attended the nativity at the same hall a year later, when Quiet had been cast as King Number One. He had the important job of delivering gold to the Holy Infant. In his defence, I suspect that there had probably been one too many dress rehearsals prior to the big event because my normally very reticent older son staged an unexpected rebellion. He adamantly refused to go on stage, loudly declaring that he was not going to walk to Bethlehem *again* because he'd been there yesterday, and the day before, and he was tired. Apparently, all the other kings agreed with him.

When I tentatively approached our wonderful village pre-school with my fourth child a few years later, I was very surprised that they even let me through the door. I am quite sure that a more delightfully calm and forgiving group of pre-school teachers could not be found anywhere else on this planet because they welcomed him with open arms, in spite of his unfortunate family connections. Luckily, the fourth time proved to be the charm as Small's pre-school Christmas show, a non-religious yet culturally diverse tale about a singing spaceman with a confusing collection of colourful crustacean cronies, passed without a hitch.

Phew! Practice makes perfect!

Eventually, having crunched my way through my toast and finished my tea, I had to stop reminiscing about plays gone past and actually get sorted for the day ahead. It was time to start that lengthy to-do list I mentioned, all the while also trying to figure out my older Barbarian boy's bizarre behaviour.

2: Subconscious

Definition: the part of the mind that a person is not fully aware of but which can unobtrusively guide their actions, responses and emotions.

Staying with the present for the time being....

Arriving back at the house, none the wiser, at about midday after ticking several jobs off my to-do list, I had a couple of hours to spare before I was going to have to launch myself into the whole after school chauffeuring routine. I quickly fed the washing machine and switched on the kettle, when the phone rang. I picked up the handset to hear my mother's lively tones echoing down a rather crackly line.

"Oh, I am so glad I caught you. I'll be quick. I know you're busy. Do you remember my friend from bridge? The one I told you about, her sister's husband's brother is on the committee for the local literary and creative arts society."

I absently wondered where she was going with this information, as I tucked the phone under my chin so I could still hear her, and opened the fridge in order to see if Quiet had left any milk for my cup of tea. My older son's breakfast these days seemed to consist of a deep serving bowl filled with the white stuff plus almost an entire box of whatever random cereal he could find in the cupboard swimming in it. I assumed that it had something to do with calcium and all that growing he was doing. He had also developed a habit of consuming a whole pint glass full of yet more milk at random points during the day, which meant that keeping the supply level equal with the demand was proving to be quite a challenge. It didn't make any difference that we were living in the deepest darkest countryside, surrounded by herds of dairy cows. Getting him to hop over the fence into the nearest field with a clean bucket was, unfortunately, not an option; I still had to go to a supermarket to buy milk by the shedload like everyone else.

I pounced on a suspiciously empty looking six-pint-sized plastic bottle hopefully, having realised fairly recently that, in order to deal with his guilt at not bothering to cross the room to put the empty bottle in the recycling bin, Quiet had taken to leaving small dregs in the base. This was probably so that he could claim there was still some left, which in his mind completely justified the typically lazy teenage act of putting an empty container back in the fridge.

While upending the carton over my mug and watching the smallest smidgen of remaining milk turn my black tea into an indiscriminately murky, slightly-less-black version, a sixth sense made me tune back into what my mother was saying.

"So anyway, I told her you'd do it?"

Alarm bells rang immediately. I'd obviously missed something important, what on earth was my mother up to now?

"I'm sorry, what did you tell her I'd do?"

"Go to the literary and creative arts society and give a forty- five minute presentation."

"What?" My world momentarily tipped on its axis and it suddenly became very difficult to breathe as advanced panic set in. "I can't do that!"

"Don't be silly darling, of course you can!" continued my mother blithely. "You gave a lovely presentation at your exhibition last May."

"Mother, that hardly counts!" I exclaimed, "I stood up for about ten minutes and waffled on about a few paintings. I shook like a leaf and probably bored everyone senseless. I can't even remember what I said. It was awful!"

"Nonsense!" she countermanded briskly. "You did very well. This would be the same sort of thing, only it's a bit longer. They'll probably want to ask lots of questions."

"Forty-five minutes is quite a bit longer!" I exclaimed faintly, feeling nauseous. "What on earth would I say?" But my mother didn't seem to register my concern and carried on regardless.

"Oh well, that's easy darling," she said breezily. "You tell them your story, show them some paintings and then talk about writing your book."

"My book!"

It was true, I had written a book. (I know there's a fair chance that you know this because if you are reading this one then you've probably read the first one, and probably the second one too, but feel free to pretend you haven't if it helps.)

"It's not a real book," I wailed. It was only a small self-published novel and nothing to be taken too seriously. To be frank, I had rather surprised myself by writing it in the first place and now that I had, I didn't really know what to do with it, so I was quite happily ignoring its existence.

"It is real!" she countered firmly. "I've read it. It's funny, and the society members will love hearing from an author. Your road to publication, that sort of thing."

"But it's only self-published."

"What's that got to do with anything? It makes it more interesting if you ask me. What about that fifty shadows woman? She was self-published!"

"You really can't compare my book with Fifty Shades of Grey mum." I said wryly. "There is absolutely no similarity whatsoever."

"And thank goodness for that, I wouldn't have posted a copy of your book off to my cousin's wife if there was! But that's not the point. Self-publishing is the up and coming thing for authors these days." My mother was probably the only person in the world who had actually bought a copy of my book.

"I seriously don't think I can do this," I sighed.

"You'll be fine. The society members are all amateur creative persons themselves, just like you, and they'll be so interested in how you've gone about it all. Just go along and have a little chat with them. It'll be easy. Some of them might even buy the book, if you take some copies with you, and perhaps a painting or two. You'll have a lovely time."

Typically biased in my favour, as parents often are towards their offspring, my mother thinks I can do anything, which is wonderfully supportive of course but not always terribly accurate. Had she not noticed that I had spent the last 46 years actively avoiding public speaking in any form? (Apart from a little divergence from that policy at my solo exhibition last year, which, while it hadn't been quite as bad as all that, wasn't an experience I was keen to repeat.) All through school I had managed to never stand up in front of anyone and say anything. It was quite an achievement, one that had taken careful planning and forethought and I didn't intend to change things now.

There was a moment or two of silence as I went into a little mental bubble of anxiety. I took a couple of deep, slow breaths to steady myself and eventually my mother continued, "Well, you have a little think about it and let me know. I have to go now, darling, I've got my tap class and then your dad and I are meeting up with friends from the French Twinning Association for coffee. I'll call you tomorrow. Bye!" With that breezy farewell she was gone. Off to the myriad social engagements my parents got up to now they were retired.

I slumped onto one of the stools by the breakfast bar, put the handset down on the surface before me and stared unseeing into the depths of my dark teacup. What was she thinking? There was no way I could ever do any real public speaking.

Satisfied that this was the end of the matter, I was quite surprised to hear a defiant little voice from the depths of my subconscious stating quite clearly and very seriously, "It's not a bad idea"

"It is a terrible idea," I countered in surprise. "I really can't do it." I said this very firmly indeed, just to make sure I understood myself.

"Why?" My inner voice piped up again to demand defiantly.

"I don't do public speaking, ever!" I said with conviction.

"You didn't think you'd write a book either," the voice inside replied. I ought to clarify here that I wasn't actually hearing things; honestly! It was just that the words seemed to spring into my head unbidden from nowhere.

"I haven't written a book." I told myself.

"Errr, I beg to differ..." (How come my inner voice sounded like a sarcastic teenager?)

"Oh, you know what I mean. Not really. I'm not a proper author."

"Authors write books, you've written a book..."

"It's not the same thing," I said, wondering why on earth I was arguing with myself.

"Lots of people would like to write a book, not many actually do it. You've done it. Give yourself some credit for once. Things change," reasoned my subconscious earnestly. "You've changed!"

'Yes!' I mentally muttered, very quietly (in case I heard myself), 'I am clearly now such a total nut case that I am having a row with myself!'

I stood up abruptly.

"I'm very busy!" I said firmly, out loud again this time. "So, stop going on about it, I've got things to do." I think it was Buddha who said: 'Rule your mind or it will rule you.' Rather apt I felt, given the circumstances! Squashing down any further subconscious responses very resolutely indeed, I bustled around getting my hessian carrier bags out so I could go and do a quick smash and grab at the local supermarket to stock up on milk and other sundries.

I hastily went through my 'leaving the house' checklist which involves a quick glance in every room to make sure the kids (or the husband) haven't left anything electronic on that might blow up or burn the place down while I'm out. Yes, I am still paranoid. Then I switched off all the lights (because teenagers are physically incapable of doing that, hence every single light in the house was on) and locked both the back and front doors. (No-one else ever seems to do that around here either.) Just to be on the safe side, I stuck a spare door key behind the skull and crossbones badge on the brim of Skelly's tri-corn hat as I passed him on my way to the car. The family skeleton was lounging lazily on a large, upturned, wooden bucket by the fence, doing an excellent impression of an extra from the Pirates of the Caribbean film. One could almost expect Captain Jack Sparrow to rock up and sit next to him any minute.

Now that Quiet was in the sixth form and some of his friends had passed their driving tests, he had a habit of hitching a lift home from school early with one of them, but he never remembered to take his door key with him and then grumped when he couldn't get in. I had taken to hiding a spare key for him so that when he rang me up and grumbled about being locked out, I could present him with a solution that wouldn't cause me any undue inconvenience. I reasoned that not many burglars would be brave enough to frisk a skeleton for a spare key, especially one armed with such a realistic looking plastic sabre and two flintlock pistols, so in my mind it was a fairly secure system.

Finally, I settled myself comfortably in Daisy, my little purple car, and we were off, satisfied that there was a fairly good chance the house might still be standing on our return. (Lightening? Twice? It happens!)

As I negotiated the ford further down the road, I started to wonder what had made me write a book in the first place. I had never had any ambitions to be an author and yet when it started, I had been powerless to resist. It was as if some force had taken over and consumed me completely until the story was told. Perhaps that's why I didn't feel it was real.

Nevertheless, while I didn't know why, I did know when. It had all started about six months earlier when we had finally accepted that we needed to put our home on the market, an act that was to have some very unexpected consequences indeed.

3: Perception

Definition: The way in which something might be interpreted or judged.

Back in the past, approximately six months earlier, soon after the house was put up for sale

"This kitchen is just no good at all," the rather haughty woman declared in a somewhat nasal tone. "I run a professional catering business. I give classes from home. I would need to have large groups watching me demonstrate."

Mentally rolling my eyes and thinking 'We've got a right one here!' I started to sidle slowly towards the door, intent on extricating myself from the general conversation as soon as possible.

It was the end of August and our beautiful cottage had been on the market for nearly two months. Rebuilding our home, after it had collapsed unexpectedly, had cost us dearly in both emotional and financial terms, hence we were left in possession of a scarily big mortgage; so big in fact that we'd given it a name. We'd christened our massive mortgage Mortimer, in an attempt to make it seem more friendly and approachable. That tactic hadn't worked particularly well, so several months before my art exhibition we had got stuck in to do all the things you are supposed to do when putting your house up for sale, with the intention of significantly reducing Mortimer as soon as possible. We've seen the daytime TV shows like The House Doctor and Escape to the

Country. It's not rocket science. Everyone knows you consider your kerb appeal, slap a bit of fresh paint around, get a neutral carpet and de-clutter till the cows come home before sitting back and waiting for an acceptable offer.

Let's look at those elements in more detail, shall we? There was no doubt that we'd been forcibly 'decluttered' when the house fell down, so that was not really an issue. If anything, we didn't have enough junk around the place. The house looked a bit too sparse, in an obsessively minimalist way. We were missing a lot of essentials, especially on the furniture front, so I had used my imagination and created several small occasional tables from cardboard boxes disguised with all-encompassing tablecloths draped over them. It was important to remember which items were counterfeit and not to accidentally put anything heavy on them or you'd get predictable and often messy results.

As for fresh paint, there was plenty of that already on the brand new walls; it was barely dry from the rebuild. Similarly, the carpets, a lovely pale biscuit colour, had only just gone down.

I left the kerb appeal side of things to my gardening and power tool obsessed husband. (There is no point having a dog and then barking yourself now, is there?) He had happily hacked away at the front hedges and then cheerfully chopped the overgrown vegetation at the roadside verge into submission as well, before turning his hand to planting up a profusion of pelargoniums in pots. There was even an abundance of flowery climbers flourishing up the fence by the garage as well.

All I had to do after that was keep the place looking tidy, which is no mean feat when you share living space with two occasionally 'back for the summer vacation' students, three untidy fellas and a six-foot skeleton with both a fancy dress fetish and a penchant for lurking in unexpected locations. It meant that nearly all my free time was spent either trying to keep on top of the housework myself or chivvying the other residents to do their fair share (which actually took far longer and was much less effective than doing everything myself, but that's not the point). Neither featured as one of my favourite occupations by any stretch of the imagination, but you really can't leave knickers drying in the conservatory on racks when any old Tom, Dick or Harriet might pop by at a moment's notice to eye up your square footage with a view to making a potential property purchase offer, can you? It simply didn't fit with the whole 'luxury lifestyle image' that we were trying to promote in order to get a decent sale price. Shame that really but there you go. Needs must!

In fact, I was exhausted after a high-speed, last minute tidy up this morning for the snooty woman currently criticising my kitchen, and I was in no mood to try and placate her or point out the many positive attributes of the room. I edged towards the door leaving our extremely patient estate agent valiantly commenting, in a gently persuasive tone, that it was a touch unfair to expect to find a professional kitchen in what was a purely domestic property. As soon as I was around the corner and out of sight I fled to my studio while the estate agent waxed lyrical about beautifully generous proportions including not only the kitchen, but also a lounge area with an open fireplace and an adjoining conservatory section large enough to contain a table that seated 12 when fully extended.

Not a small room by any standards really, unless you are feeling particularly picky. And thank goodness for that! For nearly eighteen months the whole family had often spent all day together in that one room after the rest of the house had fallen down. We had frequently slept on the floor by the fire rather than spend another soggy night in a tent during the worst of the weather.

To be fair though, while our haughty house-viewer was being a touch overbearing with her comments about her catering business, she'd probably never been in such an awful situation and therefore not learned to see life in quite the way we did, and why should she? In many ways I was glad for her, because I wouldn't wish what had happened to us on anyone. Nevertheless, that didn't mean that I had to stick around to hear her pick holes in my property. That was why we had employed the lovely Patience and her other estate agent colleagues and they were very good at their jobs.

Once in the studio, I gave myself over to prepping canvases for future paintings. At that time, I was very 'into' creating textured bases onto which I would then paint ocean or plant images. The resultant uneven canvas surfaces gave the finished pieces much greater depth and they were really exciting to paint on, as I never quite knew how each one was going to turn out. Merrily slapping glue and layers of crumpled tissue paper onto several stretched canvases, I was getting into a right old sticky mess, when Patience eventually popped her head around the door.

"She's gone," she announced with a smile." It's safe to come out now. Shame on you for not having a professional kitchen!"

"I know!" I replied, "Silly me! I should have realised she'd want one when we had the kitchen put in twelve years ago. Can I assume that she won't be putting in an offer then?"

"I think we can safely say that she's not interested, although I am not really sure where she'll find what she's looking for. Especially when you consider her budget," Patience grimaced and rolled her eyes. "It's probably a bit too remote here for her anyway. We will find you a buyer, I promise, it's just going to take some time. This is rather a unique property."

I nodded thoughtfully. "Yes, I can see that it wouldn't be everyone's cup of tea, living this far out of town, but we love it. It's so peaceful."

If it weren't for Mortimer we wouldn't dream of selling up, but unfortunately it wasn't that straightforward. It also wasn't proving easy to find a buyer because although the house was now beautifully restored and in perfect structural and general working order, the current housing market was not terribly buoyant and there were very few legitimate buyers in our particular price bracket. There was no point dropping the price because that wouldn't solve our financial situation, so we were effectively between a rock and a hard place and simply had to tighten our belts and stick it out.

Patience made as if to leave, but then turned back with what I had learned in recent weeks was her 'tactful' expression. I paused, gluey brush in hand, "You look like you have a suggestion."

She smiled and nodded, "Two suggestions, actually."

"Go on." I braced myself, placing my brush down and folding my arms in a subconsciously defensive gesture.

She cast an eye around my studio. "The rest of the house is beautifully presented, but this room isn't particularly doing you any favours right now."

I followed her gaze. It was a bit cluttered, I supposed. I often didn't bother to put my paints away because it just wasted precious painting time getting them out again. There were also several unfinished wet paintings on the go, one on the easel, a small one on the desk by the window and one propped up on the mantelpiece. Finally, the textured canvases I was working on, although small, were lined up on layers of newspaper on the floor surrounded by tissue paper and pots of PVA glue.

OK, I didn't like it but I had to concede that she had a point! Don't get me wrong though, the rest of the house was beautifully tidy. I'd spent hours vacuuming carpets and polishing stuff over the last few weeks, even though all I really wanted to do was get on with finishing the painting commissions I'd recently taken on.

"So, you're suggesting I tidy it up a bit."

She nodded sympathetically, "Quite a bit. Just in here, everywhere else in the house is fine."

"OK!" I agreed.

She didn't continue.

"And the second thing?" I prompted.

"Well," she paused.

"Go on," I encouraged. If there was something that would better our chances of achieving a sale then I needed to know what it was.

She sighed, "It's your skeleton….."

"Oh, hell!" I said, "I thought I'd hidden him. Where is he this time?"

"At the moment he's in the utility room, behind the door, on a hook hanging by the neck with what looks like a school tie….?"

That's definitely not where I left him, and the school tie really ought to be around someone else's neck right at that moment, otherwise he'd get a detention!

Patience continued carefully, "As I said, I don't think this lady was going to buy anyway, but finding the skeleton….well…."

"It put the final nail in the coffin, right?"

She smiled at my unintentional pun and nodded.

"You do know he's not real, don't you?" My fingers instinctively crossed behind my back as I asked this because, in truth, I had no idea if he was or not.

"Oh yes, but he is remarkably realistic and unfortunately I do think some people might be finding him a touch off-putting."

"Some people have no sense of humour!" I muttered.

Skelly was now, very definitely, part of the family after arriving for a Halloween party during the time that we lived in the garden, and then never leaving. His antics at the time had cheered us all up immensely during a very dark period, but I could see what she meant. We couldn't expect normal people to 'get' him particularly.

"Don't worry," I said, "I'll sort it out."

After Patience had left (no doubt to be perfectly patient at another property where I bet they hadn't got a mobile skeleton problem), I sat and stared at my canvases for quite some time. I'd rather gone off the idea of painting now. Pealing layers of dried PVA glue off my fingers, I decided that my lovely estate agent was probably right. It was going to be a painful process but this studio needed sorting out, and sooner rather than later.

Tidying up never features at the top of my list of 'favourite things to do'. It always makes me grumpy and is, therefore, usually best avoided. My reasoning follows the logic that the mess will still be there tomorrow, whereas the urge to paint might not be. (Unless my mother or my mother-in-law plan to visit of course, in which case everything needs to be tidied up immediately.) In fact, clearing up in the grand scheme of things generally doesn't appear on my 'to do' list at all, but that doesn't mean it doesn't need doing of course. Since the house had been on the market there had been far too much tidying up going on, in my opinion.

I've probably given you the impression that I'm slovenly, but that isn't the case, honestly. The house is usually reasonably neat, as I tend to keep on top of things as I go along, but it doesn't generally have the sort of polish required for a viewing in the natural course of our day-to-day lives as a family. There are too many people actually trying to get on with the business of living here for it to ever be a typical show home.

However, Patience was right, a bit more effort was definitely required in my studio and before I attempted to solve the Skelly situation, I reluctantly concentrated my efforts on tackling my cluttered creative space.

Several hours later I was exhausted. It wasn't a fun job by any stretch of the imagination, but I had to do what I could to improve our chances of getting a buyer. The sad thing was that this was going to mean some fairly drastic changes in my usual method of operation. I was going to have to restrict my painting schedule significantly in order to keep control of the state that this room got into. It wasn't something I was looking forward to. My whole ethos with art was to relax and enjoy it, to let go of constraints, forget the rules and just let colour and creativity flow. However, under current circumstances, that was now a luxury I couldn't afford.

Nevertheless, I had carefully collected up and sorted my profusion of painting paraphernalia into a number of neatly compartmented drawers and boxes. No longer were the acrylics, oils and watercolour tubes all tumbled together in a happy, haphazard heap, but regimented in strictly separate sections. Brushes, palette knives, rollers and rulers were organised into tidy rows of jolly jam jars sitting on systematically sorted shelves stuffed with outsized tubs of glue, natural sponges, and rolls of tissue paper, cellophane and bubble wrap. Sizeable sheets of mount board were stacked in ship-shape fashion behind the filing cabinet and pencils, charcoal, rulers and rubbers marched in smart straight lines in the top drawer of my desk by the window.

All of the finished canvases had been removed and stacked in one of the sheds and my easel had been dismantled and tucked behind the door out of sight.

The result was a light, bright, tidy room that looked very appealing. All my hard work had brought about pretty impressive results, but it made me feel sad. I wasn't sure I was ever going to be the type of person who was able to paint tidily and I had a worrying feeling that this was going to be a bit of a problem. However, if it meant that we sold the house then it would be worth it. I could always paint afterwards, assuming we found a house that was big enough.

Eventually I ran out of things to sort out in the studio and tiredly closed the door before heading into my 'unprofessional' kitchen in search of a sustaining snack, making a mental note to tackle the Skelly issue before the next viewing.

4: Concatenation

Definition: a whole series of things that have a connection. (I promise!)

Staying with the situation in the past...

A week or so after the big studio tidy up, at the beginning of September, I stood in a tiny, airless corridor surrounded by boxes of random stuff belonging to my younger daughter, Logic. Both the boxes and I were enveloped in the slightly stale aroma of 'eau de mildew' mixed with institutional bulk-buy bleach and, as such, I was trying hard not to need to breathe. The smell and the squeaky linoleum beneath my feet transported me instantaneously back to my long-forgotten arrival at university as a student, (more than 28 years ago, but who's counting?) and I noted with interest that halls of residence hadn't really changed all that much in the intervening period.

For various reasons I had found myself studying science at university when all I had really wanted to do was go to art college, having been inspired as a young child by my grandmother who was a very talented, amateur artist. But life doesn't generally work out the way we hope it will when we are six, does it? At the age of eighteen I had found myself studying for a 'proper' qualification instead. It was a sensible decision, made for all sorts of practical reasons and while I didn't regret it, a really tiny piece of me couldn't help lamenting a lost opportunity to follow that childhood dream.

A reminiscent sigh rolled down my spine, but I reminded myself that my role here today was that of 'dutifully supportive mother returning one of two student daughters to university for the second year'. As such, my opinion on the standard of her accommodation was irrelevant and I was only permitting myself to say bright and positive things like "How lovely!" "Isn't this exciting?" and "You are so lucky/clever/brilliant," interchanging the adjective as appropriate.

Now was not the time to start saying anything along the lines of: "Are you seriously planning to live here?" or "What on earth were you thinking when you signed the tenancy agreement for this dive?"

To be honest, it wasn't actually that bad as student accommodation goes. I'd seen much worse. Only last week I had moved my older daughter, Chaos, into a house for the start of her third year. Having been obsessed with wanting to see full structural surveys for the student house she had lived in last year, Chaos contrarily now seemed to be defiantly tempting fate with her latest rental property choice, as it appeared to have even less stability than the proverbial house of cards. I couldn't help but admire her blasé attitude.

Sadly, none of the family had got away with the whole 'whoops, the house has fallen down and we're homeless, let's go and live in a tent in the garden' experience scot-free. There had been a massive emotional price to pay after our cob cottage had collapsed. Yet while I would like to think that the nightmare of that time might eventually start to fade from her mind, I felt that Chaos' current choice of accommodation was an act of deliberately brave rebellion; an open dare to the fates not to mess with her again.

Her latest student house, on close inspection the previous week, gave all the appearance of being held together in places with little more than a combination of string, duct tape and a few half-hearted prayers. I was pretty certain that her cramped Victorian terrace dwelling was still standing only because the significantly better maintained houses on either side of it were holding it up. Neither Chaos nor her four house mates seemed to have noticed the huge crater in the kitchen floor, the hole in the back door covered with a dog-eared bit of old cardboard and sticky tape, or the missing third tread on the staircase. (I am not going to comment on the state of the bathroom!) But it didn't matter. They were happy and that was the most important thing. I reassured myself that in spite of all evidence to the contrary, it must have passed the necessary safety checks that are currently in force, as it was definitely on the university-approved housing list.

I checked.

Three times!

Now, I do appreciate that, given our recent history, I have a habit of overreacting and as a result I forced myself to take the view that if the state of the place didn't bother the students then why should it bother me? Contracts were already signed for the year and there was nowhere else available, so there was nothing I could do about it anyway.

Therefore, in view of her sister's extreme choice, it could be said that Logic's second year residential flat was quite reasonable, in spite of the creeping mould and a dodgy window (it doesn't quite close properly so there is a permanent draft which might prove an issue mid-winter but let's not borrow trouble). It was right in the city centre, so near countless bars and nightclubs which are inevitably essential for student life, and yet still only a short walk to campus. It was also quite economically priced she assured me.

Speaking of finances, let's not forget my other parental role on this day, which was to produce my credit card to solve any minor teething issues, such as forgotten duvet cases or essential kitchen equipment by purchasing replacements at the nearest department store.

Logic, energised by the prospect of the start of her second year of extra hard maths, (I know, she's crazy, but someone has to do it!) popped her head out of her new room with a bright smile on her face. "Won't be long, just need to get organised, then I'll find the kettle and make us a brew," she said and, grabbing one of the boxes off the pile, disappeared again.

I wasn't really needed to guard her possessions in the corridor, but there was not enough space in her room for the two of us at the same time. I was beginning to wonder how she was going to get all her belongings in through the door, let alone put them away, but that was definitely her problem, not mine. She's always liked jigsaws and she gave every appearance of enjoying this particular conundrum. Shifting my position slightly so that I could peer into the somewhat bijou space that was to be her home for the next forty-two weeks, I studied the cramped room through the open doorway with interest. A three-quarter sized double bed took up ninety percent of the floor area, with a small wardrobe and desk unit running alongside it. A door next to the foot of the bed opened into a miniscule en-suite, a very grand term for what was effectively a toilet located within a shower cubicle. This arrangement effectively encouraged the student to multitask on matters of personal hygiene, as one could clean one's teeth whilst sitting on the loo and showering all at the same time, if one had a mind to. I supposed it would depend just how late the student was for lectures in the morning.

While most people might consider that this was a fairly impossible space to live and work in for any length of time, I couldn't help but be quite impressed by the design. It was very cleverly engineered, practical and efficient, as well as being significantly larger than the cupboard that Logic had lived in for almost a year after the house sat down and we moved lock, stock and barrel into Hattie the caravan. That whole entertaining experience had massively modified our expectations of general living facilities, and we tend to be grateful for what we have these days, rather than bother about what we don't.

Suddenly realising that the room looked rather empty, I wondered where Logic actually was. She had definitely gone into the room but wasn't visible now. They were very dinky dimensions for her to have successfully disappeared in. With some relief I spotted her feet, encased in a mismatching pair of funky socks (like mother, like daughter), sticking out from under the bed. Aha! Obviously, 'under bed storage' was the key solution for such a compact student life style, although I am sure you're not supposed to lounge around under there for long. I bet it never gets hoovered.

There was a muffled muttering followed by some energetic wriggling which made me question whether she needed some help extricating herself from the dark depths but, other than diving in and yanking hard on both legs, I wasn't sure how much assistance I could be. Instead I stayed at my post and watched as more of her came slowly into view until eventually her head popped out too. Shoving static, crackly hair out of her eyes, she looked over at me.

"So! It's a shame about your job, isn't it?" she said, bluntly.

Ah! I'd been wondering when that particular subject would come up. I looked at my feet for a second before answering.

"Yes, I suppose so," I replied vaguely.

The company that I had been working for, for the past twenty years, was in the process of changing hands and the new management structure would not include a role for me. I wasn't particularly devastated as it had never been a terribly inspiring job by any stretch of the imagination, merely something that I'd fallen into fairly early on in life. It was flexible, paid relatively well and fitted around our growing family's needs, and as a result I had stayed on way longer than I had ever imagined I would. Nevertheless, by the coming December, I would effectively be unemployed for the first time ever in my working life and it was requiring a bit of mental adjustment.

While I wasn't actually bothered about losing that particular job, it would inevitably add some pressure to our current financial situation (remember Mortimer?), so I was going to have to find another form of income fairly soon. However, there was to be a small severance pay out which would allow some breathing space before things got completely critical in the penny stakes. Selling the house would still help massively, but there was no sign of a buyer as yet. Either way, I was going to have to get another job of some description. The only problem was that I didn't really know what sort of job to go for. Feeling wrong-footed, I wasn't really in the mood to face the sort of Spanish Inquisition style interrogation that I suspected was about to be launched in my general direction.

In that moment I realised that my adored Barbarian offspring had definitely discussed my approaching unemployment situation at length, in private, and reached what they decided was the most appropriate course of action. No doubt Logic had been given the unenviable task of 'Sorting Mother Out'!

Unfortunately for Logic, I wasn't prepared to co-operate just then. I had been up since silly o'clock in order to crow-bar as much returning student-related detritus into Daisy as was humanly possible, and then I had spent nearly three hours trekking from the Hampshire border, across the wilds of Dorset, and Devon to reach the university. Poor Daisy had been so overloaded with the aforementioned student associated paraphernalia that making it to the top of some of the hills along the way had been extremely touch and go, even in first gear with my foot to the floor. Then, having arrived, we were faced with lugging all her junk up six flights of stairs (the lift was, of course, out of order – what a surprise!) to our current location on the top floor. All that had been accomplished without the aid of any breakfast; not even a cup of tea!

Whilst off caffeine for the most part, I usually need one cup of the 'proper' stuff to start the day. However, that morning I had been worrying about the lack of potential 'rest breaks' on route and so, foolishly, had left without my usual fix. As a result, I felt I was achieving a minor miracle just staying on my feet at that point, thus the bright scholar before me would be wise not to push her luck. I wasn't as open to the experience of being organised by my offspring as I might have been under other circumstances. I really did not want to talk about my job situation, or the lack thereof, but Logic had that sensible expression on her face indicating the presence of a whole host of carefully collated questions. These were, no doubt, questions that I didn't currently have the answers to as I was still processing my change in circumstances and trying not to get stressed. Casting around for a distraction, I spotted what looked like the handle of the kettle peeking out of one of the boxes.

"Aha! There it is!" I exclaimed in relief, pouncing on it. "I'll just set this up in the communal kitchen for you, shall I?" I scooped up the box in the certain knowledge that if the kettle was in there then so would any tea and coffee making equipment; including mugs, teaspoons and probably even some milk in a little cool bag, if I know my daughter correctly. Logic is nothing if not…. well…. logical, hence her nickname. Backing away from the approaching cross-examination with indecent haste, I shoved the door that was helpfully marked 'Kitchen' with my comfortably padded rear end and disappeared inside with a fixed but polite 'I am ignoring you' expression on my face.

I knew I wouldn't get away with it for long but the words of one particular wise old Roman, Tacitus, were echoing around in my head. 'He who fights and runs away may turn to fight another day'. Hence, I beat a hasty retreat until such time as I felt a touch more resilient.

Anyway, enough of all this history for the moment; it is all connected to why I wrote my book, and I will get to the point soon, I promise, but let us return to the present for a bit, to see how things are developing.

Part 2

'Thinking, the talking of the soul with itself,'

Plato
424BC – 347BC

5: Momentous

Definition: of significant importance, having a substantial effect on future events

Do please come forward in time with me once again to the present day, early January and our heroine heading for the supermarket…

I trundled along the wintery lanes in the general direction of civilisation and a milk supply, slowing for a small herd of horses, three super-fit looking joggers and a selection of dogs of indeterminate breed exercising their associated humans. Eventually, I turned Daisy into the car park of a reasonably-sized supermarket, all the while contemplating how the events that had unfolded six months earlier had led to the situation that I now found myself in. But that was when the little voice in my head started nagging me again.

"Your mother's right, you know."

"No, she isn't" I replied firmly.

"She is," the other me insisted. "You could put a fairly interesting presentation together. It might be fun."

"No, I couldn't, and no, it wouldn't be."

"Think about it."

"Be quiet!" I replied firmly, "I am trying to park."

Silence reigned as I reversed into a space and then headed into the shop armed with my hessian bags and a wonky trolley. Several packed aisles of produce later my subconscious tried again.

"On reflection, I don't think I want to be quiet," she piped up.

"For goodness sake," I hissed in frustration. Having loaded up with twelve pints of milk, I was then marching through the frozen food section looking for peas and oven chips to go with some sausages for supper.

"Give me one good reason why you can't do this," my inner voice was developing an increasingly belligerent tone.

"I can't, it'd be too embarrassing!" I muttered.

"Seriously? That's your reason?" replied my subconscious with a fair degree of disgust. "That's pretty pathetic, you know!"

"Oh, will you just go away!" I said forcefully, frowning fiercely at my internal self.

The old lady in the thick tweed overcoat who was peering short-sightedly at the frozen peas in the freezer cabinet, stiffened abruptly with an affronted huff, before scuttling off with surprising agility for one so elderly, whilst giving me nervous glances over her shoulder.

"Oh! Sorry, I don't mean you. I'm just talking to myself. Out loud," I said, watching her rapidly retreating rear in dismay.

"Was that what you meant by embarrassing?" piped up my subconscious sarcastically.

"Aagh!" I hissed in quiet frustration. "OK, I'll think about it! I promise. Now will you please leave me alone?"

"That's all I ask," said my subconscious smugly before fading out of my mind completely with an ominously final whisper that echoed around my mind, "I'll be back!"

"Great!" I said sarcastically to myself, grabbing a large bag of Birds Eye's best and shoving my trolley towards the tills, wondering if anyone else had to argue with such an opinionated subliminal self. How come I get saddled with such an outspoken and obstinate inner identity? Surely the very definition of the subconscious is that one is supposed to be blissfully unaware of it? Hmmm! I just might have to explain that to my bolshie alter ego one day soon. If she ever lets me get a word in sideways that is.

In spite of my embarrassing argument with myself in the supermarket, the rest of the afternoon passed relatively calmly, thank goodness, and I returned to my still-standing house (phew!) to find

Quiet and a couple of his mates playing the PlayStation with Skelly in the lounge. It would seem that there was nothing more interesting happening on the Sixth Form timetable that afternoon.

Remembering my son's odd behaviour that morning, I watched him surreptitiously for a few minutes, but he seemed completely normal so I backed out of the room, closing the door on the way in order to dampen the noise of car races screeching away at a hundred-plus miles per hour accompanied by cheers and other associated teenage boy banter. I unpacked the shopping hurriedly before diving into the freezer to locate those sausages I mentioned. My plan for the evening was to go to the WI meeting in the village whilst the boys and Beloved Husband were occupied at cricket training. They are always ravenous after training, so it made sense to cook their tea before I left so that they could microwave it quickly when they got home.

A few hours later, I was settling into my seat in the village hall next to my lovely neighbour as the meeting got underway. There is usually a very interesting presentation given at each WI meeting and, while I had not paid any attention to who was speaking this evening or what they planned to speak about, they are generally of a very high standard so I was looking forward to it.

Fifteen minutes into the meeting (and bang on time) after the general news and business had been discussed, the main door to the hall opened and a tall, confident, smartly dressed woman walked in, wheeling a little case behind her. She was welcomed warmly by the committee members and ushered to a table by a screen at the front of the room where she swiftly unzipped her case and drew out a laptop with a small projector attachment. These were assembled on the table at lightning quick speed and in moments she was smiling at her audience and ready to begin.

An impressively efficient start to what was, in truth, a very entertaining presentation. This lady was a particularly awesome individual who had spent her entire career supporting women in the working environment and encouraging them to reach their full potential. In fact, she had been awarded an MBE in recognition of her outstanding achievement and services to the community. Over the course of the next hour, she made us laugh with funny yet very motivational anecdotes about some of the gifted women that she had worked with over the years. She rounded off her talk by mentioning that she was keen to interview women with interesting stories and achievements for her podcast (I wasn't quite sure what a podcast was but nodded knowledgeably anyway), and would be delighted to hear recommendations or suggestions from any of the ladies in the audience.

Well! Talk about waving a red rag at a bull. My lovely neighbour immediately started elbowing me firmly in the ribs and in a stage whisper said, "You should tell her about your story!"

Uh oh!

"You know," she persisted, "about your house falling down. Tell her about writing your book."

If you remember, I mentioned earlier that I didn't expect anyone to read my book? Well, my neighbour was probably one of the few people on the planet who not only knew about it (she's met my mother), but had also read it (she's a very kind person). I smiled at her to acknowledge the compliment she was paying me by suggesting that I might be interesting enough to draw to the attention of the awesome lady speaker. Unfortunately, that wasn't enough for my neighbour, as she elbowed me again and gesture towards the front of the room.

"Go on!" she insisted.

"I'll think about it," I demurred. The last thing I wanted was to have any attention drawn to me, but she obviously didn't agree. My lovely neighbour is a wonderfully warm woman and always seems to have a bright smile on her face, but it would be a mistake to think she is a pushover in any way. She is one determined character with some very strong opinions and, I found out at that moment, she also has extremely pointy elbows. It was quite clear that she was going to ensure that I drew myself to the attention of Lady Awesome whether I liked it or not. It soon became evident that, if I wanted to avoid extreme bruising or a couple of broken ribs from those elbows I mentioned, I was going to have to give in graciously. In a desperate attempt to protect my torso and make sure she didn't announce her idea to the whole room, I whispered hastily, "I promise, I will speak to her afterwards, but let's allow her to finish up and have a cup of tea first, she must be exhausted."

"Hmm," she replied ominously before nodding meaningfully at

me, in the same way that my mum does when she is really saying: "You'd better see that you do young lady because I'll be watching you!" Honestly, it was as if my mother was sat right there beside me in the hall in east Dorset, instead of two counties away causing mischief and mayhem for the residents of Devon.

Lady Awesome wound up her presentation to thunderous applause very shortly after that and there was a general increase in the noise level in the hall as the fifty or so ladies of the WI, who had been engrossed by the talk, were now gripped by a sudden need for caffeine. The usual refined scramble for the excellent home-baked refreshments ensued.

In the confusion that followed, I had every hope that I could avoid having to make good on my promise. I made a few fake moves in the general direction of Lady Awesome to try and throw my neighbour off the scent, feeling sure that she would eventually become engrossed in acquiring a cup of tea and a chocolate cupcake, but to no avail. She was wise to my little tricks and kept her eye on me at all times. At one point, from across the room, she even raised her eyebrows and pointed at her watch before crossing her arms and nodding forcefully in the direction she felt I should be moving. I couldn't help but quail inside. Obviously, I was not going to get away with my cunning plan of avoidance, but there was a whole group of very talented ladies of the WI lining up to chat to Lady Awesome already so I couldn't see why she would want to talk to me.

Eventually, as my lovely neighbour made a really obvious shooing gesture and moved as if to walk over there herself, I threw my hands up in the air in supplication and finally joined the back of the pack by the speaker.

All joking aside, what I didn't realise was that I was at one of those significant turning points in my life. You probably know the sort I mean, they are often unexpected and massively important when you look at things retrospectively, but at the time you generally don't recognise them for what they are. It's only with hindsight that you can see that they are fairly pivotal to future developments. With that reasoning, the next few minutes of my life were about to be quite momentous for me, if not in quite the way my lovely neighbour anticipated.

I edged closer to Lady Awesome, as the rest of the WI members eventually trotted off to dive on the remaining refreshments, and told myself that my neighbour only had to think that I had told the speaker about my book. I didn't actually have to do it. Lady Awesome turned to me with a welcoming smile and said hello. I thanked her nervously for a great presentation and asked if I could buy a signed copy of the book that she was selling that evening before realising in mortification that I didn't have any money on me.

She laughed, signed a copy of her book with a flourish and handed it to me saying not to worry; I could transfer the money to her when I got home.

"You trust me?" I asked surprised.

"You look trustworthy enough to me," she said firmly and handed me her business card with her BACs details on the back. Taking it, I thanked her and watched as she started to pack her projector and laptop away as efficiently as she had on arrival.

I am not quite sure what came over me at that point, but seeing this compelling, inspirational woman gather her things together and make ready to leave, I was unexpectedly overcome by the urge to tell her my story. However, my window of opportunity to do so was disappearing before my eyes. I suddenly remembered the copy of my book that always lurked in the bottom of my handbag and, scrabbling around in the depths of the fabric, hurriedly drew it out. I held it out to Lady Awesome muttering, "Do you mind if I give you this? It's my story, based on true events." Then before she could really respond either way, I practically chucked the thing at her and said a quick goodbye before scarpering for the loos, where I then kicked myself hard (metaphorically) for being a socially inept idiot.

"Well! That went well," said my subconscious sarcastically. "You displayed a staggering lack of confidence there and covered yourself in glory...not! She's going to think you're a weirdo."

"Oh, do shut up," I begged. Fortunately, all the cubicles were empty so there was no danger of me scaring any more little old ladies by talking to myself this time. I was fully aware that I hadn't handled the situation with any kind of aplomb and I had no idea why. I only usually get tongue-tied like that over things that are really important. Maybe my book meant more to me than I realised.

Looking at myself in the mirror over the hand basin I wrinkled my nose, sighed and said, "Well, she'll either read it or she won't. It's not the end of the world if she doesn't."

"True, no harm done!" replied my subconscious quietly in a moment of unexpected solidarity. I shrugged and then pulled my handbag more securely onto my shoulder, before going over to peer out of the ladies' room door in order to see if the coast was clear so that I could make my escape to the car and go home.

Unknown to me, Lady Awesome was intrigued (in spite of my poor communication skills) and that was soon going to lead on to some very interesting developments indeed.

6: Inquisition

Definition: A religious tribunal instigated by Pope Gregory IX in the twelfth century, notorious for prolonged and intense questioning and the use of torture to gain results

Back to the Spanish Inquisition from the student in the past…

I wasn't going to get much of a reprieve from my offspring- induced interrogation. Logic isn't the type to let a subject go until she has finished with it to her full satisfaction; a quality that I completely admire when it isn't aimed at me. I couldn't hide in that grotty student accommodation kitchen forever. Unfortunately!

Let's not forget that when dropping a child off at university for the start of a new term it is also the dutiful parent's express obligation to feed the starving student. It's in the unwritten rulebook; the one that keeps changing to ensure that you are always in the wrong. The abandoning parent must provide a sufficiently large final meal in order to keep the student nourished throughout the weeks of hardship and study to come, before deserting them and beating a hasty retreat home at all speed. Hence, I found myself sat opposite Logic in the local pub an hour later watching her diligently work her way through a suitably sustaining, hearty student meal deal.

As she daintily chomped through a double beef burger loaded with extra bacon and cheese oozing out of an outsized bun, set in a vast sea of chips and deep fried onion rings complete with a single lettuce leaf one slice of cucumber and two segments of tomato on the side (no doubt this was supposed to be the healthy balanced bit of the whole meal), she came to the point with her usual tact, declaring emphatically, "Quiet is worried you'll get bored if you're not working."

Noting her strategic use of the 'blame-a-sibling' diversionary tactic, I couldn't help smiling wryly, because the subtext on that one was so obvious. What Quiet was really worried about was that I might start interfering in what he was up to with greater frequency and effect if I didn't have a job to keep me otherwise occupied. The last thing a sixteen-year old boy wants is a mother with too much time on her hands, hence there had been any number of suggestions from my older son with regard to possible jobs that he felt I should consider applying for. Funnily enough I wasn't enamoured with the idea of stacking shelves at the local supermarket full-time or working shifts at the local fast food joint except as a last resort. Nevertheless, Small thought the latter idea was fantastic until I explained that such a job would not mean he had access to an unlimited supply of free burgers.

"I don't think that's really what your brother is concerned about," I replied dryly.

She smiled. "It may not be his main motivation, I'll admit that, but I do think he is genuinely concerned about you. We all are."

"Really?" I asked in surprise, "There's no need, I'll find something. I'm just not sure what to go for at the moment."

"That is precisely the problem," she said emphatically.

Mystified, I replied, "I don't follow you."

"It's your attitude, 'I'll find something,' for goodness' sake mum, you're forty-six not sixteen!"

Inhaling deeply, a bit taken aback by her exasperated tone, I said with studied patience, "Believe me, I am very aware of exactly how old I am."

"Shouldn't you know what you want to do with your life by now? You've been doing that office job for years and you've never particularly liked it. This is an opportunity for change. You need to do some serious thinking so that you make the right choice next. Start thinking about what you do want to do with the rest of your life." We (I mean she) had moved onto dessert by this time and she was stabbing viciously at a chocolate ice cream sundae using a teaspoon with a remarkably elongated handle, while I stared at her (and it) in bemusement. Just who exactly was the parent here? Shouldn't we be having this conversation the other way around?

I suddenly felt like I was sixteen again and not in a good way. (For me sixteen had involved a lot of puppy fat, pimples and a shocking poodle perm!) I had a nightmare flashback of the old teenage me sat opposite the remarkably uninspiring, elderly, fat and balding careers guidance counsellor; the one who told me categorically that going to art school was a really stupid idea, and to stop wasting my time because I would never make it as an artist. He then breezily recommended that I think about doing a typing course to become a secretary or perhaps consider nursing. The latter suggestion was a singularly bad idea given the number of times I had fainted that term in biology dissection classes.

On reflection, I think that particular gentleman had spent years giving that same generic gender-biased careers advice to all the girls that had the misfortune to cross his path. He was probably correct in his assessment that I was unlikely to earn enough to live on through art. I really wasn't that good, hence my desire to go to college and learn how to be better. Nevertheless, his grumpy assertion that I should get my head out of the clouds like a good girl and get on with learning to type (with the subtext being that I could get an admin job until I got married and my husband could support me) had really annoyed me even then. Nowadays, such an archaic, anti-parity viewpoint is almost too painful to type but in the interests of honesty, there it is in black and white.

Defiantly chucking away the leaflet he gave me entitled 'Opportunities in Administration', and with my very supportive parents' encouragement, I applied to study environmental sciences at university instead because I was quite good at biology and geography. Nevertheless, his damning indictment that I would never make it as an artist had lodged itself very firmly in my brain.

Here I was, thirty years later, discussing future employment suitability once again; only this time with a modern, more enlightened and, fortunately, more positive twist to it, because then Logic got down to the nitty-gritty and she doesn't beat about the bush.

"Seriously! I've lost count of the number of times you've said that you always wanted to be a full-time artist. This could be your opportunity. Why haven't you organised another exhibition? The last one was really quite successful, and I know the gallery want you back again. Chaos got an email from them. She sent it onto you and copied me in. You should follow it up. You'll have plenty of time soon to do that sort of thing."

"There's no money in art," I said unconsciously, reiterating exactly what the guidance counsellor had said all those years ago. Isn't it amazing how the things we absorbed when we were young stay with us? Subliminal social conditioning is responsible for inhibiting us in all sorts of ways, not all of them good, perpetuating unhealthy situations and attitudes down the generations without us even being aware of it.

"There won't be any money in it if you don't ever get your work out of your studio and in front of potential customers. Honestly Mum! How can anyone buy one of your paintings if they can't see them? You have to put them on display and give them a chance. Share them with the world. Why are you hiding them away? You tell us that we can do anything we want if we are prepared to work hard and go for it. We just want you to do the same."

"This is a bit different," I said.

"Why?" she asked, "I don't see how. Your paintings are beautiful. They tell a true and inspiring story that gives them an added meaning. What was it that lady at the exhibition said to you when she bought one of your fish paintings?" There was a pause while Logic went a bit cross-eyed as she tried to remember. I looked at her with interest, wondering absently if she could actually see through both eyes at the same time when she did that.

"That was it!" I jumped, startled, as her eyes suddenly snapped back to their usual straight alignment and skewered me in my seat as she continued. "She said she'd had a really tough time recently and that your fish painting made her feel that there was light at the end of the tunnel and that it represented hope to her."

I nodded slowly not really sure where this conversation was going, "Yes, she did seem to quite like it."

"But then you went and tried to give her the painting for nothing!"

"Well, I wanted her to have it, if it meant that much to her."

"Luckily for you she wouldn't accept it as a gift and went off to pay for it properly through the gallery."

I shrugged, muttering "I don't see why I couldn't just give it to her."

Logic sighed heavily yet again, "Because if you did that, you would devalue it, for yourself and for her. You have to appreciate what your paintings are worth and price them accordingly. If you don't value yourself, no-one else is going to. You have a real skill and create genuinely original work, paintings that speak to people. Painting is not some little hobby to you is it?"

I thought about that for a while, considering the obsessively overwhelming need that I experienced to complete each piece, before saying quietly, yet definitely, "No, my painting is not a hobby. It's never been a hobby."

"Start valuing yourself then and get your work out there. We all believe in you, but if you don't believe in yourself then it doesn't count for anything does it? Chaos is ready and waiting to negotiate a second exhibition with the gallery for you, and to approach others. You just need to say the word, OK?"

There was a long silence while she tipped the sundae glass up to her lips and drained the dregs of cream, chocolate and melted ice cream. Returning the empty glass to the table she grinned and said, "Just think about it, please, for us? But more importantly for you OK? That's all I'm asking."

***

And that is exactly what I did! I thought about future opportunities all the way home, as I pootled across Devon and Dorset on the A35 behind a succession of slow-moving vehicles, including lumbering lorries, trundling tractors and countless crawling caravans. I thought about what Logic had said and realised that she had a fair point when she said that my self-esteem was on the low side. I didn't know why that was but suspected that it had a lot to do with having had the stuffing mentally knocked out of me when the house had fallen down. It was definitely affecting my decisions and not necessarily in a good way. I was going to have to find a way to work on that.

Furthermore, why on earth was I still allowing the echoing words of a myopic, misogynistic careers counsellor from thirty years ago to affect me? If I were advising any of my children in my situation, I would tell them to believe in themselves and go for it. Could it actually be time for me to take a risk? Should I step out from the shadows of the past and start making the long-buried dreams of my sixteen-year-old self, to become a full -time artist, a reality? I concluded that, yet again, my Barbarian advisory team were on to something. This was an opportunity that I would be a fool to miss. I wasn't quite sure exactly what I was going to do yet or how I was going to do it, but it was definitely time to consider a new approach.

As Daisy and I pootled around the Dorchester ring road I had moved on in my mental musings to contemplate the story behind the paintings and the emotional journey I had been on as I created them. There was clear imagery of healing behind the sequence of canvases, each having been created as I climbed painfully slowly out of the dangerously deep pit of despair I had plummeted into after the house and our lives had collapsed around us. My paintings had helped that broken version of me to heal and, when seen together as a complete collection, they represented a visual voyage of my struggle up from the darkness of shock and depression into a light, bright future of hope, all created with oil paint, acrylic, watercolour and canvas.

My paintings told a powerful tale.

They told the saga of the house that sat down.

It was the concept of actually telling that story, in its entirety, which stayed in the forefront of my mind for the remainder of the journey home.

7: Modification

Definition: the process of making of minor or gradual, small changes to something

Returning to the present day, shortly after meeting Lady Awesome at the WI….

The morning that followed the incredible presentation at the Women's Institute, having spent a large part of the night annoying Beloved Husband by keeping the light on so I could read Lady Awesome's book, I woke far earlier than normal. The book turned out to be an entertaining yet knowledgeable guide to finding self-confidence and unlocking your true potential as a working woman, and considering I had low self-esteem issues, it was quite a timely read for me. Now normally I don't particularly go for self-help-guide-type books, but this was not like that at all. It was actually a very amusing read, with chapters on setting achievable goals and strategies for success, whilst still coping with life and associated family-related complications. It was rather a shame I hadn't read it before I'd had the kids, or at least whilst I still had a job to go to. That last thought trotted through my mind as I sat at the breakfast bar, yawning rather rudely at my Marmite on toast.

It was with some surprise, given the fact that it was 6.30am, that I saw the door onto the patio suddenly open and Quiet entered the house from the garden. I did my best to hide the confusion I felt at the fact that not only had he been outside, but he had obviously been up and dressed for quite some time, a previously unheard-of phenomenon. Instead of making a big deal about it, I casually offered him a cup of tea.

"No thanks, I've just had one," he replied with a quick smile as he placed an empty cup in the sink. Now I was really intrigued about what on earth had taken him outside so early for long enough to drink an entire cup of tea. Strange behaviour indeed!

"Really? Where have you been?" I couldn't help myself. I had to ask.

"Oh, just outside," he answered and looked at me with genuine astonishment, as if that should have been obvious.

Before I could start a subtle campaign of maternal interrogation (OK, probably not so subtle), he spiked my guns by leaving the room and I could hear him bounding up the stairs, several treads at a time, and then his door closed very firmly. It would seem that my curiosity was going to have to wait for the moment. I made a mental note to revisit this information later before turning my attention back to my original morning musings and my, now cold and rubbery, toast with a small dissatisfied exclamation.

"Humph!"

It was now my third week of being officially unemployed and I still had no idea what I was actually going to do to earn money. I had given a great deal of thought to the advice Logic had given me about expanding the exhibition side of my art and, while it was great fun selling paintings and a great motivator for creating more, it wasn't proving a sufficiently reliable way to earn a living. I had put together another exhibition over the Christmas period having followed up the invitation I had received from the gallery after the first event, and there was another one in the pipeline for the summer months. However, as a source of income it was erratic. I needed a way to generate more opportunities to put my work before a wider audience more regularly, but I didn't quite know how to go about that. While I had a gut reaction that there was a way to make this work, it felt like I was missing something obvious. It was as if something was lurking at the corner of my eye where I couldn't quite see it and, even if I turned my head, I couldn't bring it into my field of vision; yet it was definitely there.

It was also quite annoying that I wasn't able to take advantage of my 'lack of a job' situation by having a nice long lie-in in the mornings. For the first time in I don't know how long, I didn't have to be in the office by 9am, but the boy Barbarians still had to get to school and Beloved Husband left too early in the morning to take them in. Now that Quiet was sixteen and in the sixth form doing A-levels, he no longer qualified for a free place on the school bus but wasn't old enough to learn to drive himself there. Not that we could afford a car for him anyway. The upshot of this was that even though I didn't have to get up to go to work in the mornings, I still had to get up to do the school run because it was way cheaper than buying Quiet a bus pass.

Small would often cadge a lift in with me too, even though, being under the age of sixteen, he did qualify for a free bus pass. (I know! The rules make no sense whatsoever, which is no great surprise when you think about it. Two boys, both in full-time education, living at the same address, going to the same school couldn't possibly *both* get a bus pass could they? That would be daft!) It had only taken Small a second to work out that travelling to school in Daisy every morning was a much more comfortable option to walking more than two miles to stand on his own, at a bus stop on the edge of a random field, in the middle of nowhere on a cold, dark, often rainy, early January morning. He's not daft.

Anyway, I was still pondering what to do about potentially boosting my income stream after I had dropped both boys to school and returned to the empty house. As I blew the steam of a restorative cup of lemon and green tea, I couldn't help remembering some of the more entertaining aspects of Lady Awesome's presentation from the evening before. She'd seemed so confident and comfortable that she made the whole public speaking thing look easy. I was convinced that because she was relaxed and appeared to be enjoying herself, it had encouraged the audience to relax and enjoy themselves too and I wished I knew how to do something similar. I'd had another phone call from my mother recently and there was no way she was going to let me off the hook with this Literary and Creative Society talk she had signed me up for, so I was just jolly well going to have to get on with it.

In that weird way that can often happen, it was as if by thinking about Lady Awesome I had conjured her up, because my phone pinged to alert me to a new email and in seconds there on the screen in my hand was a message from her. I had emailed her as soon as I'd got home from the WI and completed that promised BACs payment for her, just to confirm that the payment had gone through. Her response this morning was warm and friendly, thanking me for the payment and telling me that she'd been up late the night before reading my book.

A good feeling spread through me, perhaps she didn't think I was a nutter after all. It was nice that we'd both been up reading each other's books at the same time.

She finished her email by asking if I would be interested in going along to a small informal meeting of the Brilliant Women in Business Brunch Group in two days' time, suggesting that this would be a low-key gathering I might enjoy where I could get to know some other local women who would be attending.

Before I could even begin to think of all the reasons why I couldn't go, my obstinate inner identity piped up, "Don't you dare find an excuse! You need to expand your customer base remember? You might make some really useful contacts at a meeting like this. If you can survive the house falling down and all the nonsense that went on afterwards, then a bit of brunch with some businesswomen should be a doddle! Grow a backbone girl!"

With visions of my mother, my lovely neighbour and my own subconscious ganging up on me if I even considered not going, I straightened my spine, pulled my shoulders back and gave in to the inevitable. If I am totally frank, I think I was even secretly looking forward to it; I was getting rather bored on my own at home all day. I could do this!

With some surprise that I had successfully managed to kick myself up my own backside, I sent a polite acceptance back to Lady Awesome and booked the meeting into my empty, newly-unemployed person's diary.

8: Inducement

Definition: The thing that leads someone into action or encourages momentum forward.

Continuing in the present and the meeting of the Brilliant Women in Business.

Hmmm! So much for my new-found backbone! It hadn't lasted long. All I'd had to do was rock up at the venue for the breakfast meeting ten minutes early. Actually, if I am completely honest it was twenty minutes, but I get stressed if I'm late and I was worried I might not be able to park, so the result was that I was far too early. Sadly, this meant I had too much time to lurk uncertainly outside the door of the conference room that the receptionist had directed me to and worry about what might be waiting for me on the other side. That was when the metaphorical mind monkeys hopped onto my shoulder and started whispering their poison into my ear to undermine my confidence. What was I doing here? I wasn't a businesswoman. I was unemployed for goodness sake. I would be totally out of place and wouldn't know what to say. I'd better leave now before I embarrassed myself.

What a time for my stroppy subconscious to take a sudden sabbatical! I needed her to back me up here, to tell the mind-monkeys to naff off and leave me alone. Then perhaps she could give me a bit of a stern talking to while she was at it, I thought hopefully and waited for some input from her. Sadly, she remained stubbornly silent.

I ummed and ahhed for a good few minutes while shifting from foot to foot nervously. Just as I was concluding that I probably should just give up and go home, I registered the tantalising aroma of warm croissants permeating the air and my stomach rumbled insistently. There had been no time this morning to indulge in any more than half a cup of tea, gulped down in passing before I had shuffled my reluctant Barbarians off to school (way earlier than usual) so that I could continue on, to track down the location for this meeting. I was to wonder later if my hunger had contributed to my pathetic indecisiveness about entering the room, but the comforting scent of freshly-baked croissants was to prove just the inducement I needed, and something quite extraordinary happened. Involuntarily my back straightened and I drew myself up nice and tall. Smoothing down my hair quickly and taking a deep breath, my right hand reached for the door and pushed firmly. Two seconds later I was through the doorway and standing in a puddle of warm, bright sunshine that poured down from a series of huge windows marching along the length of an enormous room.

Blinking as my eyes adjusted to the sudden brilliance, I had no time to wonder what on earth I was going to do or say, because Lady Awesome herself welcomed me the instant I appeared and enveloped me in a quick warm hug.

"You made it! You're nice and early too, so you can pick the best seat. Come on in and grab yourself a coffee."

She gestured over to a long table covered in a crisp, white cloth on which was set out a mountain of breakfast goodies, including a large tray of the aforementioned croissants. "Let me just sign you in, give you a badge and then I'll introduce you."

I had no idea to whom she planned to introduce me, because my first dazzled impression was that there wasn't anyone else there. However, my eyes slowly started to function properly again whilst I poured myself a cup of coffee and, when I turned around to survey the rest of the room, I could see one other person present, a woman with the most incredible pink hair. Not a puny, pathetic pastel pink either, I am talking about serious, mind-blowingly magnificent, 'don't mess with me' magenta! That statement colour echoed through her funky outfit too and emanated through her aura. I don't really understand the whole 'aura' thing, it's not usually something that features on my radar, but this woman definitely had one and it was undeniably pink. Just looking at her made my fingers start to twitch in artistic anguish at the lack of paints and brushes in my immediate environment. Here was a woman who exuded confidence, character, charisma and caring all by simply existing, and I instinctively wanted to capture that energetic essence on canvas.

Lady Awesome escorted me across the thick burgundy carpet towards the large conference table and made a quick introduction before excusing herself because there were more women starting to spill through the door behind us.

"Hello," said Magenta (what else could she be called?) with a bright smile. "Are you joining me?" I nodded nervously before setting my bag on the back of the chair next to hers and sitting down. "So, what do you do?" she asked.

"Oh!" I stammered. "Not that much really, I'm kind of between jobs, not sure what my next step is. I paint. I don't actually have a business, so I probably shouldn't really be here, sorry."

"You're exploring some options, are you? Don't apologise for that, we've all been there at some time or another. What would you like to do if you could?"

"Oh well, I'd like to be an artist. Properly. Full-time. I do sell quite a bit of work, but it's a fairly erratic income, dependant on exposure, exhibitions that sort of thing. I've been relying on an office job for a regular wage until recently. But that's over now."

"But surely if you paint and sell original work then you are already an artist."

"I don't have any art qualifications."

"Who cares? The real question is 'can you paint?' If you can and it's what you want to do, then you should do it. Life is too short to do a job you hate unless you have no other choice. Lots of the women who come to these groups are running their own kitchen table companies. Businesses that are based on things they feel passionately about. They're often working at other jobs at the same time to help pay the bills too."

"Really?"

"Yes, sometimes it's the only way to get what you really want to do off the ground at the start."

That was interesting, so I wasn't the only one spinning several plates whilst dreaming of a simpler but more satisfying future.

Just at that moment, Lady Awesome whizzed over to our table to collect some papers and as she did so she grinned at us asking, "How are you ladies getting on?" She looked at Magenta but jerked her head at me before continuing, "Has she told you about the book she wrote yet?"

"You wrote a book?" Magenta rounded on me, her eyes fairly popping out of her head in outraged delight.

"I was up all night reading it," confirmed Lady Awesome. "Couldn't put it down! Oh look, another arrival, excuse me, I'll be back in a minute." She whisked back off across the room to coax another lady, also tentatively poking her nose through the door, to come in and raid the coffee supplies. The sight of someone else who was clearly a bit unsure of herself made me feel less out of place.

"So, you're an artist and an author," said Magenta archly.

"I'm not really an author," I demurred. "I just wrote a book. It was only a bit of fun."

"What do you mean you 'just' wrote a book?" she demanded with a quizzical expression on her face.

"Well.... I ....." I wasn't really sure what to say. "I don't think many people have actually bought it."

"No-one's going to want to buy it if you run it down like that. It's a massive achievement to write a book. I couldn't write one. Most people haven't written one. You need to say it like this," she paused, dramatically, squared her shoulders, took a deep breath and continued speaking as she threw her arms out in a melodramatic but commanding gesture and spoke.

"I wrote a book!"

Her tone was positive, firm yet warm and her statement was clear, concise and had a significant lift in pitch at the end. She smiled warmly at me and then said in her normal voice, "I'm a voice coach. Can you tell?"

"I'd never have guessed!" I teased.

"So, you're an author and an artist. You should be proud of that. That's cool! What sort of thing do you paint?"

"Well, anything that takes my fancy really. Oils, acrylics, watercolours, it depends on the effect I want. I painted the images for the cover of the book too, which was fun." I paused suddenly as a penny dropped at the back of my mind. I'd suddenly caught a slightly clearer glimpse of that thing that had been nagging at the corner of my eye. Shaking my head, I dragged my mind back to the conversation at hand so as not to appear rude but made a quick mental note to pursue that 'dropped penny' at a later date.

"Now we're getting somewhere! You wrote a book and you painted the artwork for it yourself, and yet you tell me you're not a real artist or a real author. For goodness' sake woman! Own your achievements! Don't run them down. There are plenty of people out there who will do the negative stuff for you." She shook her head at me wryly before continuing, "We've really got our work cut out with you, haven't we?"

"What do you mean?"

"Confidence my girl, that's what you need. A good dose of self-confidence! But don't you worry. We'll soon sort you out. Have you brought a copy of your book then?" my vibrant new friend demanded.

"Oh! Yes, sorry," I dug around in my bag for one, feeling just a little bit steamrolled but, surprisingly, I didn't feel like running for the hills, which would be my usual response under such circumstances.

"Oh dear, you're one of those as well." She shook her head sadly, but I could see a twinkle in her eye.

"One of what?" I had to ask. It would have been rude not to and anyway I was rather intrigued as to what this entertainingly nutty character would say next. She didn't seem to have any traditional conversation boundaries. Although going by her extraordinarily vivid hair, why on earth would I expect her to be conventional?

"You're an 'apologiser', you keep saying 'sorry' when you don't need to. Don't apologise for your book. It's not some kind of mistake. You didn't write it by accident. If you don't value it then you can't expect anyone else to. You're not really sorry, so don't say it."

"Are you going to tell me off all day?" I asked looking into my empty coffee cup as it dawned on me that I might be requiring considerably more caffeine to cope with the rest of this morning.

"Probably," she agreed with an irrepressible smile. "It's what I do. You'll just have to put up with it. Or move seats of course. I won't be offended."

I decided I quite liked her refreshingly blunt approach. I'd love to have even an ounce of her poise and assurance, and she did have a point. It was very easy to get into the habit of saying sorry. To constantly excuse yourself and your accomplishments.

"Well, I think I'll be just fine right here." I said.

"Jolly good! Oh look, I think we are about to start."

The room had filled up with a fair selection of smart looking women all chattering away to each other while Magenta and I had been indulging in that bit of barmy banter and Lady Awesome had greeted them all. She was now approaching the head of the conference table in order to begin proceedings. The meeting started in earnest with each of the ladies standing up in turn and introducing themselves and their businesses with a quick one-minute spiel. Listening to them, I marvelled that I was there at all, it was a totally new and unanticipated environment but it wasn't an unwelcome one. In actual fact it was quite inspiring. I was definitely panicking about what on earth I was going to say when it came to my turn to stand up, but the positivity in the room was incredible.

All too quickly it was my turn and I started shaking even before I got to my feet. Mumbling my name and a few random sentences about looking for new opportunities, I sat down as quickly as I could and Magenta nudged me and leaned over to whisper, "Well done, that was a good first try. It's called an 'Elevator Pitch'. There's a real art to doing it effectively. Make sure you come to the next meeting, I'll be running a workshop on how to put them together to make the most effective use of the time."

I knew she was being kind. There was no way my pathetic attempt to emulate the women around me had been any good at all, but I didn't feel embarrassed like I would normally. No-one was laughing at me; many ladies were actively nodding and smiling. In fact, the whole group seemed genuinely intent on encouraging and supporting each other. I could feel my horizons opening up before me with potential opportunities as I sat there listening to them all. It was the most surreal feeling.

Later on, with only half an ear on the closing minutes of the meeting, I examined that 'falling penny' in the back of my mind a little closer. It kept nagging away at me, and in light of the bizarre conversation with Magenta and the inspiration of the women around me, I realised that I needed to look at my skill set in a more holistic way, rather than compartmentalising things. In fact, there might be a way for them to complement each other. The book and the art were both very creative and told the same basic story using different media. Perhaps they could work together somehow, each strengthening the other. At the grand old age of forty-six, it seemed that I was at last putting the pieces of my personal puzzle together and was ready to find out what I was going to be when I finally grew up.

Looking at the copy of my book on the table before me, I recalled the day that the writing had started so unexpectedly. As little as five minutes before I began to type, I hadn't realised what I was going to do. Even as I was tapping away at the keyboard, a part of my brain was asking quite stridently what on earth I thought I was doing. This was not normal for me, I didn't write, I painted but still I had kept on going. It was completely out of character, but once I started I found it felt so right that I couldn't stop, so I kept going. Even as I was writing I kept expecting to run out of things to say and thought that my typing would eventually grind to an ignominious halt, but it didn't.

This uncharacteristic phenomenon had all started shortly after I had cleared out my studio room, on Patience's recommendation, in order to make it more viewing friendly. It was only a day or so after my trip back from Devon, following Logic's interrogation of me about my future plans and her comments about my paintings telling a story. I don't think that she had any concept that the little pep talk she had delivered to me over lunch in the pub would trigger such a reaction (neither had I for that matter), but that was exactly what happened.

9: Adaptation

Definition: a specific process of change to meet altered circumstances

Returning to the past, approximately thirty-six hours after my return from Devon…

"What on earth is she doing?" The not very hushed whisper hissed from the doorway behind me.

There was a pause and then a shuffling sound.

"Uuuum!" Came a second, deeper, hushed voice, "Well…. it looks like she's typing!"

"What, you mean like on a computer?"

More shuffling.

"Yup!"

"Why?"

"Well how should I know?" The deeper voice came out more impatiently this time.

"I didn't know she could do that." The first voice expressed a degree of muted outrage!

Part of my mind was registering the hushed conversation taking place behind me and found it quite amusing that Small was surprised that I might have skills of which he was previously unaware. Admittedly I wasn't obviously the most technologically minded of parents but what on earth did he think I did all day at work? Use chalk and a slate to send messages? I might not know much about social media or be able to send text messages from my phone using both thumbs at the speed of light like teenagers could, but my typing skills were something I was quite proud of.

Honed back in the late 80's thanks to a combination of the advent of 'Mavis Beacon' and a need to get university summer vacation work to reduce my overdraft, my ability to touch type is something that has proven extremely useful over the years. Nevertheless, I normally kept this skill under wraps because I had learned the hard way that if your colleagues know you can touch type, you generally get all the typing jobs dumped on your desk and subsequently end up missing out on more exciting projects. Always, always make them do their own typing, it's good for them.

Anyway, back to the unsubtle discussion going on behind me. I was so focused on my 'scandalous' typing, that I was only vaguely listening to them.

"What should we do?" asked Small.

There was another pause before Quiet answered him.

"I think we should make a sandwich."

"Good idea!" There was a pause before Small continued, sounding a bit concerned, "But we don't know what she wants in it!"

"Not for her, you dummy! For us! I'm starving!"

"Oh! OK! That's a really good idea!" Small agreed before adding, "Hey! Don't call me dummy!"

The noise of scuffling ensued as the boys abandoned me for the delights of raiding the fridge. I could hear them shoving each other playfully into furniture as they raced to reach the kitchen first. Having recently restocked, I knew there was plenty in the fridge and, as such, there was no danger of them starving, so I tuned them out and focused fully on what I was doing.

My Barbarian boys' observational skills were absolutely spot on! I was typing. Now normally, as you know, I'd be painting but I was not painting today, hence the boys' astonishment. When I had got home from my shift at work having done the school pick-up en route, I had felt totally dispirited. It had been really hard to focus in the office earlier with the knowledge that I was surplus to requirements for the company's future, hence an intense feeling of disengagement had settled heavily on my shoulders and it was hard to shake off even now. I stood in my unnaturally tidy art studio and looked around.

It had been nearly ten days since the big studio de-clutter. Ten days in which I had barely been able to bring myself to enter the room. It was too organised. I daren't get anything out. If I started to work on a new piece I knew the whole room would be trashed in no time, so my instinctive impulse to create was crushed by my knowledge that the need to find a buyer was far more important and, therefore, for the first time in ages I felt no craving to paint which worried me because even though there was no spark to paint crackling in my fingers, my head felt absolutely full to the point of bursting. Confusingly though, it was not full of the usual things like images, shapes and colours anymore; this time my head felt as if it was full of something else entirely, something that had never particularly interested me before.

Words.

Lots of words.

Words and phrases had been building up in my mind over the last few days, since my return from Devon. Clauses kept creeping up on me when I should have been thinking about other things (like my soon-to-be-gone job). Grammatical constructions were starting to spill over themselves in my brain in waves, constantly multiplying, then lurking and waiting to pounce on me at unsuspecting moments, until my skull felt like it was on the point of exploding with expressions that wanted to escape.

I didn't understand it, but there was only one thing I could think of to do with them all. The scenarios that were playing themselves out, over and over again, on a loop inside my mind had to be excised somehow. If I couldn't paint, then I was going to have to find another way to create. As is often the way with me, I acted on basic instinct and simply followed the impulse. I decided that I was going to have to write the words down in the hope that they would then leave me in peace.

Turning my back on my art materials, I dug around in the bottom drawer of the filing cabinet and eventually emerged with an old laptop that Logic had left behind when she first went away to university the year before. I placed it on the desk by the window and plugged it in before pressing the 'on' button. It wasn't long before I had booted up Word and that was when I started to type.

Weirdly enough, I wasn't really conscious of what I was typing particularly, I was merely aware that the pressure in my head was easing and so my fingers kept hitting the keys, settling into a steady, rhythmic pace. The onslaught of words continued as they organised themselves neatly into sentences. Those sentences became paragraphs and then paragraphs became pages. You get the general idea, I'm sure.

Time passed. Quite a lot of time actually, which is why my boys had come looking for me, ostensibly to find out why I hadn't cooked them any supper, resulting in the conversation from the doorway behind me with regard to what I was doing. Grateful that they had decided to feed themselves (something I knew they were more than capable of doing), I focused on typing for a bit longer.

I kept meaning to stop, but never did.

Eventually the noise of the front door opening to admit Beloved Husband before being firmly shut and locked filtered into my conscious mind. This was followed by the sound of him stomping along the hall into the kitchen whilst jettisoning coat, shoes and briefcase along the way. The audible reverberation of the fridge opening and then closing followed by a few cupboard doors doing the same reached me. He was probably searching for the supper I hadn't made. Ooops!

Heavy footsteps ambled past to the lounge and I heard him address the boys cheerfully, "You alright boys? Where's your mother?"

There was a pause as Quiet, no doubt, had to extricate his brain from whichever PlayStation game they were playing in order to answer his father, "Hi Dad! She's in the studio."

"Yeah," agreed Small. "She's typing." That particular phrase was uttered in a hushed, horror-filled whisper, as if I was indulging in something decidedly indecent.

"Oh, OK!" he said, and his footsteps sounded in the corridor again before stopping abruptly. "Hang on a minute! She's what?"

"She's typing," repeated Small.

"Really?" Beloved Husband sounded intrigued and I heard several pairs of footsteps, both little and large, approach the doorway of the studio and stop as all three of my menfolk studied me intently from the threshold.

"So she is!" Beloved Husband concluded with mild surprise. "Have you boys eaten?" he continued.

"We're starving!" chorused both boys together. What little fibbers! They couldn't possibly be starving! I had heard them make several raids on the kitchen in the time I had been working. It would be a minor miracle if there was any food left but, as is inevitable with teenage boys, well one teenager and one very-nearly-a-teenager, they both had two hollow legs each and were still hungry.

"OK!" Beloved Husband said, "I'll rustle up some beans on toast while we leave your mother to get on with it."

"Get on with what though?" Quiet asked.

"I have absolutely no idea," he replied, not sounding remotely bothered. "But let's leave her alone to do it in peace, shall we? There's a football match starting on telly soon. If she's typing she won't badger us to change channel for something soppy." (For the record, I do not watch 'soppy' TV programmes; I simply occasionally prefer to see if there is something else on other than sport or gratuitous violence.)

Given the enthusiastic response that greeted the sports scheduling information, I realised that all curiosity with regard to my activities had been successfully diverted. Which was just as well because I didn't have clue why I was doing what I was doing, so how could I explain it? I just knew that I needed to do it and so the words kept coming.

Some not insignificant time later I felt a hand on my shoulder. Pausing for a second, I looked up from the screen, vaguely interested to note that it was now dark outside. Beloved Husband was standing next to me with a distinctly puzzled look on his face.

"Don't you think you should move around a bit? It can't be healthy to sit still for so long and don't say you are moving your fingers, it doesn't count. I've made you some food. Why don't you save that up and come through?" He patted my shoulder gently and left the room. "And whatever that is you are working on, have you been backing it up?" he called back casually.

Daft man! Of course I hadn't! Who does he think I am? It was a good idea though. In a daze, I registered that it was nearly eleven o'clock at night. I had been typing for well over six hours. The document before me on the screen registered nearly 16,000 words. Feeling quite sure I had never written so much in such a short time ever before, I surreptitiously tested the inside of my head and realised that it was feeling better. Less congested. Which was good, but my eyes were sore from staring at the screen and I desperately needed a wee.

He was right, it was probably well past time to save what I had written and take a break. Scrabbling around in the desk drawer I found a memory stick and proceeded to save copies of the document onto both the desktop and the USB before closing the laptop down and heading for the kitchen to find a steaming bowl of tomato soup with a chunk of fresh bread and some cheese waiting for me.

Why is it that food you haven't had to prepare yourself tastes so heavenly? I chomped ravenously on the simple fare and then fell into bed in an exhausted but happy haze, sleeping dreamlessly for several hours, until the words started to nudge playfully at my sub-conscious again and the cycle of writing began again.

10: Transmutation

Definition: conversion from one form into another

Let us continue with our heroine's bizarre typing activities in the past….

"What time did you get up? It must have been incredibly early," muttered Beloved Husband in disgust, as he leaned past me to reach for a coaster so he could place a steaming mug of tea on the desk next to the laptop.

"Hmmm….! It wasn't that early, I just wanted to make a few notes before I do the school run." I was fudging it a little because, in reality, I'd been up for hours as I had woken at about two in the morning, itching to resume my typing. It was as if there was a film playing in my head, repeatedly, and it had persisted in pestering me, preventing me from dropping back off to sleep again. I thought that if I wrote down what was happening, then it might leave me alone long enough to get some sleep. So, I'd crept downstairs to the studio in the dead of night and switched the laptop back on. I'd been typing ever since. Just as I thought I was getting to the end of what I wanted to say, there were suddenly more words backing up in my mind, urging me on and making it impossible to turn the computer off.

Fortunately, I'd had the foresight to put on not only my own dressing gown, but also Beloved Husband's big black one, because it was extremely cold sat at the computer in the dark hours before dawn, in spite of the fact that it was only September. This unique sartorial selection was one of the reasons I then resembled an overweight grizzly bear ready to hibernate for winter. I never look terribly glamorous first thing in the morning (or ever, if I'm completely candid) but the combination of dark circles under my eyes courtesy of virtually no sleep, plus two thick fluffy dressing gowns, significantly increasing my girth, was never going to improve matters.

"What time is it?" I suddenly asked in alarm. If Beloved Husband was up and dressed then surely the boys should be too. If I wasn't careful I was going to be late getting them to school.

"Don't worry. I gave both boys a nudge about twenty minutes ago. Quiet's having breakfast and Small is packing his games kit. I can take them in this morning. I've got a meeting first thing that'll take me past the school at the right sort of time anyway."

"Thanks," I breathed a sigh of relief and turned back to my screen. A hand on my shoulder stopped me.

"Just a suggestion though," he continued. "Perhaps you should take a shower and get dressed before you start that again. Why don't you set an alarm? I know it's your day off today, but don't forget there's a house viewing at one o'clock this afternoon." He smiled and shrugged as if it didn't bother him either way before sauntering from the room.

***

Luckily, I'd followed his excellent advice, because it only felt like half an hour later that the alarm in the kitchen went off, alerting me to the fact that I had only a short time until Patience and the latest potential house buyer descended on the property for the viewing. It was time for a quick scoot round to check that the house was in a suitably neat condition. I had my suspicions that sufficient tidiness was unlikely, therefore I reluctantly turned off the computer and headed upstairs to check the bedrooms.

A few minutes later I peered into Small's room with rising dismay. He had obviously made a half-hearted attempted to straighten the room for the viewing before he went to school that morning, but his opinion on what made a tidy room differed wildly from mine.

Admittedly, there was nothing on the floor, but a suspiciously large bulge under the duvet gave away exactly where everything that usually resided on the floor was now concealed. Flipping the duvet to one side,

I pulled a random collection of jumpers, trainers, pyjamas, Lego models, books, a mini wrench and a wind-up torch back on to the floor before re-making the bed properly. Then I shoved the pile of detritus over to the wardrobe with my foot and pulled open the cupboard door with every intention of scooping all the hanging clothes to one side and dumping in the haphazard jumble of Small's possessions, where they would be out of sight and able to be dealt with at some later date.

However, it was immediately apparent why Small hadn't used this space for all his junk, as there in the wardrobe was Skelly, dressed in a red and white stripy t-shirt and blue jeans. The Barbarians had evidently been playing a melded version of 'Hide and Seek' and 'Where's Wally?' with him. I sighed heavily. I'd forgotten about the 'scary Skelly' issue. Hauling him out of the wardrobe, I stuffed Small's collection of dubious treasures into the space and closed the door. Then I had to think fast. What was I going to do about Skelly?

There was no way we were getting rid of him; he was part of the family. However, a temporary storage solution was definitely required. One that meant whoever was moving him around wouldn't know where he was and couldn't retrieve him until after we had a buyer. I needed Skelly to disappear for a bit. Not permanently, but it was time for him to have a little holiday. The question was where.

A short while later, I was dragging him, wrapped in an old blanket tied up with string, out of the front door towards the boot of my car. I had decided to lock him in there out of sight for the time being, where the boys couldn't find him until after we'd sold the house. Unfortunately, there were two flaws in my cunning plan. The first one was that I wasn't actually strong enough to get him into the car. Skeletons, whether fake or real, are an awkward shape and much heavier than they look! I did manage to lift his head and shoulders up and over the lip of the car boot, but when I reached down to try do the same with his feet, his upper body fell out again and I couldn't help but wince as his head hit the pea shingle with a bone-jarring crunch. That was when I realised my second problem - he wasn't going to fit in the boot space anyway because he wouldn't bend in the middle. I didn't want to use any force in case I hurt him. (Yes, I know he's not real, but that's not the point!)

Pausing in my exertions in order to re-think my strategy, I stood up to wipe the sweat from my forehead and froze in alarm! Standing stock still in the road at the entrance to our driveway were an elderly couple staring at me, transfixed with shock, as their beautiful brown and white beagle bounded over to sniff at the large, 'dead human' shaped bundle at my feet.

Appreciating, far too late, just how suspicious my actions must appear, I tried to brazen it out by smiling and nodding politely at them. "Lovely day for it, isn't it?" I asked, inwardly cringing.

What a stupid thing to say!

Lovely day for what exactly?

A nice bit of murder?

The hiding of corpses in the boot of the car perhaps?

Seriously?

Nevertheless, my comment seemed to break their horrified trance as the man nodded back very warily, then pulled at his companion's arm whilst calling dog to heel, before they scurried off in the direction of the village.

'Great!' I muttered to myself, 'that'll be all round the county by lunchtime and the fact that no-one wants to buy the house will be the least of my problems. If I'm not careful, the police will be round here with handcuffs and a team of forensic experts wanting to dig up the patio!'

Giving a heavy sigh, I closed the car boot and started to drag Skelly by the ankles across the drive towards the garage where I rolled him up in an old bit of carpet. (I know it's a cliché but carpeting really does disguise the distinct 'dead-body' shape of a …well… a dead body so much better than a blanket does.) The carpet was a remnant left over from when the house had collapsed and had been abandoned there for no apparent reason, so I figured no-one would interfere with it anytime soon. Once Skelly was completely enshrouded, I stuffed him gently behind the massive pile of cricket equipment the boys had accumulated over the summer months. Dusting off my hands I headed back inside to have a last-minute scurry round the house looking for potential unmentionables before settling back at my laptop to wait for Patience to arrive with the latest viewers.

The immediate Scary Skelly issue was sorted! Or so I thought…

Part 3

'From a small seed a mighty trunk might grow'

Aeschylus 525BC – 456BC

11: Conversion

Definition: an adaptation of something from one form to another, a process of change.

Let's return to the present for a bit and our heroine's attempts to gain more self-confidence.....

By the time my first meeting with the Brilliant Women in Business group was over, I had rather a lot of things to think about.

Not only had I met some amazing people, all trying to do something they felt passionately about, but I had also been on a crash course in assertiveness. The group was not merely for networking, making business contacts and chatting; there was also an educational element to the meeting, which had been about politely and firmly standing your ground if you needed to. Assertiveness was something that I now appreciated was significantly lacking in my general day-to-day demeanour. This was a realisation that surprised me, because I used to be a fairly determined character when I was younger. My stroppy inner voice could well be a remnant of that former fortitude.

This week was turning into a bit of a self-improvement binge-fest, what with Lady Awesome's book on self-confidence earlier on and now assertiveness training. I hadn't really thought about it much before but the various elements that had been raised were fascinating, yet so effectively simple when used in the right way.

We are all occasionally guilty of giving in on things just to avoid a confrontation, but I was beginning to realise that it had become a bit of a habit and I was now constantly apologising as if I had no right to exist. It was definitely time for that to stop.

My encounter with Magenta was also pestering away at me on the drive home. I couldn't get away from the fact that she had been talking a lot of sense. Writing a book was an achievement and so were my paintings. It was quite exciting to think that there might genuinely be a niche for them together. It was interesting that I had never felt remotely driven or passionate about my boring old office job in the last twenty years; I had saved all that emotion and intensity for my paintings and now my writing.

As I pulled Daisy onto the drive back at the house, I had to accept the fact that the answer to my future employment dilemma was staring me in the face. Particularly in the light of my sudden 'penny-dropping' realisation that keeping the book and paintings as separate entities made no sense at all. They were essentially about the same thing and thus legitimised each other in a very unique way. They were both very much a part of me and should be treated as such.

I guess in many ways, we mothers can get a bit fragmented over time as we morph into a number of different people for the disparate areas of our lives. We are perceived by others in relation to certain specific roles as perhaps a parent, a wife, an employee or an old friend; all individual compartments with precise requirements and expected associated behaviours. It's not surprising that after many years of this we can feel a bit disconnected from our true self; as if, in fact, our whole identity becomes a bundle of connected yet dislocated pieces and needs a little readjustment from time to time to remould it into a complete whole once more.

Deep in thought, I let myself into the house where it was immediately obvious from the cacophony coming from the kitchen that I was not alone.

Following the noise to its source, I peered cautiously around the kitchen door to see not only Beloved Husband but also the Barbarian Boys. They'd all successfully made it back from work and school and appeared to be engaged in some form of *Masterchef*-related activity. They do this from time to time. Beloved Husband is actually an extremely good cook and, on the rare occasion he dusts off these particular skills (other than for merely opening random tins of tomato soup of course), we are always in for a delicious dinner, which is just as well because it has to be good to make up for all the clearing up that follows. I am not joking; it can often last well into the next week. Great cuisine apparently cannot be created without every last saucepan in the house getting involved in the process.

I noted, thankfully, that he had already rounded up the boys to act as sous-chefs and they were busily engaged in peeling and chopping mountains of colourful veg. Quiet was tackling the onions and had carefully equipped himself with a pair swimming goggles, no doubt in an attempt to prevent the onion fumes from making his eyes water. Small had been tasked with peeling the carrots and, for reasons I couldn't fathom, was wearing a red and black spotted hankie tied over his hair as well as a pirate's eye patch positioned over it so that it sat right in the middle of his forehead. (I've learned over the years that it's best not to ask.)

As my equivalents of John Torode, Jamie Oliver and Ainsley Harriot seemed to have supper well under control, there was little danger of me being co-opted in to help out as well, so I figured it was safe for me to grab my laptop from the studio and join the whole convivially-creative culinary atmosphere. Setting up to one side of the breakfast bar where I could be sure of successfully sneaking tasty morsels without getting too close to any of the sharp knives being brandished about, I booted up the computer and opened my email account.

In the cosy, warm and noisy kitchen, a glass of white wine magically appeared in my field of vision as I mulled over the ideas that had been formulating that day. Sipping gratefully at a crisp sauvignon blanc, I pulled up a few specific emails that had arrived sporadically over the previous few months. They were from people I had never met. Don't worry though, they were not from over friendly, yet sadly dispossessed foreign dignitaries demanding that I help them get their money out of their failing nations by giving them my bank card details complete with security code, passport number, home address and my mother's maiden name. While I am not very computer-savvy, I am not daft enough to fall for that one. I also deleted the one informing me that I had won millions of dollars but asking would I please send through the very modest administration fee for the release of the funds.

No, these were messages from women who had read my book. I had no connection with any of them, so goodness only knows how they had heard about the book, but these ladies had experienced traumas of their own and they appreciated what we as a family had been through. In fact, one of them actually thanked me for my brutal honesty in telling my story. Others asked, 'What happened next?' and 'When is the next book coming out?" It would seem that there was actually a demand for a sequel. They were also keen to see the paintings I referred to in the book and so I wondered if perhaps this really was what I should think about pursuing.

Recalling how energised I had felt whilst writing each chapter made me realise that this was exactly what I'd like to do with my future if I could. It was the same sort of intense buzz I got with each painting. Perhaps my Barbarians had been right all along, this little unemployed interlude was just the opportunity I needed to consider how to move forward as both an author and an artist. Maybe the two together could be woven into a solid career. I wasn't quite sure how it would work as it was a little bit unusual, but the women entrepreneurs at today's meeting were all talking about the need to have a unique selling point. Maybe the art/author cross over was mine? It was certainly worth some further investigation.

"What are you doing so intently then?" asked Beloved Husband curiously. I looked over at him, enveloped as he was in a black apron with 'Britain's Best Barbeque Chef' emblazoned on it in bright red embroidery.

"I am wondering if I should think about starting my own business," I said with a grin.

"Really?" he said whilst attacking the contents of the wok on the hob enthusiastically with a pink plastic spatula. "That sounds fun. Tell me all."

That's one of the reasons I love him, he never seems to be remotely phased by any of the less than normal things I do; like coming down early in the morning to chuck PVA and tissue paper on enormous canvases or filling every spare corner of the house with random unfinished and half dry paintings. Even suddenly deciding to start a business, when I had no idea how to do it and no reason to think it might be successful, didn't seem to bother him in the slightest.

When I had started out on that crazy writing phase I told you about, totally out of the blue six months ago, and he had been scarcely able to separate me from my keyboard for more than five minutes at a time, he hadn't given the appearance of minding particularly. Although he did admit to me later on that he had been a bit worried that I might have finally lost the plot. Nevertheless, he had ultimately decided that the best thing to do was to let me get on with it, keep his fingers crossed, hope for the best and see what happened.

Now, when he could be forgiven for telling me to pull myself together and go out and apply for a proper job to assist with the family finances, he merely seemed genuinely interested in what I was thinking of doing. You don't get many fellas like that, so I should probably keep this one, don't you think?

"It would be a bit mad but I couldn't help thinking about it today," I clarified. "Unfortunately, there's unlikely to be enough of an income from it to begin with, but it does have potential." I told him all about my day and the thoughts that had occurred to me about melding my art with my writing into a creative business opportunity. I filled him in on the meeting I had been to and all the wonderfully inspiring women who were all so driven by a love of what they did that it was infectious.

"Well," he said, when I had rattled on until I ran out of steam, "there's no harm in doing a bit of research into it is there? You'll never know otherwise, will you? Can I make one observation though?"

"OK," I replied warily.

"I think you are missing a trick with all this."

"What's that then?"

"I think you should take your mother's suggestion about doing that talk for the Creative and Literary Society more seriously. Events like that would give you a platform to promote both your book and the art. An informal and relaxed chat with other creative people can't be that scary surely?" He was right of course, which is why it was so annoying.

"It's just so completely out of my comfort zone," I grumbled.

"That's no reason to discount it out of hand. If you seriously want to consider starting a business, then you should explore the potential opportunity that this represents. You will have to learn how to promote yourself. If it doesn't work out, then that is fine but you should definitely think about it." He smiled at me and raised his bottle of lager in a toast before saying, "In the meantime, here's to new opportunities."

I nodded and raised my glass in reply with a grin. "Ok, I'll give it some thought. But it was just an idea; a little dream."

"There's absolutely nothing wrong with dreams; big or small," came the reply, "In fact, I might have one of my own!"

"Oh?" I asked in delight. "What's that then?"

He shrugged, "Yeah, it's nothing really but one of the senior guys at work mentioned that I ought to consider applying for this job that's coming up. It'll be quite a promotion though and loads more responsibility, so I probably won't get it."

"Well you won't if you don't apply." I said firmly, "I hope you are going to."

"I'm thinking about it."

"If this senior guy mentioned it to you, then that's surely an open invitation to apply? They must think you would be a good fit. You have to go for it." I couldn't help but insist; he's quite brilliant and yet always so modest about his skills and accomplishments. Why is it always easier to encourage someone else to follow their dreams and yet we hesitate with our own?

"Maybe I will, maybe we both have a goal we should be reaching for," he said. "But right now, I am dreaming of stir fry chicken with black bean sauce, egg fried rice and some rather dodgy looking carrots. Any takers?" he demanded of the room in general, lifting the wok off the hob. The enthusiastic response from the boys was deafening.

He was right (as usual!). There was nothing wrong with having a dream. Whether I could actually translate that into a reality was another thing entirely and the first step was probably to investigate possible platforms for marketing; platforms precisely like the one presented by the upcoming Creative and Literary Society talk.

There was no avoiding the situation. It was time to confront my nemesis head on; I was going to have to learn how to speak in public. Fortunately, Magenta had suggested we meet for a coffee the following week and she might be persuaded to give me some tips on how to go about it. I had a feeling I was going to need all the help I could get if I was going to succeed at this. As I looked up her email address so that I could send her a few possible dates I could hear that little internal voice of mine piping up, "And about time too!"

12: Germination

Definition: the process via which something comes into existence, the development of a seed.

Staying with the present and the need to learn to speak in public....

"You really need to get over yourself!"

Watching the steam rise from a decaf, skinny, flat white, I let those rather blunt words sink in. Magenta didn't mean any offence; she was merely being matter-of -act.

"If you are going to successfully speak in public," she continued, "you need to think about what message you are trying to get across. It's not about you. It's about what you are trying to say."

To tell the truth, I liked her 'call a spade a spade' approach. It was rather refreshing. I was here to learn and therefore her no-nonsense approach was perfect. There was no beating around the bush. She simply 'told it like it was', which meant we weren't wasting any time getting to the point over our drinks at the little coffee house in the town centre.

"If people are going to pay you to speak then you have to approach it in a professional way."

"Pay me?" I interjected, "are you saying that people would pay me to speak?"

"Oh yes," she confirmed with a brisk nod. "If you do it properly and get onto the right speaking circuits. You could, in theory, get an appearance fee plus travel expenses."

"Wow, I never knew that. I don't think anyone is going to pay me right now. I will be speaking to the literary society for nothing."

"That's fine," she said. "You have to start somewhere. You can ask them to give you feedback too if you like. Either way though, you need to do a professional job or it's not fair on your audience. So, you can't get hung up on being embarrassed. You need to write a good speech, it needs to be entertaining and insightful with just the right amount of visuals to break the time up and keep people interested."

"No pressure then," I muttered.

"Think of the one person in that room that you need to get your message across to and focus on them."

"What do you mean?" I was puzzled.

"What do you hope to achieve with your presentation? Do you even have a message? If you just want to flog books then that's OK, but it would be better if you had a proper message."

"Obviously I'd like it to be entertaining but…"I thought about it for a moment before scrabbling around in my bag to bring out a few sheets of paper. These I held out to Magenta saying, "I want to tell my story for people like her."

She took the paper and scanned it. I watched as her eyes followed the line of text from one of the emails I had re-read the day before. It was from a lady whose house had burned to the ground a year or two earlier, leaving her in a terrible position. She had read a copy of my book had then written to me using the email address I'd included on the last page. She thanked me for writing about our story because reading it had made her feel less alone with the emotions she had experienced in the wake of her own home-loss tragedy, but it had also made her laugh too; something that she had found cathartic. It was a brief, yet powerful, thought-provoking communication from a woman who had stood in shoes just like mine and suffered in much the same way. If there was one person like her out there, then it stood to reason that there would be others.

"I don't want my presentation to be too intense or depressing," I continued. "It needs to be uplifting and positive because for most of the people in the audience it will merely be entertainment, but if I can connect with women like this one at the same time, then it might potentially do some good."

Magenta nodded thoughtfully as I tried to explain what I meant and when I ground to a halt she said, "Well that's certainly a pretty powerful incentive, but we'll need to get the tone right. Let's get down to business."

The next hour was incredibly exciting as Magenta and I threw ideas together, pulled them apart and put them back together again in various configurations to see how best to achieve my aim. My notebook was soon full of scribbled notes to follow up later, including tips and advice on how to proceed. I left the café later that day with Magenta's advice still ringing in my ears as I drove home to write the first draft of a presentation entitled 'Surviving the House that Sat Down'; a talk that was to bind together the events of the last few years with my two creative passions, art and writing. As Magenta had expressed so colourfully, I had a story to tell, it was high time I got out there and started telling it.

I could do this!

Couldn't I?

"Of course you can you daft woman!" My inner voice was back to berate me again. "You wrote that book, didn't you? That's something you never thought you could do; so why not this too? It's about time you found your voice and started using it."

"What if I freeze in front of everyone?" I whispered anxiously.

"Well there's one sure fire way to find out! It's not a difficult concept. You're a bright bunny, relatively speaking anyway, so get out there and jolly well get on with it! You won't know until you try." Having cast aspersions on my general intellect, the voice of my stroppy subconscious then melted away into nothing before I could think of a suitable response. (She's such a coward!) But I couldn't fault her reasoning. It was certainly worth having a go. What harm could it do?

All of these thoughts tumbled through my brain as I picked the Barbarian Boys up from school later that afternoon. Then it was back to earth for me with a bump as I slogged my way through a whole host of housework, gave what I hoped was helpful advice on homework, and cooked several tonnes of chips to go with a chicken curry I'd thrown together the night before. In between all these activities, I kept diving into the studio for a few spare minutes at a time to jot some more notes down. Eventually I was in a position to try the speech out loud in order to work out the basic timing of it. It was going to need a lot of practice.

Interestingly enough though, there was another meeting of the Brilliant Women in Business the following week and I had been sufficiently intrigued by my first encounter with the group to go along a second time. Now that I knew what to expect from the experience and didn't feel quite so out of my depth, I found myself relaxing and started to indulge in a little people watching as I munched my way contentedly through a pain au chocolat.

Lady Awesome was equally as dynamic and inspiring as she had been on the previous two occasions I had met her, and the group in general consisted of a wide variety of confident and motivated ladies. It was quite clear that amongst the coffee, croissants and chat there were some very fine analytical business minds around the table and yet this was not an aggressive Apprentice-style competitive event; merely a gathering of intelligent and capable women focused on camaraderie and collaboration. The overriding atmosphere was welcoming, relaxed and safe.

Those attending represented a whole range of ventures from small 'kitchen table' initiatives to large scale enterprises and they were interspersed with a few other women who, like me, seemed a little unsure as to why they were there but nevertheless seemed to be enjoying the experience. However, there was one particular lady who caught my interest. She had been a new arrival at the last meeting (just like me) and had seemed particularly nervous and unsure of herself. I was pleased to see that she had come along again too, but during the course of the meeting I noticed something interesting about her manner.

The meeting kicked off with everyone delivering a one minute 'elevator pitch' each like the last time. I'd been working on mine in the interim so was a bit more prepared than I had been before. It was an interesting exercise and really made me think about what I was trying to achieve and how to get that across to someone else in a short timeframe. I had probably looked a bit mad on the drive to the event that morning because I had been practicing my elevator pitch out loud on the way. The guy who pulled up in the sports car next to Daisy at one set of red traffic lights had given me a really funny look.

Anyway, back to my point. During this lady's elevator pitch, she spoke about making and selling organic ice cream. The group as a whole radiated a significant degree of positivity towards this idea, (after all who doesn't like ice cream?) but it wasn't a wishy washy 'oh that's a nice idea, dear' type of encouragement. Lady Awesome displayed a clear and genuine interest in the concept, coaxing more information from her about how she might go about it, and several other women asked pertinent questions about her proposed methods, sources and supplies before making some very useful suggestions.

In other words, there was no question that they were all taking her and her business idea seriously. The result was that the ice cream lady started to sit up a little straighter and speak with significantly more confidence. She had obviously done a fair bit of research into her topic of choice and you could see her passion for it as she raised a number of potential pitfalls and difficulties that she was concerned about. Other people around the table started to make suggestions and identify potential solutions for her, offering both help and advice. With this encouragement, I noticed that her language as she spoke about what she wanted to do began to change. She stopped using phrases like 'I don't know about', or 'I'm not sure how to' and 'I can't' and instead she started to say 'I can find out about', 'I need to learn to' and 'I can'! I knew I was witnessing something quite remarkable. It was like watching a new flower bloom for the first time in the warmth and light from the sun and I recognised then that there was a very unique power at work here. Together the group had created a subtle yet powerful shift in this lady's perception of herself and her idea, which in turn had encouraged her to believe in herself. A new organic ice cream company was one step closer to being born and I for one couldn't wait until I could buy (and try) her product.

Lady Awesome and her Brilliant Women in Business Group were a force to be reckoned with. Discussions about potential customer bases, stakeholders, communication strategies and finances followed, yet all the while part of my mind was marvelling at how the potential hurdles the ice cream lady believed were in her way could all be overcome. A clear route forward was emerging should she decide to take that first step, and with the right attitude, hard work and some effective encouragement and support I could see her realising her dream.

It was exactly what my family were trying to persuade me to do but my family know and love me and therefore it was hard not to brush praise from them aside as being biased. Bizarrely, it is more believable if a compliment comes from a stranger. Why is it so much easier to see gifts and potential in other people and yet constantly fail to recognise them in ourselves? Without self-belief we do not have the foundation we need from which to build our dreams and reach for the stars.

Slowly the pieces of my personal puzzle were starting to slot together, and a clear picture was emerging. I was getting so fed up with feeling inferior. Like the lady with the ice cream dream, I had a lot of skills and ideas too. It was time I gave myself the respect I deserved and started to take myself seriously. The aspiring child artist in me was still there and the long-held seed of inspiration, planted by my grandmother all those years ago, was finally ready to germinate and push upwards towards the light.

On the way home in the car I told myself defiantly, "I paint and I write and I am OK with that! I am learning to speak in public and I am going to stand up and be counted. I will tell my story. I will build an unconventional business for an unconventional person, an artist, an author and a speaker. Hopefully, other people will be OK with it too, but if they aren't, it doesn't matter.

This is what I do.

This is who I am.

This is me!"

"Hallelujah!" the voice in my head replied. "It's about time you worked that out. Now let's get this show on the road!"

Part 4

For my part I know nothing with any certainty, but the sight of the stars makes me dream.

Vincent Van Gogh 1853-1890

13: Evolution

Definition: the process via which our early hominid ancestors developed into modern man

Let us return to the past and continue with that bizarre obsession with typing....

"Did you actually come to bed at all last night?"

Beloved Husband's voice broke through my train of thoughts and made me jump out of my skin. I had obviously been really far away in my little fantasy world.

"Because it doesn't look as if you've moved at all." He continued with a grin and a lazy shrug, "Just an observation."

"I did come up for a bit, but I couldn't settle so I came back down. I hope I didn't disturb you. What time is it?" The early autumn mornings were getting so dark that it was impossible to guess what time it was, but the fact that Beloved Husband was dressed did indicate that I might have to think about morning related activities, namely the school run and then work (how boring!). Even though I wouldn't be working much longer, I had to keep going until the management transfer was complete if I wanted to get a reasonable reference and my full redundancy package.

"It's 7.30. I've just given the boys a nudge. They didn't like it much, but they should hopefully be emerging from their pits sometime soon. I've also made their packed lunches and now I'm off to work. Back later this afternoon hopefully."

"Ok, thanks. Have a nice day," I said turning back to the computer.

There was a brief pause in which he didn't move, and then he cleared his throat meaningfully. Looking back up at him in confusion, I saw him give me his mock-serious look and then say firmly, "Step away from the keyboard."

Puzzled, I asked, "Why?"

"You are going to have to do the school run."

"I know."

"In about 20 minutes."

"Yes, I know."

"Have you seen what you're wearing?"

Ah!

I looked down at myself and realised that during the course of my almost all-night typing session I must have periodically felt cold and, without any real cohesive thought, gone in search of additional warm garments. The result was a random selection of coverings each piled on top of the last, which could not be considered to have any degree of elegance whatsoever. In short, I was now in the centre of a round, padded mass of fleecy pyjamas, three different dressing gowns (only one of which was actually mine), a thick jumper, Beloved Husband's all-weather gardening coat, as well as a scarf, a hat and a pair of pink, fluffy slippers.

He was right, as usual (how annoying!), there was no way the Barbarians would let me take them to school dressed like that and, come to think of it, I really couldn't turn up at work in this get up either. It was time to stop obsessing with my typing and start being a responsible grown-up for a bit! I nodded sheepishly and saved up my document before logging out and heading for the shower.

Quite a few hours later, I logged back in having completed the school run, my shift at work and a quick trip to the supermarket for basic essentials. All the time my trolley trundled through the aisles of edibles, I was only partially engaged in the real world because a fictional scenario continued to play out in my head on my own personal, internal movie screen.

Once back at the house I was in front of the keyboard again as soon as I'd put the shopping away, where I immediately resumed thumping away determinedly. Almost involuntarily, I systematically bashed out the specific details of the plot that had unfolded in my mind in the dairy food department. That led onto yet more developments and, even though I had my suspicions where this was going, I had decided not to fight it. I kept thinking that I would eventually run out of words and then this oddly literary anomaly would be done with. It was surely just an unexpected flash of confounding creativity which would eventually burn itself out and pass. In the meantime, I was quite enjoying myself.

It was something of a surprise, only a short time later, to see Beloved Husband wandering passed my studio window in the direction of the garage. He must have returned from work while I had been engrossed with my story. On checking the clock at the base of my screen, I was amazed to see that over two hours had passed and it was now nearly three in the afternoon. Minutes later he walked back in the other direction, this time carrying several large sheets of old cardboard.

I continued to type but with a degree of distraction now as I noted several more trips to and from the garage with a random selection of large pieces of junk being dragged round the front of the house to the side gate. Eventually I realised that Beloved Husband was definitely up to something and it would be wise to investigate what that something was. The estate agent had tactfully pointed out, only the day before, that the pile of discarded bits and pieces in the garage might be preventing potential buyers from appreciating the dimensions of the space available. (Why these people couldn't use their imaginations was beyond me.) Nevertheless, it would seem that Beloved Husband was now intent on sorting out the garage. This could only mean one thing. He intended to have a bonfire.

I suddenly remembered that I had hidden Skelly, wrapped up in that old bit of carpet, behind the pile of cricket equipment and other debris and thought I had better go and make sure that he didn't end up getting accidentally cremated. Hiding the family skeleton out of sight was one thing, lots of people do that, but unintentionally incinerating him was something else entirely. I was going to have to pick the boys up soon anyway, so having saved my document up quickly I then switched off the machine and headed outside, fully aware that once a bonfire was lit, Beloved Husband had the habit of chucking all sorts of useful items into the flames simply because they would burn well. It was an activity during which I knew from past experience he absolutely needed the supervision of another adult.

I still had nightmares about one particular bonfire incident that occurred while we were living in the caravan in the garden after the house collapsed. If you recall, I mentioned that we had done our best to salvage much of our furniture from the rubble but quite a lot of it was damaged beyond repair. We had spent weeks redistributing various items of all shapes and sizes to other locations, storing that which we absolutely needed to keep and donating other reusable items to charity shops. We had also lost count of the number of tedious trips to the tip that had taken place to dispose of non-repairable or non-recyclable pieces. The remaining stuff ranged from large useless bits such as cracked doors from wardrobes that wouldn't fit in the car, through to smaller unrecognisable chunks of wood and these were all piled up at the bottom of the garden.

One clear crisp December morning, Beloved Husband had woken up in the caravan with the light of a 'mission' burning in his eyes. The warning signs were there before I had even poked my nose out from under the duvet. It had been a particularly chilly and restless night in spite of numerous hot water bottles and countless fleecy layers (including gloves and hats) as the temperature plummeted drastically. In an uncharacteristically early burst of energy he was up and out of bed, carelessly allowing a huge waft of freezing air to reach me under the duvet, hence I woke up too (the rat!) and before too many minutes had passed, he was warmly wrapped up and had also equipped himself with a thick outdoor coat and boots. Deciding that I should keep an eye on this suspicious behaviour so early in the morning, I hastily dressed and followed him out to see that he was stomping around the pile of smashed wood at the bottom of the garden, scrutinising it from all angles. I decided that a strong cup of tea was definitely required to get my brain working before I investigated any further and so I trotted off across the frost-encrusted grass towards the kitchen (the only bit of the house that was still standing) and put the kettle on.

In the time it took for me to make two cups of tea and head back outside, it would seem that Beloved Husband had decided to set light to the pile of wood. What is it about fellas and fire? Does lighting bonfires fill a deep evolutionary need? Perhaps the whispered memories of our Cro-Magnon ancestors still lurk deep down in the DNA of every modern man because there does seem to be a great deal of satisfaction to be had from kindling a blaze. Just as he was leaning in with a match to set the flame, I remember thinking to myself that he would never get it alight in the freezing conditions. How wrong I was! All of a sudden, a large flare leapt from the match in his hand onto the piled wood and a dancing circle of blue flames spread outwards along the ground in all directions. This flash of fire travelled at least two metres out from the centre of the pile of wood and completely engulfed where Beloved Husband was standing.

With a squeak of fear, I dropped the cups of tea and started running towards him, although what I was planning to do when I got there was beyond me. Fortunately, as quickly as the wall of moving flames had appeared they then disappeared, leaving Beloved Husband looking stunned but unhurt.

"What was that?" I demanded in shock.

He turned to me and shrugged sheepishly. His face looked incredibly odd, but I couldn't work out why. He didn't appear to be burnt at all which, given what I had just witnessed, was quite unbelievable.

I spotted the petrol can for the lawn mower lurking near the shed and quickly put two and two together making a big, fat, furious four.

"Did you cheat and put petrol on it, to get it going?" I demanded crossly.

He refused to look me in the eye, glancing over to Skelly who was sitting on the swing nearby.

"Don't you dare blame the skeleton!" I hissed at him. "Did you or did you not put petrol on it?"

He hung his head and nodded guiltily in the general direction of his feet.

"Didn't you realise that in these cold conditions the petrol fumes would lurk at ground level and ignite rapidly like that? We're lucky you weren't injured. You could have set fire to the fence! Or the caravan. Or both! You great nitwit!"

My Beloved Great Nitwit simply nodded thoughtfully.

"Well I know that now, don't I?" he replied. "But look! It worked! It's going to be nice and warm here in a few minutes." He gestured towards the bonfire, which was burning away merrily now that the excess petrol fumes had burned off, as if that excused his dangerous actions. Giving me an incorrigible wink, he asked, "Any chance of a cup of tea?"

Growling with a confusing mixture of frustration about how irresponsible his actions had been and relief that there had been no permanent damage done, I returned to the patio to pick up the pieces of the two mugs I had dropped. As I passed the caravan, the door opened and the two boys piled out pulling thick coats on over their dressing gowns as they dashed across the grass towards the fire.

"Wow! Cool fire, Dad!" I heard Small proclaim, as he grabbed a long stick from the ground and started poking at the flames. I have long suspected that our youngest child possesses some of the very same pyromaniac tendencies as his father and therefore I was unbelievably relieved he hadn't witnessed the whole 'petrol fumes' incident, it would only give him ideas. Leaving my Beloved Nitwit Cro-Magnon Man Husband with the Barbarian Boys, I retreated, shaking my head in despair. Quite frankly, if the survival of the species via natural selection had relied solely on the fellas in our little family unit, then heaven help the human race.

Just as I stepped into the house, I overheard Quiet's voice carrying clearly down the garden in the still morning air.

"Woah! What happened to your eyebrows, Dad?"

Aha! That's why he looked so odd!

***

Back in the study, I smiled at the memory of that day. Nevertheless, I still felt it was prudent to make my way swiftly out to the back of the house to the garage to have a firm word with Beloved Husband on bonfire safety issues before I left to pick up the boys from school. Interestingly enough, Skelly wasn't where I had left him, rolled up in the rug behind the cricket equipment. Beloved Husband swore he'd not seen him but promised to be extra careful that he didn't inadvertently chuck him on the fire by mistake. The old bit of carpet was still there but not the bony contents, so it was anyone's guess as to where on earth the family skeleton might be lurking now. However, I couldn't spare the time to track him down right then. No doubt he would materialise at some suitably inconvenient time and place in the near future.

I could only wonder where it would be this time.

14: Resilience

Definition: the ability of someone or something to recover from adversity or to return the original form after an impact

Staying with the obsessed writer in the past for a bit longer…

That night, the whole 'up-all-night-writing' thing happened again, only this time Beloved Husband came into my studio in the morning to find me slumped over my desk, fast asleep. I was in imminent danger of having the topography of my keyboard permanently embossed on my forehead when he gently shook me to wake me up. Sitting up in a startled daze, I wiped a patch of drool off my cheek. Then immediately remembering the last thing I had done before dropping off, I looked over towards the printer.

It was buried under a thick wad of freshly printed double-sided A4 sheets, some of which had spilled over, slipping down to cover the floor below like giant pieces of confetti. Pushing my chair back, I stood up and scooped them all together, sorted them into the right order and turned to him with a smile. "It's finished!" I said, giving a contented little sigh.

"What is?" he asked.

"My story."

"Does that mean you can stop typing now and go and get some proper sleep?"

I nodded at him, shoving the pile of pages into his hand and moved towards the door. He looked at them with some consternation before asking, "What do you want me to do with this lot?"

I smiled sleepily at him, shrugged and said simply, "Read it."

As I was already on my way to the door, I didn't register the look of alarm that flitted briefly across his face. Had I not been so tired I would have realised that suggesting he read it was not that brilliant an idea. In the twenty-three years we'd been married, to date I'd only ever seen him read a grand total of about three books. Don't get me wrong, he can read, (of course he can!) but he just doesn't enjoy it particularly, so probably the last thing on the planet that he wanted to do was read my manuscript. Fortunately, I was too intent on getting some sleep to register his dismay as I staggered towards the stairs. It was a Sunday, thank goodness, which meant that I could sink into my lovely bed for a few hours and let my tired (but now mercifully empty) brain drift off into a deep and dreamless slumber.

***

I couldn't believe how much more human I felt only a couple of hours later, when I did eventually surface and clamber out of bed. Given half a chance, I would have gladly stayed there all day but sadly that wasn't going to happen. There was too much to do, especially when you consider how much time I had redirected from other household tasks in recent weeks in order to keep typing. Now all that was over I was going to have to catch up on a few more mundane matters.

After a large cup of tea and a restorative bacon and egg bap, I leaned out of the back door to bash mud-encrusted rugby socks against the boot scraper. I have to confess that the beauty of the crisp winter's morning was somewhat lost on me as I repeated the action with the rugby shorts and then the shirts, smacking and thwacking the worst of the playing pitch off the fabric before stuffing them all into my poor old battered washing machine. While I felt sorry for the machine, I wasn't daft enough to risk leaving the dirty kit in a pile on the floor for too much longer. In my experience, dirty sports kit has a habit of reproducing exponentially if left to its own devices and I already had enough to contend with.

As I loaded the soap dispenser, I grumbled away to myself that Sundays were supposed to be a day of rest. Surely Sunday mornings were supposed to involve lazy lie-ins, hot coffee and the relaxed reading of newspapers from cover to cover? Although where I'd got this daft idea from I couldn't possibly say. It's not something that ever happens in this house, and it definitely wasn't going to today.

We had quite a busy schedule lined up and I had absolutely no idea where Beloved Husband was hiding. He seemed to have disappeared, but the boys had already started to ask me about lifts to and from their various 'plans' for the day. Plans that were going to generate yet more dirty sports kit. The only difference being that today we would be collecting mud from football pitches not rugby ones. (Sigh!) The rest of the day would involve a convoluted schedule of lifts to meet with or pick up mates to take to two different training grounds and then on to a couple of matches. None of these plans appeared to conveniently coincide on either times, places or people. This often happens when your teens have got carried away making elaborate arrangements over Facebook without consulting the unfortunate parent/driver.

If you associate with any young people in a 'responsible adult' capacity then you will be familiar with the type of day that requires a grown-up to drive the car in silence and wait around for undetermined periods of time in the cold, without actually speaking or trying to communicate with anyone at all. This is because adults, especially parents, are so *not cool* that they should do the decent thing and pretend that they don't actually exist. That was the sort of day that was ahead of me today. No wonder I was starting to feel a bit grumpy. My Sunday had the potential to be very cold and boring and, if I didn't manage to track Beloved Husband down, I was going to have to juggle it all by myself. I could refuse of course, but as the boys had been quite patient with me recently, what with all my obsessive typing, I felt that I owed them some dedicated parenting of some sort, even if it was only my ability to drive the car (and keep my trap shut) that they needed.

So, extricating myself from the evil clutches of the utility room, leaving the washing machine to chug away to itself, I checked that my Kindle was fully charged (in anticipation of many hours of hanging around) and then wandered over to see what the boys were up to. The PlayStation was in full swing with some sort of complicated split screen, multi-player football match taking place accompanied by running commentary and loud cheering. Clearly the boys were working hard on their warm-up for today's matches.

"Any idea where your dad is?" I asked.

There was a long pause as each boy continued to press buttons and wiggle toggles on their handsets. The pause was so long in fact, that I began to wonder if I had accidentally forgotten to speak the words out loud. Perhaps I had merely whispered or only said it in my head? (As you know, I do talk to myself in my head, so such a scenario is entirely possible.) Just as I was about to repeat myself and this time make sure I used my vocal chords, Quiet took in a deep breath and said 'Uuuuuuh!' in a thoughtful way, which implied that I might get an answer, so I waited. Then he stopped, sighed and the pause began again.

It was time to deploy dastardly tactics. I shuffled round to stand in between the boys and the TV screen.

"Hey!"

"What are you doing?"

"Noooooooo!"

"You made me miss that goal!"

"Oh, good, you can speak! I thought for a minute you'd both lost your voices! That would have been a shame," I said as they tried to continue playing whilst peering around me. "Have you seen your dad?" I repeated, enunciating slowly and clearly with exaggerated patience.

Briefly, Quiet took his eyes of the screen and scanned around the room.

"Ummm. No, sorry!"

Small shook his head impatiently, leaned further to the right and fell off his chair as he tried to look past my leg.

Realising that I was not going to get anything more out of them, I gave in and moved out of the way, setting off to track their father down. He couldn't have gone too far surely? His car was still on the drive and sparkling beautifully with the ice from this morning's heavy frost. Eventually, having looked in all of the bedrooms, the bathroom the dining room, the cubby hole we refer to as his study, the main kitchen/lounge once again and the under stair cupboard (in my defence, I was passing it and running out of options so I just thought I'd check!), I ventured outside to search the garage and the sheds.

We own quite a number of sheds now as Beloved Husband has developed a habit of collecting them. I have wondered if it is a psychological reaction to that time when we had nowhere at all to put anything after the house fell down. We lost so many things in the actual collapse and were unable to store many of the precious items we pulled from the rubble and therefore we were forced to give them away. Perhaps that is why he has since amassed an impressive array of shed-type structures, just in case it ever happens again. In some respects, it's comforting to know I'm not the only paranoid wreck in the family.

However, we have got to the stage where I daren't let him go to B&Q unsupervised because I know he will find a reason to buy yet another wooden outbuilding of some description, if I am not there to firmly and repeatedly say 'No!'

Given the fact that we now have seven sheds, two bike stores, a lean-to log store and a little wooden cabin, it did take me a while to find out that he wasn't in any of them. Returning to the kitchen husbandless and completely frozen, I admitted defeat. I was totally mystified as to where he might be. Making the assumption that he must have somehow gone out earlier in an inspired (yet sneaky) attempt to avoid all Sunday related parental duties, I was forced to accept ungraciously that the only taxi driver in the house today was me, so I'd better jolly well get on with it.

Stomping huffily off towards the stairs in order to find a sufficiently warm selection of clothing, of the type suitable for hanging around a series of sporting pitches and training grounds in midwinter, I spotted that my studio door was ever so slightly ajar. That was unusual! I always make a point of shutting it firmly last thing at night as part of my 'going round the house locking doors and turning off electrics' routine. (Remember the one that I said no-one else seems to bother with?)

On closer inspection, I realised that I had finally located my quarry. In the grand scheme of things, Beloved Husband doesn't usually go into my studio unattended, hence I had not included it in my intense search of the house, and yet there he was ensconced in the chair by my desk, with his headphones on, nodding away rhythmically to some soundtrack or other on his iPod. He appeared to be reading my manuscript and, by the looks of it, he had been doing so for quite some time.

Interesting!

So that was where he'd been hiding. I tiptoed carefully away and carried on getting ready to go out with the boys. If he was going to read my book, then I was not going to disturb him.

Just before we left for the first drop off on the list, I snuck back into the studio with a cup of tea and a plate of cookies and placed them on the desk next to Beloved Husband. A bit of a role reversal, I felt; me delivering sustenance to him in my studio. Admittedly the cookies weren't quite up to Chaos and Logic's standard but that didn't really undermine my good intentions. He didn't seem to notice so I crept out and left him to it.

During the course of the day I popped back to the house a couple times, mainly to try and thaw out between silent taxi trips. This was only possible when the training/match locations weren't so far away that I was forced to lurk unobtrusively on the side-lines remembering not to draw any undue attention to myself by accidentally cheering on my own child and therefore embarrassing him hugely. While home I took the opportunity to switch the damp, but now relatively clean, rugby kit across to the tumble drier in the garage and then fed the washing machine with the next load of dirty washing from the pile.

To my surprise, when I peeped into the studio, it didn't look as if Beloved Husband had moved at all, except to turn pages, as he was quite a bit further on in the manuscript. I took the opportunity to refresh his mug of tea and also provided a selection of sandwiches. It wouldn't do to interrupt his flow of thought with a rumbling tummy now, would it?

I had fully expected him to simply skim read it and then say something vague but relatively bland about it, but he looked like he was giving it serious attention. Obtusely, this had the effect of making me worry. What if he didn't like it? Was I making a complete fool of myself? I have heard it said that everyone thinks they can write a book, but it had never occurred to me that I might ever write one. However, having said that, it had never occurred to me that my house might fall down either, so quite clearly anything is possible as Logic is always telling me.

It felt as if this whole thing had come from nothing and yet the inspiration for it was no secret.

Unacknowledged by me, all this time, my mind had been subconsciously replaying the events of the house collapse and the horrendous months following it over and over, to the point that the dark emotions generated by that time had to be discharged in some way. You cannot live well in a state of constantly high anxiety and there is no point in destroying the beauty of each new day by obsessing over what went wrong yesterday. Having expressed my distress, guilt and healing through my paintings, I was then in a position to tell the full story, to look at it all, in as unbiased a way as possible, aided by the clarity of vision that comes with time. To write it all down as fairly as possible and then move on. If I didn't, then surely, I would keep repeating the loop endlessly in my head until I went completely mad.

Perhaps this book had been an attempt to regain some perspective over what had happened; to exert a bit of power over events that had been completely beyond my control. Maybe it was a search for some meaning in that which had made us feel so completely helpless. It was definitely an opportunity to have a bit of harmless fun, to allow my sense of humour free reign and to try to look at the whole event with an optimistic, light-hearted filter.

The incredible thing was that once I started looking for the positives, I was amazed at what I found. There were so many silver linings littered through our story. So many good things came from apparent disaster. Writing my story down had enabled me to see the redeeming features. Nothing is ever all bad. There is always some light in the darkness. For everything that is black there is some white too, and all the colours of the rainbow in between. There is beauty everywhere, you simply have to open your eyes and look for it.

The house collapse was just an event that had happened. It was over. It had no power to hurt us anymore. By capturing it in words I could define it, put a full stop to it and I now felt ready to begin afresh and move forward with my life, stronger and hopefully wiser than before.

All the while that I chauffeured children around that Sunday afternoon I wondered what Beloved Husband thought of my manuscript. Would he like it? I kept telling myself that it didn't matter what he thought, it was only a bit of fun and, anyway, I liked it and that was what was important. I had to admit that I was lying to myself; I did care what he thought because as the day progressed I was getting more and more nervous. Finally, as the evening approached and my chauffeuring duties ended, I sidled up to my studio door and peered in. He was just reading the last page. As I watched, he gathered all the pages into a neat pile and placed them carefully on my desk.

I tentatively pushed the door open and looked at him. "What do you think?"

He scratched his head, a thoughtful expression on his face. Then he hummed and hawed a bit before saying in a somewhat surprised tone, "You know what? That's actually quite good."

Rather stunned, I was simultaneously torn between the utter relief that he liked it and trying not to be offended at how surprised he sounded about the fact that he liked it. But before I could comment he continued.

"I think you should consider sending it to some publishers to see what sort of a reaction you get."

Oh! He was serious!

My goodness! For some reason, I had not expected that.

15: Nascent

Definition: early indication of future potential

Moving forward in time to present day and the approaching major public speaking event dilemma....

The evening after my meeting with Magenta, I was digging around, head first, in the chest freezer in the garage, hoping to locate something I could cook for supper, when the landline rang. Abandoning my vain quest for comestibles, I hot-footed it back to the house in the certain knowledge that neither of the boys would bother to answer the shrill summons. They probably didn't even realise they were supposed to. As fully paid up members of the youth of today, they only communicate with their peers via text or social media and as such, a ringing landline would be beyond their comprehension.

Trotting hastily across the travertine tiles, I grabbed the handset rather breathlessly on at least the millionth ring. There was only one person I knew who had the patience to let the phone ring that long and the caller ID confirmed my suspicions. "Hi Dad!" I said in delight, "How are you?"

"Good thanks. Am I interrupting anything?"

"Nothing exciting. Just the never-ending task of attempting to feed teenage boys, but that can wait. What are you up to?"

"I'm just ringing to give you the heads-up on something."

"OK! That sounds ominous."

"Not really, it's just that your mother had a call from the Literary and Creative Society about that talk she told them you would do."

"Ah! Have they changed their minds?" Typical I thought, having dithered about doing it, now that I had decided to go for it, Murphy's Law would state that they no longer wanted me. "Well it did take me a while to get back to mum and agree to do it, so I wouldn't be surprised if they've found someone else to do it by now."

"Not exactly, they're still interested, very interested in fact, I just thought I ought to warn you that it might be a slightly bigger group than you were expecting."

"How big?" I already thought thirty to forty was quite big enough.

"Maybe eighty to a hundred."

"What?"

"Yes, there's been quite a lot of interest since the initial advert went out to members last week, and you know what your mother's like. She's told everyone. So, the Society committee members have decided to amalgamate the event with their annual summer fundraising dinner. The whole society will be there, with partners."

"You're joking!"

"Nope, I thought you'd want to know in advance. It shouldn't make any difference to your actual presentation but it's always a good idea to know your audience before you start. I go to lots of these sorts of events with one of my friends. He's a speaker and needs assistance with his IT equipment." That didn't surprise me as my dad is an absolute whizz with computers and is constantly being asked to help people out of technical traumas. "He always likes to know how big a crowd he's going to be talking to and what the dynamics are, so I found out for you. This will be a mixed gender group of mainly retired people. They'll all have had a glass or two of wine before you speak so they'll be nice and relaxed. I just thought I'd mention it because once you get over a certain size then the acoustics can be an issue."

"I see," I said, rather faintly. The acoustics were the least of my worries. I needed something to say first, but I could add it to my exponentially growing list of concerns. "Oh dear, I was just getting used to the idea of talking to a fairly small group Dad. I'm not sure I can do this."

"Don't be daft. Of course you can. You and your sisters never had any trouble talking when you were kids. Your poor brother could never get a word in edgewise. This is no different. You'll have no problem whatsoever. Now, I've been to events at the venue the Society are using, so I really rang to let you know that they have great audio-visual equipment. Computer, projector, mic and speakers are all state of the art. You'll be hooked up to a wireless clip-on microphone that feeds into a surround sound system. It's all really easy to use, but you must remember that there will be a small battery pack for the microphone that you will need to attach to your clothing. If you make sure you wear something with a waist band or a belt then you'll be fine, but be careful not to leave the microphone switched on when you're not giving your presentation. You don't want to pop to the bathroom and inadvertently broadcast your personal business to the whole room."

I absorbed this information in silence for a moment before replying.

"I'll bear that in mind Dad, but I'm more worried about whether I can speak at all, rather than if people can hear me," I said dryly. While my first instinct was to refuse to do the talk at all now, I was surprised to experience a small but definite seed of disappointment at the thought of pulling out. How interesting!

"You know what you need, don't you?'

"What?"

"A practice run. You need to give your presentation to a few smaller groups first. Get some feedback. Work out what bits make people laugh, that sort of thing. It'll give you a bit more confidence. Isn't there anyone in your neck of the woods you can ask?"

I realised that, as usual, my dad was offering very sound advice. It's one of the many things he's good at.

"Actually," I said perking up at the thought, "I think you might be onto something there. Thank you."

"Anytime," he laughed, "and remember two other pieces of practical advice when you are a public speaker; always take an extension lead with you to every event because the organiser will never be able to find one and the room you are speaking in will never have a power socket where you need one. Secondly, always turn your projector off as soon as you finish your talk, before you take questions, so that it can cool down.

The bulbs cost a fortune to replace and will last longer if they are completely cold before you try to move the machine to pack it away. Other than that, you'll be fine."

It may sound daft but, as a self-confessed control freak, having some practical do's and don'ts to follow was really helpful for calming me down and my dad knew that. He'd obviously learned the hard way, from the many events he had assisted at, what did and didn't work on a more technical level. While the content of my presentation was up to me, the equipment I would be using to deliver it would be pretty much the same for any speaker and I needed to know that it wouldn't let me down. The only way to be truly confident about that was to follow his advice.

Grateful that he had warned me just how large an event it was going to be, I reconciled myself to the fact that I was definitely going to need to do a few trial runs before the big day. It was time to call in the cavalry. Having chatted for a bit longer with Dad and then eventually said goodbye, I flipped open my laptop to compose an email to Lady Awesome. If anyone knew of potential groups in the area that might be interested in allowing me to give a practice talk then you could bet your bottom dollar she would know who they were.

Half an hour later, while I was dishing mountains of my homemade 'special' fried rice into vast bowls for the starving horde, a reply pinged into my inbox. Lady Awesome had found a local Ladies' Lunch Group who were interested in listening to my presentation and were prepared to give me some feedback. If the group enjoyed the experience then she was happy to consider recommending me to a few others, but she planned to attend the lunch group so that she could listen to my talk, just to make sure that she could make any future recommendations in good faith.

Given what an amazing speaker she was herself, I found it quite surreal to think that she was now going to come and listen to me. Torn between my default setting of automatic anxiety and a new burgeoning excitement, I spent the evening refining my ideas with regard to what I planned to say.

16: Incubation

Definition: maintaining an organism in conditions that promote development and growth.

Continuing in the present and the lead up to the ladies' lunch....

Time was not in the mood to stand still it would seem, and the following week whizzed by in a bit of a blur.

However, by contrast, one thing was definitely in full focus during that time and it worried me far more than any speaking event could because I observed two more occasions when Quiet ambled back into the house in the (very) early morning.

I am the first to admit that I am notoriously nosy, but I couldn't demand to know where he had been without sounding like a Victorian parent and I knew from experience that this was not the way to handle him. He was clearly safe and not in any distress, and given his age I rather hoped he would eventually give me a clue as to what was going on. Any of the other Barbarians would have, of course, but I was dealing with the intensely closed-mouthed Quiet.

The situation bugged me on several levels because I knew he was going to bed in his own room; admittedly this was sometimes very late but, let's face facts, the teenage circadian rhythm does operate in a vastly different time frame to the rest of reality. I had even started checking on him in the middle of the night, like I used to when he was a baby, although this wasn't difficult given the way the fellas in this family snore fit to wake the dead. I didn't actually have to go into his bedroom; I could hear him from down the corridor. But I still had no idea when he was getting up and leaving the house, or why. I took to lurking on the landing at an earlier and earlier hour until I finally spotted him padding silently down the stairs into the kitchen. Peeping over the bannister, I watched as he made himself a cup of tea just before five am and then, steaming cuppa in hand, he let himself out of the patio doors and disappeared. Where on earth was he going?

I crept back under my duvet to consider this conundrum. Beloved Husband's advice, when I raised the mystery with him, was to leave well alone as Quiet seemed perfectly fine, but that was never going to work for a maternal control freak like me. I needed a plan of action; I just hadn't worked one out yet.

In the meantime, everything else seemed to carry on as normal, or as normal as things ever get around here. If I wasn't feeding or chauffeuring the Barbarian Boys around to school, sports or social activities, then I was writing and then re-writing sections of my presentation or boring anyone who came within three feet of me to death by forcing them to listen to it.

"Try to relax and enjoy it," advised Beloved Husband after my first few failed attempts to deliver the earlier drafts. "Don't try to be anything that you're not. This is your story and your artwork, so it really needs to be you talking, not some rigid, formal robot. People need to feel they can connect with you. You can use your hands, you know."

"But I thought I had to stay still so I don't cause a distraction," I wailed.

"There's a big difference between having a totally infuriating twitch and merely relaxing and being you," he stated firmly. "I'm not suggesting you tap dance across the stage, but you can use hand gestures and move around a bit. Don't forget you have to fill the room, engage your audience. Get them to connect with you on a personal level." You might wonder why I was asking him for advice, but he gives presentations all the time in his job, so he does actually know what he's talking about.

"This is all so difficult," I grumbled.

"You're getting there, keep going, and for heaven's sake smile. If you look like you are heading for the executioner's block, you'll make your audience feel uncomfortable. I seriously doubt they're going to be throwing rotten tomatoes at you. Although I guess that will depend on the quality of the lunch as well as your speaking, won't it?" On that unhelpful note he gave me a cheeky grin before grabbing his mobile and making a hasty exit before I could throw something (anything) at *him*!

Eventually I realised that all three of my resident menfolk were actively avoiding me. The house was beginning to feel like the bridge of the Marie Celeste. You could practically see tumbleweed trundling through any room I entered as the other inhabitants retreated away from my approach, abandoning whatever they were doing to ensure their successful escape from being forced to listen to the latest version of my talk and then come up with constructive criticism.

Eventually I rang my mother and delivered my entire presentation down the phone to her. All forty-five minutes of it. The whole thing was her fault after all, so I figured she should suffer with me. It didn't occur to me until much later on that she probably put the phone down on the side and let me ramble away to myself for a bit before retrieving it and making encouraging noises once I'd finished. I am probably being unfair because she did come up with some very constructive comments so she must have been listening to some of it, but it's what I would have done in her place so I wouldn't blame her even if she had snuck off.

Finally, confident that I had a sequence of material that would work to tell my story but also keep the attention of the audience for the required length of time, I then had to learn it. Not word for word, of course, but I needed to know the material so well that I would be able to deliver it in a calm relaxed manner rather than scrabbling around for words as I usually do if put on the spot for an opinion. I needed phrases and paragraphs that flowed well into each other and enabled me to express myself effectively, so I had to be very familiar with how the material should progress.

After that, I had to make sure I got the timing right. There was no point having great presentation material if I merely galloped through it with no sense of control or drama.

It wasn't very long before the day of the lunch club dawned and I found myself stood before twenty delightfully encouraging ladies who had just partaken of a deliciously wholesome quiche and salad (with no rotten tomatoes, only fresh ones – I checked) and were now indulging in coffee liqueurs and huge slabs of chocolate cake with cream whilst looking expectantly at me for entertainment. With the not inconsiderable weight of this group anticipation on me while the president of the club gave the introduction, my knees instantly turned to jelly, and I could feel my insides starting to quake.

Looking down at the prompt cards in my hands, I thought 'What on earth am I doing here?' as a wave of panic threatened to overwhelm me completely before my stroppy inner voice came sharply to my rescue.

"For goodness sake girl, pull yourself together! Just open your big gob and get on with it! These ladies haven't got all day." Supressing a small laugh at how ridiculous I would look if I started arguing with myself in public (been there, done that, wouldn't recommend it), I looked up at my audience and caught the eye of one particular lady sat towards the back of the room. She smiled broadly at me from beneath her shockingly pink hair and winked before mouthing the word "Message" at me. It was Magenta reminding me that this wasn't about me; it was about the story I wanted to share. Lady Awesome was sat next to her with an encouraging expression on her face as she waited patiently for me to find my voice.

Clearing my throat, I smiled at my audience and began to speak. My voice was a bit shaky to begin with, but as the minutes ticked by, I got caught up in the tale I was telling, the responsiveness of my delightful audience and the artwork I was displaying. Before long, I realised that the fear had evaporated.

***

Later that evening, when Beloved Husband returned home from work, he came directly into the studio where I was adding huge curly black eyelashes to a rainbow coloured Jersey cow painting with a contented little flourish. Sitting on the edge of my desk he asked me how the lunch had gone.

"Pretty well, I think," I said smiling happily, "They were all really nice and gave me some very useful feedback."

"So, you weren't terrified?"

"Oh yes, I definitely was, but I got over it eventually."

"Sell any books?"

At his instigation, I'd ordered a dozen copies of my book to take to the lunch with me and I'd also made up a few dozen brightly coloured cards with prints from my paintings on them.

"Yes, all twelve sold, and I've taken orders for six more which is quite good. It felt really weird signing them for people. A good weird though. The cards were well received too. I thought I'd order some more bases and envelopes. Make up some more for next week."

"Next week?"

"There was a lady there who asked me to go to her book club next Wednesday evening; there are ten of them apparently, all willing to give me the practice and more feedback. Lady Awesome is going to recommend me to some other groups, and one of the local WIs needs a speaker to fill in at short notice on Friday. So, I said I'd do that too."

"Wow, you don't hang about do you? Today a ladies' lunch club and tomorrow you'll be taking over the world!" he teased.

"Don't be silly! It was quite fun, but these smaller groups aren't the same as presenting to eighty people as an after dinner speaker. I need all the practice I can get."

"You'll be fine, don't worry. Remember, set up a file so you can keep a note of the figures from this though, like you do for your paintings. You'll need the usual stuff, income and expenditure, especially if you're ordering books in and materials for making cards up. You'll need to keep a careful set of accounts for your tax return at the end of the year."

"That's a good idea," I replied. "I meant to do that earlier but got rather distracted," I nodded at the colourful cow painting before me. "I'll sort it out, I promise."

17: Stymie

Definition: the hampering of progress

Back to the past, the manuscript and yet another tedious house-viewing

I closed the gate with a heavy sigh and leaned on it just to make absolutely certain that it was closed, and my unwelcome visitor could not get back on my property. For the first time in my life I could appreciate some people's desire to own a double-barrelled shotgun.

You've probably worked out that things had not gone well that morning. I had been planning to get to the Post Office in the village with my freshly printed manuscripts immediately after the school run, but my mobile had rung at eight thirty and a last-minute appointment had been booked in for a potential buyer to see around the house at 9am. Apparently, he was very insistent that he had to see the property today and that was the only time he could make. Somewhat resentfully I had to put my postal plans on hold.

Usually I would need more notice to tidy up for a viewing, but as the Barbarians miraculously hadn't actually trashed the place since the last viewing, I had agreed that a short notice appointment was acceptable. If only I was in possession of the gift of foresight and had refused, I could have saved myself so much negative emotion. Five minutes before the arranged arrival time, I had received a second phone call from a panicking Patience to tell me that she'd had a puncture and wouldn't be able to show the viewer around.

The housing market was a bit odd at the time, not helped by recent political developments and the fact that it was now early November, so there weren't that many interested parties looking to buy houses just then. That detail, coupled with the fact that the cottage was rather a niche property given its size and location, meant that it made sense for me to show this potential buyer around rather than reschedule the appointment. Which didn't particularly worry me; it was a pleasantly warm, sunny day for the time of year and I was quite capable of showing people around even if I didn't particularly enjoy the process of watching strangers crawl all over my beautiful home.

For the most part, the viewers we had already shown around were really very pleasant people, generally families with young children or young couples looking to move to the country. Unfortunately though, when push came to shove, the sheer remoteness of true country life in comparison to town life was an issue. The absence of things like streetlights, pavements and takeaway delivery options were a bit of an issue. On the whole, people seemed to expect the peace, quiet and chocolate-box charm of country living but to still have all the conveniences of town life. It simply doesn't work like that, so our plans to sell were not moving along as quickly as we had hoped, and I was really beginning to wish (a little ungraciously I will admit) that people would do their research about what they really wanted before they bothered me.

One couple came out to view a grand total of five times bringing a motley collection of associated relatives. On each occasion they stayed well over an hour before they eventually admitted that they really wanted to live by the sea. Surely the fact that our home was a remote country property would have been fairly obvious to them from the start? I would have thought that the surrounding fields and woodland, coupled with the complete absence of sand and a large moving body of blue, salty water would have given that one away on the first viewing, surely? But apparently not!

However, the forty minutes prior to me very firmly closing the gate behind my latest visitor that morning had to have been the worst house viewing I had ever experienced. An ominously bad feeling had enveloped me from the moment I had set eyes on the squat, little man who had knocked impatiently on my front door. Although not terribly tall, he was of a fairly solid construction, and strutted into the house with a self-important swagger. My first impression was that he probably spent a lot of time at the gym given the vast array of over the top, muscular definition displayed by the very tight black T-shirt he had on (no sign of a coat even though it was quite chilly in spite of the sunshine). In fact, it rather looked as though his muscles had muscles, but I'm not sure if that is even possible.

With some difficulty I dragged my horrified gaze from his bizarrely distorted biceps. I can never understand why people do that to themselves; is it the pressure of social media or merely some form of obsessive-compulsive behaviour? It can't be easy not being able to put your arms down by the side of your body because your muscles are in the way.

Pulling myself together I launched into a general spiel about how the cottage used to be three hundred and fifty years old but that a significant portion had been rebuilt in recent years and was therefore of more modern construction. Not displaying any inclination to listen to me, he marched off through the house, opening doors and cupboards seemingly at random and firing blunt questions at me before belligerently belittling my answers. The man seemed to want to argue with me on every single point. It would seem that I was incapable of being truthful about anything with regard to the house. I began to suspect that he might have a bit of a death wish, as my hackles became steadily raised and my hands clenched into involuntary fists in my pockets.

One major bone of contention surfaced when I mentioned that the property had its own private wastewater drainage system. You are probably well aware that this is a very common occurrence when you live in remote country locations due to the sheer distance from any larger residential areas. It doesn't make sense for the local councils to dig up vast stretches of road to lay underground sewer pipes all the way out to every tiny little hamlet where only one or two properties will benefit. Hence many country cottages like ours either have septic tanks or individual mini sewage treatment works installed. Happily, several years previously, we had installed a state-of-the-art version of one of the latter and were very proud of it. A nice young person from the drainage company visited twice a year to check it was working to the required standard and sign all the paperwork to comply with environmental controls.

If you've never had to think seriously about the practical disposal of wastewater from your property, then you really won't get how interesting the subject can be. Take my word for it. A person can get quite invested in such equipment when there is no other option available. Three years earlier, when the vast majority of the house had collapsed, it had been a massive comfort to us to know that we still had one flushing toilet. Admittedly, at the time, we hadn't been at all sure that the roof over that toilet was stable, but having an operational loo made everyday life in the tent so much more civilised.

Nevertheless, I digress! The presence of all the paperwork for the wastewater treatment system plus photographic evidence of its installation wasn't enough for this argumentative ape. He didn't believe me when I said there was no mains drainage option available to the property and kept insisting that he would get it installed, as if he had some sort of superior power and influence. I politely (through gritted teeth) pointed out that the nearest mains drainage connection was over five miles away and creating the connection he was suggesting would cost a crazy sum of money and require not only multiple and extremely complicated planning permissions but also major feats of inconceivable co-operation from both the local council, the water company and the highways agency. But he merely waved me away dismissively with that 'don't be a stupid little woman' way that some ignorant men have. I could feel my already raised hackles rising yet further as my inner voice muttered mutinously in my head.

"Where on earth did Patience find such a knuckle-dragging Neanderthal?"

Quite frankly I couldn't agree with myself more for once, but I still had to get through the rest of the viewing without accidentally (or otherwise) knocking my visitor's teeth down his throat. I really didn't want to play this game anymore. Nevertheless, I took a deep breath and soldiered on.

What followed was a similar verbal exchange with regard to the property's gas supply. In other words, there isn't one. We use oil, but apparently Knuckles could get mains gas pipes installed as well as mains drainage. Good for him! Although I suppose if the council were persuaded to dig up half the county to put in sewage pipes for his sole benefit, then there's no reason why they couldn't lay gas pipes at the same time. Realistically speaking, there was no way that scenario was going to happen of course, but I saw no reason to argue with him any further. I had no intention of selling my home to this creep, but I did need him to leave without resorting to violence. (Let me be clear here, I was concerned about me being violent, not him. In spite of my unwelcome guest's sadly overdeveloped physique and bully boy, boorish ways I wasn't scared of him, just very annoyed.)

Then he launched into extensive and impossible plans to build a basement swimming pool complex under the entire house. Evidently, they are all the rage in London.

'Good luck with that one" Sighed my inner voice.

I did consider briefly acquainting him, yet again, with the fact that the property was within the New Forest National Park and therefore subject to the most stringent planning regulations, not to mention the complications of the Area of Outstanding Natural Beauty, Site of Special Scientific Interest and Ramsar Site statuses adorning the surrounding area too. A basement swimming pool complex simply wasn't going to be happening, but I decided that he could find that out for himself. Or not. Either way it wasn't going to be my problem.

In fact, by the time Knuckles had verbally torn apart my lovely thatched roof and then started to stalk around the garden, glowering aggressively at Beloved Husband's adored collection of outbuildings whilst looking for more things to carp about, I was starting to lose the will to live. Was he ever going to leave? Or even worse, was I going to spend the rest of my life chasing him round while he fired rude questions at me?

Trailing behind him at a safe distance, I watched as he yanked the door open to the log cabin where Beloved Husband keeps his (rarely used) gym equipment. I was surprised to see him suddenly stop short, his eyes momentarily locked on something inside. Then his face drained of all colour and he gave me a look of total incomprehension. He abruptly turned on his heel and headed for the side gate which leads to the front driveway, moving at a significant speed, where he got into his car, started it and drove away without another word.

Puzzled, but not unhappy at this sudden end to proceedings, I peered curiously in through the open door of the log cabin to see Skelly installed in all his super skinny splendour on Beloved Husband's old exercise bike; one of those more comfy constructions where you recline in a padded seat with your legs pedalling out in front of you and a screen at eye level showing you the mountains you could be cycling through, should you ever chose to cycle outside in the real world somewhere exotic like the Bahamas.

Skelly was sporting a luminous pink sweat band round his skull, a bright orange runner's singlet, complete with the number 13 printed on a square of white paper stapled to it, baggy yellow shorts and flowery flip flops on his bony feet. A small table had been carefully placed to his right, where a bottle of energy drink and a half-eaten Mars Bar lay within easy reach. He looked the perfect picture of the perils of too much exercise.

So that was where he'd got to.

18: Exposure

Definition: the revelation of something secret, hidden or potentially embarrassing.

Still in the past, half an hour later on that morning…

Shortly after the aborted house viewing, I shuffled into the Post Office with a large orange bag-for-life stuffed to the brim with neatly parcelled manuscripts. I joined the end of a fairly lengthy queue. Normally I wouldn't dream of going near the Post Office in the village on the first Monday morning of the month as it is always packed with people for some reason and the ensuing scrum is usually far too much for my claustrophobic tendencies, hence it's best avoided. However, my enthusiasm for my new writing project was sufficient to add steel to my nerves and so I braved the battleground.

It wasn't long before several other people arrived after I did, and the queue threatened to snake out of the door. Nevertheless, the lady standing immediately behind me appeared to be giving me a fairly wide birth because she was persistently refusing to close up the gap between us, in spite of polite prodding from the people behind her. It eventually dawned on me that she must have heard about the whole 'body in the car boot' scenario on the village grapevine. Her shifty behaviour made me wonder what she thought I was going to do; especially in a packed public place like the Post Office. Whip out a concealed weapon perhaps, or maybe just a blood covered body part? (I mean from a victim of course, not just one of my own body parts – although, come to think of it, either action would certainly liven things up!)

Ignoring her hostile behaviour, I settled in to observe those queueing in front of me and soon realised we wouldn't be moving for a while because someone had just requested a 'check and send' on no fewer than five passport applications. Quite clearly a passport application novice if you ask me. No matter how helpful the ladies behind the counter in the village Post Office are, no one with any sense asks for that particular service on a Monday morning? 'Check and sends' are definitely a quiet Friday afternoon job, assuming that you don't want to be lynched by at least half a dozen people waiting to pick up their Giros, that is.

Nonetheless, even though it was going to be a while before we made any progress, everyone was doing that gentle rock from foot to foot that you do when queueing and attempting to edge infinitesimally forwards as if they could speed things up by sheer effort of will. Yet still the gap behind me didn't close up, not even fractionally. Thanks to the vastly over-exaggerated rumours of my bloodthirsty and murderous tendencies, I had plenty of room. Notoriety has unexpected benefits, I realised, because at least my parcels were in no danger of getting crushed.

The situation also meant that I could keep a certain amount of personal space between the rather tall gentleman in front of me and myself. He was well over six and a half feet in height and very solidly built. In comparison I came up to about his elbow, while the rest of him loomed overhead, casting me into deep shadow. This fact didn't particularly trouble me until his mobile phone rang and he dug around in the back pocket of his baggy jeans to retrieve it. Not a particularly remarkable action you might think, except that whilst pulling out his phone the loose blue shirt he was wearing over dark jeans rode up considerably and it became evident that he was one of those men who prefer to wear their trousers in an exceedingly low-slung fashion. So low in fact that I marvelled how on earth they were staying up at all. It was also sadly apparent that he'd had the misfortune to run out of underwear when he got dressed that morning, as I was confronted with an uninterrupted view of a significantly large portion of his very hairy and totally bare backside; a backside that, given his extreme height, was in lamentably close proximity to my face. (Do they not make trousers long enough to go all the way up when a person is over six foot?)

Mercifully, his shirt dropped back down quite quickly, and I was left doubting whether I had in fact seen that which I thought I had just seen; although the image was bouncing around the inside of my traumatised eyeballs like the flare from an unexpected camera flash for some time afterwards. Unhappily, this rude rump-revealer's mobile phone conversation was a brief one and he soon stowed the handset back in his jeans pocket, affording me with a confirmatory and crystal clear view of his almost entirely naked nether regions for a second time, and I was obliged to believe the evidence before my eyes even though it left me with an overwhelming urge to go home immediately and scrub my eyeballs with bleach. I couldn't help but sympathise with his poor mother; no doubt she would be mortified to know he had left the house with no knickers on. What if he was involved in an accident and had to go to hospital?

I instinctively started to edge backwards, unlike everyone else in the queue, while looking behind me to see if any other poor unfortunate had spotted this massive lapse in true British queue related etiquette. Surely it's common knowledge that you should at least arrive at the Post Office fully equipped with pants? The ladies behind me seemed oblivious, engaged as they were in a good old gossip which involved occasionally nodding archly in my direction. I was forced to conclude that criminally concealed corpses were very probably still the hot topic of the moment rather than blatant buttock brandishing.

The passports at the front of the queue were eventually checked, found to be lacking, and a gentle but firm lecture on what constitutes an appropriate passport photo delivered by the postmistress, resulting in the current customer at the counter turning to leave with a heavy sigh. One could almost see the air of dejected defeat hanging over her head like a little black cloud as she headed for the door with her deficient documents.

Eventually it was my associate with the well-aired rear end's turn to step up to the counter. I spotted immediately that his sheer vertical proportions were going to force him to have to lean down quite considerably in order to communicate effectively with the tiny lady behind the glass screen. It was clear that his shirt was definitely going to be insufficient to cover his stern in that position, so I closed my eyes and turned away. I really didn't need to see it again and there was no way I could effectively warn anyone about what was going to happen. A few seconds later there was an audible 'Mexican wave' of horrified gasps rippling along the queue behind me and then a shocked silence descended as numerous jaws simply hung open in a form of farcical, facial suspended animation.

Oblivious to the scandal he was causing, Mr Commando finished his transaction, stood upright again and departed from the shop leaving the counter free for me. Shaking myself free of a bizarre inertia, I stepped up to the counter with my bag of parcels. The surreal spell of silence that had bewitched the whole room was only broken when the door closed firmly behind 'the behind'.

Ten minutes later I stood out on the street again, secure in the knowledge that many copies of my manuscript were winging their way to sit in the slush piles of twenty different publishing companies. Feeling exhilarated at this small success, I considered popping into the village coffee shop for a celebratory cappuccino but on spotting a certain tall and low-slung-trouser-wearing gentleman at the till, I rapidly changed direction and wisely headed home instead.

All I could do after that was to wait and see what response I might get. It was going to be a fairly long wait. So long in fact that I was to give up on the whole idea and eventually forgot about it, getting caught up in all the practicalities of the run-up to Christmas, practicing my synchronised swimming routine with the WI ladies and the final weeks of my nearly-over job.

However, some weeks later on, there was a very interesting development indeed.

Part 5

'What we think, we become.'

Buddha

19: Self-Confidence

Definition: A feeling of certainty or trust that a person can have in one's own abilities.

Moving forward in time, away from manuscripts and bare bottoms, to continue this tale in the present and the big presentation event that was looming….

Several weeks of practice and preparation passed peacefully until it was only a matter of forty-eight hours before I was going to have to actually stand up before a vast number of the Creative and Literary Society members and speak. My mother had called to let me know that over one hundred and twenty tickets had been sold to the event and I was definitely getting very cold feet. It was one thing to give a presentation to a small group of ladies on a casual basis. It was something else entirely to be the entertainment for a large gathering of creative people who had all paid not insignificant sums of money for their evening.

It was all very well telling myself to pull myself together and jolly well get on with it but, as the event had got closer and closer, I had seriously started to worry. Nevertheless, I did my best to crush the mind-monkeys on my shoulder telling me that I couldn't do it, repeating clearly to myself over and over that I was going to give it my absolute best shot and all would be well.

I was secretly quite pleased with the way my presentation had developed over the last few weeks, thanks to all the constructive feedback from the various ladies' groups. The basic premise of the talk was to quickly outline what happened when the house started falling down and how we then found ourselves homeless apart from the tent in the garden. Then I planned to describe how we coped afterwards, as well as speaking about some of the very intense emotions which had eventually led to me creating all those frantic paintings and, ultimately, inspired me to write the book. I hoped that the whole presentation had a positive and empowering feel to it, based around the concept that it is possible to pick yourself up from the things in life which blind side us and that we can move on to a happier state.

On the whole, the practice events had generated some very positive responses and I hoped it would translate well to a much larger group. I also planned to illustrate the whole thing with original pieces of art too, and now I was scheduled to drive Daisy, packed with paintings, to Devon the next day. Once there, I would visit my parents for lunch and in the evening, I was to stand before the eminent members of the Society and deliver the promised presentation.

I had my timings all worked out. The required forty-five minutes was broken up into handy sections, alternating between telling elements of the story and showing paintings and describing how events had unfolded. Beloved Husband, the boy Barbarians and even the girls, on quick trips back from university, had spent quite some time helping me to establish a relatively professional delivery style. There were even several jokes, at least the Barbarians seemed to find them funny, unless it was merely hysterical laughter in the hope that I would go away and leave them alone. However, whether the Creative and Literary Society members would find them amusing remained to be seen.

On the whole it was intended to be a light-hearted, entertaining yet ultimately inspirational performance. All I had to do now was actually deliver it without falling to pieces, a prospect I was contemplating with mounting concern as I dashed into town to do some essential banking jobs the day before I was due to leave for Devon.

After I finished my business at the bank, I started back across our little town towards the car. Whilst simultaneously stressing about the upcoming talk but also trying to keep myself calm about it, I took a short cut down a small alley where a chic little boutique was tucked away. The sort of place I never ever visit because I am simply far too intimidated to step through the door. I always tell myself that the clothes would be well beyond my budget and avert my eyes as I go past to avoid temptation.

Failing to avert them fast enough this morning, I suddenly found myself stopping dead just past the shop. I doubled back, to take a second look at the display in the window. There before me were the most divine pair of shoes I had ever seen. Now I have always appreciated the look and shape of shoes, but I rarely buy them because they generally have a 'too high' heel or 'too pointy' toe for my great plates of meat to feel even remotely comfortable. But these beauties had a graceful mid-height, spool heel and were decorated in bright blue with cheerful yellow sunflowers. They were totally mad but at the same time utterly gorgeous.

In only a few seconds I suddenly could appreciate what is meant by the phrase 'statement shoes' and the statement wasn't "Buy Me", although they definitely said that too. I realised that the longer I stared at them through the window, the more I was in severe danger of falling completely in love and actually drooling on the recently cleaned shop window. Yet, try as I might, I could not tear myself away.

I looked for a price tag in a vain hope that it would put me off. No such luck, even though the little white printed slip in the sole stated quite a significant sum. Not enormous by designer standards, after all we weren't talking Jimmy Choos here, but it was still way more than I would normally consider. However, there were some additions to the price tag, four incredible, little red letters.

S.

A.

L.

E.

Oh no!

Another lower figure was etched below the original amount. It was still quite high but not ridiculously so. There was nothing else for it; I was going to have to investigate further.

I checked furtively both left and right before reaching for the door handle. Why on earth I did that I don't know. Did I think that a police van would suddenly screech to a halt with sirens blaring? Perhaps half a dozen heavily armed officers would jump out and point guns at me and use a megaphone to yell, "Halt! Step away from the shoes!"

Tentatively opening the door as unobtrusively as possible, I slipped in and moved across to a small table where there were several samples of the most beautiful shoes on display. They were all very colourful and hence so very appealing. I was beginning to develop a very deep desire to have new shoes, in spite of the fact that when I had left home that morning it had been the furthest thing from my mind.

Oh dear!

Dismissing the really high-heeled shoes at the back as unrealistic, I narrowed down my possible choice to three different styles, but it was going to be a very difficult decision. I tried to be sensible, taking the time to work out which of the outfits I already had in my wardrobe might work with each of the bright designs, and found myself coming to the unfortunate conclusion that I had absolutely nothing suitable to wear with the gorgeous blue shoes with the sunflowers on them. In spite of that fact, they were the ones I really wanted. In fact, I liked them so much I could feel myself generating reasons why I was going to have to treat myself to a whole new outfit in order to justify buying that particular pair of shoes.

Slipping them on, something incredible happened. They made me feel a million dollars. I'd never understood that phrase before, but standing there in that little boutique in those shoes I felt that I could conquer the world. I could certainly give a forty-five-minute presentation, no problem!

I could do anything!

It was like a madness descending.

I needed those shoes.

What on earth was I thinking? I had only just been to the bank and I'd seen my bank balance. It wasn't good. There was no way I could afford them, let alone a new outfit. This was absolutely not a good idea at all. But I couldn't help it. I simply had to have them. Out came my purse (entirely of its own accord, I do assure you) and I headed for the counter with an uncharacteristic, yet steely, determination in my step.

It seemed that, while I was arriving somewhat late to the whole shoe-addiction party, I was about to buy my first ever pair of fabulously funky designer footwear and it felt incredible!

20: Incongruous

Definition: not fitting in with other aspects.

Staying with the present and the trip to Devon for the presentation.....

Twenty-four hours later my new shoes, packed carefully in tissue paper in their beautiful matching designer box, sat on the passenger seat next to me in Daisy while I set the satnav destination. I do actually know the way to my mum and dad's house but I was nervous and taking no chances. The Barbarian Boys had kindly assisted me in packing my little car full of original artwork, projector, screen, laptop (I knew they had the necessary IT at the event but I was being over-cautious, as usual, and wanted my own equipment too, just in case), a cash float and boxes of books, cards and prints.

Having done their duty by their nervous mum, the boys were now indulging in an epic battle of some sort whilst waiting for Beloved Husband. He had kindly offered to take them to school for me so that I could head off early and beat the rush hour traffic past the local town. But I knew that he had a big day ahead himself as the preliminary interviews for that job he'd mentioned were today. Hence, at that moment he was trying to get himself organised for the day ahead while the boys lurked by his car.

Watching them in my rear-view mirror as they pounced on each other on the driveway behind Daisy, I couldn't help but wonder why everything had to be quite so physical with boys. At that moment in time

Quiet, wearing a long black cloak over his jeans and a sweatshirt, was forcefully bashing at his younger brother with the leftover cardboard inner tube from a used roll of wrapping paper and displaying far too much enthusiasm for his actions. While I thought it was nice to see him contributing to the family attempts to reuse and recycle things, I did wonder if I should step in and prevent him actively causing any real injury. Nevertheless, as the battle raged on, Small seemed to be fending off his brother's blows quite effectively with his own cardboard tube until, thanks to an unlucky mis-step, he was forced off the driveway towards the ditch. I watched my younger son desperately try to maintain his footing on the overgrown verge outside our property boundary. Instead of giving his brother some quarter at this point though, Quiet started hacking at Small's wrist and yelling:

"I

am

your

father!"

(Ah! That old chestnut! Obviously, he's not his father, but I *now* knew what they were doing! It was *role play*. They were acting! It was educational, how enterprising of them!)

Small dropped his cardboard tube and disappeared into the ditch screaming dramatically, "Nooooooooooooooooo!" while Quiet swirled his black cloak around him and stalked off.

Goodness only knows what the neighbours would think of it all. However, they were clearly re-enacting one of their favourite films. Star Wars in this case, or rather The Empire Strikes Back, when Darth Vader declares, mid light-sabre fight, that he is Luke Skywalker's dad, they fight a bit more and then Luke's hand gets chopped off. The boys do this from time to time, especially when the PlayStation is out of action for whatever reason. I rather wish they'd choose some less violent scenes to recreate but have to accept that there's probably no fun in that.

As a mother I wasn't too worried by Small's current location in the ditch because I knew it wasn't that deep and we hadn't had any rain recently, so it was probably empty and there was no danger of him drowning. My only concern was the state that his school uniform would be in when he eventually climbed out and I briefly considered getting out of the car to haul him out to check it over but then decided against getting involved. Beloved Husband stepped out of the house and unlocked his car which caused Small to leap out of the ditch and race his brother (now minus the black cloak) to the front passenger door where a friendly scuffle over who was to ride shotgun ensued.

Beloved Husband raised his eyebrows at me and called out. "Go! You are supposed to be getting a jump start on the traffic. I can sort these ruffians out. Good luck and don't worry. Let us know how you get on."

Smiling, I waved at him and put Daisy into gear, pulling away from the scene of mayhem and considered how, contrary to all appearances, our Barbarian boys actually got on incredibly well as brothers but no-one watching would ever believe that. Neither of them could resist the urge to scrap with the other at the drop of a hat and I did sometimes wonder if that was normal.

I can still clearly remember the look on Quiet's face, over twelve years ago, when I had arrived home from the maternity hospital bearing a plastic, padded rock-a-tot car seat containing the latest (and last) little bundle of joy, dressed head to toe in yellow. We hadn't intentionally kept the gender of the new baby a secret but a very uncooperative foetus at all scans (a sign of things to come perhaps?) had resulted in none of us really having a clue if it would be a pink one or a blue one. It was my fourth time around, so I definitely had my suspicions but kept quiet as I didn't want to raise anyone's hopes either way. The minute we arrived home my four-year-old son had his eyes glued to the new yellow baby bundle with a rather desperate expression on his face.

"What is it?" His voice was barely louder than a whisper indicating just how badly he wanted the information. Do please remember that this was back in the days when he earned his (now rather incongruous) nickname 'Quiet' by rarely ever speaking at all.

"It's a baby, silly!" replied his older sister smartly. I forget which sister, which is a terrible admission for any mother to make but in my defence, I was only six hours post-delivery and hormones coupled with exhaustion had fried my brain.

Quiet merely closed his eyes.

"Please tell me it isn't another girl?" he begged with a disgusted sigh. It was a heartfelt plea if ever I heard one. So, I sat tentatively on the edge of the sofa next to him and placed the rock-a-tot carefully on the floor before us.

"Then let me introduce you to your little brother."

His eyes went round as he looked at me disbelievingly. Obviously, he had been bracing himself for the worst, but now he perked up and examined the little yellow scrap of humanity in the baby car seat with a bit more interest.

"He's a bit small!" He made this pronouncement doubtfully after an intense scrutiny and, in that moment, my second son gained his own, now completely contradictory, soubriquet. It doesn't take much in this family to get a nickname.

Given how relieved Quiet had been at the arrival of Small to even up the gender balance in our home, it was surprising just how many times over the years that the two boys have tried to inflict benign physical damage to each other. I have made the assumption that this is merely a 'boy' thing and try to ignore it unless serious injury, death or destruction of property seems a probable outcome. At the same time, they have learned the hard way that I don't react well if there is blood involved, so they do try to avoid it. For the most part, I just send them outside to perpetrate their own personal brand of pandemonium where I don't have to witness it but today all I had to do was point Daisy in the general direction of Devon and leave them for their doting dad to sort out.

I had bigger fish to fry, a little further along the coast.

21: Unwonted

Definition: unaccustomed, unusual or unprecedented

Returning to the past and the wait for a response from a publisher…

It was several weeks after my encounter with Mr Commando in the village Post Office that I was trundling contentedly past the autumn fields and hedges in Daisy and enjoying the low, late afternoon sunshine, looking forward to the prospect of getting home to a peaceful evening.

Having finished work an hour earlier, I had executed an efficient raid on the local supermarket before swinging by the Barbarian Boys' school to pick them up after rugby training. This was why Small, smothered in mud, was currently crow-barred into the back seat along with industrial-sized packs of all sorts of edible loot as well as enough rolls of loo paper to sink a battleship. I had taken great delight in packing several bags of fruit and vegetables around him, in the certain knowledge that this might be as close to them as he was ever going to get willingly, and that was only because he didn't want to have to walk the five miles home from school. Very sensibly, I carefully packed any sweet treats well out of his reach in the boot where they stood a chance of making it back to the house rather than being surreptitiously consumed en route.

Quiet, on the other hand, was sat in the front passenger seat juggling a number of mega-sized containers of milk loitering around his legs in the foot-well, with four multipacks of yoghurts piled on his lap whilst patiently listening to a litany of strict instructions from me to not allow any of the two-dozen eggs balanced on the top to get broken. All of a sudden, my nagging was rudely interrupted by a shiny, silver BMW roaring around a blind corner and forcing Daisy to veer right off the road.

Regrettably, such inconsiderate driving is not an uncommon occurrence on the local lanes these days, but at least one of us (I mean me of course) hadn't been travelling too fast and I was therefore able to skid skilfully into a handy, if muddy, gateway thus avoiding a messy accident.

"Woah!" said Small, "Did you see that BMW?"

"We could hardly have missed it!" muttered Quiet with his own signature brand of serenely soft sarcasm.

"I *did* miss it," I pointed out with some pride. "Quite expertly actually, but we were very luck this gateway was here or we could have landed in one of those." I nodded out of the window at the deep, murky, water filled trenches on either side of our present location.

"That would not have been very good for the eggs," pointed out Quiet in a massive understatement.

Shaking my head in condemnation of the other driver's poor road skills, I coaxed poor Daisy into reverse, edged cautiously out of the muddy gateway and back onto the tarmac before shifting into first to continue forwards and around the corner, only to slow right down again almost immediately at the sight of one of those square, squat, refrigerated supermarket delivery lorries stranded in the road ahead; or, rather more accurately, *not* in the road ahead.

Creeping closer, very slowly, we could see the vehicle was leaning at an awkward forty-five-degree angle. The bulk of the main storage compartment was resting heavily against the hedge as the two offside wheels had slipped into the deep drainage ditch that was lurking beneath the undergrowth at the side of the road, no doubt with the express intention of swallowing up any unsuspecting suburban drivers.

It didn't take a genius to arrive at the conclusion that this vehicle was clearly another victim of the badly driven BMW. The poor driver had not had the fortune to be anywhere near to a handy gateway. It was pretty clear that the selfish speedster had blasted past forcing this poor delivery person to pull out of the way onto what he mistakenly thought was solid verge, only to find out that there was nothing solid about it and the results were before us for all to see.

"Ooops!" mumbled Quiet. "I bet his eggs are broken!"

"Do you think he's dead?" Small's helpful contribution came from the backseat in a dramatic whisper.

"Let's hope not," I said slowing the car down and coming to a complete stop right in the middle of the road (no way was I going anywhere near those ditches). "We'd better go and find out. Stick out the red triangle Small, back by the bend is probably best. I'll go check on the van driver."

Climbing out, I opened Daisy's rear door to help Small extricate both himself and the warning triangle from under the bags of shopping and left him to run down the road to set it up. Then I cautiously approached the van to peer in through the windscreen to see the driver hunched over the dashboard. He definitely wasn't dead because he appeared to be busy head-butting the steering wheel repeatedly and uttering profanities. This struck me as fairly odd behaviour but then I've never driven into a ditch; maybe this is standard practice.

Quiet, having carefully divested himself of eggs, yoghurts and milk, joined me next to the van with Small on his heels. He reached up to haul the cab door open asking, "Are you alright mate?"

The startled driver stopped his stream of rather fruity language and turned to look at us with a grimace, "Yeah! But I think I might be about to lose my job!" He laughed self-consciously before adding, "It's only my second day too!"

He appeared to me to be about twelve years old as he unfolded his long, lanky frame from the driving seat and swung himself to the ground. Obviously, he can't have been quite that young, but I would have put odds on him only recently having passed his driving test and that was nothing to do with the position his vehicle was currently in. He had the sort of frail emaciation that you see in some mid-to-late teenage boys when they are in the grip of a major growth spurt. You probably know some, when their height has outgrown their strength and their bones haven't yet been fleshed out with the muscle and general bulk that will eventually develop.

While I was making sure that this Lanky lad with the impressively varied vocabulary was not hurt, Quiet dangled his brother into the ditch by his feet (hopefully taking care to keep his head above the murky water) so that he could get a good look under the van and assess the damage. This probably sounds like a daft idea but, for a twelve-year old, Small knows a surprising amount about engines and general vehicle mechanics gleaned from many dedicated hours watching YouTube videos and has developed a worrying obsession with all things Top Gear related (more specifically the old series with JC, in case you were wondering).

Eventually, Quiet hauled Small back out of the ditch having finished his assessment of the mechanical situation and my youngest Barbarian dusted himself down efficiently before declaring firmly that the underside of the van didn't appear to be damaged at all.

"We probably just need to pull it out really carefully," said Small earnestly to Lanky. "Then you can get it checked over back at your depot." Everyone turned and looked at poor Daisy and all reached the same conclusion fairly rapidly. Even if she was possessed of a towing hitch (which she wasn't), there was no way that Daisy was going to be able to come to the rescue. She was simply far too dainty. However, this was the country and we all know there are usually a high proportion of handy tractor drivers per head of rural population, so it couldn't be that difficult to find suitable assistance. Just as I was considering the logistics of trying to squeeze Lanky into the back of Daisy alongside Small to go looking for a tractor driver, there was the welcome sound of rumbling reverberating through the air, accompanied by a ground shaking tremor. Around the corner trundled an immense vehicle of precisely the type we required; the sort fitted with big bouncy wheels the size of double decker buses and a massive girth that seem to sweep right across the country carriageway from hedge to hedge leaving no room for anyone or anything else to pass. Perfect. Isn't it amazing how life can sometimes provide us with exactly what we need just when we need it?

Perched high above this impressive array of agricultural horsepower was one of the local farmer's many offspring who had no doubt been occupied in some late harvest-related activity in the area. From his lofty vantage point in the cab the driver appeared to be simultaneously chatting into a mobile phone held in one hand, whilst also eating an apple that was gripped in the other. One could only marvel at his multi-tasking abilities; after all talking, chewing and swallowing all at the same time isn't easy. However, I was more concerned with the fact that, as both hands were visibly occupied with other tasks, it wasn't terribly clear how he was steering the vast vehicle that was bearing down on us (but perhaps I didn't need to know). Our knight in shining agricultural machinery pulled to a stop within inches of Daisy's back bumper, tucked his phone into his shirt pocket and chucked his apple core into the hedge before dismounting from the cab and striding towards us with a big friendly grin on his face.

"Let me guess," this new arrival said nodding at the van. "Close encounter with a silver BMW?"

"Wow, how did you know?" said Small in an incredulous tone.

"He just tried to play chicken with me too, only I didn't lose. He landed in a field back there."

"Well, he forced me to veer off into a field though a gate too, so as long as he isn't hurt, it serves him right," I said with feeling.

"Oh, he didn't go through a gateway, but never mind. I am sure the hedge will soon recover. I stopped to see if he wanted any help, but he was too busy swearing and kicking his car. I thought I'd give him a chance to calm down and left him to it. I'd much rather help you out. Is there much damage?"

Quiet shook his head, "None that we can see, it really just needs a bit of a tow to get it out."

"No worries, I can do that. Can you shift the little car? I'll get the van out in no time."

Dragging a very disappointed Small away from all the mechanical excitement, Quiet and I thanked him, wished Lanky every good luck and got back into Daisy to head for home and ten minutes later we pulled onto our drive.

Given all the extra excitement of the trip home, I was completely smashed (I mean tired – not drunk!) by the time we finally made it inside. Hence, I didn't immediately spot what was lurking in the pile of post on the doormat. I was so intent on unpacking the shopping and making a restorative cup of green tea that the mat and the mini mountain of mail on it were simply shoved to one side as we traipsed in and out with bags of supplies from the car. I then promptly forgot all about it in the commotion of putting the shopping away.

A large, thick, cream envelope sat, partially obscured by other letters, advertisements, a gardening catalogue and a plastic wrapped 'WI Life' magazine and waited patiently until I finally remembered the mail and went to collect it off the floor. That was when I spotted the unusual package and was very surprised to see that it was addressed to me. The only post I usually get consists of bank statements or the automatic TV license or car tax renewal letters, plus general circular stuff like adverts for pizza delivery firms and charity letters, that sort of thing. This was definitely not any of those. What on earth could it be?

It looked official. Worryingly official! Potentially something legal, perhaps? I employed my perfectly honed skills of procrastination for a while, first carefully putting my car keys and handbag away, before hanging up some coats and then tidying up the shoes that the boys had abandoned just inside the door. Then I moved all the other unremarkable pieces of mail and dealt with them, leaving the big envelope where it was on the floor by the door. I was simultaneously intrigued and perturbed by this item of post. I don't like the unknown and this mysterious missive represented exactly that to me.

Whatever could it be?

22: Recalcitrant

Definition: having an obstinate and uncooperative attitude towards the expected way to behave under certain circumstances

Staying with the past and the intriguing bit of mail that has arrived....

Eventually, I tentatively picked the large envelope up off the doormat and transferred it to the breakfast bar in the kitchen where I could keep an eye on it while I started to cook supper. It was still sitting there patiently an hour later when Beloved Husband came home. He'd taken a short detour past the station on his way back to meet Chaos off one of the trains, because she was visiting for the weekend, laden with the inevitable ton of dirty washing.

"Oooh!" he said, nodding at the envelope. "That looks exciting! What is it?"

I shrugged and muttered, "Don't know," in a small voice, just in case it could hear me.

"So, open it then. It's addressed to you."

"It looks official," commented Chaos peering over his shoulder. "I wonder what it is. Want me to open it for you?"

Beloved Husband, who is well aware that I can ignore the things I don't want to deal with for a very long time, picked it off the counter and put it in my hands. "Open it yourself," he said firmly. "Now!"

Fumbling to get my thumbnail under the glued flap, I managed to rip across the top of the expensive envelope and drew out a dark blue glossy document wallet. There was a small window cut out of the front sheet of card that allowed the title of the document within to be read. My jaw nearly hit the floor as I read the following:

Publishing Contract!

Almost dropping the whole thing in shock, I looked at first Beloved Husband and then Chaos and tried to speak. There were no words, or rather more accurately, *I* had no words.

Chaos had plenty of them.

Her squeal of delight drew the boy Barbarians' attention briefly away from their electronic endeavours. They weren't daft though and only poked their noses through the door long enough to find out what was going on, before retreating to a safe distance. They recognised her tone from previous experiences with two excitable older sisters and fully appreciated that there was a significant danger that they might be accidentally hugged by an over-enthusiastic female relative if they got too close.

With shaking hands, I opened the wallet to find a hefty written document inside from a small, London-based publishing firm. Obviously one of those submissions I had sent out that day from the Post Office had reached their destination. Quite unbelievably, it would seem, this firm wanted my book! Wow!

As Chaos grabbed me by the arm and did a jubilant little jig of hyper-excitement, I smiled in a dazed fashion, all the while feeling oddly disconnected from proceedings. My stomach felt all fluttery and my legs went all wobbly and weak. This was a pretty sensational event, but contrarily I didn't quite know what to think. It definitely called for more than a cup of green tea though. Beloved Husband smiled at me across Chaos' enthusiastic chatter and opened the fridge to bring out a bottle of chilled Prosecco (it had been lurking there for ages, so it was about time we opened it). He gestured towards me with the bottle and raised questioning eyebrows and I smiled and nodded. As he popped the cork, the news slowly sank in to my befuddled brain and, by the time I took my first sip of refreshing bubbles, a goofy grin was starting to spread across my face accompanied by a pleasant tingly feeling that literally started to spread outwards from my core to my fingertips, enveloping my entire body in warm waves of cautious excitement.

Of course, sometime later that particular bubble burst when I sat down with the contract and read it from cover to cover, including the almost endless small print. Beloved Husband came into the studio just as I was placing the last pages down on my desk.

"I've done some research on the internet," he said, "and we can get some advice on the contract from the Society of Authors, apparently. Maybe find out the name of a recommended lawyer to check it over before you sign it. What do you think?"

"There's no need, I won't be signing it." I said firmly.

A beat or two of silence passed before he replied carefully, "OK! Whatever you think. Care to share why?"

"Sure," I riffled through the pages to find the one I wanted and handed it over to him. He read it thoughtfully, right the way to the bottom and I watched as understanding dawned.

"Fair enough," he said, nodding in agreement.

"There's no way I can sign that. It would be like signing away one of the children." In short, by signing the contract, I would effectively be signing over the book and all associated rights to the publishing company for very little return. They wanted all publishing rights, including translation rights in multiple languages, as well as film and TV rights and control of any related memorabilia (for which I read to mean my paintings), leaving virtually nothing to me whatsoever. The contract gave them the right to change my story too, as well as the right to never publish it at all if they chose to do so and they wouldn't have to give a reason.

My decision wasn't based around money; it was about governance. I didn't want these strangers having such complete control over my work. My story. I had lived every painful second of it and the resultant book told a tale that had been haunting me for months until I had finally been compelled to write it down. Now that I had done so, there was no way I was going to let anyone tell me what to do with it.

"Nice to get offered a contract of course, shame I can't sign it."

"Why not?" asked Chaos from the door way and Beloved Husband looked inquiringly at me. I nodded permission for him to hand the contract page over to her. It didn't take her long to read it. "Nah! I wouldn't sign that either."

"Never mind," said Beloved Husband, "better luck next time."

I smiled at him but was distracted by the look on Chaos' face. "What are you thinking?" I asked her.

"Well," she said, breezily, "I think it's pretty obvious what you should do."

"What's that then?"

"OK, the very fact that they have offered you this contract pretty much proves that you have got something with this book, doesn't it? That it's a marketable entity."

"I suppose so, yes."

"Why don't you publish it yourself?"

Well that was easy enough to answer. "Because I don't know how," I laughed sheepishly.

There was a pause before she responded. "Yes, but I do."

Oh! How stupid of me! She was right! That was exactly what I should do. Why hadn't I thought of it before? Chaos had already self-published two books, so she knew exactly how to go about it. I sat up straighter, bubbles of excitement starting to fizz inside me. There were obviously pros and cons to self-publishing, but the major benefit to this plan of action would be that I would have complete and utter control over my work, from the detail in the story to the artwork on the cover. It would be completely and utterly mine, and the control freak in me really liked that concept.

"And you'll show me how to do it?"

"Duh! Of course!"

"OK, let's do it."

***

There were times in the coming weeks when I wished I hadn't started it all, as the sheer complexity of the technical computer stuff involved dawned on me. My brain threatened to melt and pour out of my ears on several occasions as I tried to follow what Chaos was accomplishing through the self-publishing website. There were an awful lot of official forms that had to be filled in to complete the process, and a whole series of editing, proofing and quality control-type issues that needed to be sorted out before my book could come into existence. But it was also very exciting.

Then I needed a cover for it and spent an entire weekend dithering about which of my paintings should be used, before finally creating something suitable on Photoshop so that it could be uploaded and added to the written content that was already being processed as part of my project.

At last the day dawned when my book finally hit the online bookstore shelves and it felt amazing. The very first thing I did was to officially buy a copy and extravagantly arranged for an express delivery the next day. The poor postman must have wondered what on earth was going on because I don't usually pounce on him the minute he sets foot on the drive. (I mean that I don't *ever* pounce on him; I am really not like that, honest!)

I couldn't believe how surreal it felt to hold the first ever physical copy of my book in my hands. A book that I had written! The Barbarians laughed when they saw me immediately head for the patio in order to sit down with a cup of tea and read it; as if I didn't already know what was going to happen in it. I don't think they quite understood how special that moment was to me. I genuinely didn't expect anyone else to ever buy my book or read it. It was just supposed to be a bit of fun and I was pretty certain that I would be my only customer, but it didn't matter.

My book was in print.

It felt incredible!

23: Consolidation

Definition: the combining of several elements into a single more effective and stronger whole entity

Coming forward in time again to the present day and the nervously prepared for big speaking event.....

You will no doubt have heard the phrase 'silence is golden', but it occurred to me that there are many types of silence to be experienced in life. On the downside, there are the cold silences of hate and disapproval, or the painful silence of regret. Then there are many much more positive silences, such as that wonderful wordlessness that can denote happiness so intense that it cannot be expressed. Of course, any parent among us cannot forget the suspicious silence that arises from quiet children getting into mischief either.

So, with a wealth of silences to choose from, the silence around me just at that particular moment was a thick and rich one, packed full of anticipation. It was an ocean of silkily expectant silence with silver overtones that I was expected to dive into and fill.

This was the Creative and Literary Society's annual summer evening party where more than sixty couples were arranged around ten circular tables, draped with snowy white linen in a beautiful ballroom at a stunning hotel on the edge of the cliffs overlooking the sea. A delicious three-course meal (with no tomatoes!) had been consumed by all present, as had the contents of many bottles of wine. All that was needed now was a bit of entertainment to round the evening off in style and I was providing the entertainment, so no pressure then! This wasn't exactly the small and relaxed gathering my mother had originally proposed.

Standing in the silence near a projector and laptop arranged on a small table on the low stage at the front of the room, I could feel a tremor starting in my legs and reminded myself of Magenta's words of wisdom, "Don't be afraid of the silence, if the audience isn't silent then how can they be ready to listen?" This was the moment of reckoning. Here was the reason I had been working so hard to learn the many skills of speaking in public. Now was the time to find out just how good a student I had been.

I made myself look at the sea of still faces all turned eagerly towards me and absorbed the expectation. Feeling as if everything was happening in slow motion, a split second passed in which I acknowledged that this was the moment to panic if I was going to. Strangely though the panic never came, despite the fact that my brain was completely empty, because this wasn't the paralysing blankness of 'nothing'. Instead it was a space for absolute and complete focus. For the first time in my life I had something I wanted to say, and I was about to say it.

I took a deep steadying breath, smiled and said hello. I could hear my voice over the audio system as I launched into my opening phrases, slightly wobbly initially but soon settling into a calm and clear rhythm that filled the room with my words. Taking care to talk directly to my audience and not at them or above them, I spoke to all sections of the room in turn, making eye contact with individuals and drawing them into my tale as I produced original pieces of artwork to illustrate appropriate points.

The presentation I had prepared was simple and honest, and I spoke from the heart about the events that had inspired both the paintings and the book. As my mother had predicted, the audience were delightfully responsive and followed my words with a flurry of fascinated questions. I was almost sorry to find the President of the Society drawing the question and answer section that followed my presentation to a close. Almost sorry, but not completely so, because I had been on my feet for over an hour and was quite exhausted; if exhilarated at the same time. The whole presentation and the books and art had gone down a storm.

It would seem that as usual my mother was right. (But don't tell her

I said so, or who knows what she'll sign me up for next!)

***

I headed for home the next day, after spending the night at mum and dad's, and pootled along the A35 in a happy haze of success. Sadly, the speedometer did not once rise above a frustrating forty miles an hour thanks to a succession of roadworks. By the time I arrived at the house, I was completely drained which was a combination of the days of stress leading up to the event, followed by a very late night, no doubt.

So, I was not really in the mood for a sudden phone call from the estate agent before I'd even switched off Daisy's engine. Oblivious to my state of mind, Patience politely asked if a viewing that was booked for later that afternoon (that I had totally forgotten about) could be pushed back from one o'clock to two thirty.

Supressing a sigh and agreeing to the time change, I hauled my weary body out of the car, unlocked the front door and went inside planning a strong cup of tea followed by a swift tidy round. Chucking my keys on top of the piano in the hall as I passed it, I went into the kitchen only to stop short on the threshold, staring in confusion at the scene before me. What on earth had happened to my kitchen?

Never the tidiest room in the house to begin with, it was now completely unrecognisable. An unidentified white powder seemed to be coating everything, and everywhere I looked there were piles of shredded paper and tubs of slime. Chunks of what I could only describe as 'goo' clung to the walls, cupboards and door, and a trail of bits of old newspaper led off into the conservatory.

I stood there stunned, trying to compute what might have resulted in such a strange scene; perhaps we'd been visited by the Ghost Busters or some rather confused burglars? Perhaps the boys had decided to throw a bizarrely themed party or … what about……? No! I was completely stumped and had no idea what was going on. Then I became aware that I was not alone. Beloved Husband was peering sheepishly at me through the patio doors.

"You're back!" he said. (He's very good at stating the obvious.)

"I am!" I agreed. (I can state the obvious too.)

"It's a bit of a mess," he said. (He's a veritable master of the understatement.)

"Yes, it is," I confirmed. (So am I.)

There was a pause before I continued, "Can I ask why?"

He scratched the back of his head. "Well, I thought it would be a good idea to encourage the boys to do something non-electronic."

"That sounds like a very good idea," I agreed, still not sure how such a concept might be linked to the total destruction of our kitchen, but I was willing to be enlightened so nodded encouragingly.

"I know you've been worrying about Quiet, what with him disappearing off in the early mornings, so I thought if we did something creative together he might feel like chatting about it."

"And did he?" I asked hopefully, thinking that perhaps all this wreckage was worth it.

"Did he what?"

"Did he chat?

"No."

"Oh!"

How disappointing!

"You'll have to think of something else, sorry. But we did make a snowman," he said cheerfully.

"Pardon?"

Honestly, after twenty-three years of marriage, you'd think I'd get used to the way my husband's brain works but even after all that time, I am still pretty much in the dark. I was definitely losing track of the direction of this conversation.

"We made a snowman. Look! I just put him outside so I can start to clean up."

Sure enough, there in the garden was what looked like a four foot snowman.

"It's June! How on earth did you make a snowman?"

"Papier-mâché, of course." He said it like it was obvious. "I saw it on Blue Peter when I was a kid and I've always wanted to make one."

Looking around I realised that this activity did explain the suspicious white powder coating every surface; it must be flour and therefore not something from a dodgy drugs den. It also explained the piles of shredded paper and the tubs of slime. I could only assume that the chunks of 'stuff' I could see hanging off the walls, doors, ceiling and cupboards were escaped bits of papier-mâché that were superfluous to requirements. Beloved Husband followed my line of sight and coughed, "Yes, the boys did get a bit carried away. I hadn't realised that it was possible to have a papier-mâché snowball fight. They were kind enough to demonstrate. I did plan to clear it all up before you got back."

"Oh," I brightened, "so you remembered the viewing then?"

He paled, "Ah! That had actually slipped my mind. Oh heck, they're coming at one, aren't they?"

"It's been put back to two-thirty, so don't worry there's time. If the two of us get going, we can be ready. Bagsy you clean the kitchen though. I'll sort the bedrooms out." I grinned, knowing I was getting the better deal. To be fair it was usually me causing creative chaos, it was nice that someone else had indulged for a change.

***

Several hours later, following an extensive application of elbow grease, the house looked so much better.

Beloved Husband met me at the bottom of the stairs as I was coming down laden with dirty washing. Still sporting a streak of flour through his hair, he hefted the huge bundle off me and asked, "Where do you want this? Utility room?"

"Can you stick it in the back of your car?" I asked.

He looked at me askance. "Why?"

"Because I want to hide it, not wash it. I was going to put it in Daisy like I usually do, but she's full of paintings. I haven't had a chance to unload her yet. I'll do it after the viewing." I followed him out to the car to open the boot for him, so I could keep talking, "I'm really starting to hate these viewings you know. Hopefully this lot will be better than the last one. He was mental. It's such a shame we can't just take the house off the market and stay here forever."

"Well perhaps we should think about it," Beloved Husband said with a shrug.

"We can't afford it," was my blunt reply. "Remember Mortimer?"

"Yes, but the only offers we've had have been way below the asking price and we can't afford to accept those, can we? Time is passing and yet, somehow, we do seem to be managing each month to make the mortgage repayments. Perhaps we should consider trying to ride it out.

And don't forget, if I get that promotion it'll mean quite a jump in salary."

"Well, I know you're on the shortlist which is great, and you are brilliant of course, but there's still the final interview to go, and I continue to be unemployed so let's just wait and see. In the meantime, now the housework is sorted, why don't you take me out for a coffee while Patience does the whole patience routine with these viewers?"

"Sounds like a plan," he said, "and then you can tell me how your presentation went."

"Deal, but first we have to remember to hide Skelly so he doesn't frighten off this lot of viewers. Have you any idea where he is right now?"

"Yup, Skelly went into school this morning with the boys, so he's not a problem we have to worry about today."

Beloved Husband managed to get that whole sentence out with a completely straight face too. Incredible!

"Dare I ask why?" I said, not really sure that I wanted to know.

"Biology, show and tell, I think. Don't worry! He went in wearing full school uniform and Small even packed him some lunch. He'll probably help him eat it too."

I thought it best to leave the subject there, but I did wonder what the Headmaster would make of our smallest Barbarian dragging the family skeleton around with him at school all day.

Only time would tell.

24: Potential

Definition: latent qualities that might develop into future success.

Staying with the present and that celebratory cup of coffee I mentioned…

"I never thought I would say this, but I really enjoyed it." I said, once my hands were wrapped around a decaff, skinny cappuccino in the cute little coffee shop squeezed between the village shop and the Post Office.

The shop was absolutely heaving with local mums having a last-minute cuppa before heading for the local primary school playground for pick up. We had been very lucky to get a seat at all, let alone prime position by the window where we could see across the village green and watch the various comings and goings to our heart's content whilst commenting idly on recent events.

"I thought you would, when you got going. It's a good presentation and you can be quite funny when you relax."

I stared at him. "Funny 'good' or funny 'weird'?"

He paused for a moment and wrinkled his nose at me before saying wickedly, "Definitely funny weird, of course," and then ducked as I threw the little biscuit lurking in my saucer at him.

Catching it deftly he popped it in his mouth, and chewed and swallowed it in seconds, "Yum! Thanks!"

"And I got so many comments on my funky new shoes!"

He looked at me doubtfully, "Seriously?"

"Yes!" I insisted. "You're a man, you wouldn't understand it, but so many of the women there complimented me on my shoes. It really helped to break the ice on a social level. You know I'm not the best at mingling with a bunch of strangers but the shoes provided a talking point. There isn't a woman alive who doesn't like shoes? Hence there's an immediate connection. Plus, I could stand all night in them and they didn't hurt."

The expression of total bewilderment on his face at that point was an absolute picture.

"Honestly, they were such a good investment!" I declared.

"Yeah, you keep telling yourself that," he said with a grin. "More importantly, did you sell any books?"

"I did, yes. I sold out."

"No way! I thought you took three boxes?"

"I did. I just kept signing them until a lady asked me if I had any more and when I said 'yes, look in the other box', she said 'I have, it's empty' which was when I realised I'd run out."

Reaching over, I nicked the mini biscuit sitting on his saucer and chomped on it.

"That's a shame. Not a shame you sold them all, just that you could have sold more."

"Aha! But I did sell more," I exclaimed happily. "I just took a list of names and addresses and they paid me the cost of the book in advance, plus a bit extra for postage. I am going to place an order this afternoon and then when it arrives, I'll sign them all and post them off to their new owners."

"Seriously? Well done for thinking on your feet!"

"It was the shoes," I quipped. "I told you they were a good investment. I sold loads of cards too."

"I am not surprised about that," he said. "They are nice and bright and quite unusual. Also, they're a good memento of a fun evening, I should imagine."

"And each one advertises my book on the back too, so I might get a few more sales off that as well. I also got chatting to a really nice woman from a mental health charity. She was really interested in the concept of the paintings telling the story of my recovery from depression. She mentioned that there was a big fundraiser coming up and when I offered to donate a painting for the raffle, she asked me if I would consider speaking for them."

"That's a good idea. So, all in all would you say it was a fairly successful event?"

"I haven't got to the best bit yet," I said.

"Well don't keep me in suspense."

"I sold *two* paintings. Big ones."

"But I thought you put quite high prices on them."

"I did. But the buyers didn't bat an eyelid at the amount. They just handed over cheques and took the paintings home with them at the end of the evening. I probably should have waited for the cheques to clear before releasing the paintings because they could bounce, but I don't think they will."

He gave a low whistle. "If you keep that up we really can take the house off the market, you know."

I shook my head at him seriously, "I don't think so. It was probably all a bit of a fluke, but it was a really fun evening nevertheless, and I wouldn't mind doing that sort of thing again if I get the opportunity, but it's unlikely to happen."

"Don't underestimate yourself, let's just see what happens."

"OK," I nodded in agreement and then changed the subject. "Now, what are we going to do about Quiet?"

"Ah! I was thinking about that while I was scraping papier-mâché off the ceiling" he said and leaned in towards me, "I have a cunning plan!"

Given that his last idea involved creating a four-foot snowman using flour, water and a torn-up copy of the Yellow Pages, I couldn't wait to hear what he'd come up with this time.

Part 6

‘There is nothing impossible to him who will try.’

Alexander the Great
356BC 323BC

25: Prorogation

Definition: a period of time between the ending of one thing and the beginning of another

Let us travel one final time into the past, to see what happened after the official publication of the book…

Several changes occurred in the next few weeks following the publication of my book. Christmas was over, as was the old year, and the final weeks of my job were complete. My twenty-year status as a gainfully employed person was over and I was set adrift on the ocean of redundancy.

You have probably noticed by now that I do not handle change terribly well and this was no different. Instead of doing something practical about it, like looking for another job, I ignored the situation and buried myself in my studio. With no overwhelming urge to write taking predominance, I returned to my first love. Painting!

It must be borne in mind that the house was still on the market, so I had to try to paint tidily, which was proving a challenge but not stopping me. On the whole, we were still trying to exist in an unnaturally (for us) organised and neat way, or at least I was. I could be pretty certain that the boys weren't trying too hard to be tidy judging from the state of their bedrooms. Unfortunately, there is only so much stuff you can ram under the bed or behind the wardrobe, and we were reaching the stage where a major reshuffle or 'spring clean' was going to be needed. You could say that this might be a better way to occupy my newly-redundant time, but I merely told myself it wasn't quite Spring yet, closed my studio door to it all and opened tubes of paint instead.

The result was a series of small, brightly coloured random animal pictures; a field mouse, a trio of gossiping giraffes, an elephant or two and a happy looking hippo. These creations helped the icy cold months of January and February to slowly slide past.

It was during that time that two developments became apparent to me. The first was that my youngest son had definitely lost the ability to hang up wet towels, which I believe is a stage that all teenage boys reach at some point or another, usually around the time their parents start repeatedly insisting that daily showers and hair washes are an absolute necessity. One morning, totally stumped by the mysterious disappearance of every towel in the house, from my posh Egyptian cottons (they were a present, ages ago, and only used on special occasions) to our usual Tesco's basics, I was forced to investigate Small's bedroom where I was to discover that he had amassed an impressively festering collection of bath sheets over several weeks.

Retrieving the manky, mouldy mound of fluffy fabric from under the bed and heading for the utility room, I walked past the front door to see that the postman had been. There was a littering of letters lounging nonchalantly on the mat. Setting the washer going on what was to be the first of many washes with my fingers crossed that the ancient apparatus would cope with all the towels, I wandered back to retrieve the post.

This was when the second development I mentioned manifested itself with the suspicion that my mother was up to something. One of the items of mail was a very pretty pink envelope addressed to me from my sister's godmother. (No, I am not psychic! There was a little return address sticker attached to the back of it; the type that sensible, organised and properly grown-up people use. I might even get some, one day.) Now I adore my youngest sister's godmother, she is wonderful, but she and I are not in the habit of exchanging snail mail on a regular basis, so something was definitely afoot. As I mentioned previously, I rarely get proper mail so I was intrigued and hence I opened it carefully and with relish. A proper old fashioned, written communiqué is something to be enjoyed and treated with respect, don't you think? Inside was a gorgeous, flowered piece of writing paper covered in traditionally cursive script.

Reading the beautifully written sentences it contained, I smiled and reached for the telephone, dialled quickly and perched myself comfortably on a stool at the breakfast bar in the kitchen as I listened to the resulting dialling tone. As soon as the call was picked up, I got straight to the point.

"What are you up to, Mum?"

There was a pause before she replied, "Me? I don't know what you mean!" There was an air of mystified innocence behind the smile in her voice, but I wasn't fooled.

"Ok," I agreed, playing along, "Then perhaps you can tell me why I've just received a really lovely letter from one of your very good friends saying how much they enjoyed reading my book?"

"Oh, how nice!" she sounded absolutely delighted, "Your first piece of proper fan mail. Who was that from then?"

"Hardly fan mail, Mum. But who on earth do you think it's from? I assume you must have given her a copy."

"Oh yes I probably did, but…." she sounded genuinely mystified, "I couldn't possibly guess who might have written to you."

"Well how many copies have you given to people then?" I asked in surprise.

"Hundreds!" interrupted my Dad's voice. He'd obviously heard the phone ring, worked out it was me and picked up the second handset upstairs so he could join in the conversation. "She's sent so many copies out to her friends that I've lost count!"

"Seriously?"

"Don't exaggerate!" Mum said in an exasperated voice. "I've only sent out a few. Although I have given some as presents recently, and I mentioned it to the ladies at my dance, keep fit and yoga classes. Then your Dad's mentioned it at his French conversation group, the Twinning Association, the sailing club and the Rotary Club. I suppose there are quite a few people it might be."

"Why?" I asked, rather stunned.

She laughed, "Why do you think, you daft girl? We enjoyed it and thought they might like to read it too. Isn't that why you published it?"

"I suppose so. I just didn't really think anyone would want to read it."

"Have you looked on Amazon recently?" That was my dad again. "You've got some reviews! Four and five star reviews."

"No way!" I exclaimed in amazement.

"Yes, have a look!"

"That's unbelievable. Hang on let me pull up the website and see what it says." I flipped open the iPad and quickly Googled both Amazon and the self-publishing website to see reviews and any recent book sales activity. As I hadn't expected anyone to buy it and wasn't promoting it like you are supposed to on all social media forums (I didn't really know how to, even though Chaos had tried to show me), I hadn't bothered to look at the sales report page before now.

"Wow! Mum! How many copies did you buy?" I asked incredulously when I saw the report.

"Yes, how many did you buy?" echoed my dad with a more suspicious tone.

"Oh not that many, maybe ten….possibly twelve… or so… I forget. They were just a few presents for people, that sort of thing, you know how it is," she tailed off, vaguely. I wasn't fooled though, she's as sharp as a tack and I've used the same ambiguous tactic myself to deflect my own husband's queries with regard to my spending habits. Who do you think I learned it from?

Looking at the website I could see far more activity than a dozen book sales, but there was no way she could have bought them all. The sales graph showed a healthy selection of spikes of increasing significance over the last few weeks.

Then I opened another tab to look up those reviews Dad mentioned, and he was right. Several four- and five-star reviews were listed under the page for my book. There was a one-star review too but that didn't faze me. Show me an author who hasn't had a one-star review. It's practically a rite of passage and you can't please everyone. All the other comments were really positive. How amazing!

"Well that's interesting." I said, "I probably ought to dig out the bit of paper I wrote Chaos' marketing instructions down on and try a bit of advertising."

"Ah!" Something about my mother's tone got my attention from the reviews on the screen in front of me.

"Mum?" I queried. "What else is going on?"

"I take it that you haven't been on Facebook recently then."

"When have I ever been on Facebook? I know Chaos set me up an account with an author page, but I haven't really bothered with it. I had no idea what I was supposed to write on it."

"Oh, don't worry! She's been doing that for you. At least I think it's her."

"She's supposed to be studying." I said, repressively.

"I am sure she is, but no doubt she is able to multi-screen as well as the next student and who else is it likely to be? There have been some very exciting posts on your page. Apparently, you're going on a book tour."

"I'm what? When? Where?"

Dad broke back into the conversation to say sensibly, "I think you probably ought to give her a ring and find out what's going on?"

"Yes," I agreed faintly, "I think I probably should. Thanks."

A few minutes later after a flurry of hurried goodbyes I finally put down the handset and sat in a rather dazed heap, wondering if that conversation had really just happened. Then, checking the time and seeing that Chaos would be in the middle of a lecture (assuming she was studying as she was supposed to be and not moonlighting as me on social media) I fired off a quick email suggesting that we needed to have a chat and asking her to ring me as soon as she was free.

Sticking the pretty little letter of congratulations that had triggered all this to the fridge with a magnet, I returned to the iPad determined to remember how to log into Facebook and find out what 'I' had been up to in recent weeks.

It was a most illuminating experience.

26: Skulduggery

Definition: Secret activities conducted under the radar

Remaining with the social media mystery in the past…

A couple of hours later, as I was just putting a dish of lasagne into the oven for the evening's supper, a Skype call came into the iPad. I accepted it to find Chaos and Logic both looking at me from the one screen.

"Hi Mum!" they both chorused. "How are you?"

"You're together!" I said bluntly in surprise. They were supposed to be in different counties at different universities.

"Yup, I'm visiting Logic for the weekend," Chaos confirmed.

"That's nice," I said, deciding not to point out that it was only Wednesday (it was none of my business) and concentrated on how lovely it was that the two of them visited each other by choice. Although why I was surprised I didn't know, they've always been close.

"You wanted to chat," prompted Chaos.

"Oh yes, what's this about a book tour, and what on earth have you been posting on Facebook?"

"Just promotional stuff, I noticed you weren't logging in so I just thought I would run a Facebook ad for you. I'm an administrator on the page so it's easy enough to do. It's no big deal. It's reached quite a big audience already and has another two weeks to run. What do your sales figures look like? Has there been a response?"

"Well yes, I think so. I've definitely sold some, which is pretty incredible. I had no idea."

"That's good. The tour starts the week after the advert stops."

"Chaos, I can't possibly go on a book tour in two weeks' time. I know I don't have a job anymore, but I can't go travelling round the country at the drop of a hat. Who would look after your brothers? Your dad's working." I tailed off as I spotted that both girls were laughing. "What have I said?"

"It's not an *actual* book tour, Mum!" Chaos grinned.

"It's a virtual one," added Logic, as if that explained everything.

"What does that mean?" I demanded, trying not to get cross at my own ignorance.

"It means that your book will be hosted on a series of blogs and other websites all around the country, and you'll be interviewed and small sections of the first few chapters made available to try and drum up some interest in it," explained Chaos, looking exceedingly smug.

"What do I have to do?" I asked with mounting concern. I wasn't sure I liked the idea of being interviewed.

"Not much actually, I've organised most of it. I'll send you the interview questions. There aren't that many, so it won't take you long. Send them back to me when you are done and I'll send them on to the right sites. Then on each day of the tour you need to make sure you spend some time sharing posts, retweeting, blogging and reposting everything."

"You need to make sure you thank everyone who shares stuff about the book and retweets links too." Logic added as if it was the simplest thing in the world.

I felt rather sick. There was no way I could do that. I had barely been able to remember how to log in.

Spotting my look of mounting horror, Chaos said soothingly, "Don't worry Mum, I'll be home with you for the first two days of the tour and I'll show you what to do. I'll also share and post from my social media accounts too. It'll be fun."

"Sure it will," I answered with a studied nonchalance I did not feel, and then because it seemed expected, "Thank you."

"No worries, this is going to be great," smiled Chaos. "I'll see you in two weeks."

"We're off to the library now," said Logic.

"Yeah, and then the pub," said her sister. "Bye!"

With that the screen went blank and I wondered what on earth I was getting into. Then I thought about those little baby sales figures and the unexpected reviews and I couldn't help feeling a little fluttering of excitement.

Perhaps Chaos was right, perhaps this could be fun.

27: Crepuscular

Definition: associated with the twilight hours

Returning to the present day, at a disgustingly early hour of the morning…

It was still dark, but as soon as I heard Quiet's bedroom door open I was wide awake. It was time to make my move.

Beloved Husband's plan was really simple. I was going to join Quiet for his morning travels; not follow him, not try to speak to him or question what he was up to, or even ask permission, I was to merely 'join' him as if it had been planned all along and see what happened.

Dragging on some tracksuit trousers over my pyjamas and grabbing a fleece, I slipped my feet into my trainers and padded down the stairs as silently as I could. Once in the kitchen, I took a mug out of the cupboard and placed it on the surface next to the one Quiet had just put out for himself. He looked at me for a few seconds before nodding faintly and dropping one tea bag into each mug. We didn't speak as the kettle boiled, nor as the tea bags were squashed, or the milk added.

Neither did we speak as we let ourselves out of the patio doors and wandered down the garden in the gentle silver-grey light of an almost-full moon. We clambered over the fence at the bottom, taking care not to spill our drinks, and then headed off into the forest together.

It was beautiful, clear, cool, companionable and stunningly peaceful.

We ambled a fair distance until we came to a stream where a tree had fallen some time ago; the trunk provided a convenient seat. This is where we parked ourselves and drank our tea together, listening to the sounds of the waking forest. Eventually as the light began to change and the sun started to rise, my son spoke.

"I miss it sometimes," he said in a low voice.

"What do you miss?" I whispered back.

"Being outside late at night and early in the morning. It's calm. It balances out all the things that happen in the day."

I waited for him to go on.

"I know it was a hard time for us all living in the tent in the garden, but it wasn't all bad. We were so much closer to nature and that was good."

I thought about it for a minute and I recalled the dancing bats in the trees and hedgehogs scurrying past the tent in the dusky evenings, the call of the owl at night and the fresh clear views of the moon. There was a magical beauty to being so close to nature and feeling the rhythm of the earth enfolding us at the start and end of each day.

"Yes," I confirmed softly, "Some of it was good."

Then he surprised me by speaking again.

"I think I'd like to do some camping this summer. Small said he'd like it too."

"Really?" I replied, "I thought none of you kids would ever want to camp again after what happened with the house." In fact, to tell you the truth, I'd spent many fruitless hours worrying about how all those events might have affected them.

He grinned at me, "Nah we're good. It happened, it's over, and we've moved on."

"I'm so glad you told me," I said with an answering smile. "As for camping, well that can be arranged."

We sat in silence for a bit longer before he nudged me gently and nodded further up the stream. Following his gaze, I could see movement. A deer was approaching the water to drink and, as she moved in the long grass, we could see that she was accompanied by a fawn.

"Oh, wow!" I muttered softly. I simply couldn't take my eyes off them but was aware of Quiet grinning at me.

"Just you wait till you see the badgers."

"There are badgers?" I whispered. "Where?"

"Next time," he promised in a low voice and turned back to look at the deer.

I tucked the delight that there was going to be a next time carefully into my heart with a contented sigh and watched my boy as he watched the deer. In that moment, I focussed on simply acknowledging just how much I adored him. How lucky I was to have him and all his siblings to cherish. As mums we can get so wrapped up in what is expected of us; the right way to be a parent. Making sure our children behave themselves, eat the right food, go to school, pass exams, conform with society's demands, turn up to music lessons, sports training and the rest of the whirl of everyday life. Yet somehow, in amongst all of that, it is vital that we take the time to simply appreciate them for the wonderful miracles that they are.

Here was this lovely young man, who clatters through our home on his long limbs and tackles his brother at random moments, before eating everything in sight, whilst rarely saying a word, teaching me that taking a moment to simply sit and be, to acknowledge events for what they are and then move on, is so very important.

28: Coalescence

Definition: the convergence of many elements to form a new whole

Staying with the present day once again as this story finally draws to a close….

Later that same day, in glorious contrast to our peaceful early morning, chaos was reigning in the kitchen. I mean the actual chaotic type of chaos in this case rather than my gorgeous grown-up-daughter-Chaos, although she was present too, singing loudly, and not necessarily accurately, along to something only she could hear, thanks to the happy application of ear buds. Logic was also singing only, unfortunately, it wasn't the same song, which made for an interesting 'mash up.' (Hark at me; I am so trendy, with my technical modern music terms!)

Both girls were sat at the breakfast bar supposedly doing university work on their laptops, although I had my doubts about that, as every so often one or other of them would suddenly laugh out loud at something for no obvious reason, leading me to conclude that they were probably studying but also on some form of social media at the same time. How their brains manage to multi task effectively like that is beyond me.

The boy Barbarians were indulging in a more physically demanding type of multi-tasking, enmeshed as they were in some sort of karate/judo/all-in-wrestling 'mash up' contest of their own, in the middle of the kitchen floor. It's a stone floor, so I was fairly sure some of those 'take-downs' must have smarted just a touch, although no one squealed and no bones seemed to have broken either. However, there was quite a lot of alarming grunting going on.

At the same time a large pan of something was bubbling furiously away on the stove. I wasn't sure what it contained or who had put it on but took the view that whoever it was hopefully knew what they were doing, so I was trying to ignore it.

In fact, I was doing my best to ignore everything.

If I didn't acknowledge it then it couldn't possibly be happening, which is a technique I advise any mother to develop very early on in her maternal career. If no-one is actually dying, then there is no problem to stress about. Hence, I was sat at the conservatory table wearing headphones and ignoring everything. My headphones were of the big clumpy variety that were trendy way back in the dim and distant nineteen eighties but have come back into fashion again recently. I am sure you've seen them around, the sort that the youngsters of today think are a completely modern invention and hence 'cool' or 'sick' or 'rad' or whatever the word of the moment is for something that is 'on-trend'.

The up-to-date jargon changes so quickly I've given up trying to keep pace with it. But really, we used to wear headphones like these decades ago back when 'cool' really meant…um…well… 'cool'!

However, I was not listening to music and I was definitely *not* singing along. I was trying to concentrate and was using the headphones more as ear defenders than anything else, as they proved very effective at cutting out the pandemonium my darling Barbarians were generating around me and allowed me to focus on the laptop before me on the table. I was wading through what seemed like hundreds of emails that had arrived overnight. Interestingly enough they didn't seem the usual sort of miscellaneous junk from random sales companies, fraudulent enterprises and scam artists.

After ploughing through delivery confirmations from several online retailers and an online banking circular, I came across one from the nice lady in charge of the Literary and Creative Society evening event, thanking me for coming along and sharing my story. Apparently, she had received some rather flattering feedback from the Society members and wanted to let me know.

She finished her email by saying that she hoped I didn't mind but she had passed my particulars on to several other groups she knew who were always looking for good speakers. She felt that my signature talk was refreshingly different and entertaining that she was quite certain that other event organisers would be interested in contacting me. In fact, she suggested I would be 'snapped up'. It was really good to know that my presentation had been genuinely appreciated, not merely politely suffered by the audience.

Funnily enough the next three emails I read were inquiries about possibly booking me to speak at further events, so she hadn't been joking about passing on my details, or about there being a demand. The event organisers were obviously not hanging about.

This was quite exciting, and I had so effectively tuned out everything else that was going on around me that I didn't even hear the landline ringing stridently. None of the kids reacted to it either but then we've already discussed how they don't seem to bother with landlines, haven't we? If it's not mobile then it can't possibly be a phone. It was still ringing as Beloved Husband burst through the kitchen door.

"Is anyone going to answer that phone?" he demanded. "I could hear it from outside." Looking up I watched him dump his jacket on the side and take a flying leap over the bundle of brawling boys on the floor to grab the handset before it stopped ringing. As I pulled my headphones off, I noticed that his aerial acrobatics act had successfully got everyone's attention and the noise level was significantly reduced almost immediately.

Perhaps he should do it more often!

The boys briefly stopped hammering at each other and the girls stopped caterwauling (ahem - I mean singing!), and all looked on with interest to see what he would do next.

"Hello?" he said, trying to catch his breath after such an unaccustomed burst of exercise. He was attempting to use his 'stern' voice, the one that was supposed to convey in a single word the fact that he would be most displeased if there was a cold caller on the other end of the line. We do seem to get quite a lot of those, so he has spent time perfecting this skill.

His eyes widened as he listened to the voice on the end of the line. Then he looked directly at me and started to frantically flap his hand in what I think was a request for complete silence. It was already quite quiet in the room so we all held our breath and waited.

"No, this is her personal assistant speaking. She's not available for a press interview just at this moment but you could email her, or alternatively I can take a message for her and she will get back to you."

He wiggled his fingers in the air, and his eyebrows too. Logic reacted by shoving a pad of paper and a pen under his hand so he could write down a name and number. Just as he was thanking the caller and hanging up the handset, my mobile started to buzz away next to me on the table. Picking it up, I saw a number I didn't recognise and swiped to answer it. A polite female voice enquired about booking me to speak at an art event for charity, at a fairly big venue, in the nearby town the following month. Flipping open my diary, I agreed, made a note of the particulars and ended the call, but my mobile started ringing again as soon as I tried to put it down. This time it was a lady from one of the local WI's asking if I could fill in for a speaker who had been forced to cancel at short notice due to ill health. The date she needed me was in two days' time. I agreed and again made a note in my diary. At the same time the shrill bleat of the main landline started up again. Giving me a quizzical look, Beloved Husband reached to answer it, just as I swiped to disconnect my mobile only for it to ring almost immediately once again.

Eventually we both got off the phones and just looked at each other.

"Well, you seem rather popular all of a sudden!"

"How bizarre!" I agreed.

"What was that about a press interview?" asked Logic.

"Not really sure, but I didn't hand the phone over to your mother when I realised it was a journalist because I don't think you can be too careful with the press. Best not get caught unprepared. He's going to send an email, which should give us an idea what he's after and allow you time to decide if you want to respond or not," he looked at me as he said this and shrugged.

"Yeah, that's wise," said Chaos, nodding thoughtfully.

"What about the other calls?"

"A couple of ladies want you to call them back, one about some book group and the other about a ladies' social event. I took names and numbers."

"Oh, that's nice, I'll give them a ring a bit later on."

"I think we'll have to assume that you are a bit of a hit!"

"So it would seem."

"You know, there might genuinely be something in this," said Chaos. "We might need to upgrade your website!"

"I have a website?" I asked in surprise.

"Oh yeah!" she admitted sheepishly, "didn't I tell you? I created it for your exhibition last year. We can probably expand it considerably now."

"What do you mean?"

"Business-wise. You are going to need a speaker's page with the details of your talk and upcoming events. You are going to charge to speak, aren't you?"

"Well, I thought I might charge a speaker's fee, plus a minimal mileage."

"Good! That could prove to be a nice steady income stream, then there's a second potential income stream from the books that you will sell at these speaking events. Then there's the main income from your art work, in the form of exclusive original paintings, then prints, cards, inspirational quotes and the like. I can design you a whole online shop too, if you like. I'll have to take into account all the necessary regulations, the new data protection laws and security, so it might take a while." She started muttering about jpegs and dots per inch at that point so lost me quite quickly, but Logic seemed to be following her and nodded along as if she wasn't talking gibberish.

"She's right," agreed Beloved Husband, nudging me. "You have a ready-made market there. If you get regular speaking gigs, that'll give you a platform for the book and also your paintings. You have all the ingredients of a potentially successful business with three main elements to it, as an artist, an author and a speaker."

"Triangles are supposed to be the strongest geometric shapes," interjected the resident maths genius. We looked at her for clarification, "I'm just agreeing with you," Logic explained a touch defensively. "I think it could make a very effective business model, especially as it is all underpinned with a very positive human-interest story. If the press are interested already, then you might even get some great publicity too."

"That's true, but PR is important, you'll have to think about your brand." Chaos looked even more thoughtful, if that were possible.

"Your accounts will be important too. You'll need to make sure you keep a record of all transactions, so you can pay the right tax. I'll do some research to find out the best way to do this," Logic said, turning to her laptop and typing furiously into it. The two girls started murmuring between themselves and enthusiastically making a list of all the things they thought I needed to consider.

"Perhaps this really is the perfect new job for you," rumbled Quiet thoughtfully, as Small broke free of the headlock he had absentmindedly held him pinned in for the last ten minutes, and delivered a swift kick to the back of his older brother's knees. Both boys tumbled to the ground and as I watched them, my thoughts went into freefall with all the potential possibilities.

"I think he might be right," agreed Beloved Husband. "It's a really good mix of your skills and so very creative which is a far cry from that job you've been doing all these years. I think you should go for it." There was a pause during which he reached over and took my hand gently and gave it a little shake to get me to look right at him. Then in a low voice that reached under the Barbarians babbling around us, "You know, with this and my new promotion we stand a real chance of turning our finances around."

I looked at him for a moment trying to work out if he was saying what I thought he was saying. "You mean….?"

He nodded. "Yes, I got the job. They told me just as I left the office this evening. You are looking at the new Director."

"Oh! Well done!" I flung my arms around him and hugged him tightly. "I am so proud of you."

"And I am proud of you," he countered. "I think you should go for it. And I think we should do the other thing we mentioned too."

"You mean…" I could hardly dare say the words.

"Yes, I think I do."

"Really, can we?"

"Let's give it our best shot."

His smile was enough to have me launching myself at him again and throwing my arms around his neck. Laughing in absolute delight I said, “Can we do it now?” (Do get your mind out of the gutter please? I am not talking about that!)

He disentangled himself from my arms with a chuckle, “OK!” he said, “Just let me find a screwdriver. He opened the cutlery drawer and rummaged around a bit before he drew out a large yellow and black multi-headed screwdriver. Please don’t ask me what it was doing in the cutlery drawer because I have no idea.

“Come on then gang, let’s do this,” he said, grabbing my hand and pulling me towards the front door.

29: Exhilaration

Definition: A sensation of great happiness, excitement, elation.

Staying with the family in the present at this momentous instant......

Realising something significant was afoot, the Barbarian girls abandoned their laptops and the Barbarian boys untangled themselves. All four of them followed us outside to the driveway where we interrupted Skelly doing some weeding in the front flower bed complete with a frilly apron, a wheelbarrow and a long-handled hoe.

Small ensured that Skelly took a break from his labours and joined us as we all stood around watching Beloved Husband, armed with his trusty screwdriver, advancing on the For-Sale sign that still skulked over the hedge. He attacked the fixings anchoring the wooden pole supporting the board to our gatepost. After only a few moments though he gave a rude exclamation and chucked his screwdriver on the ground before heading determinedly for the garage.

Quiet stepped up to the gate to examine the fixings for a minute and then said knowledgeably, "Yup! The screws have sheered."

"That's a nuisance," agreed Small.

Logic shuffled over to me and asked, "Is Dad doing what I think he's doing?"

"I hope so," I replied. "Otherwise I'm not quite sure what else he could be planning to do with that." I pointed at Beloved Husband who had re-emerged from the garage armed with a chainsaw trailing an extra-long electrical lead. He stalked right up to the Estate Agent board and started up his weapon before chopping right through the post holding it up. The board put up a token resistance but quickly gave in and toppled to the ground, as the noise of the chainsaw died away almost as soon as it had started.

"This is our home." Beloved Husband said defiantly. "We're staying right here!"

I couldn't help the warm happy tears that welled up in my eyes as I heard the huge cheer that erupted at his words from the Barbarians. There would be no more awful viewings and I could mess my studio up to my heart's content but, more importantly, we were going to stay in this crazy old/new house of ours, all the way out here in the middle of nowhere, in this incredible countryside with its forest full of deer and badgers; the home in which we had shared our lives so far and where, in spite of everything, we were so happy. It must be confessed that a certain amount of group hugging went on (yes, even the boys and Skelly) before we headed back inside, chattering and laughing together.

A short while later, armed with a celebratory cup of tea, I wandered out onto the patio. Sipping my drink thoughtfully, I surveyed the garden where we had lived in both tent and caravan for so long. The scuffed and damaged grass had recovered completely so that there was now no sign of either temporary residence. Towards the bottom of the garden on the gorgeous green grass, Skelly, now sporting full cricket whites including a helmet with a face guard and wicket-keeping gloves, was standing by a set of cricket stumps complete with bails resting on top, no doubt waiting for the boys to come and play with him.

The sun was shining and bright, cheerful birdsong hung in the warm air as I surveyed the peaceful scene. Looking back at the house I thought of all that had passed to bring me to this moment and I really wished that for just one instant I could go back in time to the old me standing on the drive watching the walls of my home disintegrate before my eyes. I wanted to give that poor broken mother a hug and say 'it's going to be all right! It's going to be horrible for a bit, and there are going to be times when you think this is going to destroy you, but it won't. You are stronger than you think. You can do it. Your husband and children will be fine, and you won't believe where all this is ultimately going to take you, so hang in there.'

I was a very different person now from the one I used to be, as a direct result of what happened the day our house sat down. That self-knowledge gave me courage. Sometimes, in the very depths of darkness, a small glimmer of light can effectively guide the way. My art had enabled me to express my deepest feelings without having to find words and then, when I was getting better, the words had found me and a story was born. I had a tale to tell and there were people asking to hear it. This wasn't about me, but about sharing a story; something human beings have been doing for thousands of years.

We weren't the only family to have come up against a difficult situation. There were, no doubt, countless other people just like us out there, struggling to hold families together against impossible odds. Life can throw countless difficulties into our path to trip us up and sometimes we simply don't feel we have the resilience we need. The obstacles before us can seem impossible to overcome. Hearing about another person's journey through a tricky time can potentially cast new light on otherwise apparently insurmountable situations.

Let us not forget that in order for a mighty oak to grow, first a tiny seed must fall and become buried in the earth. It must then fight to find a way through the darkness to reach sunlight in order to live. I had survived the collapse of the house and then battled my way through the darkness of both the emotional turmoil and the physical strain of the subsequent situational fall out. Now, having germinated and broken through the surface of the earth like a tiny sapling, I had found the strength to develop and grow, nurtured by the knowledge that I was a survivor. All I had to do now was to move forward in that new strength and understanding. Knowing the direction that I wanted to travel in and having the drive to take the first steps was immensely empowering. What seemed initially like a first tiny baby step was proving, in fact, to be quite momentous. I felt energised and motivated and completely driven to succeed at my goal.

I could bind my paintings with my book, and now my speaking into the same package, each supporting the other. After all these years I could genuinely call myself an artist. It wasn't going to be easy, I had a lot of hard work ahead of me, but I was certain that I could do it. I had changed and was still changing as a direct result of what had happened, and I was beginning to respect and even to like the person I was becoming.

How extraordinary! I had never felt like that before.

Who would have thought that such a long-held childhood dream to pursue a creative career would finally come true? Perhaps the spirit of my grandmother was watching over me, with a smile on her face saying 'At last, my girl, it's about time you followed your dream! Even if it took the house falling down on you to make you recognise it.'

Smiling at my mental musings, I shook my head.

Turning towards the house I could see that the girls had brought their laptops out onto the patio and were settling into the comfy chairs there to type companionably away together in the sunshine. Then the sound of running feet and laughter heralded the arrival of both boys, at speed now, equipped with cricket bat and ball, tripping and tumbling over each other on their way to join Skelly at the crease.

I looked at my Barbarians and wondered where their dreams would take them.

Behind the boys, at a more dignified pace, came Beloved Husband, ambling over the grass with his own cup of tea in hand. On reaching me, he put his free arm around my shoulders and we stood together in the cool shade of the old oak tree and looked at our house; a house that, like us all, had been through the wars yet was still a home in which our family could flourish

There we all were; the slightly barmy but happy family from the house that sat down.

Epilogue

Definition – a piece of text bringing closure to a story

And there we shall leave our heroine, dear reader, at the end of one incredible journey and the beginning of the next. She is content in the company of her crazy but fabulous family as the whole tribe are reunited, complete with skeleton, to enjoy the summer sunshine together.

None of us know what the future will bring but the fact that everything is alright in this one perfect moment, right here, right now, is a blessing that we should not overlook.

There is a saying that time heals. I wonder if that is true or perhaps time merely enables one to gain some perspective; the ability to see events from a more holistic point of view, a change in perception facilitating a greater understanding of the bigger picture. None of us exists as an island and all events are inextricably linked. Perhaps time allows the brain to process information, to permit the marrying of an emotional response with a more practical or philosophical one. I don't know. Sadly, some hurts never heal, and we have to learn to live with them somehow, but the making of irrevocable decisions whilst in the grip of major emotional responses should always be avoided if possible, until distance and perspective can be gained.

Our heroine has certainly been through the mill, but who hasn't in life? The overall outcome of these events has been a good one, in spite of everything. Her house may have sat down, and her security might have been torn apart, but she has grown stronger and a little bit wiser in the aftermath. The yin and yang of life has achieved a balance once again.

It always does in the end.

A Few Added Extras From The House That Sat Down

What happened to Skelly?

In case you were wondering, Skelly has found a degree of fame in recent times. He now has a job at the local sixth form college where he happily divides his time between the biology laboratory, assisting with anatomy lectures, and the art department where he is employed as a model for the life (?) drawing class.

Nevertheless, he still spends the school holidays advising Beloved Husband on his latest gardening obsession (he is currently attempting to grow a wide variety of vegetables that Small will no doubt refuse to eat), and occasionally deigns to act as a sophisticated scarecrow sporting a wide variety of Harry Potter inspired outfits.

Ultimately though, his favourite occupation is always going to be that of loafing around at the house that sat down. He can generally be located at the bottom of the garden, under a large floppy hat, lounging in a hammock in the sunshine with a good book. He is often accompanied by a four-foot papier-mâché snowman.

The Comforting Recipes of Chaos and Logic

Crispy Cakes

Ingredients

To make this Crispy Cakes Recipe you will need:
1 x 100g bar milk or dark chocolate
90g/ (3 oz) rice crispies
12 small paper cake cases.

Method

Melt the chocolate in a bowl over a saucepan of simmering water. Once melted carefully remove the bowl from the saucepan.

Add the rice crispies and stir in to the chocolate mix until entirely covered in chocolate. Spoon, evenly, into the 12 paper cases.

Sprinkles on top make a really cheerful finishing touch.

Leave to cool in the fridge.

Chaos would like to remind you not to forget to scrape the bowl out thoroughly at the end though, as it is the cook's privilege. Although Logic does state that if you have small children or Barbarians on hand that you need to keep quiet, then it is acceptable to hand it over (assuming safe supervision of any glassware of course). Anything for a bit of peace!

Fridge Cake

Ingredients

250g (8oz) digestive biscuits or rich tea depending on preference
150g (5oz) milk chocolate
150g (5oz) dark chocolate
100g (3½oz) unsalted butter
150g (5oz) golden syrup
150g (5oz) raisins
Handful of mini marshmallows (optional)

Nuts are also optional but be careful with regard to any nut allergy sufferers among your guests.

Method

Use cling film to line a 20cm (8in) shallow, square-shaped tin. Leave additional cling film to hang over the sides.

Bash the biscuits into pieces using a rolling pin. Logic would dictate that you could put can them in a strong plastic bag first before hitting them with the rolling pin so they don't go everywhere! Or you could follow Chaos' method that involves just put the biscuits in a really large bowl before bashing down with the end of your rolling pin and simply enjoying the mess that ensues. I guess it rather depends how much time you have allocated for clearing up.

Melt chocolate, butter and golden syrup in a heatproof bowl set over a pan of simmering water. Stir occasionally.

Remove the bowl from the heat and stir in the broken biscuits, raisins and mini marshmallows (optional but really, really nice – makes it a bit like rocky road).

Spoon the mixture into the tin. Level the surface and press down.

Leave to cool, in the fridge for 1-2 hours to set.

Turn out the cake and peel off the cling film being careful not to miss any little bits. Logic respectfully reminds you that no one likes chomping through forgotten bits of old cling-film.

Cut into squares and enjoy.

Please note that Chaos invites you to believe her when she says that they won't last long, so you probably better double up on your ingredients next time you order on-line, save the delivery driver the extra trip.

Chocolate Chip Cookies

Ingredients

150g butter
160g sugar
1 large egg
220g plain flour
0.5 tsp bicarbonate soda
0.25 tsp salt
200g chocolate chips

Method

Preheat the oven to 190C/375F/Gas mark 5.

Melt the butter in a bowl, add sugar and beat in the eggs. Add the rest of the ingredients and mix well. Put a tablespoon of the mixture on a baking tray and back for 8-10 minutes to see how far it will spread during cooking. This will give you an idea how many you can cook on the tray in each batch without the dough running all over your lovely clean oven.

Logic would suggest lining your tray with baking paper but Chaos would ask why bother? Again, it's got a lot to do with the cleaning up and how organised you are feeling I suppose.

Bake the remaining dough in batches until all is used. Then leave to cool for a few minutes before transferring to wire racks to cool further. Logic recommends this as they can break if moved too soon although Chaos maintains that the broken ones are testers for the cook to taste to ensure quality control. You can decide which method you concur with.

Personally, I prefer to remain impartial, as long as my ready supply of biscuits continues why on earth would I step in?

Serve with a large cup of tea.

You deserve a break.

The Barbarian Boys' Favourite 'Special' Fried Rice

Ingredients

Whatever you can find in the fridge that hasn't gone off
Eggs, beaten with a little milk if you have it but not if you don't
Rice freshly boiled, and drained
Soy sauce
Pepper

Directions

Chop up whatever you found in the fridge (that hasn't gone off like onions, peppers, ham/bacon/chicken etc.) really small and fry in a wok until cooked through.

Then beat however many eggs you have (the more eggs the merrier in the Barbarian Boys' opinion), chuck in a bit of soy sauce and add to the wok, plus a slug of milk to stop it all drying out and stir. Keep stirring.

Then once the eggs start to scramble, add the rice and keep it moving until the eggs are cooked through and everything is heated through thoroughly and nice and hot. Add pepper to season but no salt as the soy sauce is salty enough.

This really is just a way to feed teenagers when you've run out of almost anything and everything, but you are unable to (or can't be bothered to) go to a shop to buy something more suitable. Fortunately, my boys love it. Beloved Husband is less enamoured, but then he can always shift for himself, can't he?

Making a four foot snowman without snow

You will need:

Gardening gloves plus wire cutters

Chicken wire plus extra thin wire for fixing

Flour

Water

Strips of newspaper or waste paper (Your old GCSE notes are good for this, assuming you passed and don't need to re-sit of course)

Tissue paper or paint

Orange card cut into a semi-circle and rolled up to make a nose resembling a carrot

Two black buttons for eyes. PVA glue

Plenty of time to clean up

Directions

Using the gardening gloves to protect your hands, bend the chicken wire into the shape of a snowman's body and head and then fix in place with bits of thin wire.

Mix flour and water using half and half quantities until you have a runny white mess. Dip in strips of paper and lay over the chicken wire frame. Build up several layers and then leave to dry. Do try not to indulge in a soggy wet paper fight with your partner in crime at this point as the results will be fairly disastrous. Once dry, you can either paint the colour of your choice or stick scrunched up white tissue paper all over your snowman.

Add eyes and nose, then hat, scarf and pipe. Enjoy!

Innovative Games for Bored Barbarian Boys

Catch for ruffians

Equipment

1 large sheet of paper carefully scrumpled up into a tight ball, this could be newspaper, wrapping paper or simply an old envelope or empty crisp packet. (Even better use your older sister's A-level physics notes – such fun to see her reaction!)

1 room in your house. It is preferable to choose one where there are plenty of potentially breakable ornaments as this adds to the general excitement of the game.

2 or more ruffians. The more the merrier.

Rules of the game

Pass (throw really hard) the ball of paper systematically between you without dropping it. Points are awarded for how close you can get to potentially breakable items without actually causing any damage. Additional points are awarded as appropriate for the maximum possible annoyance that can be caused to any siblings choosing not to play.

NB: Please note that this is not a good activity to engage in if you wish to remain on good terms with your mother.

In door cricket for the very brave thug

Equipment

Much as outlined previously but please add a long cardboard tube as is generally found inside a roll of kitchen towels or even wrapping paper. (Feel free to unravel one that isn't finished yet and leave the unused paper lying around to get in the way. No one will mind.)

Rules of the game

You've seen cricket, it's much like that. Make it up as you go along. (Who needs rules?) Changing the (non-existent) rules as you go along is an excellent way of winding up a participating sibling too.

Enjoy!

NB: see previous warning note. You really don't want to upset your mother.

Talks by Alice May

'Surviving the House That Sat Down!'

'Surviving the House That Sat Down' is my signature presentation. It is a positive and uplifting talk based on the events of 2014 when my house partially collapsed one day and my husband and 4 children and I were forced to move into a tent in the garden.

As a direct result of what happened that day and events which followed my life has been completely transformed; proving that you can triumph in the face of adversity.

Using my own personal artwork as illustration, my signature talk gives a flavour of my inspiring journey from the ruins of our home to my life now as an author, artist and public speaker.

Chasing Rainbows – Dreams can come true

In this second presentation, I discuss the potential to boost our general resilience through creative activities, whilst sharing a selection of my own original art and painting demonstration videos.

The world is an increasingly stressful place and it is so important that we find ways to deal with the pressures of everyday life. Find out about the many different types of creative therapy available to us today. Hear some of the theories on why it can be so effective.

This presentation draws on my personal experience of the healing power of creativity, an inspirational story that has enabled my dreams to come true.

Details of all my talks as well as my books and artwork can be found on my website: www.alicemay.weebly.com

About the Author

Alice May

As a direct result of the real story behind The House That Sat Down, I am a huge advocate for self-care and resilience through creative activities and I speak regularly on the subject to a wide variety of groups.

I am a working mother with four (not-so-small anymore) children and I am fortunate enough to be married to the most patient man on the planet. We live in, what used to be, a ramshackle old cottage in the country.

My conservatory is always festooned with wet washing and my kitchen full of cake. I love listening to the radio.

Inspired by some shocking true-life events (our house really did fall down) and fuelled by some very frantic painting sessions, this tale wouldn't leave me alone until it was written.

I really hope you enjoyed it.

If you have any comments about this book please send them to me at alicegmay@hotmail.com

Other links:
Website: www.alicemay.weebly.com
Twitter: @AliceMay_Author
Or find my Alice May Author page on Facebook.
Alternatively, you can see me painting on YouTube by searching for 'Alice May Artist'.

P.S. Please note that no Barbarians, skeletons or snowmen were harmed during the writing of this book.

Printed in Poland
by Amazon Fulfillment
Poland Sp. z o.o., Wrocław

51465497R00327